Against All Gods

Against All Gods

Miles Cameron

This edition published in Great Britain in 2023 by Gollancz

First published in Great Britain in 2022 by Gollancz
an imprint of The Orion Publishing Group Ltd
Carmelite House, 50 Victoria Embankment
London EC4Y 0DZ

An Hachette UK Company

3 5 7 9 10 8 6 4

A CIP catalogue record for this book is
available from the British Library.

ISBN (MMP) 978 1 473 23252 5
ISBN (eBook) 978 1 473 23253 2
ISBN (audio) 978 1 473 23264 8

Typeset at The Spartan Press Ltd,
Lymington, Hants

Printed and bound in Great Britain by Clays Ltd,
Elcograf S.p.A.

MIX
Paper from
responsible sources
FSC® C104740
FSC
www.fsc.org

www.gollancz.co.uk

To Greg Mele, swordmaster, fantasy writer and historian of Mesoamerica, without whom these books would never have been written

Some Notes on Measurement

Characters in *Against All Gods* express distance in paransangs and stadia (singular stadion).

The parasang is approximately five kilometres, or the distance a fit man can walk in an hour of hard walking. It's not an exact measurement. This is, after all, the Bronze Age.

The stadion is approximately six hundred feet (roughly two hundred metres, give or take). The foot is the measure of a man's foot – not standardised. There are thirty stadia in a parasang in Noa and Dardania; fewer in the Hundred Cities, more in Narmer. But don't be fooled; there are no standardised systems of measure. Every city measures everything from weights to distance, from grain to volume, in a different way. I have chosen to use the archaic Greek/Persian stadion and parasang (and the 'foot') to keep it relatively simple.

There is no money. This is a barter economy, and the relative value of gold, silver, grain or any other commodity varies from place to place and from transaction to transaction. Precious stones, like emeralds, rubies and lapis, are all useful for trade, but again, have no standard value.

There are no maps or charts, although Narmer and Ma'rib have 'world pictures' that begin to approach maps. People tend to express travel as a set of waypoints: 'I went to A, then B, then C.' Written down, these itineraries are the way pilgrims and merchants learn their routes.

Most people cannot read; the ability to read is almost a magic power. Scribes hold that power, and a good scribe can read most of the languages, 'modern' and 'ancient' of the world. There is no paper. Everything must be written on either papyrus (mostly in Narmer) or inscribed on clay tablets. Book-keeping and accounting, like reading, are near-magical powers.

Finally, the most durable metal is bronze. Iron is almost un-known, and its ownership is illegal and taboo. It is worth noting that a good work-hardened bronze blade is the equal or superior of much ironwork; only steel would exceed bronze, and bronze can be worked much more easily. This is an age of bronze, extended and enforced by the gods.

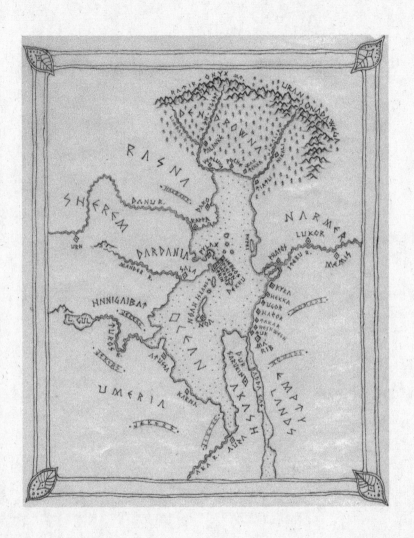

Glossary of Names and Titles

Protagonists

Atosa – Chief jeweller of the Palace of Hekka.

Daos – An orphaned child with mysterious powers.

Era – An epic singer and dancer, swordswoman, abandoned daughter of a godborn father and a Narmerian dancer.

Gamash of Weshwesh – Godborn aristocrat, master magos, and past tool of the gods.

Hefa-Asus – A Dendrownan smith from the far north, in Poche. A great maker.

Nicté – A tough woman of Northern Dendrowna, apprentice of Hefa-Asus.

Pollon – Scribe, musician, archer, and man of reason. A little patronizing at times.

Zos – Godborn sell-sword, cynical and past his best.

Hakrans aboard the *Untroubled Swan*

Aanat – Master sailor, 'captain' of the *Untroubled Swan,* senior husband.

Bravah – Youngest husband of the family, a little jealous, a little too fond of anger.

Jawala – Strongest and wisest of the Hakran crew/family, senior of Aanat's three wives (and with two fellow-husbands).

Miti – Youngest in the family, independent, and stubborn, wife of the *Untroubled Swan* crew/family.

Mokshi – Middle husband of the family, older, superb cook, steady and reliable.

Pavi – Middle wife of the Hakran family, veteran sailor and merchant.

Other Characters

Agon of Mykoax – God-King of Dardania.

Anenome – Short, blond, and long limbed, reputed the best warrior in the world, a godborn sell-sword.

Atrios the Great – War King of Mykoax, killed by his wife after the failure of the Holy War against the Hakrans.

Axe – Tall, dark, and old, a killer mercenary who has survived many wars. Partner of Anenome.

Bror – A stuffed bear.

Cyra – Goddess Queen of Noa, old and powerful, and very competent.

Dite – A mysterious, exotic and very powerful woman.

Hyatti-Azi – Former Hattussan prince, and a great captain among the Jekers.

Kussu – A market rat boy.

Makeda, Tisa, Theklassa – Three nomad warriors.

Maritaten – The new goddess-queen of Narmer, often referred to as 'Lady of Narmer' or 'Lady of the High House'.

Mekos – God-King of Kyra, a powerful city-state too close to Narmer.

Mura of Samar – Pollon's lover and landlady, a merchant of nomad birth.

Nannu – A persistent donkey.

Persay of Mykoax – A mad former slave and failed bull-leaper.

Spathios – Scribe for the god-king of Hekka.

Taha – A former slave from Py and veteran scout.

Thanatos – God-King of Hekka, neighbour to Kyra and very rich.

Thayos – Lord of Dardania, Captain of the *Wave Serpent*, a merchant and a pirate.

The Old Gods

Antaboga – The World Serpent. The Last Dragon.

Arrina – Narmerian Sun Goddess, lover of Enkul-Anu, now banished to the Outer Darkness.

Nanuk – Old pantheon god of the Sea, by his Northern name. In the south, Nammu. Sometimes a big man, sometimes a sea monster. Supposedly killed by Timurti.

Ranos – The Father and Lord of the old pantheon.

Shemeg – Old pantheon sun god.

Taris – Former Queen of Heaven and top god of the old pantheon, killed by Ara in the last 'War in Heaven'.

Temis – Also the Dark Huntress, Black Goddess – One of the Sisters. Lady of Animals, sometimes a goddess of death and chaos. The only one of the old gods to still hold a place in the new pantheon.

The 'New' Gods

Anzu – The winged lion-headed god of rage and insanity, a dangerous killer.

Ara – God of War and Strife. Only marginally sane. Still, a Greater God.

Druku – God of Drunkenness and Orgies, who is tired of being treated like a drunk. A Greater God.

Enkul-Anu – Bull-headed God of the Storm. Master of the pantheon. Just trying to hold it all together.

Grulu – Goddess of Spite and Envy; completely mad or perhaps just senile.

Gul – God of the Underworld, Lord of the Hosts of the Dead. A Greater God.

Illikumi – A snake god, God of Liars, also many merchants. Not very powerful but very clever.

Lady Laila – A sort of demi-goddess. Apparently, just a servant. Apparently.

Kur – The underworld, where Gul and Urkigul rule as Enkul-Anu rules heaven. Seven layers of hells, most of them rumoured to be very cold.

Nerkalush – The son of Gul, a junior god looking to increase his power.

Nisroch – Herald of the Gods, a son of Enkul-Anu with plans of his own.

Resheph – A junior god with a high opinion of himself, son of the God of War.

Sypa – Goddess of Lust; a Great Goddess and consort of Enkul-Anu.

Tyka – Also the Blue Goddess, the Antlered One – The other 'Sister.' The goddess of death in childbirth, of fertility, of things reborn and things dying and rotting and being healed and reborn.

Telipinu – The chamberlain of the gods, son of Sypa and Enkul-Anu, a very junior godling.

Timurti – Goddess of the Sea, totally lost to age and madness. A Great God.

Urkigul – Gul's wife, Lady of the Underworld. A Great Goddess.

Uthu – The 'new' sun god. Almost powerless.

Titles

Ra-wa-ke-ta – The champion of the god-king.

Ra-pte-re – The chancellor of the god-king.

Basilios – A great lord.

Wanax – A king who is not also an appointed god-king, a Dardanian term also used for generals and powerful lords.

God-kings – Mortals appointed by the gods to rule important centers, usually given immortal resin (ambrosia) to prolong their lives and powers.

Godborn – The literal descendants of the gods and god-kings, either the current pantheon or their predecessors. Few of them have any real powers, but their claim to superiority remains mostly unchallenged.

Prologue

Auza, Home of the Gods

'What the *fuck* just happened?'

Enkul-Anu, lord of the hosts of heaven, He-Who-Holds-The-Thunderbolt, towered over the other gods, his size marking him as the most dangerous, the most powerful and the most beautiful god.

The other gods flinched away – even the older gods who didn't fully understand … anything.

Enkul-Anu, god of gods, Storm God of Auza, sat on his great black marble throne. His skin was the polished deep red of carnelian; his eyes shone like molten gold in a massive bull's head, with neither iris nor pupil, and his long black hair fell from his polished golden horns. He was taller than an elephant, and by his side was a great basalt bucket of thunderbolts that growled with suppressed power and showed malevolently in the *Aura*, powered by the souls of his victims ripped from their bodies.

He ruled the Great Palace of Heaven, the magnificent and many-roomed palace atop Mount Auza, Gate of Heaven, where megarons were layered, hall on top of hall, with working spaces and deep caverns hiding the many treasures and secrets of the gods.

Many, if not most of the countless minor deities thronged the hall as courtiers, sycophants, soldiers and messengers, but he alone was seated. This was not the Hall of the Gods where all lay on their magnificent couches, nor the Hall of Judgement where no mortal ever passed; this was the Hall of Hearing, where petitions came, where the occasional mortal visitor saw an endless vista of heavy black marble columns supporting a massive vault of dark stone inlaid with a thousand scenes in ruby and emerald, ivory and diamond. In lurid, god-lit colours and glowing traceries, Enkul-Anu conquered his enemies, destroyed the former seat of heaven, overthrew Titans and demons and enslaved humanity, his brilliant scarlet skin carefully lit so that the eye could follow his triumph on every surface.

The other gods were represented: Ara, the God of War and Violence, slew Taris, the former Queen of Heaven of the former pantheon, on the steps of her temple on distant Dekhu; and Timurti rose from the depths, a hideous crustacean, to wreck a human fleet; Druku lay in drunken abandon in most scenes – he was after all, the God of Drunkenness and Orgies; Sypa, Goddess of Lust, consort of the Storm God, coupled with him even as they fought monsters.

And across the back wall, they all were represented lying in state – all the great gods in their aspects, and even the two Enemies: Temis, the Dark Huntress and Tyka, the enigmatic Blue Goddess, standing alone as if banished from the table of the gods. All in a magnificent mosaic of precious stones that was forever lit from within by mage-fire.

Enkul-Anu thought it was all lurid and rather tasteless, but it served its purpose. And he seldom really looked at it any more, because he had to watch his fellow gods all the time. A thousand years after their conquest of heaven, some weren't wearing well.

Several of the older gods stood apart, or leant against the veined marble of the walls under colourful depictions of their own great deeds, but their slack faces and absent expressions gave an impression of inaction at odds with their youthful vigour and perfect immortal forms. They were silent, except for Timurti, the great Goddess of the Deep Sea, who muttered to herself, striking her immortal thigh repeatedly and rhythmically with her fist. Grulu, Goddess of Spite and Envy, stood alone and locked in her own world. Uthu, the new Sun God, was one of Timurti's brood and not even able to make light yet, although he had her Bright Spear.

Because Arrina was the real Sun Goddess ...

Enkul-Anu frowned and turned his gaze away from the deities that surrounded him, his senses tuned to the world below his feet. He looked down from Auza, sensing the rage of a distant and important worshipper – sensing that something had slipped. Somewhere over to the east, one of his mortal powers was cursing the gods. A mortal power who should have been dead. *Too gods-be-damned much has slipped these days*, Enkul-Anu thought. *When we took heaven, it was different. What happened?*

A thousand years – that's what happened. Most of them can't handle it. Senile fools. And the young are worse. Weak. Soft.

'Summon the Herald of the Gods!' Enkul-Anu bellowed.

He hadn't meant to bellow, but almost everything sent him into a rage these days – perhaps because he had to do everything himself.

Fucking idiots.

A dark-skinned godling – one of Sypa's many brats – tapped a magnificent gold-encrusted spear on the black marble floor and summoned the Herald of the Gods by name.

'Nisroch!' he intoned.

Teifani? Telafanos? Teolophi? Enkul-Anu couldn't remember the young pup's name. His chamberlain. Handsome. Definitely Sypa's. He preferred his son by Arrina ...

Her name could no longer be spoken aloud. She had betrayed him, and she was gone to the Outer Darkness for eternity.

Arrina ...

He shook himself as his son, the herald, Nisroch, appeared on eagle's wings, his feet touching the floor lightly as he landed – a huge waste of power, as he'd summoned a gate and stepped through it. The flight was some sort of artistic flourish.

Fucking idiots. We gave them too much power. They have no idea what they're doing with it.

'What just happened?' Enkul-Anu roared.

Nisroch didn't *quite* shrug. 'All sorts of things, Great God. The god-king of Narmer is recruiting charioteers against your express order. The god-king of Kyra prepares to make war on Hekka. In Mykoax, the god-king—'

'Someone did something stupid. At Weshwesh. I can feel the fucking stupid right through the scarlet marrow of my bones. One of you children...'

Nisroch blinked. And looked around. 'I don't like to carry tales—'

'That's what you do, *herald.*' The great god glared down at his messenger. 'You are my eyes and ears. My spy. *You carry tales!*'

The Storm God made a gesture, showing that in his hand he held a thunderbolt glowing with its own titanic energy.

No one in heaven was sure if Enkul-Anu's thunderbolts could actually kill a god, but the balance of guesswork was that they would. And no one was in a hurry to be the one to test them. Even after a thousand years, the threat was enough.

Nisroch flinched away, all his elegance gone.

'Resheph,' he said. 'Resheph... has slain... the daughter of a mortal.'

Enkul-Anu looked at his herald, and then around at the gods on their couch-thrones of ebony and gold.

Ara, God of War, looked blurrily at him.

'My son,' he said. He wasn't always coherent, so it was quite a cogent statement. 'My *son!*'

It was true. Resheph *was* Ara's son.

4

'What mortal?' Enkul-Anu demanded in a voice like the thunder he controlled.

'Irene, daughter of Gamash of Weshwesh,' the herald said cautiously. He didn't *quite* cringe away.

Enkul-Anu sighed heavily. He looked at the herald, and the thunderbolt glowed malevolently.

'Fucking idiot,' he said quietly. 'Didn't I send him to kill Gamash himself?'

Silence.

'Didn't I?' Enkul-Anu bellowed at the great black marble hall of the gods. 'Didn't I so order it?'

The gods all froze; all except Sypa, who wore a winning smile, Druku, singing an ancient drinking song to himself on his couch, and Lady Laila, who was herself somewhere between godhood and serving status – Sypa's confidante and everyone's favourite ...

'You did,' Nisroch admitted.

And then the greatest god, god of gods, tilted his head to one side.

'Well.' He sat back on his great throne.

And then he allowed himself a slight smile.

'Why didn't you say?' he spat. 'A has-been. His worshipping days are past and he's not been good sport for twenty years.' His laugh was as infectious as his frown was terrifying. 'So ... why did Resheph kill her? I ordered him to kill the old fool. Not the daughter.'

The herald shrugged, taking a subtle cue from his father.

'Why do gods kill mortals?' he asked rhetorically.

Enkul-Anu began to laugh. And when it was clear that he was amused, all the other gods laughed with him.

But then he turned, all business, to Nisroch.

'Tell the king of Narmer to stop recruiting charioteers or I'll fall on him with fire,' he said. 'And tell the king of Kyra to stick to something he understands, like incest. Make my views clear. And tell the king of Hekka ...' Enkul-Anu, great Storm God of Auza, smiled over a recent memory, and then glanced at his consort and turned away. 'Never mind. Tell him he is in my thoughts.'

The herald bowed deeply. 'And Resheph?'

Enkul-Anu shrugged majestically. 'What's a mortal life? Gods will be gods.'

Nisroch nodded. 'Yes, Great God.' He paused. 'And Gamash of Weshwesh?'

Enkul-Anu found himself increasingly interested in his consort's smile. In fact, she licked her lips, and when Sypa licked her lips, the results were staggering.

He waved a scarlet godly hand in dismissal.

'He's old – he'll soon be dead, and he's had his warning.'

'But ...'

Nisroch couldn't follow his father's decision-making. And he liked sending demons and godlings to kill mortals. It felt ... important.

Enkul-Anu went over to Sypa, scooped her in his arms, and walked from the hall.

Nisroch sighed, and glanced at his half-brother, Telipinu, the chamberlain, *ra-pte-re* of the gods.

'Any idea what this is all about?' he asked.

Telipinu was a surprisingly friendly young godling, and they *were* half-brothers. He shrugged.

'Never even heard of this mortal, Gamash,' he said. 'But my mother is all in a rage about Hekka. There's a priestess there ... Let's just say the great Storm God's been indiscreet.'

Nisroch shook his head. 'Of course, that's what it's about.'

He went back to his secrets and his spies. He liked to know things. But some things he didn't want to know.

Book One

The Rebels

Chapter One

Gamash

Rage. An old man's rage.

The Temple of the Sisters in Weshwesh had more than a hundred steps – one hundred and forty-four, in fact, as the old seer had reason to know. But he climbed them without counting; indeed, without seeing them. Rage carried him, and as he leapt up the steps, his age and pain were forgotten in an anger that so enveloped him that, even as his old knees trembled, the weight of his daughter's corpse was nothing; nor the spreading stain of her blood on his embroidered robes, nor the terrible wound where a sword had ripped across her womb and killed her and her unborn child.

Rage.

The Furies were coming to surround him. Not one, or two, but a murder and then a flock of Furies – an uncountable host of dull red-black wings beating in the air over his head. The souls of those unjustly killed, or so priests said.

Gamash had been a priest; ordinarily, he hated and feared the damned things, sent by Gul from the underworld to torment the living. Now they tasted his rage and his despair and they drank deep when they came close, and they were never glutted.

Those that drank deepest learnt her name, and sang it.

'Irene!' they sang. 'Irene!'

A hundred discordant voices, and all they did was make his rage burn the hotter.

He had reached the top, his steps never faltering as he walked towards the one temple in all of Weshwesh that men feared – the one temple with no lush maiden, no fat priest, no well-fed keeper. Just the brown stains of the sacrifices on the old green marble.

He passed under the magnificent pediment forty feet above him, clear against the lightning-swept evening sky, where Tyka, the Goddess of Fortune and Death, stood over the reclining couches of the other gods and goddesses, the two gold rods of her sign, the *occulae*, radiating from her forehead and gleaming like a stag's horns. And by her side, leaning in as if to speak, her sister Temis – the Dark Huntress – in black basalt with gold accents, wearing a man's tunic and carrying a bow and a sword. It was like most of the other statue groups in the finer temples; the greater gods lay at their ease. There was the voluptuous Sypa, every sculptor's favourite; and Druku, the god of drunken revelry, sitting on a stool, his beautiful male body the parallel of Sypa's; the brutal God of War in gold and bronze – Ara, killer of men. In the centre stood Enkul-Anu, god of gods, storm lord of Auza, ruler of the universe, He-Who-Holds-The-Thunderbolt. He was flanked by a dozen others, every statue painted in bright colours and the whole lit brilliantly with *auric* magelight to show their eternal power, all of them facing the two 'Sisters'. The 'Enemies'.

No one was supposed to worship either of the Sisters. But they were occasionally appeased, and widely feared ... and, truth be told, there were some worshippers. Secret worshippers. Especially of the Huntress.

Gamash no longer cared for the rules of men or gods. Nor did he look up. He knew the gods far too well already, and none of them were likely to help now.

None except the Enemy.

He entered the *pronaos* and no priest ran to stop him. There were silver vessels waiting for a sacrifice, but no acolyte to tend them, and no guards.

Tyka and Temis were too dangerous to need guards.

Rage carried him into the dark porch of the temple. The Furies above him lit his way with the glow of hundreds of red eyes and the beat of their glowing wings, which looked like red-hot metal in the imperfect darkness, and he went through the sacred door to the inner sanctum without a hesitation, almost *wanting* them to see his despair and punish his sacrilege.

There, in the deeper black of the *cella*, was the altar. Once a year it was choked with blood; but Tyka, the priestless deity, lacked the donations and the slaves that might have left her altar gleaming and clean in the Furies' light. Every godborn aristocrat claimed descent from the dozens of gods, greater and lesser, who benighted the world, and they ran to serve their putative ancestors. But not one of them claimed to be the offspring of Tyka or the Virgin Huntress Temis.

Instead, the room stank – the cloying, sweet stench of rotting meat and old blood.

The man put his daughter down on that rank surface with a gentleness that belied his dark fire, and he had a moment of clarity to say her name aloud.

'Irene.'

The one good thing. The one ...

His voice echoed in the cavernous sanctum and mixed with the tiny Furies' chant. They glowed red with his hate.

He raised his arms.

'Temis!' he said to the silence.

'Temis!' he cried.

He drew a bronze dagger from his robes, wiped it in his daughter's clotting blood, and then slashed it across his own hand so that a long, slow drop ran down his wrist and fell on the altar.

'Long ago I did your bidding, Huntress. Now all I ask is vengeance.' He raised his bleeding hand, and said, 'Tem—'

And *She* was there. An icy but gentle hand on his face, the crisp lapis-blue of her flesh and the golden horns above her eyes revealing her identity.

He sank to his knees in awe.

Not Temis. But *Tyka*. Not a remote voice.

A presence. An immanence.

Terror.

Tyka – whose name was too fearsome to speak, and so most priests called her *the Enemy*. But it was the forbidden name which came unbidden into his head.

The Blue Deity reached out with her lapis hand, and talons of shining, pure gold, and the same hand which had touched him now stroked Irene's cheek, and came to a rest on her neck.

Where one gold talon pierced his dead daughter's throat.

And Irene stirred, and sat up.

'———Mine———', Tyka said through Irene's dead mouth. Her voice was hard, like the buzz of an ill-tempered hornet.

The Furies fled. Their red light vanished, and the deity's blue light was the only light.

Even the old man, with nothing whatsoever left but death, quailed before the dark deity and her obvious anger.

'Yours?' he asked. The words escaped him before he could think, and he waited for her lash.

But his purpose remained. He raised his hands, no longer caring which immortal answered him.

'I beg a boon!'

He fell to his knees and reached out a hand.

'———Blessing-Curse———' replied the corpse's mouth, almost as quickly as he could speak, and Tyka reached out with her free claws. He shuddered and closed his eyes, and felt the deity's touch as if a statue had come to life.

He could not withdraw his hand. And she was silent for so long that the cold became pain, and the pain became agony – agony that reached him even through his rage. The cold was incredible – seeping up the length of his arm and working towards his heart.

He waited for death.

But instead Tyka spoke – now with calm clarity, the sound of a perfectly tuned lyre playing.

He opened his eyes and saw her nails were no longer gold. They were black, like terrible rose thorns, and as he watched one punctured his skin. He felt it as pressure – the cold had stolen any feeling of pain – but he saw the black talon sink deep into his palm and then...

He heard *her* voice in his head.

I hear you! Your rage calls to mine, man, and I hear it and use it. Do not mistake me for one of THEM. I am other. I am neither human nor god but I will lead you to a vengeance.

He tried to meet her eyes but they were too intense, shining like molten gold. He couldn't keep her black-blue face in his field of vision; it was physically painful, and he was so afraid that he could not form words. Thanks? Awe? Terror?

Listen to me, mortal man. My hand will touch the wheel, even as I touch you now, and the wheel will falter.

He fell on his face.

Her cold hand touched his head.

I mark you for my own. Now attend! When the stars fall, you will know my metal. Do with it as you must, and know my will shall be done.

The cold hand was drawing the warmth from his body. And in the place of that warmth came a terrible chaos...

Take this poisoned chalice, man. See how all you believe is a lie.

13

He couldn't breathe as he wrestled with the weight of her meaning, a labyrinth of knowledge exploding within him with her words.

There are not four elements, and the world was not born in fire.

All of your magic is but the clumsiest structure for something infinitely finer, while the gods no more control the Aura than a cat controls mice.

I am no deity. I am neither man nor woman, and I am not immortal. Nor are any of your so-called gods.

Resheph killed your daughter in vengeance for your winning the battle of Vetluna years ago, and he did so on Enkul-Anu's orders. He was ordered to kill you, man. But he is a fool.

There were no discrete words. It was a profusion of alien thoughts, images, conclusions he had never himself reached to problems he had never imagined – all growing in his head like summer vines in every direction – so that he wondered at the movement of planets he had thought were stars while simultaneously watching the formation of—

It was too much; his sanity was swept away in a moment of utter negation.

Everything you believe is a lie.

His world turned to absolute black, and then it in turn was shattered by the sound of a baby crying.

'Tyka is taking my child,' Irene said, in her own voice. 'Oh, Father, I loved you.'

And then the old man was alone, his rage burnt out like a sudden fire of bark, leaving only ash, and he was weeping by a stinking altar.

There was no corpse.

No dead child.

It was as if Irene had never been.

'Oh, Gods,' Gamash said with a groan. 'What have I done?'

★

He managed to drag himself down from the temple undiscovered, and when he awoke a day later, his slaves creeping about him in terror, his first thought was that his heresy was discovered.

His second thought was rage at the manner of his daughter's death.

He was supposed to kill you.

But that rage led him to his memories, and that labyrinth within his mind – the untameable eternity of thought that Tyka had put in his head with her hand – and he fell to the floor, and his slaves feared he was having a fit and put him to bed.

The second time was better than the first, and he was a tough old man, a victor in twenty battles, a veteran of pain and humiliation and many defeats. He lay on his bed while slaves hurried to obey him, but his first foray into the vast complexity that now sat in his head and ... he was lost again.

The third time he awoke, he had some possession of himself, despite the omnipresent labyrinth, and he ate some figs and drank sweet wine and lay on a couch and stared up at the night sky.

A night sky that made more sense and less – that had new meanings. And had lost old ones.

He lay and watched the stars and tried to process what he had learnt, though it had been more violent than learning, as if a master had beaten some philosophy into a slave with a bronze rod, and he was still bruised – not least because he had prided himself on the depth of his knowledge, the power of his erudition.

I was the great warrior mage.

All gone. All wrong. All foolish and vain.

No wonder the priests call you the Enemy if this is your gift, he thought. But he thought it with wry amusement, not anger.

By the seventh day, he had remade himself. That is: he'd

accepted the images of heresy in his mind and begun to try and work through them. Many were, mercifully, already fading; a mere mortal mind could not contain all the knowledge, all the thought, all the interrelations, that he'd been forced to accept.

He felt intellectually violated and satiated at the same time.

He cast a horoscope, saw that the Octopus was in the Gate and the Sisters were wandering, and knew that even the heavens reflected the new chaos in his soul. And the chaos to come.

There was really only one decision to make, and it was simple enough: accept the revelation and turn his back on everything he'd ever been and done, or refuse it.

His rage was still there. And because of it, he saw the revelation for what it could be, assuming it was all true, of which he was not yet convinced.

It was a weapon. A mighty weapon. He didn't really think he would live to see it used, but he was as excited as he had been when he was young, and first learnt to make light in darkness using only the ritual binding of the sun. That magic was a lie, it turned out. A lie that worked, but a lie nonetheless. Understanding the roots of the lie made him almost ridiculously powerful; ironically, he no longer cared much for worldly power.

The old man chuckled to himself. He saw with the clarity of age and experience – a man who had done both good and great evil and knew the difference.

The truth will set them free.

After a great many of them die.

And will most of them actually be better off?

Every night, he watched the sky carefully. He always had; most things could be read in the stars, if you had the wit to see them and the time to learn what they were saying. It amused him that though everything he had learnt about reading them was based on falsehoods, in this one thing, the Lady Tyka was mirroring

16

the other gods. Gamash had always been patient; patient as he learnt, patient as he taught, patient in destroying his old enemies, and now he was patient in the pursuit of his revenge. Sometimes he thought that he was mad – had he spoken to a god?

To the wrong god? The Enemy?

It was a crime just to say her name. How much worse to speak to her?

Had he really heard his grandchild cry?

Or had he thrown his daughter's corpse in some hole, or in the sea, and the memory was lost to him, like the face of his wife and blood of his first kill? And now his broken mind spun fantasies or stars and planets and gates in reality...

But every night he went to the roof above his rooms in the tower of the inner citadel where the god-king – his great-nephew – lived in the constant squalor of adolescent bliss. He ignored the orgiastic moans and groans, and eventually the stars told him part of a tale, and then he guessed more, as he was, after all, a seer. And he smiled at the stars; a cold smile that his long-dead enemies might have remembered, except none had survived him.

Among the many changes, his access to the Greater *Aura* – the golden magic of the upper airs that powered all the most powerful arcanae – was increased tenfold. Or more.

The irony was not lost on Gamash; after a life of striving for power, he was suddenly almost godlike; and that only when he rebelled. The cold smile lingered.

He tucked that smile away deep now, and doddered deliberately to the king: the same king who had not saved his daughter, the same king who would not heed his advice. The god-king, who was young and stupid, in a world that seemed to value those attributes in a king very highly.

The real gods like their satraps to be stupid.

17

'Great lord, serene god,' he said, laying himself full-length at the foot of the ivory throne.

His knees creaked as he fell to them, and the champion lounging by the throne laughed. The warrior wore a great cuirass of hardened bronze and a helmet to match, with two long horns of a black ibex to show his status and a huge ruff of plumes. Bronze greaves encased his shins below a spotless scarlet kilt. He was big and handsome, just the way the god-king liked them.

But the god-king leant forwards.

'Old man, lying on cold stone like that must be a torment for your bones. Get up! I can hear your joints pop from here.'

Warriors around the throne sneered. They saw themselves as lions, but the old man knew lions well, and these behaved more like hyenas.

He rose slowly, cursing his diminishment, his lack of grace, the laughing warriors secure in their bronze and gold. He was acutely aware of how small the god-king was, compared to the deity he had seen.

'Great Serene One, I ask a boon.'

'You are an old servant of this house. How can I refuse you anything?' the young god-king replied.

He was beautiful to look at, and made more so by the kohl under his eyes and the elaborate gold breastplate he wore. It made him seem to glow; and he exuded an almost palpable glow of power. And he was performing a role, now: *the great king is kind to an old retainer.*

He glanced at his warriors for their approval.

But then he leant forwards.

'Be quick, old man. What do you want? I have some entertainment on the way.'

Ah, entertainment.

The old man would have smiled. Because his revenge was

very much a betrayal and, up until that moment, he hadn't been sure that the golden god on his throne and the hyenas around him deserved what he had in mind.

Now he put doubt behind him.

'My lord,' he said, standing in the formal declaratory mode. 'My lord, I have seen a great event foretold in the sky. I wish to be present for its occurrence.'

It was as if Tyka had put those words in his mouth. The truth. The pure truth.

'Be my guest,' the god-king said, and the derisory laughter of the hyenas rose in pitch. No one wanted him around, and now he would take himself away.

'I will need money, a chariot, a horse and a driver. Two pack mules...'

His nephew's attention had already moved on.

'See to it,' he said to one of the priests – a scribe.

The writer cut the relevant sigil carefully into a clay tablet with a stylus.

Behind the old man there was the sound of snarling. The sound of wild dogs raised the hackles on the old man's neck, but he held his ground.

The warriors all turned to look, however.

The god-king looked, and then glanced down at the writer, who presented his tablet of wet clay on a slab of wood.

The god-king fastidiously affixed the magnificent carnelian seal from his belt, and the writer bowed deeply and backed down the dais to the old man.

'Wet dirt,' the god-king said. 'It is the cheapest clay, and yet by these signs a man can order armies or gold.'

He said this, but none of his attention was on the old man. All of it was on the wicker cages which held his dogs.

The old man didn't know what the dogs were for, and he

didn't want to know. He took his sheet of damp clay with a display of gratitude.

'Bring the servant,' the wanax ordered. 'You know the one...'

He smiled, a wicked child about to pull the limbs off a human insect.

Gamash backed out of the great hall between the towering stone pillars and into the sun of the palace courtyards as quickly as he could on his untrustworthy legs. And then he picked up his staff where it had rested, untouched, against the marble, and he hobbled past the graves of the old kings to the palace ovens as quickly as he could. He didn't want to know.

Or rather, he already knew too much.

I am old in evil, and so I will allow another innocent to go down. But now, I do it for a purpose. Because we will have our revenge. I have been promised.

Another old man, a baker's servant of a low grade, or perhaps a former slave, with one eye and a spectacular facial scar, placed his wet clay delicately on a broad, flat stone and slid it into the oven as if he was baking flatbread.

In fact, Gamash thought that was probably what the man did, for the most part.

'See that it comes out golden-brown and toasty,' he said. His first attempt at humour since Irene's murder.

'Delicious,' One-Eye joked. 'Mind if I have a bite?' He laughed. 'Sorry, lord. Just my little way.'

The old man smiled. 'No one calls me *lord* any more.'

'Aye. Well, all the world's nothing more than living hell, and then you die and your shade blows away on the wind.' The slave shrugged.

Gamash reflected that the one-eyed man had always thought this, whereas he had once believed otherwise.

'You may have something there, old friend,' the old man said. 'But the gods—'

'Fuck 'em,' the one-eyed man said. 'Beggin' yer pardon, lord. I'm jus' an old fool.'

That one eye was bright and clear, though.

'I have not heard many men curse the gods,' Gamash said.

'Don't take two eyes to see that everything's shit.'

The baker opened the oven door and extracted the clay tablet, now baked.

'Don't touch it, mind,' he said.

'You really don't have to tell me that.'

'You say that, lord, but palace fuckers get burnt every fucking day. And who do they blame? Me. Ten blows with the cane. Because they are, pardon my language, fuckwits.' He looked down at the signs. 'Could be yer death warrant,' he said. 'Who knows what it says?'

'I do,' the old man said. 'See? There's a chariot wheel. There's a cart, and there are two donkeys.'

'So there are.' The baker laughed. 'Although the great king, son of the gods, might have ordered a horse and two donkeys to drag you to death.'

'Do you talk like this to everyone?' the old man asked.

'Only old people, lord. Those of us with one foot in the grave, we see things differently...'

He had an odd moment, because the one-eyed man's smile reminded Gamash of...

Reminded him of something...

And when he turned away, he thought he caught the faintest whiff of the sea.

Five days later Gamash was riding along the edge of the sea, with the desert on his left and the black sea on his right, and yet his blood ran cold when he finally remembered.

The smell of the sea. And the rumour he'd once heard in a

far off land that Nanuk, the old pantheon's god of horses and the sea, had never been finished off by the new pantheon.

He'd seen an illegal statue of Nanuk once, a bearded giant with just one eye. And that smile was one which said, 'I own you all.'

What have I gotten myself into this time?

In his dreams a blue woman brought him bolts of silver lightning, and he gave them to the most unsuitable people: a slave with a bull's head tattoo; a dancing woman; a warrior; a scribe, but most of all a smith and his apprentice.

He cast bones. He made his sacrifices, and left the butchered sheep carcasses behind at every camp as he rode south along the ocean shore, and then into the desert west of Tur, the southernmost major town of the Hundred Cities. All of them vied for dominance on the eastern shore. Before he turned inland, he made camp in a circle of giant rocks on a headland that looked out over the sea. Ma'rib was perhaps five days' travel to the south – a mighty city that distanced herself from the eastern shore. The great mountain of Auza, where the gods dwelt, was just a glimmer in the evening haze; it would grow more visible every day that he travelled south. As he passed pilgrims on the road, his bitterness and rage had swelled again.

The next camp had fires, and a festive atmosphere. There were pilgrims heading south to worship the gods at the mountain, and a caravan of tin traders coming north from far-off Akash, plus a whole clan of nomads.

The nomads were kind enough; they knew him for what he was, and they feared his magics and wanted his gold. He left them the cart and his young driver, who had managed to be afraid of him and contemptuous of his age at the same time.

The next day he turned his horse inland, away from the coast road, his two donkeys laden with fresh food following him.

After fifteen days of dreams and sacrifices and rage and sorrow, and one rapid flight from a trio of Dry Ones he'd seen hovering in the distance, he came to a rocky outcropping with a deep cave – a campsite, established here for many long ages. The nomads had told him where to find water. One of the donkeys had died, but the other was doing well enough, and the horse, which mostly walked by his side, seemed to like the desert. He let it wander in the rough grass by the cave, though there were many signs of the Dry Ones and he was very cautious about making loud noises. No one knew what the Dry Ones wanted, or why they sometimes traded with people and sometimes attacked them. There were tales of Dry Ones saving people lost in the desert, and as many of their attacking human settlements and killing everyone, leaving desiccated corpses and complete, ruthless destruction in their wake. They were tall, elegant, with insectile wings and features, said to be touched by the gods themselves…

His brain was spinning like a chariot wheel. He calmed himself, and built his little camp deep inside the cave – having checked the back of it first, from habit, to make sure his throat wasn't cut in the night by man or Dry One. Then he ate sparingly, and watched the sun journey across the sky. The heat felt good as he lay back and sweltered in the sunlight, and his joints hurt less than they had in years.

That night a star slashed across the sky, burning so brightly that it left an afterimage on his closed eyes. He felt, or heard, its impact far to the south, in the Empty Lands by the distant sea of Badda Cas.

The next night there were several – probably more than he saw, because, with elderly frailty, he fell asleep.

The third night, the falling stars became a shower, which was perhaps the most beautiful thing he'd ever seen. They descended like the spears of a victorious army of gods, slashing across the signs and sigils and goring the whole of the zodiac like an omen. The shooting stars lit the night so brightly he could see the sigils he'd traced in the sand – wards to protect himself from the dead and anything else wandering the cool night air.

After he nodded off the second time he withdrew into the cave and lay down to dream, and Tyka came to him and showed him a deep, smoking crater, and then seven more, in the midst of northern snows. He woke, cold in spite of the heat, and stupid with sleep as he fumbled for his cloak. He was just unrolling it to sleep when the sky...

Flashed...

White...

There was a light like all the lightning that had ever been and a sound like every thunder that had ever clapped, all together between one heartbeat and the next.

Only the rocky cave saved him, and even then, the ceiling shook; rock and dirt fell all around him and his hair was filled with dust. A wind burst down the cave and ripped his cloak away, plastering it against the far wall for a moment like a living thing, while a storm of sand and stones outside swept away his horse.

Then true lightning forked across the sky, and Gamash knew awe and fear. In its light he saw the gods, although he could not tell if what he saw was play or war. Their gold and ivory and scarlet and ebony forms were visible in the clear night air, passing low over the desert as if searching for something, and then they were gone.

He fell on his face and waited for death.

He awoke to a clear blue sky and a headache like a hangover, and climbed the mound above his cave slowly to survey the scene, then stopped, his mind almost unable to take in what he was seeing.

At his feet...

He looked away, and back.

At his feet was a great pit – a crater. The crater from his dream. The more he looked at it, the more it became manageable, at least in his head and his heart. It was more than a hundred paces across, and the air over it was distorted with heat.

He backed away to the relative sanity of his cave to sit down and take it in, and saw his horse's carcass hundreds of paces away. As if deliberately avoiding the crater behind him, he spent the day butchering the animal. He wasn't particularly good at it, but his skill was adequate to the task; he'd been a warrior once, and he'd hunted the great deer in the Rasnan wilderness far to the north and west, and bears in the woods of Dendrowna. It wasn't too long before he set a dozen slabs of meat on the rock to dry in the ferocious sun; within an hour he'd been reminded that the apparently empty desert was full of scavengers.

It was three days before he could get to the black rock in the middle of the crater. On the first, he was understanding the surprise. For the next two he could smell the forbidden star-metal, but it was still too hot to approach.

Star-metal was taboo – a pollution of anything it touched. He had assumed that the Enemy would send him such; he knew what it was for, and he was fixed in his purpose. But to see it was shocking; to touch it was to touch a deadly curse, or so the gods told people.

And even when he could, it was too big and heavy to move, not even the width of a hair. It was almost three times the size of his head and shaped like a trumpet in reverse, the top pitted as if the contact with the gods had corroded it.

But the more he searched the crater, the more shards of the black stone he found. Shards he could collect, until he had picked up a dozen that together made half a donkey-load. He used his folded cloak to move them, and did his best never to touch them.

He survived ten days across the desert. Perhaps more remarkably, so did the donkey.

He rode along his own back trail, pleased that he could navigate his way back from camp to camp, until he reached the oasis where he had left the nomads.

They were gone.

Gamash walked on with the donkey until he returned to the pilgrim camps on the cliffs above the sea, and there he bought a pair of precious horses. Once he would have prayed. Now he didn't bother. He watched the sea, ate with pilgrims going south, and then he rode south himself along the well-travelled road.

At some point, he admitted to himself that the hand of the Enemy was on him. If his survival in the desert was not enough, his travelling alone, alive and unrobbed along a path positively engorged with broken men and bandits, while carrying a pound or so of gold and a donkey-load of star-metal, was proof.

He rode south, along the edge of the desert, until he came to Ma'rib. He'd been there once before, as part of an embassy; he knew its towers and its great walls, the streets canopied in wisteria, the mountain that rose from the sea, crowned in hippogryphs, and its scent of manure and frankincense. And its reputation as a city of smiths.

He visited a dozen, and they all shook their heads. More than one threw him out angrily, and he moved tavernas twice in case they'd informed the king about his enquiries. He grew more cautious once he discovered how deep the taboo about star-metal ran in Ma'rib. He narrowly avoided a run-in with a godborn warrior, after which he sat in his inn and contemplated failure.

After an evening of too much wine he tried another tack,

and met with a fellow seer – a man called Shafi he remembered from his embassy. His name meant 'The Pure', though he hadn't seemed particularly pure to Gamash, and right now the man's venality was a positive recommendation.

Gamash sent a request with some hesitation, knowing seers were like cats: they were territorial and didn't tend to encourage visits. But age mellows even the most aloof, and the boy he sent returned with a positive answer, and his host, Shafi, a fellow seer, was convivial, at least at first, and didn't poison him, or even offer grandiloquence. He merely declined to be involved.

'You have the mark of the gods on you,' the Saabian seer said. 'I can see it and it warns me to keep my distance. And what you seek is like incest – forbidden even to the powerful. Walk away.' He leant forwards. 'More wine?'

Gamash caught the note of duplicity in his voice and poured the second cup of wine into a hanging plant – a rare lotus that, in certain conjunctions of the stars, was reputed a powerful aphrodisiac. He made an excuse and left.

He went to a temple in the high citadel, a huge temple dedicated to the whole pantheon of gods, with a portico that allowed pilgrims a framed glimpse of the distant mountain of Auza, and he found a chapel with a lapis pillar, the only sign of devotion to the Blue Goddess. Here in Ma'rib the folk called her 'the Blue One.' Women thought she eased the pangs of childbirth, and men thought she aided fertility; Gamash thought both were a comment on people's desires and fears. And not for the first time, he wondered who or what they were, and with what he had become … entangled.

But he was enjoying the entanglement, because he was *doing something*. So he filed in past the knowing gaze of a temple guard in a red cloak and nothing else, and there he made an offering, and prayed. He felt odd, praying, with her library of counter-knowledge in his head and her assertion that the gods were neither real, nor immortal.

A fly landed on the capital of the pillar – a ton or more of lapis lazuli, veined in gold – and when the fly lifted away the old man followed it hoping for a sign, but the fly went to the top of the huge columns and then out into the world. The seer decided that either she was toying with him, which was all too possible, or it was a false sign.

He had visited three anxious, dismissive, superstitious bronze smiths, and was going to a fourth when he saw a chariot parked at the mouth of the alley, and a file of soldiers lounging about, bothering the women who passed.

He turned away, collected his bags, and trudged to the city gates, regretting that he had let his donkey go. Before he even reached the gates, he saw a small boy with an enigmatic smile and, on an instinct, followed him.

The boy said nothing. But after the seer followed him a way, hefting a bag with some of the heavy fragments of black stone inside, he came to trust his instinct. The boy could in fact be a girl, or even a woman. Or even something arcane, because the faster he walked, the faster they moved, and remained the same distance ahead of him all the time.

They walked unchallenged through the south gate of the great city at the edge of the Empty Lands, and then south along the shore just as the sun was setting out on the western rim of the world, far away across the Ocean.

He followed them when they left the road. Paths intersected the trade road everywhere; this was one of many capillaries vanishing into the wilderness at the edge of the Empty Lands. He knew trails like this; the rules of kings and gods extended only so far, and there were always places like this on the edge: hard to reach; difficult to tax.

They climbed a rocky slope, the trail cutting back and forth on the slippery shale, and the sun sank, and so did the old man's heart. It was a long and difficult climb to the top, especially carrying the bags of star-stone.

Once he reached the top, his guide was gone, but Gamash no longer expected anything else, and the desert was waiting for him. It was, so men said, the same desert he'd seen in the north, in Narmer. The dunes stretched away like waves of sand on a golden sea, but there at the base of the first dune was a hold – walled with mud bricks, painted in dried dung and whitewashed. With a well. And the reek of burning charcoal, although he could not see a chimney anywhere.

He walked to the low door in the mud-brick wall surrounding the hold. There was a bronze bell – a remarkable thing so near the terrors of the Empty Lands. The Dry Ones lived close.

He rang it. It had a comforting sound. The sound of civilisation, of the hands of men.

He waited.

It was good that he'd spent old age cultivating patience because he waited a long time; and likewise, he didn't ring the bell again. Something told him not to.

A man answered, opening the wooden door – solid wood, the kind of wood that came from Dendrowna, far to the north. That door was more valuable than the bell and more out of place.

He was tall, like a Dendrownan. Very tall. And very well muscled and tattooed. Not 'like a Dendrownan'. He was Dendrownan, from one of the big cities.

'I'm working,' he said in Trade, the simplified Dardanian familiar to all the peoples of the lands surrounding the Ocean. No annoyance – just a flat comment.

'You are a smith?' Gamash asked.

The man gave him a glance – the look of a parent for an annoying child. 'Yes.'

'I am Gamash,' the seer said.

'I am Hefa-Asus,' the man answered. He inclined his head. 'I suppose you want to come in.'

'I do,' Gamash answered.

Even when you feel as if you are in the hands of one of the immortals, a night at the edge of the Empty Lands was a thing to fear.

'Come,' said the man.

And without further conversation, he let the seer inside.

The smith had to bend almost double in the low entry tunnel. Even Gamash had to duck as they passed from the gate into the hold, and so he was doubly surprised after scrambling in the dark to emerge into what seemed like a low cave. Oil lamps lit it, and the red coals of a huge hearth with a mud-brick chimney overhead.

It was cool despite the heat of the forge fires.

The size of the forge was one thing; the four other people in the forge were another. Somehow Gamash had imagined that Hefa-Asus lived alone – a foolish notion, the sort of assumption that could get you killed.

There were four soot-blackened apprentices, young, and sweaty and big. Three men and one woman.

A woman smith. Gamash shook his head.

'All this, and yet you answer the gate bell yourself?'

'Always better that way,' the smith said. 'Fewer surprises. Less stupidity. What do you want?'

As he spoke, the woman and the biggest man took up a form like a clay log and held it upright in bronze tongs. Up close, the seer could see that all of them were covered in small burns and abrasions, and the tattoos of the north. One of them was singing, a high-pitched nasal song in a voice that would not recommend him anywhere, at least not in the Hundred Cities. His copper skin shone in the ruddy firelight.

The muscular woman manoeuvred the baked-clay log into place on the massive hearth and they set the thing upright and began to bank red-hot coals all around it. They worked quickly and with great efficiency.

Gamash could hear the spell that the northern boy was working. He sang of mixing, of making, of blending, of cutting, and of protection. It was a strong, old song, and Gamash admired it. He saw it bend the light and the air, and move the *Aura*, the background magic of the gods.

No. Not the gods. That was the old lie. It just was. The gods had nothing to do with the Aura.

Gamash smiled to hear the song, and after a few moments was able to recognise the Dendrownan language; *Poche*, he thought. He spoke it, a little, and had been there, in his war years.

As he sang, the boy tapped a crucible with a hammer. It made a good sound.

'I am in need of a smith,' Gamash said. 'You are from Poche?'

'Yes,' Hefa-Asus said, watching his people work.

'And yet you live here?'

The seer was genuinely curious; Poche lay at the margin of the vast forest of Dendrowna at the other end of the Ocean, all the way across the salt. Three month's travel by sea, if the pirates and the Jekers didn't get you, or the sea monsters or the Dry Ones.

The smith seemed annoyed to be interrupted. Gamash didn't really blame the man.

'What do you want with a smith?' Hefa-Asus asked.

'I'd like to stay the night,' the seer said. 'For starters.'

'Of course,' the smith answered. 'We are at the edge of the Empty Lands. We never refuse bed or board to any traveller who is still human.'

A chill struck the seer. 'Still human?'

Hefa-Asus gave him a glance, and Gamash shook his head.

'And then I would like to know if you can forge this,' he said.

Fifteen smiths in two days had told him that the black rock was not metal – a remarkable claim, as each one of the rocks weighed like metal and some had a dark shine like bronze but paler, almost like tarnished silver. He had taken an enormous risk, just asking them, but then, he trusted his blue deity.

Who said she was not a god.

Trust was an odd word.

Gamash opened his bag, and the smith took one of his black rocks.

'Hmmm,' he said.

The boy who was singing lifted his crucible. In one strong, practised movement, he poured molten bronze into the throat of the clay mould that the woman held upright in a volcanic mound of red coals. The metal flowed like water, and the mould smoked, and there was a smell, almost like blood. The smell of copper, and a little tartness to indicate tin.

Bronze.

Hefa-Asus tapped two of the black stones together and raised an eyebrow.

'Star-stone?' He dropped a flake on the stone floor, and it rang like the bell outside. 'Hmmm.'

The boy pouring the metal was tempted to turn his head; you could see it, and you could see him resisting it as he continued the pour, and the second young man tapped the clay mould with a hammer.

The woman had a stone hammer, and she tapped the mould more rapidly, as if they were a pair of good drummers. The man's hammer beat the rhythm; the woman's was a melody, the song the other boy had sung.

The mould vented, and a little molten bronze ran over the side. The pourer stepped back.

'A crime against the gods,' the smith said conversationally. 'Star-stone is sacred. Taboo. Not meant for men.'

Gamash was old enough to know the value of silence.

So, apparently, was Hefa-Asus. But then he looked up with a smile.

'Tell me, persistent seer. Do you dream of a blue woman?'

Gamash blinked. 'Yes.'

'Then I have waited a long time for you,' Hefa-Asus said. 'I came here for this, more than three years ago.'

The smith dropped each of the pieces, one by one, on his filthy, cinder-strewn stone floor, and they rang like metal bells; but the twelfth, the largest, made a different note, and he put it aside.

'There's an impurity,' he said. 'I'll have to take it out.'

'You'll work it for me?' Gamash asked.

The smith smiled. 'I assume you want a sword fit for a hero?'

Gamash looked away, the memory of his murdered daughter rushing back.

'No,' he said. 'I would rather a dozen spears. Or a hundred arrowheads.'

The smith's smile widened. 'I like to make spearheads,' he said. 'Though it will take time.' He sat back, brushed his lank hair from his eyes, still staring at the stone. 'Star-stone has a smell, one the gods can detect. The moment I begin to work it, the sand begins to run through our hands, and when the last grains fall, the gods will strike us dead.'

Gamash pulled at his beard. He didn't know whether the smith was completely insane or whether this was all part of getting too close to immortal things, so he nodded, as if he understood.

Hefa-Asus met his eye. His eyes were neither bright nor fevered, nor did they have the hard glitter of the broken mind.

'The moment I begin to heat this, the gods will know.' He put the bag down. 'I must sleep on this – both how, and when, to forge it.'

'The Blue Lady told me ...' the seer began, amazed at his own temerity.

'She spoke to you in a dream?'

'I saw her.'

Now he had the smith's attention.

'You *met* the Blue Lady?' he asked.

'Yes. They told me where to find the star-stone. They showed me more of it, in the snows of the north.'

Hefa-Asus gave a half-smile, half-frown that was at once amused and bitter.

'I came all the way here, apparently, to meet you. I built a secret forge to prepare for this, and now ...' He glanced at his apprentices. 'Fucking gods. Do you think you can find the star-stone in the north?'

'With help,' Gamash said. 'A great deal of help.'

He explained that there was star-stone as close as the desert west of Tur. The smith waved a hand, dismissing it.

'The gods will retrieve most of that,' he said. 'I guess it was left as a distraction.'

'It was left?' Gamash asked.

'This is an old game,' the smith said with a wry smile. 'You're just a new pawn in it.'

Gamash struggled with that for a moment, and then returned to smaller worries.

'So you think we should head for Dendrowna?'

'Yes. You've been?' the smith asked.

'As far as Palanke, in my prime.' The seer looked at his ancient hands on the low table. 'I was a kind of warrior, once.'

The smith's hands were knotted with heavy work and heavy blows.

'As was I,' he said. 'Once this is done, we'll need to get out of here very quickly.'

'A ship, then,' the magos agreed. 'Which means Ma'rib, which will probably be full of people looking for me.' He frowned into the oil-lamp flame.

'We'll be cautious. All we have to do is buy a boat.'

The old magos shook his head. 'You want to exercise caution? I'm in rebellion against the gods. My life ended when my daughter died.'

'Hmmm,' Hefa-Asus rubbed his chin. 'I hadn't thought of it as *rebellion against the gods*.' He was quiet for a long time, and then said, 'But I suppose you are correct. We are rebels against them.'

Gamash nodded. 'And I suppose you are correct – we can rebel. But we can still act with caution.'

Heaven

'How much star-stone fell?' Enkul-Anu asked with quiet ferocity.

There were more than a dozen of the younger deities gathered before his throne in the Hall of Judgement. Nisroch hated going to the Hall of Judgement; its black basalt interior was gloomy and threatening and too dark for any version of 'paradise'. And the Storm God most frequently used it as the hall of humiliating his underlings.

Nerkalush, one of Gul's sons – something in the pantheon of the dead – had a belt of human skulls that Resheph admired; the two of them were loud and stupid with youth and power. Resheph, the war god's son, already had a title – God of Pestilence During War. Nisroch thought it was a terrible title, but the adolescent god gloried in it.

'I bet I can kill more mortals than you,' Resheph bragged.

'My dad's the god of, like, death,' Nerkalush said in his strange sing-song voice. 'Like, war is awesome for killing, but death … man, it's death. I can kill more mortals than—'

'We could have a contest,' Resheph said.

'Cool,' Nerkalush said. 'I mean, with powers?'

Enkul-Anu raised his left hand, showing the thunderbolt pulsing in his palm.

'Are you two fucking idiots?' he asked harshly. 'No, I *know* you are fucking idiots, but are you actually too stupid to shut up in my presence?'

Nerkalush flinched. Resheph grew brown with rage.

'I'm not a fucking idiot,' he said. 'You can't call me—'

Enkul-Anu reached out, grabbed him by the neck and flung him into the wall.

'Moving on,' he said.

Resheph slumped to the floor. Servitors hurried to help him; ambrosia was provided, which he swallowed hastily. The beautiful honey-coloured resin worked its usual miracle, and his body knitted; bruises healed.

Illikumi, God of Serpents and Liars, raised a tentative hand.

'Ssstar-ssstone fell in the Eassstern Dessssert,' they hissed sibilantly.

Nisroch looked away. Illikumi was a virtually powerless god who would say anything to get attention. Also, their scaly skin and androgynous form was ... off-putting.

He took a half-step forwards.

'Great God, I have reports on the fall of star-stone and I have queried our usual sources.'

The gods had monitors all across the earth – spy devices called god's eyes that were installed in most palaces and temples. Nisroch was constantly attempting to broaden the reach of the god's eyes, and his Watchers – mostly junior priests recruited for their devotion – were the fastest growing part of the god's bureaucracy. Together they formed the *Nexus*; Nisroch's spy service. It was his power base in the endless struggle among the junior gods.

He liked to imagine that eventually, he'd be able to watch a sparrow fall, anywhere in the world.

Enkul-Anu leant down from his throne.

'Do you fucking idiots know what star-stone is?' he asked.

Nisroch raised his hand.

'I know *you* fucking know,' the storm god snapped to Nisroch. 'The rest of you?'

Illikumi raised a scaled talon. 'It isss ... deadly,' they hissed.

Enkul-Anu narrowed his eyes. 'Not bad, worm.' He looked

around, golden eyes burning with his power. 'It's fucking *iron*. There's no other iron on this world. I made fucking sure of that before we came here. It's deadly to us. And every time our *enemy* wants to make trouble, she drops some iron. So go and fucking find it, before she raises an army of her stupid pawns and tricks them into fighting us. It's messy and wasteful. Do you understand?'

Nerkalush looked scared. Resheph was contemptuous. Nisroch had known the score before he was summoned, and enjoyed knowing it. Illikumi was impossible to read, as they appeared to have no facial muscles – just a snake's head. Telipinu, the new chamberlain and aspiring storm god in waiting, looked excited; it was his first chance for action.

Nisroch worried about Telipinu; he was the child of Sypa and Enkul-Anu, destined to be a favourite.

And my mother is banished to the void, he thought.

The junior goddesses and one of Sypa's handmaids just nodded; in Nisroch's view they were only there to look nice. And there was Lady Laila; she didn't have a god title. She did something for Sypa, and Nisroch wanted her; her athletic body, black hair and brown skin were more to his taste than the lusher figures of the handmaids. He tried to get her attention, but she was talking to one of the other women. Some nonsense, no doubt. No one expected the goddesses to find the star-stone.

He'd do that himself, and get the credit. And perhaps put some of it away...

Chapter Two

Era

Era was lying face down in pig shit.

Short of killing herself, it seemed the best way to avoid gang rape and slavery, so she lay there, wishing that she'd left Hazor a day earlier as she'd planned, and hating the idiot men and their endless wars, and hating the gods even more.

The smell was incredible and the foulness beyond outrage. But Era had not survived so long by being shy of a little dirt.

She rolled onto her side and tried to breathe. One of the three pigs nuzzled at her, and she saw its teeth and felt a sharp moment of fear through her disgust. She'd heard that the scum lords fed their victims to pigs, and suddenly playing dead seemed dangerous, too.

'Pigs!' shouted a male voice. 'Fucking pigs!'

'Pork on the hoof!' called another.

'There's the bacon!'

She closed her eyes and prayed to her goddess, the Virgin Huntress Temis.

Hazor had started out well enough. Era had played in a waterfront taverna, eaten squid, drunk decent wine and bought a new cloak. She knew the arc of a town – arrival, fascination, the early days of wide appreciation, the increasingly insistent pawing of men, the rising anger from the spurned – and eventually, if you stayed too long, it all turned to shit...

It was like a bad refrain. Always the same notes.

She'd stayed too fucking long. She'd been distracted by the dark-haired beauty with the cow eyes who came from the brothel every night after work, and who had become a rare and eager partner, and Era hadn't had enough eager partners that she wanted to spurn one, especially one so very...

It is very difficult to wallow in pig shit and think erotic thoughts, and Era had a stab of horror at what her dark lady might be enduring, now they were both caught in a city under attack.

'Gods! Stinks like the fucking underworld.'

'They's just pigs,' the first voice said – the youngest.

'Stay with 'em if you like 'em so much,' said the thicker voice. 'Fuck 'em if that's what you fancy.'

Era lay perfectly still in the muck and tried to tune out the snorting of the pigs and the debate between men who would kill her if they knew she was alive, and tried not to listen to the fighting further away, or the screams of desperation. Hazor was dying, taken by storm. Era had no idea how it had happened or where the attackers had come from, or even who they were.

But she knew the sound of a city falling to storm. It was a horrible song, melding the screams of dying men and the despair of free women whose fate was to become chattels. Combing wool and making babies who were destined to become more warriors and more textile workers in turn.

Protect me, Huntress!

The keening sound was rising. The high-pitched screams suddenly redoubled.

The attackers must have reached the Temple of Sypa, full of godborn women praying for protection. They always prayed. Though Sypa never did shit to save them.

The godborn make great slaves. They believe in authority. Who had said that? Her mother?

Had the men left the pigsty?

Era was trying to breathe shallowly, without moving, but terror and the stench combined to make that excruciating.

Are they still fucking there or not?

Terror, as Era knew, had no time limit.

Another pig snuffled at her.

She wore a long woman's *heton* that, prior to the pig shit, had been of good quality, saffron coloured, utterly unrevealing, and the shoulders were pinned with long, straight bronze pins – every woman's last line of defence.

She moved slowly, subvocalising a song-spell to keep the animal placid.

The pig kept nuzzling her, with more interest now, and she remembered that flash of teeth.

So much for that.

She pulled one of the pins from her shoulder, and stuck it in the pig. She did it viciously; she had no hesitation in hurting anything.

Huntress, are pigs even part of your kingdom?

The pig gave a short scream, and it retreated rapidly.

'What the fuck?' said a man.

He wasn't a big man, but standing above her, silhouetted against the sun, he looked like a Titan. He was one of the three who'd been talking.

Era wasn't a big woman. But she was a dancer, trained to an exacting standard in Narmer, and she came out of the slime like a dreadful, stinking, vengeful apparition.

'Gods!' The man stumbled back and hit his head against one of the posts. 'Ara Sword-God! Fuck!'

It occurred to Era that a woman coated in pig muck probably didn't look human.

Era wasn't big, but she was fast and graceful and she had an opportunity. She went over the railing, the drenched, shit-slimed wool of her *heton* like a snare to catch her, and some part of the fabric caught on the wood of the sty and ripped.

She still got a hand into the man's throat. A knee into his groin. And again.

He had no real armour – just one of the armour-shaped linen tubes they put on poor men to make them brave.

'Where are the other two?' she asked.

'Gods!' the man said. He was choking with pain and from the reek of her.

Stinking. Her new weapon.

Era looked out into the street. There were a dozen fallen bodies, though most weren't dead. Not yet. Two men were beating a naked woman, their blows thudding home. Their victim wasn't moving.

Bile rose to gag Era.

'They went to take slaves …' the man whispered. 'I stayed … I had pigs at home …'

Era thought about that for a single beat of her heart. Here was a good enough man that he had stayed with the pigs instead of going to capture slaves.

Too bad.

Her pin sank into his temple in the soft spot and he died, and she let him fall.

She was smaller than he was, but she wasn't weak. She directed his fall onto the pigsty railing, and then lifted his feet and tossed him in.

Pigs, it turned out, really did eat people.

As the sun began to set, someone set fire to part of the upper town, and Era understood who their attackers were.

Jekers.

She saw their lords, their commanders, in their horned bronze helmets, herding their slaves to the beach.

She saw them in the squares of the city, as they made fires, and roasted the dead, and feasted on them in celebration of their victory. They offered rare meat, carved from the fallen, to the newly captured men; those who ate, they accepted as their own. Those who refused, they killed.

And roasted.

Then she saw something she wasn't supposed to – something that made her squint in puzzlement and not in horror.

Something came out of the heavens like a thunderbolt, leaving a streak of brilliant light across her retinas, and landing in a sweep of broad eagle's wings and a cloud of dust that hid its true form for a few moments.

One of the gods was among them.

For a moment, despite her distaste for them, Era hoped for the rage of a war god to smash the hideous cruelties of the Jekers. To deliver some revenge for the pointless slaughter.

When none came, she moved. She slipped from the safety of the barns and slaughterhouses, the pigs and sheep and cattle, into the narrow streets where the poor lived.

Everyone was dead.

She stepped over corpses with their hearts cut out, over men carved up like farm animals. She moved as cautiously as she could until she could see into the dust cloud …

Her own smell choked her. Hopelessness choked her. But before she could run, she had to know if her love had survived.

She got to the taverna; there were the beaded curtains, the hanging oil lamps, the rough outside tables at which she'd been happy. So happy. Her dark-eyed Puduhepa had worked here, lain with men, lain with her.

Puduhepa was still here. Era found her lover on the wine- and

43

bloodstained packed earth – a big woman from far-off Atussa, who'd died with a bronze dagger in her hand.

Somehow, that freed something in Era. Some day, she'd weep for the woman, but death with a bloody dagger in hand represented a better end than those Era had imagined for her. She breathed deeply, crawled under the taverna tables from where she could see into the main square to the lower town. And crawled on.

And on. Closer and closer to the main square.

And there he was.

A god. Taller than the biggest Jeker with the biggest helmet, he towered over them, gleaming in gold and lapis and jade, his massive white eagle's wings beating from time to time, or twitching, as if to show his power.

There was no revenge here. The god was *talking* to the *Jekers.*

Behind the god, women and children – the survivors – walked hollow-eyed like the unquiet dead – of whom, Era knew from experience, there would be quite a few by morning. A few hours ago, they had been worshippers. Now they were slaves.

Only this morning, they had been smiths and scribes, mothers and daughters.

She choked on her rage at the waste, her hatred for the brutality. But the long lines of slaves were expressionless; there was no hope here, and no revolt.

Long lines of women and children, mostly; a few men had been deemed worth keeping. And the smell of death, and fire, and cooked human flesh. Even covered in pig shit, it made her gag.

The broken captives were herded west, through the port and along the seaside beach on to the ships, the Jekers jabbering in a dozen foreign tongues and her own, and she hated them, including the god. Most of all when they laughed – aggressive laughter from large men, pleased with their simple brutality.

Eventually the god turned, and in a single, beautiful motion, leapt into the sky. In that moment, Era saw the golden staff of his office, and knew him.

It was Nisroch, Herald of the Gods.

What betrayal is this? she wondered. *Our gods strike against us now?*

As she watched, the most brazenly attired Jeker, a huge man in a green cloak lined in what she saw with sickening certainly was human hair, began to bellow orders. He was meticulous; demanding that supplies be found and water refilled.

She *knew him.* Or rather, she'd danced for him when he'd been a prince among the Attusans, visiting Narmer. *Hyatti-Azi,* she thought. *Someday.*

As soon as the herald left them, the Jekers began to shout, to prod their captives, to move faster. By sunset the ships had lifted their anchor stones, pushed their sweeping bows off the landing beaches and into the water, and were gone into the Great Green. Era was alone with the moans of the wounded and the silence of the dead, and the smell of burning wood, burning flesh and pig shit.

The gates were open, the guards dead or fled, as she walked out into a lovely evening. The Maiden star was rising, brighter than all the rest, and Ara was already an angry red in the north. The Gift constellation shone over the water, a perfect circle of brilliant emerald stars.

There were bodies everywhere. The Jekers had landed north and south of the city, too, she could see – trapping the fleeing people and butchering them, killing the men, taking the women and children.

Jekers.

And one of the gods.

Rumour said that, more than a hundred years before, some

of the southern cities had collapsed; their irrigation systems had filled with sand, their farms were lost, and the survivors had turned first to cannibalism and then to raiding. A hundred years before, they had been fearsome bandits.

Now, they were a rising tide which destroyed anything they touched, and turned people into more of their own. Era passed over a stream with a sluice-dam for irrigation; the Jekers had destroyed it. And killed the keeper and his family, and eaten parts of them.

Beasts.

Except that not even desperate animals were like this. And she loved animals.

Before the sun had completely set she had left the last of the dead behind, and she was in the open country – farms of course, but trees of the kind that grew in the delta. She'd left the donkey here, in the pine grove…

The donkey was right where she'd left it. At first, Era thought she was sleeping.

Closer up, she saw the animal was dead. She had been shot repeatedly with arrows, and then the arrows had been dug out of her flesh. Because bronze was valuable.

She had been shot hundreds of times.

Because men were horrible.

Then Era wept, as she hadn't for Puduhepa, or for the godborn maidens reduced to sexual slavery, or for the men killed and eaten before her eyes, or even for the poor farm boy she'd killed herself. But her donkey had been with her for so long. And she'd cared for her – got her through last year's attack of tiny worms.

'Fuck!' she cried.

She had very little left to say except curses, and she cursed them all, and then, stinking and unwashed, she cried herself to sleep. It was not the first time. Merely the first time in a long time.

In the morning, Era woke. Her donkey was dead. She knew as soon as she raised her head from its skin, the hair clotted with blood, her beautiful thick-lashed eyes, finer than the most beautiful dancer's, now horrid red-brown ruins. Flies buzzed.

She cried again. But while she cried, she gathered stones; her musician's hands took a beating, but the donkey had been her friend, her conveyance, her entertainment.

'Fuck,' she muttered.

It takes a great many stones to cover a dead donkey.

No one disturbed her. In the end, it took most of the day, and her nails were split and her fingers hurt from plucking stones out of the ground, but there was volcanic stone everywhere from the War of the Gods.

She stacked rocks until she thought it was unlikely that any scavenger would disturb the site.

Then she sat, and without any instrument she made music. She sang a song about the emptiness of life and the goodness of donkeys. And then she let herself feel for more than just a donkey. She let herself feel.

She sang for Puduhepa, and how a woman could be a better friend than any other person. And she dedicated her song to the Huntress, and called her by her true name – her magic name.

Which made the sound *Ta-Mi-Te* in the ancient tongue.

And she used the sounds as she made ink from her own blood and a little soot, and wrote them on the cairn, and cursed anything alive that touched it. She felt the power move. She saw her *Aura* darken with the power of the curse, and she didn't care.

When she was done, she knelt and raised her arms.

The Dark Huntress, Temis, was standing right in front of her. She was taller than a mortal, her skin a perfect, non-reflecting black – an absence, and emptiness. Her hair appeared to be spun

47

from gold, and her eyes were the same, too bright to look upon, and she wore nothing, and carried a bow and a sword.

'I see you,' the goddess said. 'I hear you, mortal.' The beautiful head turned, as if someone else was speaking. And then she said, in a rich, passionate, youthful voice, 'I am the worm in the apple of immortality.'

Era had no idea what she meant. But her voice was beautiful. As were her feet, the only part she could look at.

The goddess raised one hand in front of Era's eyes, and Era saw her nails were a vibrant, living gold.

'*Listen, child. My hand will touch the wheel, and it will falter. Your rage calls to mine, and we are not alone. When the stars fall, follow the old seer to the sea. Do what you will with what you find there, and you will do my will. Your vengeance will be in the tapestry of my vengeance, and all will be restored.*'

No voice had never been so clear. But the moment she finished speaking, she was gone.

Era lay weeping for a long time – for her loss, and for the beauty that was the Huntress.

Darkness fell, and she stank, and she had not eaten in two days, and both her donkey and her lover were dead.

She slept.

In the morning, she scrubbed herself clean in the sea and emerged from it naked, because once she had washed, the pig-shit-encrusted *heton* was unwearable. It could not be cleaned, it was torn, and the smell was appalling. She pulled her pins from it, and the knife she wore around her neck, and she had the small gold ring on her finger, and she made her way back to the city, swimming each time the road came to a beach. The gates were still open, and the corpses were still rotting, but she could feel that there was life somewhere within.

Nudity attracts evil attention the way raw meat attracts

scavengers, so as soon as she was in the upper town where the stone houses stood, she went into one.

It had been looted, but looters never wanted linen or wool. In two hundred beats of her heart, she had better fabrics than she'd possessed since childhood. She made a roll of them, like a sleeping roll, and went into the women's room to find *zones*, the tablet-woven belts all free women wore.

She wished she hadn't. Someone had killed them all, in a particularly horrid way, and taken their hearts. She wasn't disgusted; instead, she stood and looked, as if by seeing them clearly she could honour them, and measure her hatred for those who did such things. And one great advantage of nudity was that it was easy to wash things off skin. Life had taught her that again and again.

They were dead, and they no longer needed their *zones*. She took several; tied her roll with three and wore two, one around her waist, one crossed under and over her breasts like an athlete.

She found food in the kitchen with the dead slaves.

Who kills slaves? she wondered, as she found she couldn't cook in the house full of the dead.

She went to the next house – more of the same – and the next. But somewhere along the second street she tried, almost at the edge of the burning, she looked up and stood still. She all but flinched when she saw the deer antlers over the door – the secret sign of a house of a devotee of the Huntress. She was shocked, because she had spent two weeks in this city and never met another devotee, and yet the antlers were publicly displayed.

Or they had been placed for her. Temis was not a deity anyone worshipped in public. But women of a certain inclination used the antlers to find each other, and there were men who followed the Huntress as well, especially warriors.

She saw a child, but it ran before she could speak.

Era tried the door, and it was unyielding, so it took her time to find a way in: over the wall to the courtyard, then in through the kitchen. She had her small knife in her hand, waiting to be attacked, but there was no one.

In the kitchens she found grain, and some oil, and sausages, newly made and gathering flies – though not so many, when they had so many corpses in which to lay eggs.

She found a quern and ground the grain. Her hands hurt from her cairn-building, and her stomach bit at her, and the dead women seemed to lurk everywhere.

Then she started a fire. Fire, like nudity, could attract attention, but she had to eat. When a noise came she was ready, and she was very fast. Her free hand struck out, and she had him. The boy was small, and very dirty.

And very serious.

Era had never wanted children. She didn't particularly love them, although they were often charming and honest.

This one didn't flinch from her. He looked at her steadily, like someone very old. He had a gold ring on his finger, like a noble, but his accent didn't match it.

'This is my house,' he said.

His Narmerian was curiously accented, as if he was from somewhere else. Nobles in the Hundred Kingdoms usually spoke Narmerian, at least this far north.

'Yes,' she said.

'Are you my mother now?'

She gagged, and had no words at first. She didn't want a child with her, not for what she planned to do.

What on earth am I planning to do?

He was old enough that he might not be too much trouble, though. Some muscle, already.

She weighed the idea, and he looked at her.

'I like bears,' he said. 'I have one upstairs. She's very brave. All the time. She helped me hide.'

'That settles it,' she said, as if they were normal people having a normal conversation.

'You like bears?'

'Very much,' she said.

He nodded, very formally. She thought he might be godborn, or just well trained. His hair was filthy, but could be blond; common enough in Mykoax and not unknown in Narmer, blond hair was almost unheard of in the Hundred Cities.

'You smell terrible,' he said.

'Yes, I do. But I'm making dinner. And then I'm leaving. Will you stay in the house, or come with me?'

'Where are you going?' he asked.

'Somewhere better than this,' she said, hoping that was true. It wouldn't be difficult.

'Will you come back here?'

'Probably not.'

'Good,' he said. 'They killed my mother and my father. Bror, my bear, told me to hide, and I did. But now I want to leave.'

Huntress, she thought. *And I think I'm hard.*

But they both had to eat and the food wouldn't cook itself, so she took a clay pan, and tried to heat it and it broke because she hurried too much. It was years since she'd done these domestic things. She took another, blessing the orderliness of the woman who had directed this kitchen, and this time she got the charcoal to heat the clay pan slowly, and she added oil and then fried the sausages. The smell almost made her retch; the boy was no better. He was so eager to eat that he was almost attached to her leg.

'Does your mother ...? Do you have a garden?' she asked.

'Yes,' he said, as if she was not very bright. 'On the roof.'

She climbed to the roof and found cucumbers, which she grated and made into little fritters using the flour she'd ground and eggs from a basket on the chopping block.

The fritters and sausages fed them both; she ate hers before they were cool, and burned her mouth, and kept eating.

'May I call you "Mama"?' the boy asked.

'No,' she said. One look at his face and she shook her head at herself. 'Yes,' she decided.

He burst into tears.

They lasted a long time.

There were things they would need to survive. The boy's father had probably been a courtier, but not a scribe. There wasn't a sigil in the whole house, which was a prosperous house of six rooms.

But he'd taken a Narmerian woman as a wife, even though she had been a devotee of the Huntress. Everywhere that bordered on Ocean, the Lady, the Blue Goddess, was the enemy of men – the tester, the terrible avenger – and the Huntress was her 'sister', the virgin goddess, and not usually a friend to man either. The 'Sisters' had no temples of their own and few enough representations in the temples to all the gods, and priests of Enkul-Anu said that the Huntress was the goddess of evil.

Era's mother had felt differently. And apparently, so had the boy's mother.

Followers of the Huntress had another, deeper secret. They knew how to harness the *Aura* without the intercession of the gods. Even their own goddess. It was a powerful secret, and probably explained the hatred of the other gods. Era used her power very sparingly, but she needed light and she made a small blue magelight to search.

It felt like a violation to go through their things, but she did it. The woman had several musical instruments, like many followers of the Huntress. She found the woman's castanets, and knew she had been a dancer; she found the ivory phallus that suggested that she had followed the Huntress in other ways.

And then, under the bed, she found the woman's kithara. It

was a small one, made for small hands, from the shell of a small turtle, beautifully polished and inlaid. A very precious thing.

Men would kill for that.

Men will kill just to possess my body. Taking the kithara is hardly an extra risk.

Era took every gold and silver ornament she could find and dropped them into her bag with her collection of small precious stones and metal scrap, and she added the kithara. And the big bronze knife from under their bed.

She couldn't sleep in their bed – in *her* bed. Having been through her possessions, Era felt she knew the dead woman – and Narmerians believed it was dangerous to come too close to the dead. Era had thought such beliefs long behind her, but now, in that house, she feared that the dead woman would possess her and she would *become* the boy's mother if she did not keep her distance. She felt the woman around her, in the instruments and in the bed, too close, too much like her.

They slept on the roof.

She slept well, and in the morning woke with the boy wrapped in her arms.

An hour later they were walking.

The boy looked back.

'I've never been so far from home.' Then he looked at her. 'I guess every step I take will be farther.'

'Yes,' she said.

'You look like my mother,' he said.

Era bit back the words, but her fingers made a sign against death magic, and she was tempted to throw the kithara in the sea. But she didn't, and they walked along the beach together. She swam three times, but getting her hair wet just accentuated the smell of pig shit.

'What's your name?' she asked.

He looked at her as if he'd never considered having a name

before, his head cocked to one side like an intelligent puppy's head. After a bit he said, 'Daos.' It sounded like a Dardanian name, not a local one.

'A fine name,' she said.

'Yes,' he said solemnly. He was a very serious boy. 'Where are we going, Mama?'

'I think we want to take a ship, and get far from here,' she said slowly. 'Jekers usually come back. And eventually they come to stay. But until we find a ship, we walk south.'

The boy nodded. 'Bror says we'll board a ship. After we walk a long way.'

Era pulled the stinking hair off her face and looked out to sea.

'Bror is a very smart bear,' she said.

It was possible that the boy was mad. But she thought instead that he was god-touched by Temis, and had no reason to doubt him.

'I have a little food. We'll camp on the beach, and then we walk.'

Heaven

Lady Laila lay on Nisroch's couch. She was naked, on her back with one leg cocked at an angle, and she was without a doubt the most beautiful thing he'd ever seen.

She looked at him.

'I gather you're finished,' she said with a smile.

'Yes,' the Herald of the Gods said. 'Yes, and you were so ... You are so ... It's so wonderful ...'

She smiled. 'I'm not finished,' she said. 'So don't run off and get dressed. A lady does like to be ...'

Nisroch liked to know things, but the world of sensuality that Lady Laila inhabited was alien to him, and while he'd managed a few dozen human maidens, she was not like them. At all. For example, she clearly thought that she was in charge.

'I'm very busy,' he said with less force than he'd intended. He hated the sound of his own hesitancy. He was master here – she was but a chattel.

She gave him a look that made him uncomfortable.

'Ah, really?'

Her voice had a purring quality to it that moved him. He hesitated on the pins that held his magnificent purple-red chiton, a tunic of the finest wool available to the gods.

He looked down at her perfection, and lost his train of thought.

'Er ...' he said. 'Yes.'

She sat up slightly, and her breasts drew his gaze from the glory of her throat. She sipped from the two-handled golden cup of nectar by the bed and handed it to him.

'Tell me!' she said, breathless with interest. 'Your work is so fascinating...'

'You wouldn't be interested,' Nisroch said. 'It's just routine...'

Her eyes had the most remarkable flecks of gold set in the bright jade of their principal colour, as if she was a living statue. He found himself leaning forwards...

'Yes, well...' he said. 'No.'

He found that one of his hands was on her right breast. He squeezed it. He liked that, so he did it again, and she winced.

She put a hand over his, and moved his fingers lightly over the nipple.

'Like this, pretty boy,' she said. 'Ahh. Better. Now, what is so very important that you must use me like a slut and then run off?'

He gasped. 'No! I mean no discourtesy.'

He paused because, of course, he had in fact meant to finish with her and go back to work because...

He was lost in her eyes.

'I have plans,' he said into her bosom.

'I'm sure you do,' she said, her hands exquisitely firm, light, heavy, wet, dry, cool, hot.

She kissed him, and suddenly she was on top of him – a movement of her leg, a rotation like something from a wrestling move.

'Oh,' she said, almost cooing at him. 'But you said you had to go!'

He tried to shake his head. She leant down.

'What's so important?' she asked.

He heard himself talking, even though he was lost in her; there was only her scent, her eyes, her lips...

'Star-stone fell in the desert,' he said into her mouth. She did... something, and his arousal reached a terrifying peak. 'Oh, goddess! And … Narmer is sending gold to Kyra,' he blurted. 'To destroy Hekka. And I should have told the Great God!'

Lady Laila, handmaiden of the goddess Sypa, was astride him now, and he was buried within her, and she smiled down at him.

'You should have?' she breathed.

She rose above him like lust embodied, and he couldn't think, even to tell her more.

'Perhaps later, when I'm done with you,' she purred.

Druku was in a hermaphrodite form – man, and woman, too – and that made Laila laugh with delight.

'The little bastard Nisroch is plotting something,' she said. 'I could read it in his … Well … In his confusion, let us say.'

Druku drank deep, not of nectar, but of good red wine.

'They're always plotting,' Druku said into her neck.

She rolled over to let them do what they were doing more thoroughly.

'Star-stone, though. That threatens all of us.'

Druku grunted happily.

'Star-stone!' she said with emphasis.

They moved her leg in a particular way, and she clung to them.

They were looking down at her.

'I'm the god of gambling,' they said. 'And I wager your orgasm against a pillar of salt that the star-stone is just a little bluff.'

'Oh, god,' she breathed.

'You called?' They laughed, and began to do another clever thing.

Laila's eyes were huge. 'Narmer … is paying … Kyra … to destroy … Hekka,' she said in gasps.

Druku didn't pause, having considerably more experience

of being a woman than Nisroch would ever have, with all the consequent skills and understanding.

'Hekka?' Druku asked. They were only lightly drunk, and they knew the place. Good wine, for one thing. 'Enkul-Anu shouldn't be letting anyone destroy any city. There aren't enough mortals left to worship us now as it is.' They kissed her, and then said, a little breathless themselves, 'In fact, I could swear that Enkul-Anu ordered Kyra to stop making war on Hekka...'

They changed positions with the skill of old lovers. Laila looked a little glazed, but her mind was quick enough to penetrate ecstasy and still think.

'Narmer is always at the root of it...' she began. And then she turned, licked their nose, and grabbed their great shaggy head. '*You* are very popular in Narmer,' she accused.

Druku laughed, rolling her over.

'I'm a harmless old polysexual drunken lecher,' they said. 'Ask anyone.'

And they laughed together.

Chapter Three

'Just keep shooting, Baldy!' the old man yelled.

Pollon was, in fact, bald. All the palace scribes were bald, by ancient custom. It took careful attention to maintain – tweezers, hot rocks...

He drew and loosed.

'That's the way,' the old man called.

He drew and loosed. He loved the rhythm of archery – so like playing his lyre, so relaxing...

'Don't look at what ye did, you idiot. Just keep pumping them out.'

Pollon drew the string to his ear, breathed, and loosed.

His fingers found another arrow by his hip, found the alignment of the fletchings, put the nock neatly on the string, all without a glance. The bow hesitated, rose like a bird bursting from cover; he settled on the target, and the string sprang free of his fingers.

His eyes *didn't* follow the arrow to the target this time. He had the next arrow on the string, and it all seemed to flow. Nock... draw... loose – not one action, but a dance.

Then he was out of arrows.

'That's the way, laddie,' the old man said.

The old man was called Jawat and he was a peasant-born

59

warrior who had survived to be old. Even the god-king's god-born warriors paid him respect, though he only commanded the militia. Pollon outranked him by so much that in the order of precedence, he would have entered the god-king's hall, enjoyed a feast, and have left before the old man was seated.

Pollon liked to believe that such things had little meaning. And, because he wanted to be as good at archery as he was at minding the god-king's taxes, he listened and obeyed the orders.

The old man looked at the line of archers. Pollon was aware that he was among the best, and also aware that the bar was low. They weren't warriors. They were the militia.

'Ye're a good archer, Baldy,' the old man said. 'But when ye're in the shit, ye ha' to draw an' loose. Draw an' loose. Ne'er watch the result. Don' get flustered. Don' let yer mind be afraid. Draw an' fuckin' loose.'

Pollon bowed to the old man.

'Ye're humourin' me, Baldy. I know who ye are.'

The old man looked out at the line of straw targets, fifty paces away. Many of them were as clean as when they'd been set up. He looked back, where a wealthy young man with a fine Narmerian bow he couldn't really draw was haranguing the slave set to retrieve his arrows.

'I hear Kyra is marching on us and it ain't no cattle raid,' the old man said.

'I cannot comment,' Pollon said with slow dignity.

''Course you can't, Baldy. Tell you *what*, though. We ain't ready.'

'Our storehouses are full,' Pollon said, glancing around.

Here outside the walls, in the cleared area where, truth be told, there was supposed to be a ditch but none had ever been dug, there were no god's eyes to spy on them. But he was cautious nonetheless.

'Oh, yeah?' the old man asked. 'Ye do taxes, right, Baldy?'

Pollon found that he was stung before he even tasted the words.

'I am a writer to the god-king. I'm a scribe of the palace.'

'Uh-huh.' The old man turned and bellowed down the range. 'Arten! Get yer useless arse off the range until dimwit there shoots his wad! Druku's throbbing member, boy, the way Nofru shoots, he could hit yer!'

He turned to Pollon.

'When we go back through the gate, let me show you something, Baldy.'

'See that?' the old man asked.

Pollon looked at the unbaked clay tablet in the top basket – one which detailed the latest stores returns. He had no trouble reading the script. Or the seal on the tablet. It was his own seal.

Which he had not affixed.

He stared at the hard evidence of a crime before him, and his breath caught in his throat.

Someone was stealing the stores, and forging the receipts. Pollon stood with the small tablet in his hand for as long as a man might make a prayer to the King of the Gods, and then he carefully replaced it and pushed the basket up onto its place in the shelf.

His hands were shaking. 'How did you know?'

The old man shrugged. 'I'm old but I ain't stupid, lad. These stores is militia stores, see?'

Indeed, there was the broken chariot wheel sigil which stood for 'Militia'. An unkind choice of symbol, Pollon thought.

'Yes,' he agreed.

'An' I know ye, laddie. Ye're tall and bald an' honest, and frankly there ain't no one else like ye in the militia.'

Pollon took several careful breaths, as his secret practice taught, and his hands steadied, and he left the storehouse as quickly as possible. He had no real idea how vast the conspiracy he had stumbled on was, but it must be large. His seal had been forged, and stores were being stolen, and someone was making false returns ...

'Say nothing about this,' he said. 'It may be an error.'

The scale of it made him feel sick.

A writer must be involved.

The old man grinned bitterly. 'Listen, writer. We're so fuckin' short on shit that if the Kyrans really come, we're well an' truly fucked. Ye hear me? Hardly matters who did it then.'

Pollon was thinking, *Writers were supposed to be incorruptible.* The whole survival of their civilisation depended on accurate record-keeping. You learnt that on the first day they shaved your head.

If famine came, and you didn't have enough grain, everyone died.

Or if an enemy besieged the city, or if the gods didn't receive their share ... everyone died.

Pollon went to the privy, sat on one of the seats, and put his head in his hands.

Someone had forged his seal. Even now, it hung from his waist sash on a cord of silk – real silk traded from the Dry Ones. It was carved into brilliant scarlet carnelian and had his writer's name in the old script that only writers could read, along with a hippogryph, an ancient animal he'd chosen on a whim. He had watched the jeweller carve it on the glorious day that he had won his name, answered the riddles and declaimed the old poems. A hundred boys had started the training and only six had been granted their seals.

Pollon looked at it, and remembered the ease with which the jeweller had cut his name into the surface. He'd done it with hard stone tools, in less time than it had taken to deliver an oration.

So ... it stood to reason that an expert jeweller could copy his seal from one of its imprints.

There must be a difference between the original and the copy. However small, any detectable difference would clear him, and help incriminate the thieves.

He got up, but not to return to the storehouse. Instead, he crossed the square in front of the gate and received the salutes of the guards, then walked up the ramp into the massive palace that dominated the city below it. The ramp led through a warren of passages and then into a courtyard arcaded in heavy pillars painted bright scarlet. He exchanged bows with two officials of his own rank, gave way to a senior priest leading animals for sacrifice, and went in through a servants' door. He passed the steward with a nod, passed two giggling maids on the shallow steps, and went up into the main hallway – the wide one with frescoes of the War of the Gods.

His desk was in the chancery, where the god-king's treasures were enumerated, his laws promulgated, his rare boons made into clay reality, the information of his kingdom collected and shared. There were forty writers sitting cross-legged on the cool stone floor, their shaven heads reflecting the bright sun outside. It was his favourite place, and he'd worked his whole life to be master of it.

And in that moment he realised that one of the men sitting on the floor had probably betrayed him, and his oath.

He passed along the first row – his best and fastest copyists, and also his companions. Spathios and Kizzura lived in the palace-workers' barracks. Both held minor priestships to go with their palace duties.

Both would wish to be in his place some day.

Spathios had a wooden folder open, with wax poured into each of the wooden frames. These tablets let expert writers take notes at councils and in the throne room when the god-king made law. Anything which had to be recorded more permanently was noted in clay, and baked.

'Great council,' Spathios said, as his stylus moved smoothly along the complex pictographs they used for business.

Pollon got his second shock of the day as he read over Spathios' shoulder.

'Why, under heaven, would the god-king of Kyra attack us?' Pollon asked. 'Attack his brother of Hekka?'

'Because he's a greedy bastard.' Kizzura was expert at speaking out of the side of his mouth — easy to hear, but difficult to know exactly who had spoken.

'Darling, they're all greedy bastards,' Enmida whispered. He was the senior scribe of the second row — just seventeen years old and already fast enough to move to the front.

Pollon raised the bronze pen case that hung from his belt.

'Silence, writers, we are better than this.'

Amah kept writing, and Pollon read over his shoulder.

'Where does Kyra get so many men?'

'How does he feed them?' Kizzura asked.

'Maybe he won't feed them,' Enmida said.

'Narmer!' Amah hissed.

'Writers!' Pollon said.

'Apologies, sir,' Amah said.

'Pollon!'

The writer turned. The *rap-te-re*, the god-king's human viceroy, stood in the marble doorway.

'Great lord.'

'Come with me. The god-king is going to the gods.'

Pollon looked down at his sandals and then at his hands, to make sure he was clean enough to be in the presence of the gods. He still had his archery wrist brace on his arm.

'As you will it, great lord.'

He took a clean wax tablet from the stack on the table at the front of the chancery and nodded to his people.

'Good luck,' Kizzura said softly.

Pollon met his eyes. Like most writers, they were outwardly pious, but inwardly…?

Pollon hoped his doubts didn't show on his face. He had no time to worry about the thief – not when he was going to meet his gods.

The Temple of All Gods was clad in white marble and it crowned the acropolis of Hekka, inside the walls of the inner fortress, which had never fallen to any foe. The magnificent temple had twenty-six columns in two rows, an inner and an outer; the roof was of beautiful dark red tile; the statues were cast in bronze and gilded, with painted eyes and skin. Enkul-Anu, the Storm God, stood, four times life size, supported by a trio of columns. Pollon had heard sailors say that on a sunny day you could see the spark of the Storm God's head from across the surface of the sea – so far that navigators used him to find their way.

He followed the god-king and the raptere, six priests, a dozen acolytes and four virgins carrying bronze thuribles burning a musky incense. He was the least important non-priest present and he climbed the steps as silently as possible, head down, making the obligatory prayers to each god and goddess as he passed their statues. There were more than thirty of them, including the stelae for the last god-king and the one before, whom the priests said were now gods themselves.

Pollon, like all writers, had doubts.

Those doubts, about which he never spoke, were based on the evidence of his senses. The god-king climbing the steps ahead of him smelt of male sweat. The gods never did. Unlike the gods, the old god-king had died. Pollon had taken down his last attestation and he knew how a dying man smelt.

These were not appropriate thoughts for the steps of the greatest temple on the eastern shore. There were god's eyes all along the parapet and on every step – the enhanced sigils that allowed the gods to watch their flocks. Some said they could do more than just see.

Pollon knew all about that.

He climbed, head down, and hoped that the gods could not read his mind.

At the top he looked east, at the chaotic carpet of farmlands, green and gold patches, which rolled to the edge of the desert. A desert that he was sure was closer today than it had been the last time he'd climbed to here.

Why does the desert grow?

Why are there always more Jekers?

Why don't the god-kings care?

He pinched himself to drive those thoughts away, but then, as a choir sang and temple dancers began to perform, his thoughts drifted back to the tax records.

They had used his seal. Which meant, he now realised, that unless he could prove the forgery, when the cheat was exposed he was going to die a horrible death.

He shivered, suddenly cold on a brilliant, sun-hot day. The sun was reflected almost perfectly from the clean white stone of the temple's forecourt, and the beautiful young women of the dance troupe and choir flowed as if their muscles were liquid, their movements better drilled than the god-king's godborn warriors.

They were dancing the story of the Rise: the moment when the gods overcame the barbaric demons of the dark past and brought the world to peace and prosperity; when Ranos was toppled by Enkul-Anu and took the throne of the gods from the enemy and made himself all-powerful.

Pollon couldn't help but wonder why this was best acted

out by twenty petite dancers, regardless of their skill, swaying expertly, but the god-king was clearly very interested in their interpretation. Rumour was that the loveliest, the gold-bedecked chief priestess with golden skin and jet-black hair, was the god-king's favourite. Rumour suggested that some of the other priests were jealous of her.

She was almost shockingly beautiful, her movements precise, beautifully trained ...

The tax records are not an academic problem. They are an immediate and vital problem.

The thought popped into Pollon's mind, as if the dancers had promoted it.

The dancers withdrew to one side, their golden leader glancing back at the god-king with a smile.

The god-king smiled back.

Then he motioned and the procession, led by the image of the city's patron, approached the temple itself. The priests chanted and the whole procession, except for the god-king, knelt on the last three steps and sang the paean.

And then they entered, passing through the pronaos to the high altar. The women with the thuribles censed the altar and sang, their high voices magnificent in the echo-chamber of the *cella*, while the acolytes used aged cedar to light the altar fire on a clean marble hearth.

Two priests came from one of the side rooms – the sacristy – leading a black ram and a small, pretty boy with dark locks and drug-dulled eyes. The dancing priestesses came and lined the path to the altar.

The hierophant was handed the ritual knife – a shining black splinter of obsidian, perfectly polished. He killed the ram with a careful cut to its neck, and its front legs buckled as the red of its life came out into a bowl. Before it was dead, the knife opened its abdomen and spilled its guts on the altar. The high priest stirred them with the knife and nodded sharply to the god-king.

'Proceed,' he murmured.

The god-king took the black knife even as the scent of roasting lamb carried throughout the temple. The musk, incense and rich lamb fat mingled unpleasantly, or so Pollon thought.

The god-king took the child's hand, pulled back his hair, and slit his throat. Expertly, he turned the boy so that his blood flowed into the same bowl that the blood of the ram had almost filled.

His drugged eyes were wide with shock, and Pollon met them. He didn't want to, but he couldn't look away. The boy couldn't scream, or fight; the life flowed from his eyes the way the blood flowed from his open throat.

The god-king lifted him onto the altar and opened his abdomen with the knife, and the priests began to separate his organs.

The hierophant threw his heart into the fire and the choir burst into song.

The god-king took the bowl of blood, drank of it, and then poured the rest slowly onto the altar, and as he poured he invoked the ritual names.

'God of the Storms, Lord of the Gates, mighty leader of the host of heaven, Enkul-Anu, conqueror, come to us.'

Pollon was almost choking on the mingled scents of musk and death. The silence went on too long; the hierophant looked down at the boy's corpse in consternation, and the golden priestess glanced at one of her dancers. Pollon was an initiate; he could reach the *Aura,* and he saw the power from the sacrificed blood go to the God.

And then the god spoke.

'Hekka!' said a hundred deep voices. They seemed to come from everywhere.

Pollon was already writing. *Hekka* was one glyph – three lightning strokes with the stylus.

'Great god!' called the god-king. He sounded afraid. 'Enkul-Anu! I call to thee with the blood of an innocent, by the covenant—'

'Fucking idiots! Who calls me and why?' spat the impatient voice. It was everywhere, and it echoed in Pollon's head.

'Great God of Storms! I am Thanatos, God-King of Hekka. Great god, I call upon you for aid. My brother, Mekos of Kyra, is marching to attack me.'

'Your squabbles are nothing to me, Thanatos. Raise more soldiers. Raise taxes. Fight hard.' There was a pause. 'But since you have my attention, I have a command.'

Thunder rolled.

The god-king flinched visibly. 'Speak, lord!'

'There is the curse of star-stone in your land – I can smell it. Ask your priests if any stars have fallen from the sky in the last ten days.'

The hierophant looked at his priests.

Pollon knew the answer. He squirmed; no one ever wanted a scribe to speak. Then he raised a hand very tentatively; no one noticed.

'We will endeavour to—'

'Don't *endeavour*,' the god said. 'Find it. Now. Or your brother of Kyra won't be the only one attacking you.'

'I can't send my warriors!' the god-king said with a barely perceptible whine. 'The Kyrans are already inside the borders. Today or tomorrow—'

'Some of my children want to play,' snapped the god. 'I'll send Ara's son, Resheph, to you.' The great god's voice changed. 'Have the priestess dance. The golden girl.'

The hierophant motioned at the chief priestess of Sypa, and she began to dance in front of the storm god's statue.

The statue was seen to smile.

As she danced, the hierophant spoke very softly.

'Ara, God of War.' He pointed to the appropriate statue in the sanctuary. 'Resheph, god of the disease and plague war brings, is his son.'

The hierophant's voice rose in fear.

'We do not want him to come here. Even to aid us.'

The god-king was as pale as ivory. When the gods walked the earth, men died. And so did god-kings. The gods weren't known to discriminate much, or take sides. Especially the young ones.

They just killed.

'That's—'

'I'll send Resheph. He can look for the star-stone, too.' The great god chortled, obviously in a better mood.

'I will find it,' said the terrified god-king.

He looked for the hierophant, unused to speaking unaided to the gods, but the hierophant was standing, rapt, before the statue of the goddess Sypa.

'Of course you will. Or I will *find* a new god-king.' The storm god's statue grinned, a terrible sight. 'I may require your high priestess to visit Auza.'

The god-king looked at her, and blinked.

'Of course,' the hierophant said smoothly. 'I'm sure she would be honoured.'

'Good. Find the star-stone. *Do it now.*'

The god's presence vanished with a snap. Pollon was a writer, but he was also an initiate. He understood that his sensing the god meant he had an innate connection. A dangerous connection, at least today. The gods claimed to have made the *Aura* and they were most definitely the most powerful forces within it.

The hierophant turned, and led the king to the massive basalt statue of Ara, God of War. He whispered in the god-king's ear.

Pollon watched, his knees shaking, and tried not to listen, but he couldn't help overhearing.

'Beg ... can't ... Resheph comes here ... we're dead.'

Thanatos nodded sharply. The god-king of Hekka hadn't held his throne this long without having a backbone and some ingenuity in the face of the gods. Nervously, he adjusted the high crown, and he raised the long sceptre in his hand.

'Great Ara, God of War, lord of hosts, killer of men, stand with us now against Kyra!' the god-king intoned.

Silence.

'Another sacrifice,' he hissed.

The hierophant didn't hesitate. He grabbed one of the women from the dance choir. Pollon was shocked to see that he'd grabbed the chief priestess. The golden dancer. The one that the Storm God had just requested.

The god-king turned his head away.

She hadn't been drugged, and she fought after the first, stunned moment, but two priests caught her wrists. The hierophant forced her head back and held out the black stone knife with his free hand.

'Quickly,' he spat to the god-king.

'Not that one,' the god-king replied.

'Do it!' the hierophant said.

He pushed the knife into the god-king's hand and hissed something that Pollon didn't catch.

Wincing, the god-king cut her throat. He did it badly, or the obsidian caught on something in her neck; perhaps her finely trained muscles were more than he was used to cutting through. She managed a convulsion, got a wrist free, slammed a hand into the hierophant's face, her nails raking him as her hot lifeblood splattered everyone within range of that horrid fountain.

'By Druku I curse you,' she managed. Her blood gushed

from the wound, and yet she had the will to continue. 'Before tomorrow is done, you will be carrion, and I will be the lucky one.'

Grimly, the hierophant pushed her back onto the altar. Then he took the knife from the god-king, who stood, stunned.

He opened her with the black knife, and the priests who had held her wrists emptied her chest cavity. The hierophant threw her heart into the fire.

'Say the words!' he demanded.

'Great Ara, God of War, lord of hosts, killer of men, stand with us now against Kyra!'

The god-king was still looking at the dead woman's face, and his words were slurred.

The statue of the war god remained animated, and his stone face gazed down.

'My son!' he roared.

And then the statue returned to being warm stone.

No one but Pollon glanced at the statue of Druku, god of revels and drunkenness, but Pollon saw the look of anger and revulsion. And beyond, the statue of the goddess Sypa, mother of lust, had a nasty smile.

When the god-king had returned to his throne room, Pollon bowed deeply to the high priest, trying to ignore the slug's trail of blood across the man's golden outer robes and the sleeves of his once spotless white linen, and the four deep scratches across his face.

'Excellency,' he said. He kept his head down. 'I am Pollon, of the writers. I know of the falling of the stars. Astrologers reported—'

'I know what the astrologers said.' The hierophant was washing the blood from his hands in a golden bowl held by two small slave children.

'Your pardon, Excellency,' Pollon said. 'I also have heard other reports. A shepherd saw stars falling in the high desert, well to the east.'

Now the hierophant stopped washing and looked at him directly.

'What reports are these?' he snapped. 'I need more. Immediately.'

'Two reports, and then silence,' Pollon said quietly. 'They were reliable people.'

'Get me the exact locations of the cursed star-stone and you will be richly rewarded.'

'Excellency.' Pollon bowed deeply, hands together.

'I will tell the god-king.' The hierophant managed a bitter smile, and winced at the pain, and blood ran down his face.

'I will send nomads to gather—' Pollon began.

'Do all you can, and I will remember you. If your nomads return, which I beg leave to doubt, report to me immediately.'

A slave brought a linen towel – a week's work for a woman somewhere; he wiped the blood from his face and threw it in a fire.

'I seek only to serve.'

Pollon stepped away with a deep bow, and caught the raptere looking at him.

'What did you say to the priest?' the raptere asked.

'I told him about the reports of fallen stars in the east country.'

The raptere frowned. 'I remember no such report.'

'Great lord, I passed it on days ago. With the other reports under the green seal.'

Reports sealed in green wax came from spies and gossips, and sometimes from the Watchers and the Nexus, the priests who worked for Nisroch, the Herald of the Gods, who watched over all of the god's eyes.

The raptere shook his head. 'I don't think you did,' he said irritably. 'And if you did, you should have made more of a point of it.'

'Great Lord, before this moment I had no idea it was important.'

Pollon hated the sound of a whine in his own voice, but he also hated it when the raptere covered his own faults by claiming that underlings had failed him. Which he routinely did.

The raptere shook his head. 'You must learn what is important,' he said piously. 'There are four men who could fill your job. Do you want to sit in the market and write letters for peasants?' He leant on his gold-shod staff of office. 'I do not want this to become a matter for warriors. The attack from Kyra must be dealt with – that's their job. Find someone to go east and search for this star-stone.'

Pollon knew that the palace officials were always at war with each other – that the *ra-wa-ke-ta*, the champion, the leader of the god-king's warriors, was at odds with the raptere and the hierophant.

'I will do my utmost,' he said.

At the same time, the cynical part of his mind wondered if the raptere had any idea how vast the Eastern Desert was.

Again he bowed deeply, and this time he made his escape. He was shaken, as much by the two human sacrifices as by the machinations of his superiors and the problem of the forged seal. A bad day.

Any day with the gods is a bad day.

He stopped in a dark corridor to collect himself. The rooms were lit by windows, and the climate was so clement that they were unglazed. But the corridors were always dark.

He took three deep breaths and tried not to think of the beautiful dancer, and her death. Then he made his way to the chancery. He looked in; everyone was working.

'I'm off on a mission,' he said. 'Kizzura?'

'Aye!' his friend said.

'You have the desk. I expect we will be asked for an inventory of armour and chariot wheels before the hour has fled.' Pollon tried to sound commanding. It wasn't his best quality.

'Aye,' Kizzura called with satisfying alacrity.

He glanced around the workroom: low-ceilinged; cool with the breezes from the sea coming in through the open doors to the balcony outside. A god's eye stared from the middle row of bricks; the scribal room rated three, because security here was essential. The far wall had a depiction of the great god surrounded by animals – a fresco he'd seen at least ten thousand times.

Someone is falsifying my seal. That's going to get me killed. But who can it be?

Pollon nodded, more to himself than to his scribes, and moved on. He entered a little alcove with a curtain, pulled the curtain closed, and raised his own *Aura*. He did it with very little ceremony: a pinch of myrrh on the alcove's brazier and a hasty prayer to Nisroch – outwardly. Inwardly, he prayed to his own secretive goddess.

He spread his *Aura* between his hands and touched the glowing glyph that indicated the Watchers.

As the Master Writer, he had access to them. The Watchers were adepts whose only purpose was to monitor the god's eyes. The gods could also see through them, but the Watchers aided the gods in policing and enforcement. He located the god's eyes in the lower market, and accessed one. He saw camels across the market; hence, the nomads were there.

He was tempted to look at the hierophant, or the raptere's office, or to read the *anaphora* reports he'd learned to access; the collations of other writers like him from other places. He knew how to, but to do so was a capital offence. If caught.

I've never even thought of breaking these rules before.

With a grimace, he closed his *Aura* and made an obeisance to the statue of Enkul-Anu. Then he pushed through the curtain, glanced over his writers, and headed out into the courtyard at the centre of the great palace.

He wasn't rich enough to afford a personal slave, so he showed a bronze coin to a dusty, naked boy who hovered at the edge of the gates, avoiding the horse dung and the grumpy donkeys and watching for tips.

'Attend me,' he said.

'Yes, great lord,' the boy said with a smile. The smile spoke volumes of the boy's wit; it also showed he was as cynical as Enmida.

'I want to find some nomads,' he said to the boy.

'Follow me, noble master,' the boy said.

'What's your name?'

'Willing Slave,' the boy said.

Pollon rolled his eyes. 'All right, Pearl of Wisdom. Take me to the nomads.'

'My proper name is Koso. My father was a bronze smith.'

The boy looked up with what appeared to be need, or ready devotion; Pollon wondered if the boy was old enough to be able to fake all these facial expressions.

'Better. Also more likely. Koso, let me give you a little advice – you are using elements of your true name in your use name. Stop. People can bind you with it.'

The boy stopped walking and looked at him.

'How do you know?'

'I am a writer,' Pollon said. 'It is my business to know.'

He followed the boy out of the lower courtyard, which most men called the Donkey Bowl, and they walked down a steep ramp to the citadel gate. The walls of the citadel were six times the height of a man, and the whole sat on a rocky spur at the end of a long ridge, well above the plain and the sea below. A

76

stone-grit headland fell away from the rock of the citadel, and there were beaches on either side of the headland, allowing ships to come in regardless of the wind's direction. Ramshackle warehouses lined the beaches, and between them, in the only flat ground below the citadel and the palace, sat the marketplace, itself defended by four mud-brick towers. The town itself was a vast spread that filled the headland behind the acropolis.

As he stepped through the gates, he looked out over the plains to the south, and saw the dust cloud.

He stopped.

Koso nodded.

'The enemy comes, great lord. The market will be empty.'

Like our stores, Pollon thought. He narrowed his eyes. *They're that close?*

He wondered. He wasn't *exactly* a spymaster, but he had his sources of information; no one survived in the palace without them. And while he knew that the god-king of Kyra intended war, this was not just a threat. This was the dust cloud of the God of War, raised by thousands of marching feet, rolling chariot wheels, ox-carts and horses' hooves.

'My errand is all the more urgent,' he said, as much to himself as the boy. 'Listen, boy. From now, your name is Kussu.'

'Kussu is "shield" in the old tongue,' the boy said. 'I like it.'

'And it will protect you ...'

Pollon was distracted, and he wondered at himself. He did not usually give advice, especially not to beggars.

They were coming to the bottom of the citadel ramp. There were four guards – three freeborn and a godborn in full bronze armour, head to foot with a huge tower shield of bull's hide. Pollon had never seen a godborn guard here, and he bowed.

The man frowned, but Pollon had a carnelian seal in his sash and was a writer. He and the boy walked past the guards, and the line of god's eyes that watched the gate. The market was down a flight of steps, broad and flat and paved in slate where it wasn't the foot-smoothed bare rock of a thousand years of use. The wealthier merchants and more skilled craftsmen's shops lined the three outer walls, but in the middle there were tents and booths for the smaller sellers.

Ordinarily, that was. Today, there were two scared-looking farmers, factors for the big slave farms upriver, one with a cart of dried chickpeas and the other with a massive wagon of fresh melons. Otherwise, the market was virtually deserted.

Pollon used a piece of scrap copper wire to buy them both melons, and they ate them as they crossed the square until the boy pointed and said 'Nomads' very quietly. Pollon saw the camels before he saw the nomads, exactly where he'd expected, though there were fewer of them, and he noticed that the whole west wall of the enclosed market was almost as empty as the farm stalls and the meat sellers.

'Where is everyone?'

'Oh, you know,' the boy said. 'Kyra is attacking us, and there's plague out east.'

Pollon thought, *I know that, but how do you know?*

And at the same moment, he thought, 'It must be the rawa-keta. He is bribing one of my people to undermine me, to destroy the raptere.

He concocted a plan to locate which scribe was involved. While he was at it, he considered how many jewellers there really were in the palace, and in the city behind the palace.

'Nomads are right here, boss,' the boy said.

Pollon walked over to the camel, which had a remarkable smell. There were three nomads with a selection of items for sale: a large, very blue chunk of lapis; a beautiful nugget of raw silver; bags of myrrh; some cinnamon.

He squatted down with them. Mura, his landlady, dealt with

nomads every day; he'd learnt a little of their language from her, and a little trust, too.

'Friends,' he said.

The older male had blue eyes, rare among the peoples of the eastern coast. He blinked.

'Friend,' he said, in Nomad.

'Shiny-head,' said the woman.

Pollon understood that much. He laughed.

'Yes,' he agreed.

The nomad woman reached out and touched his head, and he let her.

She smiled at him. 'Shiny. Buy something – make us happy.' Now she spoke Trade Dardanian, the trade language of the whole sea.

'I will have forty grains of myrrh,' he said. 'But I really want to pay you to do something.'

All three frowned.

'It is legal!' he said, worried that he'd broken a taboo. 'Listen – ten days ago, there was a star that fell from the sky.'

'Not just one,' said the woman.

'At least ten,' said the younger man, holding up all his fingers like a child.

'He doesn't mean ten,' the older man said. 'He means hundreds.'

'Yes,' said the woman.

'Did any of them strike the ground?' Pollon asked.

The nomads shrugged, and moved uneasily.

The woman whispered, and then came back. 'At least four. One was very big and made a hole in the world.'

The boy squirmed, clearly afraid of the nomads and the idea of a hole in the world.

'How much to go and find out more, and then come back and tell me?' Pollon asked.

The woman shrugged. 'They say there is plague among our kind, out east.'

'Fate waits for no man to come to dinner.' The older nomad shrugged.

'Seventy grains of gold,' Pollon said. 'And food from the royal stores when there is a drought. If you leave today.'

'We're packing already.' The older man rose to his feet. 'I won't even bargain, although it hurts me not to. But you've already done well for me – I'll pretend I forced you to it.'

The woman smiled. She wore a brilliant red shawl that covered her entire form, head to toe, and wrapped around her head to reveal only her eyes. But he could see the smile in those eyes, and he knew she'd be covered in tattoos if he could see more.

He liked them. Nomads were very easy-going. He was aware that they murdered travellers and probably ate babies, but they were excellent in conversation and they always had news. Sometimes, in his fantasies, he ran away and became a nomad.

'Find the place where the falling star struck and made the hole and I'll double it,' Pollon said.

'There, again, you do all my work for me,' the man said.

The woman was already rolling up their carpet. The younger man handed him a bag of myrrh.

'Make your sign for us so we can find you,' the man said. 'I am Eglash.'

Pollon walked to the public scribe, who was sitting in a booth built into the wall, bored. He made his mark in clay and had it baked on the spot.

'There,' he said.

Eglash spat in his hand and they shook.

'That's it?' asked the boy.

'That's it,' Pollon said. 'Here's the bronze bit I promised, here's two more for being silent.'

Pollon had enjoyed the outing, but he had work to do and

the streets told him that the war was imminent. Hekka hadn't seen a war in many years.

And someone had betrayed him.

Pollon knew nothing of war, but he did know that Hekka was in trouble. There were towers on the city walls that were supposed to be built of stone, but were merely mud-brick on stone foundations. He knew this because he kept the records. He knew that the outer defensive ditch had never been dug, and instead several godborn had used the cleared ground for chariot racing. And for gambling. He knew that their stores were low, and they could not survive a siege. The chariot racers ... Where did they get new chariot wheels?

He couldn't stop thinking of how many ways a person with access to a writer's sigil could steal.

By all the gods ...

Back at the chancery, two of his scribes were copying out lists of armour and chariot parts, as he had expected. Kizzura vacated the table as soon as he entered, and he worked with them until the sun began to set. The god-king had issued a volley of orders and it was up to the chancery to phrase them correctly and see them dispatched, and Pollon sent Amah to the runners for ten messengers.

The sun took a long time to set and Pollon and his staff used every minute. By the time darkness arrived and the moon was up, the orders were away, the runners complaining about running in the dark. The writers were annoyed to be kept from their dinners, but Pollon took a last moment to enter the niche where he wrote his secret reports. There, he engaged the god's eye and told it about the four fragments of star-stone, one big enough to make a hole in the earth. He did this because it was his duty. In time, the report might reach Nisroch, Herald of the Gods. It made him feel ... holy. And conscientious.

He hurried back to the scribes, who were standing in the near-darkness, complaining.

'My wife hates eating in the dark,' a junior clerk said.

'Mine leaves food for me and goes to bed,' another said.

Pollon listened to their banter. He couldn't imagine any of them as a traitor; certainly, listening to them as they cleared their seats away and swept the floor, he had a hard time imagining any of them was bloodless enough to commit such crimes and then stand around making jokes.

Enmida lived in the barracks.

'The oil lamps will be lit,' he said, 'and it won't be my money paying for them.' He laughed.

He and Kizzura exchanged a look. Pollon suspected the two men were lovers; it was almost expected of writers.

But it was too dark to read every facial expression.

Amah came up out of the murk.

'You worried?' he said.

'Yes,' Pollon admitted.

'Gods. Why is Kyra invading?'

Pollon ushered his friend out and worked the cunning lock in the door.

'I will not speculate.'

'You are too straight an arrow,' Amah said.

'Listen,' Pollon said. 'This time tomorrow we could be under siege. Make sure everyone you love is safe. And make sure you have food stashed under the floor. Do you understand?'

'Isn't it illegal to store food?'

Pollon pushed his friend down the steps towards the servants' door.

'Not really,' he said softly.

'Meaning it is, but I should do it anyway.'

Pollon shrugged. 'Yes.'

★

Pollon lived on the upper floor of a small house like a tower facing the western wall, across a street so narrow that he could jump to the parapet walk from his window. He had two rooms, a brazier on a balcony where he could cook, and pegs in the walls for his precious possessions: a fine ash bow from the north; his arrows; his father's lyre, which he played sometimes on the balcony. The lyre was his secret obsession, and he often saw things in terms of music.

One of the things he saw through music was Mura, the Samar widow who owned the house and the one next door. He paid her well for his third-floor room, for access to the roof on hot nights, for her cooking, and for the privilege of sleeping with her when it was mutually agreeable. She enjoyed his music, and perhaps his company, and he was more than satisfied with the arrangement.

People in Hekka didn't speak of love. Love had been banished when the gods triumphed over the old gods. But Pollon enjoyed Mura so much that he endured her irritation that he was home so late without reciprocating.

'You expect me to feed you, you useless bureaucrat? Were you carving clay with your stylus, or do you have a boyfriend hidden away somewhere? I don't care who you fuck, but if you want to eat my cooking, you get here in time to eat it hot.' All this was delivered in a single flow of invective while Mura crouched over her fine bronze pot on the clay oven.

'There's an army on the way,' he said. 'And wars are fought in clay before they are fought with bronze.'

'Very poetic,' she said. 'Real war? I'm from Samara. I've seen a fucking war. I saw people leaving today. You know what will happen to them? They'll get picked up by the other side and made slaves. That's what happens to people like us.' She smiled bitterly. 'Slaves. Or the Jekers ... they'll *eat* you.'

83

'How's *your* food supply?'

She put a bowl, a quite pretty bowl from far-off Noa, on the low table in front of him.

'Eat, writer.'

She was his own age; her mother was a nomad, and she'd lived an exotic life for someone not godborn. She owned a butcher's shop in the market and dealt in the meat brought in by nomad hunters. She was good at it.

He took a spoonful. It was a bean soup, rich in meat and full of fennel. It was delicious, but he ate mechanically.

'That's my cooking!' she said. 'Try to enjoy it.'

He smiled. 'Are nomad hunters coming to your shop?'

'Only one in the last two days,' she admitted. 'Nomads know when the shit is coming.'

'Couldn't you just ride away?' he asked.

She shrugged. 'With the Banye, maybe. Only I haven't seen a Banye in months. They'd take me. My mother's band...' She looked away. 'A Lypse hunter told me that my mother's band were massacred by Bright People. You know... the Dry Ones. Or by Narmerians. But you know that.'

Pollon could remember it. It was the only time he'd seen her cry. And the only time she'd come to his room.

He began to scrape the bowl.

'You can have more,' she said.

'You are a magnificent cook,' he said. 'And I worry about you.'

She smiled and her eyes flicked up to his. He was very fond of her, despite their commercial arrangement, and he found her attractive, not least because she could work numbers and speak intelligently, and she had that look – the impish look...

'I suppose that if I can show you my bed,' she said, 'I can show you my other secrets.'

She took him to her bedroom. He'd been before, but he'd never been encouraged to linger. This time, with his help, she moved the bed. Under it was a beautiful rug, and under the rug, a door.

He opened it, and she laughed.

'When I was a girl, I dreamed of having a secret world,' she said. 'It's not a very big world.'

Beneath the door were four huge jars – the kind people were buried in. Also a small bronze bound chest, and another in cedar wood. And room to stand.

'I could live down here,' he said. 'It's larger than my room.'

'Don't be silly,' she said, 'and hold the ladder.'

It was very cramped, with them both down there.

'All the *pithoi* are full of barley,' she said. 'Sixty days' worth, for five people.'

She opened the cedar box. The space under her floor smelt pleasantly earthy, and the cedar smell was beautiful.

'I like your secret kingdom,' he said. 'Oh, gods!' he said, looking into the cedar chest.

There were woollens in there – embroidered *hetons* and *ymatyons*.

'That's a fortune!'

She was taking them out, folded. She closed the chest and piled the folded wool on it.

She gave him that look; the look he loved. 'I have always had a little fantasy,' she said.

She unpinned one shoulder of her garment. She put the pin down carefully, displaying the complex whorls of the tattoos over her breasts, then lay back on the magnificent woollens and smiled.

'You do the rest,' she said.

★

In the morning, they looked out from his window, as, to his surprise, they had ended in his bed. They could see over the wall. Far out over the fields, they could see the dark and spreading stain of a large army making camp.

'You should pack your things and go,' he said. 'It's going to be bad.'

She was lying on his bed, on her stomach, looking out.

'Everything I have is here,' she said. 'Including you. Now don't be insufferable because I've admitted that I like you.'

'If you go, you'll be alive,' he said. 'I have … deep reservations about what could happen if you stay.'

Then what she'd said got through.

'Mura, I have always liked you!' he said. 'In fact, it's because I like you, that I think you should take a camel and run.'

'And get made a slave? No thanks. When I sell meat, I get paid in silver. When I want sex, it's by my will. When I cook, I know the people who eat it. I know what they do to people out there.' She spoke fiercely.

He shook his head. 'You could die.'

'We could all die, every day. That's the world in which we live.'

And that was so true that Pollon chose to be late for work.

Pollon walked in later than he'd ever been before, but there was surprisingly little sense of urgency. He sat at the big writing table, listing the tasks he expected from the day.

Amah leant over him. 'There was a herald from the raptere,' he said, obviously impressed, or scared – or both. 'He didn't leave any message.'

Pollon was puzzled and it showed on his face.

'Is the militia summoned? he asked.

He was an archer, and he had a tower assignment. He'd

brought his bow with him; it was now hanging on a peg behind his desk, with his quiver and twenty-four flint-headed arrows.

'Nothing yet,' Amah said.

Pollon leant back and looked at the fresco. Making love to the widow had freed his mind of the panic of his discoveries the day before, but it all came back to him the moment he sat at his desk, and he wrote down what he knew in the wax to order his thoughts, then erased it, afraid of his own knowledge.

He wondered if he should take what he knew to the raptere. The man had never favoured him or been his friend, and Pollon was aware that he held his position by skill alone; he had no friends among the factions, no lovers in the harem, no voice to speak for him. He thought, for a moment, of how safe he'd felt in the widow's secret place.

The double entendre of it made him smile despite his fears, and he got up.

Enmida came in, and Amah was already writing, copying out a list of grain taxes, so Pollon left them to their work and walked across the courtyard to the workshops. Here, the god-king's craftspeople made wonderful things. Some items went to decorate the god-king's surroundings, and some went to his favoured servants; others went as a gifts to people he sought to please, and the very best went to the gods.

He found Atosa, the jeweller.

'Master,' he said with a bow.

'Don't *master* me, you shiny-pated rogue,' the jeweller said. 'Now what brings you, boy? I've work to do.'

Pollon had already untied his seal.

'How difficult would this be to copy?' he asked.

The jeweller looked at it. 'Did I make this?'

'Yes, master,' Pollon said.

'Nice work. Good stone. I must have liked you.' Atosa nodded. 'Really copy it? So that no one could tell?'

'Yes,'

'Fucking hard, if you'll pardon me. Look at those entwined snakes!' The old man laughed.

'Someone has a copy,' Pollon said. 'I don't know who, but I've seen an imprint of it …'

Atosa shook his head. 'Damn,' he said. 'Damn!' He looked up. 'You're a Master Writer!'

'So I am, by the help of the gods.'

'That's fucking serious. A master writer's seal copied? Druku's joy!' The man shook his head again. 'Get me the forgery, and I'll tell you who did it.'

'Really?'

'Every engraver has their hand. We're like scribes, eh?'

'That's what I'd hoped,' Pollon said.

Noon, and all through the city, the militia was finally receiving weapons from stores. Pollon had two reports of storehouses being woefully short of the spears and linen armour they were supposed to have. He passed the news on to the raptere and waited to be summoned.

No summons came.

He sent word asking for an audience.

No reply.

He turned to Amah. 'I'm late getting to my militia post,' he said. 'This is foolish.'

Amah shrugged. The writers kept working, mostly because no one had told them to stop.

There was a rumour that a god was coming in person. The hallways of the palace had an electric feeling; men were scared, and the maids were nowhere to be found.

Finally, Pollon decided to act on his own. He went to the counting house, feeling vaguely like a thief, but he had reason to look at the records of the storage of spears.

As he had feared, his sigil was on the clay tablets releasing hundreds of spears from the armouries. He took one from the tax records and one from the spear inventories, left coloured straw in their place to indicate to a writer that a record was missing, and took the two tablets to Atosa.

The master jeweller looked at them for a long time.

Then he looked up. 'I know who made this,' he said. 'But I don't know why.'

'Will you testify for me, if I go to the raptere?' Pollon asked.

'Yes, though I'll be sad to lose the boy. He's very talented. Someone must have bribed him.'

'You are sad – I, on the other hand, am terrified,' Pollon admitted.

He felt much better for having an ally. And he was already concerned that he'd be punished for not getting to his guard post.

The two of them walked through empty corridors to the wing where the powerful officials sat; the raptere and the rawaketa and the others had courtyards of their own.

'Something bad is happening,' Pollon said.

'I feel it too,' Atosa agreed. 'Let's go back.'

'What can happen inside the palace?' Pollon asked.

'Don't be stupid, boy. One blade in the back and the god-king is replaced by a new man, who wants new officers, new girls, new boys. I've seen it. More blood than a butcher's shop.' Atosa stopped where the main corridor to the god-king's apartments crossed the side corridor where the great lords had their courts. 'They say there's a god on the loose. A war god. When that happens, men die. God-kings die.' He turned to go back.

Pollon caught his arm. 'Please? I'm being framed for a whole set of crimes.'

Atosa shook his head. He had a fine bronze knife in a sheath around his neck and he touched it and prayed for a moment.

'Let's go,' he said.

They went along a low corridor until they came to the garishly painted forecourt of the raptere's chambers. Pollon announced himself to the steward and was surprised to be taken immediately to a large side room with a view of the outer court.

The two men waited, making small talk, until the raptere entered, reading from a wax tablet. He glanced at Pollon.

'I would have thought you'd have plenty to do today,' he said.

'There is an urgent matter,' Pollon said.

'More urgent than the orders of the God of War and the demands of the king?' the raptere asked. 'Speak!'

Pollon took a breath. He was shaking.

'Someone has a copy of my seal,' he said.

The king's first minister looked at him.

Atosa held up the two records.

'I can prove it,' he said. 'You see, great lord...'

He started forwards, holding the tax record, but as he did so Pollon saw the look on the raptere's face and he assembled all the data correctly, if a little too late. Before him was someone else who could write. And who was rich enough to pay a court jeweller to copy a seal. And who might have a favourite he wanted to promote.

Pollon was being deceived by his own boss, and had come straight to the man who had betrayed them all.

The raptere glanced at Pollon with withering contempt.

'Equos!' he roared. 'Warriors!'

The rawaketa's court was ten paces away, and the king's bodyguard and their servants poured into the room.

'Take him, and hold him somewhere' the raptere ordered. 'This man has betrayed us to the enemy.'

Pollon had the readiness of mind to shout 'That's a lie!' and then he was hit. Hard.

Pollon and Atosa were marched away to the gate towers, where criminals were held. Both men shouted; Atosa was one of the god-king's most prized men and he knew it. But no one even turned their heads. There were soldiers everywhere, and the streets were otherwise empty.

They were beaten thoroughly, and when a brutal soldier broke Atosa's hands with a club, Pollon knew they were going to die, and it was going to be very bad. He had no hope of rescue, no friends, no patron.

Atosa had been one of the god-king's favourite craftsmen. And they were breaking his hands with bronze rods.

The two men were thrown into a common cell. Pollon lay in an agony of outrage and physical pain, but in his mind all he could see was the dancer's throat being slit at the altar. He still couldn't believe that the hierophant had sacrificed the god-king's lover; he couldn't believe that the torturers had smashed Atosa's wonderful hands. It made no sense.

It's the way of the world.

As if reading his thoughts, the jeweller said, 'You never think it'll be you.' For a man in terrible pain, he sounded calm.

Pollon whimpered, and was appalled by the sound.

He lay in a black terror for a little more than an hour.

And then the cell door opened, and the brutal guard came in with three others. Pollon had a moment of hope, a flare of resistance, and then one struck him on the head with a bronze rod.

The rod didn't just break his jaw. It broke his will. He knew exactly what those bronze rods were used for, and he screamed in anticipation.

He and Atosa were bound to chariot wheels, and their limbs shattered with blows from the bronze rods. Before it was over, Pollon had stopped screaming, finding that the pain took him to a distance, and at that distance he could begin fingering his lyre, and thinking of music. It made no sense to him, but he was, to all intents, already dead. And nothing made sense.

He came back to awful reality when they were raised on their chariot wheels and lashed to a heavy tree trunk, so that they were held upright, broken limbs hanging to maximise the agony.

He went out.

He came out of deep unconsciousness when a third victim was raised. The man wasn't screaming, and seemed already dead. And the soldiers raising him looked unfamiliar, but Pollon was too far gone to concentrate or care.

Heaven

'Are you a fucking idiot?' Enkul-Anu asked his son, Nisroch. 'You fucking knew that Narmer was paying for Kyra to attack Hekka? And you're only telling me now?' He leant down from his throne and Nisroch quailed.

'I was going to tell—'

'I had to find out from some slimy fucking *mortal* aping the manners of his betters!' the great god roared. 'You, my supposed bright scion, left me standing there with my *dick* in my hand!'

'I was . . .' Nisroch's mind flashed to what he had been doing instead of his duty, and he flushed and stammered.

'I don't care if you were re-ordering the thirty-seven deepest layers of hell for my future adversaries' torment,' Enkul-Anu went on. 'Or beating off in your room with a statue of Sypa!'

Several of the younger gods could be seen to wince. At least one young goddess fanned herself.

'Your role here is to know things, and pass them to me. I need to know things. I need to know things before fucking mortals know them. Am I making myself clear to you, my supposed son?'

Enkul-Anu leant forwards, grabbed his herald by his hair, and suddenly . . .

They hung in the utter black of the void. The Outer Darkness. The nothing, that had been, according to the gods, before the world was made. Enkul-Anu gave off light. Nisroch gave off none. He hung by his hair, in utter anguish and deep humiliation.

'I can just leave you here and make a new son,' Enkul-Anu said.

'I put your mother here and I can do it to you. Don't ever fuck up my information flow like this again. Am I clear on this?'

Nisroch nodded in abject surrender.

They were back on the floor of the Hall of the Gods. Nisroch threw up on the black marble floor. And in that horrible moment, as his father threatened to unmake him, Nisroch vowed vengeance. It wasn't the first time.

'Now …' Enkul-Anu said in a normal voice. 'Now tell me what you know.'

Nisroch rubbed his throat and tried not to touch his head. Blood – ichor, really – was running down from his scalp.

'The high priest of Narmer says that the god-king of Narmer is paying Kyra to destroy Hekka,' Nisroch said with the shreds of his pride.

Enkul-Anu looked at Azag, captain of his guard and Prince of Demons.

'Send a flock of Furies,' he said. 'Find Ak-Enkul, God-King of Narmer, and rip his soul from his body and consume it. Do it now.'

Azag looked delighted, and saluted.

'Destroy his family. Eliminate them all, root and branch. Leave none alive. Make it horrible.' Enkul-Anu waved. 'Go.'

Azag leapt into the air and vanished.

Enkul-Anu nodded. Then he looked around the Hall of Judgement. It was vast; all black marble, veined in greys and whites, accented in gold and silver, lacking all the tasteless self-promotion of the Hall of Hearing. No mortal was ever allowed here, and the mood was … intimidating. Just the way he liked it.

His eyes fell on Ara, the war god, and his mighty – if somewhat dim – son Resheph.

'Resheph,' he said, and crooked a finger.

The boy was too stupid to be afraid. He bounded forwards,

arrogant in his power. And he had some. Already, he'd made several battlefields of mortals into hells of putrid decay; he seemed to love killing mortals. And in Enkul-Anu's great mind, he, Resheph was responsible for this mess in some indefinable way.

'Go to Hekka,' he said. 'Destroy the armies of Kyra.' He looked at the boy. 'Don't fuck this up.'

Chapter Four

Zos

He tried to watch the bull. The great beast's tiny eyes watched him.

About halfway along the sand was the man who'd gone first. He'd hesitated — a fractional pause — and now he lay with his ribs broken, the bull tattoo on his chest covered in blood. He was alive, for now. He'd either die, or recover and be sold as a slave.

One of the priestesses was shouting, and Zos knew that the first leaper's failure was a terrible omen.

Zos had trouble taking his eyes off the man. And his failure.

The magnificent bull, black as night, glossy with perfumed oil and sweat, stood across the central court, and his right hoof pawed the flagstones. His horns were gilded, and a wreath of roses was woven between them.

'Zos!' the watching crowd bellowed.

He bowed to the bull, extending his front foot ... His chest was so tight he thought he'd fail to breathe. Fear was like bands of bronze around his ribs. The first boy had failed.

Gods.

Secretly, he made the sign of the Huntress.

And the magnificent beast charged, the personification of the god.

He ran at the bull. Training overcame terror. And when Zos was afraid, he generally attacked.

The bull ran at him, his hooves like thunder on the stone.

He was one with the bull, his naked feet one with the hooves, sharing the thunder.

The great head lowered, the golden horns aimed at his waist.

He was flat out, his paces long ...

He leapt ...

'Zos!'

Mekos, God-King of Kyra, waved his golden spear.

'Calling for you, sir,' his *papista* said.

Aiois? Taios?

Zos pulled himself out of the daydream of his first bull-leap, and blinked.

He went through a lot of shield-bearers. This one was young and brave and too likeable to live long.

What is his name?

Zos was just getting his bronze body armour placed on him. He still didn't really like armour, but it was essential in a siege. Two slaves held it open like a clamshell. He folded himself in and they closed the sides with pins.

'Coming!' he shouted through the walls of his tent. 'What the fuck does he want now?' he asked the air over the slaves' heads.

'He said something about storming the sally port, lord,' the *papista* said. He was standing outside, where he could probably see the god-king and his entourage.

'Tyka's shrivelled tits, boy,' Zos spat.

One of the slaves had caught his wool *heton* in the jaws of the closing armour. Both flinched at his blasphemy and his tone. Godborn warriors were dangerous at all times, at least to slaves.

The slave boy flinched again when his hand moved.

'Open it up and do it again,' Zos said. He was a big man – big, imposing and older than most warriors. And still alive, because he cared about the details.

The boy was trembling so hard that he couldn't pull the bronze pins.

'Breathe,' Zos said. 'I will not hit you.'

The boy got a pin out and dropped it on the dirt of the tent floor.

The other slave winced and looked away, expecting a blow.

'Pick it up,' Zos said slowly.

Both slaves flinched. They weren't his – but any godborn could strike a slave at any time. Or kill them, if he was willing to pay their value.

'Tyka!' Zos said again. 'Get it done!'

'*Zos!*' called the god-king.

The breastplate slid closed. The pins went in easily now, because no fabric was trapped in the halves. He knew the *heton* was probably ruined – five weeks' work by a dozen slave girls, destroyed with one careless act by another slave.

The way of the world. Zos was too poor to have slaves of his own, so he'd have to sew the damage up in secret, because the godborn could not be seen to do manual labour.

He was godborn. One of the descendants of the gods, supposedly. Perhaps that had once been true. They were not a race; godborn came in every colour of the rainbow, as did the gods themselves, their only common trait an expectation of superiority. Now, it was more a rank than anything else. A rank to which he clung.

He took the white leather sword-belt off his armour-stand and dropped it over his breastplate so that the sword hung, hilt up, tight under his arm. He moved inside the armour, and found it comfortable enough. This new breastplate fitted snugly; the older ones were like metal pots that rattled when you walked, but this was both more handsome and more practical.

'Helmet,' he said.

His *papista* came back in with his helmet – the great incisors of forty wild boars, every one of which he'd killed himself, carefully split and built over layers of sinew by a master craftsman. It was one of his favourite possessions, although not as nice as his father's had been. He had a moment of bitter reflection. Above the peak of the helmet rose a half-moon of gold supporting a mane of scarlet horsehair, a little faded from the years. The half-moon was for Tyka, the Blue Goddess. In Mykoax, she was considered to be the same deity as the Huntress; here in the east, they divided them in two and called them the 'Sisters'.

Worship banned, Zos thought with his inner rebellion. The Huntress remained a very popular deity among Dardanians, but her worship had been banned many years before. Zos' crescent was his secret observance, and even with that, he was scarcely a pious worshipper of any god.

More just an old warrior who won't change his spots.

His reverie was interrupted by the helmet slipping over his head. His *papista* tied the laces under his chin and put a single bronze half-gauntlet on his sword hand.

'My thanks,' he said curtly.

He tried never to mistreat a slave, for reasons of his own.

He ran around the corner of the tent and then dropped into a leisurely walk. The godborn only ran when war was involved.

'Zos!' the god-king of Kyra roared. King Mekos was standing tall in his magnificent chariot.

The chariot itself was covered in thin, magnificent repoussé gold plaques – not just protecting the quivers of arrows and javelins, but plates covering the charioteer and the handrails, too. The plates were covered in figures telling the whole story of the Theomachy, the War of the Gods, episode by episode. On the front plate, Urkigul, Lady of the Underworld, and Ara, God of War, speared Shemeg, the old pantheon's God of the Sun out of his golden chariot drawn by mighty stags.

If I were a god, I'd never fight anyone again, Zos thought.

Then he shook off the thought. He thought too much; it always got him in trouble.

'Heaven-sent!' Zos greeted his current employer. 'Great Mekos!' He tried not to show a trace of anything but cheerful compliance.

'I have waited *hours* for you,' the god-king complained.

'Heaven-sent, I had prayers, and my armour…'

Zos had, in fact, been asleep. He'd been up all night with the diggers, building siege lines, and scouting. He had survived past the best years of his youth by being careful and attentive off the battlefield so that he could be a monster on it.

'I have ordered an attack,' the King Mekos said.

Zos looked out over the wind-blown barley fields and already-burnt farm villages around Hekka. Five hundred paces away, just out of extreme bow-shot range, the towers of Hekka stood above the heat shimmer. Sweat began to run down his back.

'An attack, Heaven-sent?' Zos asked.

'We will assault the gate. The side gate with the little door.' Mekos made a gesture. 'There. That one.'

'The sally port, Heaven-sent? Or the postern beside it?'

'Whichever I like,' Mekos muttered. And then louder, 'Whichever I like!'

He was slightly overweight, and well into middle age. He had golden blond hair and skin to match, and his armour was either made of gold or plated in it. In the glare of the sun on the Hekkan plain it was rather hard to look directly at him, but under the gold was a paunchy man with a petulant expression.

Zos had been here before. He patted the silver-nailed bronze sword at his side for reassurance and smiled.

'We will, of course, do as the god-king commands us,' he said with a deep bow. 'This morning, it was your will that we starve the city.'

'Yes.' After a pause, Mekos said, 'That's dull. I want the city quickly, and I want to be entertained as it falls.' He looked at Zos. 'The gods have spoken to me, you know.'

There were two more godborn standing by his chariot – both veterans. One was huge, like an ox built of human flesh. Men called him Axe. He was quite old, for a warrior; his hair was white.

The other man was his companion: Anenome. He was small, long-limbed like a monkey, and reputed the wisest warrior in all the twenty-seven kingdoms. He had a ruddy face and pale blue eyes, a sharp contrast to Axe's blue-black skin and liquid brown eyes. But both men wore their fortunes in bronze and silver – superb armour, magnificent weapons.

They were sell-swords, despite their outward show. Just like Zos.

Anenome shrugged at Zos, as if to say, *Don't ask me. I tried.*

Zos suspected that reasoning with the god-king was pointless, but he tried.

'Heaven-sent, you said you wanted the city. We hit them before they could harvest. All we need is time.'

'We are bored,' the god-king said. 'My astrologer cast a horo-scope.' He gestured at the magos, who stood in his long white wool robe in the second chariot.

The magos nodded. 'My heaven-sent lord is correct. While we are entering the Crab, the aspect of Ara is strong in the Dragon, my heaven-sent lord's house.'

The god-king smiled. 'See? Do as I say, there's a good lad. Assault the little door.'

'And as you know, Heaven-sent, the gods may take a hand.' The magos spoke with the confidence of a counsellor of weight. And the benign air of a man who wouldn't dirty his sandals or come near the sling stones and arrows of the wall.

Zos knew better than to protest that they would take losses.

God-kings never cared about such stuff. He considered the alternatives, glanced at Axe, and saw the older man wince.

'As you will it, Heaven-sent,' Zos said with apparent obedience. 'Will you be watching?'

The god-king nodded. 'Of course.'

He had a perfume cone in his wig, above his mask of beaten gold, and the scent made Zos gag. The new fashion was very sweet and musky – something bought from the Dry Ones. It probably had their resin in it. The literal stuff of immortality – or, at least, of youth and vigour, so it was said.

'The Hekkans have powerful bows, Heaven-sent. I worry—'

'Who would dare?' the god-king said. 'Send them word I am coming to watch. If one arrow comes towards my chariot, I will kill one hundred of their peasants.'

Zos doubted whether the god-king of Hekka cared any more about *his* peasants than Zos' temporary boss did. He cast about desperately for a compelling reason, and tried a real one.

'If we lose too many spearmen, Heaven-sent, we won't have enough to man the siege lines.'

The god-king shrugged and spoke in the tones of a kindly father to an erring son.

'Then we will come back next year.' Then he smiled, like a child winning an argument. 'Besides, Ara is in my aspect.'

Axe made a noise that he managed to turn into a sneeze. Anenome stepped closer to the god-king's chariot.

'Perhaps—'

'Get it done!' shrieked the god-king. 'Make it happen or I'll bury you all in anthills! I'm paying you for this!'

Zos knew when he was beaten.

'Yes, Heaven-sent.'

The king's astrologer glanced at him; he shook his head. Zos knew he was doomed. It wasn't his first time to be doomed, and he was fatalistic. He'd outlived almost all his contemporaries as a warrior. He'd outlived his kingdom and his family.

Perhaps it was time to die.

'If you'll cover me,' he said to Anenome, 'I'll at least scorch the door.'

Axe shook his head. 'We're out of this one.'

Anenome didn't even bother to look sheepish.

'While you were giving orders to the cattle, we talked him into letting us rest today.'

Zos hesitated. It was tempting to tell the two godborn what he thought of them. But he had got ahead by not burning bridges, and besides, he couldn't fault them for avoiding a suicide charge. And he'd served under them in the past; he knew they took care of themselves and their own – even their slaves. And no one else.

'Retrieve my body?' he asked.

Axe shrugged. 'If I can, I will,' the giant said. 'Gods favour you, Zos.'

Anenome put a hand on his arm. 'Twist your ankle,' he said seriously. 'Trip and fall. Don't be proud.'

Zos shook his head. 'Not my style.'

'Gods favour you, then, brother,' Anenome said.

Zos managed a grin, while his insides turned to water.

'They don't,' he said.

The assault on the postern gate would be pointless and was absolutely without military merit, but Zos tried to do things well, from habit. He threw a band of hundreds of peasant militia against a far wall, with ladders, and then he put ladders against the wall to the south by the sea. Finally he brought up a battering ram and had it chip away at the stone base of one of the towers, which he suspected was only mud-brick. The city garrison were pulled here-and-there trying to defend, and they were tardy getting to the tower. But the tower filled with archers, and they began to slaughter the peasants and slaves manning the ram.

But slaughter takes time. And Hekka's militia were both badly trained and, as he observed, apparently short on arrows.

'Now!' he called.

He led the attack himself. He had to. The king's warriors were not particularly good; if they had been, he would never have been 'invited to enjoy their company' or been showered with gifts by them, which was the godborn's way of expressing that Zos was a well-born sell-sword and they had hired him. As they had hired Axe and Anenome.

Hired because they suck. And we're good.

In fact, the cynical part of him was asking, *Where did all the gold come from, and why are we really here?*

Warfare between the Hundred Kingdoms was endemic, but it was a little war of cattle raids and slave raids, burnt villages and ambushes. This sort of straight-on assault on another god-king's citadel was...

Becoming more common.

And that gold comes from Narmer, and you know it.

He ran forwards from the cover of one of the great chunks of basalt that littered the plain. Almost immediately the arrows started to buzz around him, each one carrying a message of mortality that he understood perfectly.

He didn't look back, but he could tell by the sound that either they weren't following him, or they were well behind.

Fuck them.

He knew his own failings: he knew that he was too smart to believe in anything, even the code; he knew that he was arrogant in a way that would eventually get him killed; he feared that *eventually* had just begun to merge with *now*.

His sandals crunched on gravel and he kept his shield up.

An arrow hit it, and his whole arm moved.

And another. And another.

Something washed over his body like a taste of death – a curse, averted by either his amulet or his shield. He had no *auric* power of his own. He had to buy or borrow it.

Under the bronze rim, when he lifted it, he could see the wall and the postern. It was closer.

An arrow hit his shield and slammed off the rim, bending it, and somehow he managed to step on the shaft, shattering the cane and getting a long splinter in the side of his foot. He didn't have the breath to curse.

He made it to the wall. His shield was heavy with arrows, but not one had penetrated more than a finger's breadth, and now he held it up above his head. He looked back.

Just for a moment, he hated his employer more than any enemy he'd ever faced.

The god-king's chariot had stopped at bow-shot range, and the god-king had strung his bow. He was lofting arrows at the walls.

All his warriors were around that chariot with their shields up, protecting him.

Perhaps a dozen had followed Zos. Two were down and the rest were still running, because they were soft, and slow.

Zos wished he'd brought his *papista*. The boy was slave-born, but trustworthy – or, at least, predictable. Eager to make some kills and be free. A far, far better man than the godborn warriors who lorded it over him.

Another man went down. Zos realised that no one was shooting at him. He looked up, understood the difficulty any archer would face shooting straight down, and dropped his shield.

He hadn't brought an axe. Instead, he had something better.

He had brought a huge stone hammer with an axe wedge

on the back. He'd found the head out on the plain; there were quite a few of them. Old weapons, left over from old wars. He'd cut a shaft for it, fitted it himself. Now he pulled the cord over his head, carefully, so as not to catch it in his helmet or his plume. Then he sheathed his sword and picked the heavy weapon up, hefting it.

A thousand years old? More? What war was fought with stone weapons?

Zos managed a bitter smile.

This one.

He slammed it into the door.

It bounced. Good wood. Old and dry, but good.

He got angry.

He whirled the axe over his head and roared his name – defiance, rage, posturing, all together.

'*Zos!*'

The heavy stone head split a wedge of old wood from the door. Good wood was expensive and god-kings were cheap, too busy forcing maidens and swilling lotus wine to replace the doors and the mud-brick with sturdier defences.

He swung eight more times. He'd done this before, and he knew where the hinges were set in the mud-brick which should have been stone.

The last swing broke something.

There was a man – a terrified man – just inside the big wooden door when it fell.

He had a bow, and he loosed an arrow, so close he was almost touching Zos.

And that's it, Zos thought.

The archer missed.

The stone hammer exploded his skull.

Zos threw the hammer into the darkness and drew the short bronze sword from under his arm.

'*Zos!*' he roared.

He didn't look back. No one was coming anyway; he assumed they'd stopped to retrieve their wounded. Godborn were like that.

He stepped into the cool darkness of the postern gate, and the men inside flinched.

A tentative spear licked out, and did no more than brush the tip of his blade.

Why am I even doing this? Zos asked himself. *Must I prove to myself, every day, that I'm not old? Not weak?*

Not what Atrios tried to make me?

Prove it right up until the moment when . . .

But he was a bull-leaper, and they were not. They had no idea what he could do.

He leapt forwards and up and got his feet on the wall of the tunnel. He ran two steps along the wall as three men approached him, tumbling into a controlled fall and coming to his feet with his bronze sword in the third man's throat. The first man was just discovering that he was dead, the short sword having punctured through the top of his skull during his sideways run along the wall.

Zos thrust forwards, passed back, and stabbed the second man, behind him, in the head. His sword sloped up under his victim's jaw to enter his brain from below – a perfect blow that never left the blade stuck in the wound or allowed the bronze blade to get bent or broken, and always killed.

There were now no enemies behind him, only a man who had appeared before him with a tower shield, a big bull's hide wall that almost filled the tunnel. Zos could see the man's eyes above it, and hear his terrified breathing.

A blow hit him in the shin, where his linen greaves covered him, but it hurt as if a red-hot wire had been pushed into his skin. He bellowed, and then his left hand darted out and caught the top of his opponent's shield, slamming it to the stone floor. He jumped, got a foot on the shield's bronze boss, and his short sword went over it, glanced off the man's helmet, slid, and bit into his neck where it met the shoulder. Not quite perfect. The blade would be damaged.

He jumped back, his armour slowing him, and landed badly on the corpse of one of his victims. He'd thrust too deeply and lost his blade, locked in the wound and probably bent.

Foolish.

A distant godborn voice ordered 'Charge!' and the defenders came forwards.

It was dark in the tunnel and they didn't see him lying with the corpses until it was too late.

He drew the dead man's sword as he rolled to his left, slashing the first man's feet so hard that he severed one. This sword was shorter than his own, broad and heavy, with horns that went back over his hand. He slammed the blade down on someone and pushed forwards with all his rage, and anger, and fear and blood. He kept pushing, and killing, using the shorter weapon from very close range because he was very good at this. His feet pushed and his shoulders and back pushed, while his hands and arms and brain killed, and he climbed, rolled, fell, and leapt and killed four men in a hundred heartbeats.

He was, technically, inside the city of Hekka.

His eyes finally adjusted to the light, and he could see that he was fighting thirty men, with more coming every moment.

But he'd pushed through the thickness of the wall. If he had fifty good men beside him, the city would be his.

Only he didn't, and it wasn't.

They backed off, forming a ring, eyes wide with fear. But they weren't all afraid; an archer on the wall aimed and released carefully. Zos had warning and flicked the arrow away with his sword, but he knew that he was going down in heartbeats.

The man took a second arrow from his quiver.

I'll die here. And for what?

Fuck this, he thought.

He backed a step into the pointed arch of the postern gate and the tunnel. And another.

No one followed.

He had no choice and one chance. Halfway down the tunnel, he found the dead man with the tower shield, and he took the shield. He found his own sword and took a moment to put a foot on the corpse and free it, worrying about the blade. It was a fine sword, and good bronze swords only came from Dardania.

It came free and he backed again.

He backed out of the postern, and kept backing away. Slide the back leg, then the front. Half-turned sideways, so that his big shield covered most of his body.

He knew he had to back at least two hundred paces, far enough that the archers couldn't hit him. Any one of their arrows would punch through his bronze armour.

But not through this shield, he hoped.

He slid his right foot back, seeking secure footing, and then changed weight and got his left foot back.

And again.

And again.

As he left the lengthening shadow of the wall, the archers found him again. He didn't have the shield high enough and an arrow slammed into the crest of his helmet and he thought, *There I am, fucked.*

But his goddess was there for him, in her own strange way. Or he was just lucky.

Back.

Back.

Back.

In a way, it was boring.

In another way it was terrible, and the fear was like a dark cloud that killed any real thought.

His right foot slid back, and the left.

The pain in his left shoulder, where he held the shield out and up to intercept arrows, was real. He wondered if the shoulder would recover; he wasn't young any more.

But it always recovered.

Back.

Thump.

An arrow went so deep into his shield that the bronze head came out by the handgrip and scraped down his thumb. He didn't let go.

Thump. Another arrow, this one near the rim. It came halfway through – two handspans of arrow reaching for his face.

Someone on those ramparts, or safe in a big tower, was godborn. Someone had a great bow, and was trying to kill him with it.

Thump. Out near the rim, it hit the oak that framed his shield and shattered. But it hit so hard that it spun the shield, and a lesser arrow glanced off the rim as it twisted in his hand and buried itself in the scale armour over his heart. It hurt.

But it didn't go through for the kill.

Right foot back. Change weight.

Shield up.

Thwang!

He never saw what struck him. Something even more powerful – or god-guided, or perhaps magic. It knocked him down.

But his shield held.

Zos couldn't read, but he did know a charm, and he said it, lying on his back on the gritty sand.

Tamite. Ta-Mi-Te.

He invoked the name, the true name, of the Huntress. She

was a complicated deity – usually for women. Less a malevolent child than the others. His mother had loved her; she had run on the hills with other women in the dark of the moon in her honour. She'd woven charms in his clothes. Taught him the prayers in the secret language.

Fat lot of good she did you, when the Mykoans stormed the palace and …

He banished the thought.

He was eighty paces from the wall – maybe more. Most men couldn't hit anything at eighty paces.

He got to his feet, and the shield slapped against the arrow sticking out of his chest, and the pain …

Arrows were falling like sleet, and he got the shield up again. He suspected that turning and sprinting was now an option, at this range, but he was damned if he was going to run.

Fuckers.

He shuffled away.

Ta-Mi-Te.

And backed.

His shoulder raged, and the arrow over his heart shrieked with pain.

The godborn archer had most likely become bored. Wasn't that always the way?

Zos peeked over his shield, and then he really couldn't hold it up any longer. He was two hundred paces from the wall.

He wanted to raise his sword over his head and bellow his war cry, but the shaft in his chest precluded that.

So he turned instead and, with as much arrogance as he could muster, walked slowly away from Hekka.

He walked all the way to the god-king's magnificent chariot, seeing that his sword was bent, and he'd lost the stone hammer.

He'd get another rapier eventually, his preferred weapon, which he had trained with since childhood. And he could get another stone hammer. They littered the plain here, around Hekka, left over from one of the battles of the War of the Gods, or so the temples said. Fought right here, some time in the murky past.

The god-king was drinking.

'A cup for my hero,' he said.

Someone put a cup of lotus wine into his hands. He drank it off.

'You see?' the god-king said. 'That was exciting.' He smiled. 'I saw that little leap you made, even from here. You are very fast.'

Zos bowed his acknowledgement and received more wine.

'You are a bull-leaper,' the god-king said. 'We thought your kind were a legend.'

Zos could think of nothing to say. That is, many things came to mind, but none of them fitted his mood. Or his employment status.

Off to one side, beyond the cluster of godborn, his *papista* shook his head. Zos mimed silence.

'But, Zos...' the god-king said. 'I told you the little door. I meant the other one.'

Zos nodded. The wine, unwatered, with mead and lotus and something powdered, was just hitting him. What he needed was water. His hands were shaking. His knees were suddenly weak.

'I'm sorry, Heaven-sent.' His tone probably gave away that he wasn't sorry, he was angry, but the god-king let that pass, or never caught it.

In fact, the god-king actually smiled.

'Never mind, it was a good try. You went *inside*! Wonderful! We'll try something else tomorrow.'

Zos nodded. 'Can we just starve them now?'

He didn't want to imagine how many peasants and slaves had just died – much less the dozen or so poor bastards he'd just killed himself.

I never used to think this way, he admitted. *Is this old age?*

'No, no,' the god-king said, annoyed. 'Tomorrow you attack the other little door.' He smiled. 'The one I *told* you to attack.'

Zos shook his head.

His *papista* clapped a linen towel over his mouth.

'Yes, Heaven-sent,' Zos said, after managing a convincing show of taking the towel and wiping his face.

He looked around at the god-king's godborn warriors. None of them met his eye.

But when he turned to walk to his tent, Axe followed him. The giant warrior put a hand on his shoulder.

'You'll just die, doing it their way,' the big man said. 'They don't care.'

Zos' *papista* winced.

Zos managed a lopsided smile.

'He tells me that all the time,' he said, indicating his shield-bearer.

Axe shrugged. He was a very intelligent man, but he looked like a brute – heavy jaw, heavy forehead.

'Lad,' he said, leaning forwards, 'you just fought your way, *by yourself*, into a god-king's city.' He lowered his voice. 'And he didn't even give you a *fucking* gold cup. Or a slave. Nothing.' Axe nodded, as if in conversation with himself. 'That's how little we are valued. And that's the level of... effort... they deserve in return.'

He held out a skin, and it proved to be full of watered wine. Zos drank quite a bit, and immediately needed to piss – a bad sign.

'Go,' Axe said. 'Try not to die.'

'Or make us look bad,' Anenome added. 'Not everyone got to grow up as a bull-leaper.'

Zos shook his head. 'No,' he said. 'Not everyone *got to*.'

He thought of the boy lying, *ribs broken, the bull tattoo on his chest covered in blood*.

He shook his head.

Later, in his tent, his *papista* cleaned the wound. A pair of royal slaves brought him a magnificent *heton* in salmon pink with a tablet-woven border, and a gold belt to match. He was not particularly greedy, but he loved to look fine, and the *heton* did something to assuage his anger. It was fine stuff.

'Do you really fight naked sometimes, boss?' his *papista* asked.

Zos nodded, looking at the gifts.

In the great scheme of things, the gold belt was not very heavy and the textiles were just so many hours of slave-work. He drank more wine, thinking.

'The way I was trained, armour is a hindrance.' He shrugged. 'I'm old, boy. Everyone wears armour now. Including me.'

And my whole body hurts. I'm too old to fight like a bull-leaper.

More slaves came. They brought a fine breastplate with scales of bronze and some kind of exotic horn, and a magnificent bronze-headed spear with a long, complicated blade. Heavy. Intricate. The whole shaft had been worked in spirals and knobs, and it felt wonderful in his hands.

Better.

And then they brought three slaves – a very young boy and two women.

By then Zos was lying, naked and oiled, on his sleeping pallet, and he had a good buzz on from the lotus wine. Everything should have been good.

Instead, everything seemed odd.

The boy was afraid, and bravely trying to hide it; the two women were naked, blank-faced. One thrust out her hip and rubbed a hand under her heavy breast; the gesture was meant to be voluptuous, but it was not. Worse, both women were heavily drugged. The smaller of the two had the finger-stains of *apana*, the life-taker drug. Both had beautiful smooth skin, and bruises all over.

It was Zos' curse to see such details. And, in his present mood, to hate them.

Tyka had been too close to taking him away. Dead.

What's wrong with me? Zos asked himself.

'Are you mine?' he asked.

'We are only loaned,' the boy said.

Zos swirled the wine in his cup, contemplating whether using their bodies would make him feel better or worse. Then he sat up and drank the rest off.

'Go back to your master and tell him I was asleep,' he said.

When they were gone, his *papista* grunted.

'I might have wanted a ride,' the man said.

Zos lay back. 'Find your own,' he said. 'Do you really want some disinherited noble's daughter, high on *apana*?'

Aiois grunted again, and then said, quietly, 'You're quite the killjoy, boss. I guess I don't, now you put that ugly thought in my head.'

'Welcome to my world,' Zos said bitterly. 'Massage my back.'

'Sure. We fighting tomorrow?'

'Perish the thought, boy. I'm too fucking old to fight two days in a row.'

'That leap was something, boss,' the boy said.

Face on his arms, Zos thought, *Oh, once I could leap like that all day. Now, I'll pay for it for days.*

Fuck ageing.

He went to sleep alone.

In his dream, a blue woman with fire instead of hair offered him a chariot to drive. In the way of dreams, he was not the chariot warrior, but the driver for a female warrior. In the way of dreams, he accepted that. The Blue Goddess smiled and showed all her teeth, filed to points, and then . . .

A boy was beside him, and behind him was a wall of fire, and in his hand he held . . .

And then he was in the palace of his youth, facing the bull. And there was the man who had failed, curled in a ball around his wounds, his blood all over the sand, and the high priestess screaming at him . . .

And now the man who had failed was at his side, his spear killing men over Zos' shoulder. The man with the bull tattoo.

And then he was on the sands again . . .

Zos vomited into the bowl that his *papista* had left by his side. He was cold, and afraid, and he lay for a long time staring up at the shadowed peak of his tent. All his joints hurt; yesterday's wound had a hollow ache that he feared.

I am too old to fight as a bull-leaper. And then, for the first time in a long time, *I wonder what happened to the man with the bull tattoo.*

That could have been me.

If I'd gone first, would he have made his leap?

Did I only succeed because I saw him fail?

He didn't want any more lotus wine. He got up and found his pottery canteen hanging from the central pole, and he drank the vinegar and water in it, spat outside, pissed, came in and drank more water.

He lay down, and no sleep would come. Outside, the unfeeling stars whirled in their dance, and his mind did the same. He thought of the men he'd killed and the women he'd had in his bed; the treasure he'd won and lost.

Tonight, he owned the clothes in the tent, some fine armour, and a good shield he never used. Two very mediocre chariot horses, and a chariot that he repaired himself when he was sure no one was looking.

He was ten years older than the oldest warrior he knew except Axe. And Axe was almost a god.

The darkness was deep. The emptiness was overwhelming.

When it was light, he went out into the dawn and prayed. He had no time for gods; they were uniformly unfeeling and jealous, but it paid to keep them away. Then, wearing his old, torn *heton*, he walked off out of the camp, stepping carefully because no one in Kyra believed in proper latrines. He walked far out into the tangle of barley and millet fields with low stone walls – boundary markers really, for the Hekkan peasants who were now slaves to the god-king of Kyra. Other peasants would come and till them in the future.

Three fields from the camp, beyond the cook fires and the horse lines, he found the hammers. Signs of the Old Ones always delighted him; his father had all but lost his kingdom trying to study the past, and he'd imbibed some of the curiosity. The stone hammers were for big men – a hammer head, shaped round and beautifully polished, on one face, and an axe blade on the other. The hafts were long gone, but the scattering of human bones and a smashed skull suggested a battlefield to him.

It took him a while to find an unbroken hammer head. When he did, Zos loved it; the stone was red, the polish still intact so that it shone like lustrous blood in the rising sun. He raised it, and sang a little hymn to the God of War.

He casually stole a tent pole as he walked by, leaving the linen sheet to flap on the morning breeze. He spent an hour with a chert knife, scraping the good northern oak until it was a haft for the stone hammer.

Before he joined the two, he set a tent peg in the ground to read the sun angle exactly, and then he used a little disc amulet he wore around his neck to make the calculations. He made three marks in the dirt by his tent, and he didn't join the new-cut haft to the stone head until the third mark was reached. He sang a song at each mark, and watched the glow run up the shaft.

Astrology and craft went hand in hand. These weren't god-born skills, but then, he had not lived a godborn life.

When he was satisfied, the slaves were being driven into the no-man's-land between the besiegers and the city, to build trenches and haul brush for fires. He put on a loincloth and a big old straw hat full of holes and joined them, seized a giant armload of brush and carried it forwards while an overseer roared at the slaves around him. He knew it was no disguise, and several slaves gave him sideways glances, but he wasn't worried by the overseers. He dropped his brush on a pile where a hasty redoubt was being built to cover the forward edge of the camp and then dropped into a gully, moved along it for seventy paces, and emerged onto the sun-baked soil of an untilled field. The city walls were closer now, and Zos crawled on his belly up to an abandoned hut of sun-baked brick, crawled in through the low door, and found a window on the far side that looked, as he'd hoped, right at the gates, about two hundred paces away. He took a long look, and then crawled out again, moved across an animal pen and someone's tiny garden, and then along another wall to an alley. The walls were even closer. He could hear the guards on the walls, and hear an overseer behind him demanding a head count.

Now he could see the tower to the right of the gate. It stood perhaps sixty feet tall, and it had a definite construction problem; the longer he looked, the more he was sure it had a very slight lean to the right, as if the wall on that side was weak.

Zos didn't want to go closer, but he did. He crawled again, right up to the last little slum of shacks against an abandoned out-wall. These little mud-brick hovels were no bigger than coffins. They had no windows. They weren't even whitewashed.

He moved, as low to the ground as he could manage, until he could see around a corner.

He was now at the edge of the cleared zone. Probably, until very recently, the slums had run right up to the walls. But the local god-king had burnt a swath through it, seventy paces or so wide, right in front of his walls, to create a killing zone.

There were always things you had to know, if you wanted to win. It was always worth the time to scout, to plan, to know your enemy.

At least, it was if you planned to grow old as a warrior, and Zos had no other triumph available to him.

Unless I go back to Mykoax and kill the king.

He looked at the leaning tower for a few moments, and then turned and began the long crawl back.

By the time there was a stir around the god-king's tent, Zos had been awake for hours. He'd had a bowl of honeyed boiled wheat, and two cups of Narmerian ka, and was already in his armour.

He went around the camp, directing the listless slaves and equally listless peasants forced to carry spears.

It was well after noon when the god-king mounted his chariot. Zos attended him as the unwatered wine circled. Axe and Anenome were sent to reconnoitre three towers on the far side of the city, that looked as if they had no stone in their construction at all. Zos was beginning to suspect that *none* of the towers had stone above the second or third course, and he knew the others had been lucky to get away before the god-king grew bored. Someone suggested a challenge to single combat and Zos volunteered to carry it. The god-king glared. But he subsided, drank more, and Zos had reason to think he'd been forgotten.

But that was too much to hope for. Zos was a novelty – like a new concubine, or an acrobat.

'Zos! Let's see you attack the little door!' the drunk god-king said suddenly.

He sloshed his wine and it ran over his gleaming oiled wool *heton* covered in minute red flowers – a winter's work for five women.

'Idiot!' he snapped at his cup-bearer and waved. A warrior strangled the cup-bearer on the spot.

'Why can't I get graceful service?' the god-king asked.

But it was as if death, even a slave's death, whetted his appetite. His face grew red.

'Zos!' he shouted.

Zos had done all that he could to prepare. And he felt surprisingly good; perhaps Tyka meant to take him at his best. Or this sense of well-being was a gift from the notoriously odd Huntress.

He was thankful. It was good to be strong, and have beautiful armour. He was wearing the magnificent *heton* and the new scale shirt.

He would die looking his best. Maybe that was as good as it got.

'That tower by the gate is weak,' he said. 'I'd like to send a party to finish undermining it.'

The king waved his hand. 'Whatever you like. Just attack the little gate and make it fun!'

Zos knew his efforts were doomed, but he put a lot of effort into the attack. A stunningly incompetent band of spearmen carrying huge tower shields of bull's hide went forwards hesitantly against the same gate he'd attacked yesterday, moving cautiously through the ruined suburb he'd just scouted. They prevaricated, pushed hesitantly into arrow range, and then lost their formation, such as it was. Some of them ran, dropping their shields. Others ran back out of arrow range and huddled together like cowards, shields wobbling as the desperate men crowded together for protection from the deadly arrows.

The garrison jeered.

The second attack had more spirit, and was led by a dozen godborn from the god-king's warrior guard. Zos was sure he could trust them to try; he'd embarrassed them yesterday. And sure enough, they got ladders against the leaning tower wall.

The terrified slaves with the battering ram had a shed of animal hide to protect them, only it took them too long to push it forwards, so by the time they were picking at the socle of the tower, all the godborn warriors were dead and their bodies had been ritually maimed and thrown from the walls. The ladders were pushed down.

Zos smiled. He wasn't particularly fond of his own kind, and no one was going to miss them.

Zos saw it all unfold, because he was lying on his back in the shadow of an abandoned tower shield, wearing his new armour and carrying a round shield on his arm. He was too tired to fight like a bull-leaper today. His *papista*, stripped naked like a peasant spearman, was holding the shield. The incompetent spearmen were his pick of the peasants, and he'd offered every one of them a wife and ten silver bars if they fought with him and made it into the city. And as yet, they hadn't run, though they were all hiding in the huddle of mud-brick houses that had until recently been the main farming community outside the walls of Hekka.

'Keep looking terrified,' Zos said from where he lay, still watching the action.

'Not that hard,' his *papista* muttered, as another godborn arrow slammed into the oxhide face. But the big peasant shields were built to withstand arrows, and this one had been chosen from all of them.

'And ... now ...' Zos said.

The defenders had waited longer than he would have – perhaps their god-king was as useless as his own – but then the sally port opened in the long curtain wall. Out came a flash of bronze, then another, as if a fire was burning in the sun.

Godborn warriors just like him. The sortie. Off to kill the slaves who were busy undermining the tower. The godborn were usually eager to fight, especially if their opponents were unarmed and untrained.

'They'll go for the battering ram,' Zos said. 'Then we run for the sally port. Everyone ready?'

The enemy warriors did indeed make a dash for the peasants and slaves picking at the corner of the tower.

'Go!' Zos called.

He rolled to his feet and started for the open sally port. His little band of spearmen followed him; he could hear their feet, their heavy breathing.

Better than the godborn.

He glanced to his right, because something was going on at the weakened tower.

It took him too long to understand the subtle change. The enemy men of bronze were just reaching the corner of the damaged tower; the slaves were turning to run, abandoning their tools and the ram.

And then he saw it, all between one heartbeat and the next.

The tower was leaning even more.

He looked back at the gate. A man in bronze stood there, looking both ferocious and indecisive.

Back to his right.

The tower was leaning further still, its incline becoming a lean, sliding to the side faster and faster until the mud-bricks collapsed, and in its place was a great plume of dust.

Somewhere behind him, there was cheering. And in the city,

beyond the dust, a shaft of gold like a second sun shining down through the clouds. Something was moving fast, through the air.

Time to go.

He had the hammer slung across his back. His sword was in his hand, carefully straightened, and he went shield-to-shield with the bronze warrior at the gate. He went low, but it was like hitting a wall.

The big man kneed him, but he caught most of it on his shield, and he clearly hurt the man's leg in the process. He had to back a step, but his opponent wobbled, and the man's long sword licked out.

His *papista* caught the sword arm with his long spear, and Zos was in, passing under the spear and burying his sword under the man's upraised arm.

He pulled to withdraw it and the sword broke at the hilt, where it had bent the day before.

And there we go, Zos thought. Weeks to make, as valuable as twenty weaver-women, and now it was just scrap metal.

The sally port was a proper gate under a gate tower, unlike the postern fifty paces along the wall, and the moment he tried to enter, red-hot sand fell through a trap in the ceiling of the entry tunnel.

He ducked back into the thickness of the wall.

His *papista* grinned at him.

'You just earned your armour, Aiois,' Zos said.

Damn, I got his name right.

The shield-bearer grinned. 'Not bad, eh?'

He was, in fact, wearing the old bronze that Zos had worn the day before. He was more reliable than most godborn, because he *wanted* things – women, gold… fame.

Zos had seen it all before.

Stop thinking, start fighting.

'Now!'

Zos led them through the entry tunnel. He had the hammer in his hand and the red stone caught the light from the open trap, but six of them made it through before the defenders could upend another cauldron of sand.

The seventh man fell, the new red-hot downpour burning his entire naked body. The men behind him were hurt, and the gatehouse was filled with their screams.

Zos slammed the stone hammer against the inner doors. A shard of it split off and shot away, but the rest of the head remained intact and he swung it again. Above him, he could hear another trap opening – hot oil, or more sand.

He swung again.

Aiois lifted the tower shield over him. He stepped to the left, saw that the hinge was on his side of the door, and that someone had profited themselves by using a small bronze hinge when a large one had been required.

One blow for the lower hinge.

One blow for the upper hinge.

Six desperate men threw themselves against the doors and they burst open, the left-hand door falling flat into the city.

He was up, moving forwards, the hammer cocked back. A godborn warrior stood his ground and Zos' peasants ganged up on him and stabbed him the way men hunted lions, and he died on their spears.

They were in a narrow square – probably a market on a normal day, with a well. Streets so narrow that a man might have to walk crabwise radiated in four directions; mud-brick houses had sprouted up like toadstools... To the left, a pair of mighty gate towers rose over the market square, the entrance to the palace.

There was a rush from the wall – a counter-attack: four godborn in good armour with a dozen spearmen and an archer. The rest of Zos' bribed peasants were coming through the gate as if they were themselves godborn, screaming with fear and eagerness to kill.

The market square became a butcher's shop. It wasn't neat; there were no lines, and both sides were constantly bolstered by dribbles of men.

Zos fought, using the axe-hammer to smash his way through a trio of godborn, and then let Aiois cover him while he ducked back and sent a bloody-handed peasant as a messenger to his own god-king. He breathed for a snatched moment, drank watered wine from his canteen, and then sprinted forwards, killing the man facing his shield-bearer with a single deceptive turn of his axe. He whirled, smashed a shield to broken boards, and then it was over. The Hekkan counter-attack was reduced to a pile of corpses, and his peasants were moving into the city like hungry lions looking for a weak gazelle.

The first of the god-king of Kyra's warriors came through the sally port behind him.

And then there was a burst of colour, and a scream. Zos turned in time to see a brilliant figure leap from a building into the market square, faster than a cat.

Twice the height of a man, with armour of burning gold and jade green, and skin like ivory, the titanic being was blank-eyed and horrifying, with black vulture's wings on his back, folded for now. Even in awe and terror, Zos noted that every part of his armour was covered in magnificent designs – repoussé, enamel, niello. His shield was inlaid with gems that blazed in the sun and were lit from within by mage-light.

There was a real god among them. He was a blur of sheer *power*, and he roared.

Zos flinched. Men did not fight gods. Men just died.

The god raised his hand. A sickly green lance struck the peasant in front of Zos, burnt through his shield, and his chest exploded in a release of superheated steam and black rot.

The corpse was nothing but slime and sticks before it fell to the ground.

Zos stood, paralysed. It was more than fear. It was terror. And awe.

This was Resheph. The God of Pestilence During War.

The god swung a sword of dull black-green silver, like a bar of ugly shadow, and beheaded another two peasants – one on the fore swing, and another on the backswing. The god's shield smashed ribs and broke bones; his left hand dealt pale green death while his right hand dealt black death. All his victims rotted as they fell.

Aiois thrust with his long spear. The shield-bearer struck the god in the upper thigh, and the bronze head of the spear slipped harmlessly along the inviolate flesh of the god's pelvis. He did rock the giant being, though, and the force of his blow unbalanced the god for a moment.

The shadow sword cut down, through the *papista*'s oxhide shield, through his head and his armour and his groin, and sliced the man in half.

His war-servant's death snapped Zos out of his reverie.

So this is how it ends, he thought; then: *Fuck this, I liked this one. Aiois. Fucking gods.*

Anger filled him, and a sort of hopeless hope. A desire for an end. He leapt forwards, over the steaming offal that had been his man, and cocked back the hammer. He went between the god's weapons, as he had trained himself to do with men; the god towered over him, twice his height, but clearly unused to being forced to play close.

Then he swung the hammer, full force, into the side of the god's right knee.

The god shrieked like a woman in childbirth, and his left hand came down on Zos, the rim of the enamelled shield knocking him from his feet. He fell heavily, his fall broken by corpses; a dead man's teeth gashed his hand.

But he was still alive.

And the god was bleeding. He saw the bright too-red non-human blood clearly, in contravention of the rules of the world. The blood burned with colour as if lit by mage-light – as if it defined the colour red, ennobled it.

The god's knee was shattered, and he dropped the shadow sword and clutched the citadel wall to keep himself from falling. The beam of death from his right hand blew a hole in the wall, splashed harmlessly along a catwalk and messily destroyed half a hundred Hekkan godborn coming to fill the breach. They died in putrid horror.

Zos rolled away, his crested helmet impeding his movement, as the god tried to finish him with his shield rim. He managed a kick, got a hand on his hidden knife ...

Ribs broke. And then something else. Zos felt it give inside him and knew he was dead.

He'd lost the hammer. and all the feeling in his limbs.

'*You hurt me!*' the god screamed, his head raised to the sky, his perfect teeth visible.

Then those massive vulture's wings unfolded, and the sweet terrible smell of carrion wafted over Zos so that he gagged, and Resheph threw himself into the heavens, still screaming.

Zos lay in agony for some time. He didn't really know how long; he came and went, and then there were warriors everywhere. He could smell smoke, and hear the screams of a city being sacked.

His mind was empty of thought, because it was full of pain, and though he scrabbled for reason it was lost in aeons of pain, a red-black time in hell. He managed to get a hand to his back, and the pain became a lightning bolt.

Now he lay staring at the sky.

Ara, God of War, my back is broken.

Huntress, take my black soul.

And then Zos felt the Blue Goddess' touch, and he assumed he was dead.

I will save you, warrior. Do not forget this, came a voice, and then someone was bending over him. Zos found enough clarity to see it was Axe.

'I'll just put him down,' the big man said.

Anenome's voice floated, disembodied. 'I wouldn't, Axe.'

'He's done for,' Axe said. 'He'd a' done it for me.'

'God-king's orders, Axe,' Anenome said.

He leant down, very close to his friend. Since Axe was leaning over Zos, the wounded man could hear every word.

'*There's a fucking god's eye watching us right now, so bring him alive. He hurt a god, Axe.*'

Axe shrugged. 'Sorry, mate,' he said to Zos.

Zos' world faded away.

When he came to again, he was bound, and could not move, although there was surprisingly little pain. His thirst on the other hand, was terrible.

He could turn his head. He saw a man, his limbs broken, lashed to a chariot wheel that was tied to a tree. He was trying to scream, but only managing a sort of rasping heavy breathing.

Zos realised that he, too, was lashed to a chariot wheel, and his limbs were shattered, the swollen appendages hanging like rotten fruit.

But my back's broken, and I can't feel a fucking thing. Huntress, if you were planning to save me, now would be a fine time.

Except that my back is broken, and there's no future for me but death, and I can't ... feel ... anything!

Except thirst.

128

Heaven

The Black Goddess, Temis, goddess of the hunt, traitor and survivor, entered the Great Hall in a beautiful white tunic that had tiny embroidered patterns in white, almost impossible for an observer to read. She moved with immortal grace, with her bow unstrung and her sword sheathed, and as she walked up the Hall of the Gods the courtiers whispered behind her.

She had very few friends in the great Hall of the Gods. But she was a convenient scapegoat, and they all watched her.

She ignored the lot of them and walked on until she stood next to the Goddess of Lust, Sypa, whose radiant, magnificent near-nudity and sharply musky smell kept the courtiers about her in a state bordering erotic fervour.

'You...' Sypa purred. She hated Temis and her puritan restraint. 'As always, my dear, you look like you need a good fuck.'

The Huntress glanced at her with a girlish, virginal smile.

'Putting on weight?' she asked with apparent innocence. She had the voice of a young woman, fierce and musical, but the sarcasm of her tone was ageless.

'I'm not a stick figure like you, child,' the Goddess of Lust spat back. She ran her hands down her flanks and a nearby minor deity moaned aloud. 'I'm perfect.'

'Keep telling yourself that,' the Huntress said, kindly. 'It's important to admire yourself, or how can you possibly control others?'

The shining gold eyes of the Huntress went to Enkul-Anu, and then to Laila, Sypa's 'friend'. Laila was magnificent, but she stopped short of Sypa's outrageous beauty. Where Sypa was ashy blonde, Laila had a waterfall of black hair. Where Sypa's breasts overflowed any garment she wore, Laila's were merely superb. And at the moment, her eyes were downcast, demure, and she knelt in a subservient position, her tailored jacket and flounced skirt doing little to hide her charms.

The Black Goddess gave her a wink, and Laila licked her lips.

'Next case,' Enkul-Anu said from his black throne. His eyes slid past his consort as she stepped forwards.

Sypa pouted. 'I have a case and he's ignoring me,' she said to the Huntress.

'I wonder why?' Temis asked the air.

She turned her back on Sypa and stalked across the hall. She was looking for god's eyes. She wanted to know where they all were.

Ara, great God of War, strode forwards. As tall as Enkul-Anu, he was the golden red of bronze, perfect in his masculinity from toe to the top of his ruddy brown hair. He wore magnificent silver and bronze armour, so vastly ensorcelled that its *Aura* was almost as potent as Enkul-Anu's own. His mane-crowned helmet was flipped back on his head; the mane, people said, was the scalp of the former Queen of Heaven, Taris, whom he'd killed in single combat on the steps of her own temple on distant Dekhu, a thousand years before.

'Ara,' Enkul-Anu said.

'He shouldn't be allowed to go before me,' Sypa hissed to anyone who would listen. 'Druku is chasing my handmaidens and I won't have it.'

'Oh?' asked Gul, God of the Underworld, with a complete lack of interest. He had the kingdom of the dead to rule and seldom visited heaven.

'I'm the goddess of lust. Druku's poaching in my territory.' Bitterly. 'And he can be any gender he wants. Why can't I do that?'

'Indeed,' the death god's consort said in her dead voice. 'So inconsistent.'

'That's what I mean!' Sypa spat.

The Black Goddess permitted herself an eye-roll from her new vantage. But she'd seen what she wanted to see – six new god's eyes watching all the entry gates, even the secret one. She moved back towards Sypa.

In the centre of the hall, the war god seemed to be at a loss for words. The handsome face lightened in recognition and managed to raise a hand in salute to Enkul-Anu, but the tall war god could only shake his head. After a moment, he opened his mouth. Closed it. And then…

'I…' he said.

Enkul-Anu blinked. 'Take your time, brother,' he said with icy calm.

'I… My… My son…?' Ara said. And then, suddenly, his face filled with fury. 'Death!' he roared. 'I'll kill them all!'

'I know that your son was injured in the fighting at Hekka,' Enkul-Anu said with obvious patience. 'He's already receiving ambrosial resin. He'll be fine.'

'Heal him!' Ara demanded. 'Or I'll… kill them all!'

Enkul-Anu made a slight motion, and two of the younger deities – both his grandsons, he thought – came forwards, heads bowed in deep respect. But they stood very close to the war god.

'My son…' he said again, confused. 'I am Ara! War god!'. Suddenly he drew his sword.

Lesser creatures fell on their faces in fear. Even the Blue Goddess, who had moved forwards shyly until she was standing close to her 'sister' the Black Goddess, near Sypa's couch, felt the weight of terror that sword commanded. Sypa, at her side, burst into tears and hid her lovely head. Laila who was known to be brave, was cringing. Telipinu could barely stand.

The two grandsons were flat on the white marble floor, unable to move for fear.

The war god was very powerful, and his artifacts were as powerful as he.

The Black Goddess watched Enkul-Anu slowly rise from his throne.

'Sheathe your sword, old friend,' he said.

'My son!' the war god screamed, and the marble roof-tiles shook and rattled.

'Sheathe your sword, before I become angry,' Enkul-Anu said gently – a cautious man speaking to a rabid animal.

Out of the corner of her eye, the Black Goddess watched as gods and goddesses, some quite powerful, crept from the hall, slithering away through the many arcaded doors like snakes on their bellies.

It made her smile.

Sypa shrank against Tyka, the ultimate enemy. The Goddess of Lust was no coward, but she liked to be in a position of absolute authority, and she wasn't good when taken by surprise.

'I demand justice!' roared Ara.

Enkul-Anu took a long step forwards to his brother.

'Sheathe your sword,' Enkul-Anu said again, raising his voice, 'and all will be as you request.'

'I demand ...!' But then something changed – some spark of recognition, of memory. 'I request,' Ara said. 'I ...'

The great war god, handsome and young, looked down as if he had no idea where he was. He looked at the drawn sword of terror in his hands, and shook his head.

'I killed her,' he said suddenly. 'I killed her, didn't I? *I killed Taris!*'

Ara stared for a moment at the sword in his hand, and then sheathed it and burst into tears.

'I killed the queen!' he shouted, and then whimpered, 'You made me.'

Enkul-Anu kicked one of his grandsons.

'Get him out of here,' he said sharply. And then, with one hand theatrically on the god of war's shoulder, he said, 'You will have justice for your son. The mortal who dared raise his hand against a god shall be tortured to death in a manner so spectacular as to resound down the eons.'

The Black Goddess smiled over at the Blue Goddess; a quick look, and then she caught the Goddess of Lust around the waist and hauled her back from the path of the Storm God as he turned to his throne.

'Are you sure you aren't putting on weight?' the sable goddess hissed.

'Fuck you,' spat the lovely goddess. 'Men get hard just looking at me.'

'Oh,' the Huntress said with withering contempt. 'Men would.'

She glanced at Laila, the handmaiden, who was making an obscene gesture at the great god Druku, across the hall. But then Laila glanced at her, and a message was passed between them – a glance, a nod. And another for Tyka, and it was done.

The Black Goddess set the Goddess of Lust on her feet and stepped boldly to the side of the Storm God. Around her, the other gods and goddesses were recovering according to their age and power; the oldest were the fastest, the youngest were almost as affected as mere men.

'Great God of the Storm,' she said formally. 'I clasp your knees.'

He was still standing as Ara was led away, shoulders slumped, sobbing.

He whirled to face her.

'Huntress,' he said. 'Why the fuck are you here?'

She smiled crookedly. 'I'm here to help, as always.'

'I don't need your help,' he spat. 'Get gone.'

She nodded.

He turned and went back towards his throne.

She followed, greatly daring.

'You're making a mistake,' she said.

'Don't listen to her!' Sypa shrieked. 'I am not fat!'

Off to his left, Druku, the drunken god, made an absurd gesture. He was one of the older gods, already over his terror, and using the confusion to whisper to Laila. The nymph pretended to be uninterested while fanning her mistress. But a tiny smile licked at the corner of Laila's mouth, and Druku wore an expression that was far too intelligent for a drunk.

The Huntress, tall and matt black, young and virginal and deadly, looked away before her interest was revealed ... back to the storm god, and she saw the decision come and go on Enkul-Anu's scarlet face.

'Bide,' he said.

He sat on his great black throne, and the hall stilled.

'This Hall of Judgement is suspended,' he called, and his voice rang through the heavens. 'Chamberlain Telipinu will rearrange your appointments.'

He shot Telipinu a glance, and the chief steward of the gods nodded, and began to work his Eternal Tablets.

Enkul-Anu rose, and all, even the Black Goddess, fell to their knees and bowed their heads to the floor. The Blue Goddess was nowhere to be seen.

'Come, Huntress, Enemy of my people,' Enkul-Anu said, and led the way through a tall golden door behind the throne – a door that hadn't even been there an eye-blink before.

The great god threw himself onto a magnificent bronze and marble couch supported by heavy pillars of semi-precious stones; lapis and jade predominated, but there were carnelian and turquoise as well, so that the underside of the great god's couch was finer than any temple in the world of men and women. The couch was covered in pillows, every one of which was covered in minute, perfect tapestries by the finest artists of Narmer and the Hundred Cities. The pillows all repeated parts of the Theomachy, the War of Heaven, when the gods had overthrown the decadent gods of the past and made the New World.

'You are making a mistake,' the Black Goddess said again.

'You're the only one who thinks so,' Enkul-Anu said, sounding bored rather than angry.

'It's my job,' the Black Goddess said. 'No one else dares. Listen – you do *not* want the death of this human to ring down the ages. You want him to be completely forgotten. He fucking *hurt* Resheph. Who, by the way, is a complete fuck-up.'

Enkul-Anu lay back, and a trio of identical human sisters poured wine into his mouth. He was so used to their ministrations that he just tilted his head back, took the wine, then straightened, looking at the Black Goddess.

'None of these adolescents is worth a shit,' he admitted.

'And your contemporaries are losing their minds,' the Huntress said.

Enkul-Anu looked at her, his eyes narrowing.

'That's ... not true,' he said, sounding defensive.

'It is true and you know it. Sypa is losing her grip on anything that isn't her body. Ara is nothing but senile rage. Timurti cannot even remember what her powers are – she never goes swimming, much less controls the sea. Druku is probably the smartest one left in your generation and he's a lecherous drunk.'

'That's all the useless fuck has ever been,' Enkul-Anu said.

The Black Goddess smiled.

'Why do I listen to you?' Enkul-Anu said.

'Because I make sense,' the Black Goddess said.

'You are the enemy.'

'That's just a name you give us because we don't agree with you, Tyka and I. But we live here, too.'

'But you hate us.'

The Black Goddess shrugged. 'I hate waste and stupidity. I hate that you set the mortals against each other.' She smiled at him. 'Let's talk about this human. You want him quietly dead. So no one remembers him. I specialise in such stuff. Let me take him.'

'He deserves to be punished,' Enkul-Anu said.

'Don't believe your own propaganda, great god. The poor fool led the attack for the king of Kyra, and he was so good that he got into the city.'

Enkul-Anu shook his head. 'That is impressive.'

She nodded. 'Whereas your precious mini-god started slaying the moment he arrived. He used weapons out of proportion to the threat, as they always do, and blew a hole in the city wall. Rather than protecting Hekka, he created a portal so the Kyrans could get in! And then he attacked this human, and *lost*.'

Enkul-Anu closed his eyes, as if in pain. 'Fucking … idiot.'

The Black Goddess was relentless. 'Then the city fell. Did they tell you that, All-Father? Hekka, one of the greatest cities to pay you tribute, dead as a month-old corpse. All the men killed. All the women sold as chattels. You should know how it goes – it's the world you fucking made.'

'They're cattle,' he said automatically.

Her anger overflowed.

'Fucking farmers take better care of their cattle!' she yelled. 'Are you paying attention, great god of storm? They're dying! The desert is creeping in because they don't have the skills and time and money to irrigate! The Jekers are sweeping over them like a fucking infection! Where do the Jekers come from? From

136

fallen cities and wasted agriculture, that's where. And who's helping make more? You are!'

She stopped, breathing hard. Enkul-Anu narrowed his eyes but he waved.

'Go on,' he said slowly. The tone was dangerous.

The Black Goddess didn't care. 'And they fight among themselves because your children all want to rule their own bloody little kingdoms! Or yours!' She took a breath, then went on because he hadn't summoned a thunderbolt to silence her. 'If they are cattle, then we are farmers who allow our cows to be abused until they give no milk, and our bulls to fight one another to the death while we grow no fodder to feed them and we slaughter all their children as meat. Negligent farmers—'

'Shut up,' Enkul-Anu said. 'I've heard all your weak-kneed rants before. You forget we are stronger for their little contests. My children fight among themselves to see who is worthy of more power. That is how the world works. And unlike a farmer with his cattle, there are always more mortals. They are like lice.'

'They are not,' the Black Goddess said. 'In a few generations, you'll see it. They'll die out, and what the fuck will you have then?'

Enkul-Anu shrugged. 'We are gods,' he said. 'We'll make something new.'

'They deserve—'

'They deserve nothing! They're insects! We took this world from their puny gods and made it ours. You, Huntress, surrendered. I *spared* you. Shall I remind you of that?'

The Black Goddess shook her head. But her own decisions were already made, and she didn't even know why she bothered.

'Never mind, great god,' she said, dully. 'I surrender to your greater wisdom.'

'You always do,' Enkul-Anu said with a chuckle. 'Just as you did back when it mattered. That's why I'm the great god and you are merely the enemy.'

She nodded her apparent acceptance.

Enkul-Anu looked away, took wine from his lovely slave trio, and looked back at her.

'I see your other point, though,' he said. 'If we make him famous, we admit that gods can be hurt. How'd he do it?'

He leant forwards, and one of the trio of slaves fell from his chest.

'I don't know,' the Black Goddess lied. She was a good liar. She was, after all, one of the Enemy.

'Star-stone?' Enkul-Anu asked. 'There's a rumour that some fell to earth in the lands east of Hekka.'

'Must be,' the Black Goddess said. Inside, she smiled to see him take her star-stone hook.

Enkul-Anu slapped one of the trio of human women out of the way when she mistook his movement for a demand for wine.

'Fucking idiots. I just told the king of Hekka to look into the star-stone. And Resheph was supposed to defeat the king of Kyra as a warning to Narmer. And then find the fucking star-stone.'

'Resheph managed to ruin all that,' she said. 'And he's the one who killed Gamash of Weshwesh's daughter.' She was delighted to plant a barb. 'Is he plotting something?'

Enkul-Anu put his head in his great red hands. 'I'm surrounded by idiots.'

'You chose them,' the Black Goddess said.

'You just keep playing that tune, don't you?'

The Black Goddess shrugged. 'Well, you have a real problem with Narmer now, Great God, because they're moving south, and they're taking the Hundred Cities.' She carefully helped the human woman up off the marble floor and casually healed her broken arm. 'Let me deal with the man.'

'I'll have no trouble with Narmer because Azag has just removed the entire royal clan. They'll fight a thirty-year civil war.'

The Black Goddess raised an eyebrow.

Enkul-Anu nodded. 'See? I am on top of things. But as to this mortal? Be my guest. What do you want in return?'

The Enemy smiled. 'I want what you want,' she said carefully. 'Stability. This one is free.'

He looked at her. 'I mistrust you when you want nothing in return, Enemy.'

She nodded. 'Very wise of you.'

'You are the one stirring the people of Narmer against me,' he said.

She almost grinned. 'Not at all. Your children make my job easy, Great God. I don't have to stir up rebellion. It bubbles up of its own accord. Narmerians are very stubborn. They haven't given up on their old gods. The Sun. The Great Dragon—'

'I will crush Narmer like sand under my heel.'

The Black Goddess shrugged. 'Argument by analogy is a foolish game, but sand is very hard to crush…'

The Storm God smiled tolerantly. 'Sand doesn't spend a lot of time rebelling, either. Maybe we're better off without Narmer and her riches and size and imperial ambitions.'

She nodded. 'Of course, Narmer is the richest kingdom of mortals. It maintains the best defences against the Dry Ones, and it has the finest irrigation systems.' She was backing out of the throne room. 'So after you crush it, the Hundred Cities will probably fall anyway.'

Enkul-Anu's eyes met hers, and instead of rage, she saw fatigue.

'You think I don't know that?' he asked.

They looked at each other.

Enkul-Anu bent his great head. 'Let me tell you something you don't know, Enemy. Someone, by which I mean one of the gods, is supporting the Jekers.'

The Black Goddess blinked. 'That's insane.' For once, she was totally truthful.

Enkul-Anu made a movement with one hand, and suddenly the two of them were alone on a featureless plane of glittering black, as if the universe was made of obsidian.

'Where are we?' she asked, trying to keep her voice level.

'We're on a plane of existence that *I just created*.' Enkul-Anu smiled like a child about to crush a mouse under his heel to see what happened. 'And I can just leave you here, immortal. You won't die. Ever.'

The Black Goddess took that in.

'I'm not fucking around here, Enemy. You piss in my wine, steal my cattle, whatever. You are the Enemy. But the Jekers are a plague on all our worshippers. Are you behind them?'

'No,' she said.

He looked at her for a short eternity.

'I believe you, but I still think it's useful to remind you of my power. You think my comrades are senile? Well, I am not. We could re-fight the War of the Gods tomorrow, and I could win it by myself. We could re-fight it and all of you could join the useless old fucks we put down, and I'd still beat you.'

The Black Goddess bent her head in acknowledgement.

'And the World Dragon?' she asked quietly.

Enkul-Anu stiffened. 'Is bound,' he said. 'Bound for all eternity.'

He waved, and she was absolutely alone on a vast plane of... nothing.

She was there for only the briefest of eternities.

He returned. He moved his left hand, the gold nails flashing in the unlight, and they were back in the megaron of heaven.

'Now,' he said lazily, 'would you care to advise me on what to do about Narmer?'

She nodded slowly. 'Sure,' she said.

She was shaken. His power was incredible. It was, quite frankly, godlike. But she refused to bow to it. She always did.

'Sure,' she repeated. 'Lighten the taxes, end the human sacrifice, allow them to worship their sun god openly again.'

Terror was still tight in her throat. Enkul-Anu had been right about one thing – she had begun to forget how powerful he was.

His head came up, and his eyes were a red gold.

'Never!' he muttered. 'Their fucking sun god was a pathetic old mortal woman whose charms went to her head. Unless you mean Shemeg, the old, old Sun God.'

'You know who I mean, Storm God. Your paramour, the Sun Goddess Arrina. I remember when you didn't think she was pathetic *or* old.'

'Do you know what Sypa would do if I allowed the worship of Arrina ...' he began, and then shrugged. 'Never. They'll forget.'

She opened the golden door behind her, although now, instead of the Great Hall of Auza, it showed only a blue sky and a distant carpet of clouds, as if she was about to step out from a great height.

'They'll never forget her,' she said. 'Narmer is older than you, Great God.'

He glared at her. 'I did not dismiss you.'

She smiled. 'I don't really obey you, unless it's convenient.'

He nodded. 'Posture away, little rebel.' And then, as she was stepping into the sky, he said, 'Do you really think Sypa is gaining weight?'

She smiled, and fell away into the azure heights of day.

The moment she was gone, the great god of the storm summoned Nisroch. The Herald of the Gods wore a new cloak of peacock feathers, so cunningly constructed that it seemed to be covered in glittering eyes. It was new.

'She's up to something,' he said.

'Always, Great God,' the herald said, his face to the marble floor.

'Find this man who hurt Resheph. Kill him and dispose of him quietly. Beat her to it. Send a demon.'

Nisroch wasn't just the herald of the great gods. He was his father's spymaster, when things needed to be kept quiet, and Azag, Captain of the Demons, was his killer. Although demons had their own problems, as anything they were assigned turned into a literal bloodbath. Nisroch thought it over and decided that as Hekka was already destroyed, there was nothing to be lost by sending a demon.

He bowed. 'As you command,' he said evenly.

'Do it now,' Enkul-Anu said.

When Nisroch was gone, the Storm God sat with his nectar and ambrosia, and contemplated pissing on fires.

The Black Goddess, Temis, looked at her 'sister' Tyka, the lapis goddess with the golden horns. The one who never spoke.

'How are we going to rescue this broken man?' she asked the enigmatic golden eyes.

There was a companionable silence.

'I know,' the Huntress said, after a moment. 'Just trust you.'

The silent Blue Goddess nodded once.

Chapter Five

Aanat and Jawala

'Bring her up into the wind,' Aanat said.

He'd run into the bow to get a better look, and it was every bit as bad as he'd suspected when they saw the columns of smoke out over the horizon.

He was looking at a disaster, and trying to decide what to do about it.

Jawala, one of his mates, came aft. She belayed the line that held the big lateen and looked at him.

'I have no idea what's happened,' he admitted.

A few stadia away, most of the shipping on the beaches of Hekka was afire. And the palace itself, high above the rocky headland, was burning.

'Incredible,' Aanat muttered.

'Jekers?' Jawala asked. She was always practical, even in a crisis.

Aanat shook his head. 'No fleet,' he said. They all knew the signs; Jekers were the biggest threat his little ship faced on the open sea. 'Besides, the fishermen said the Jekers were away south at Hazor.' He sighed. 'Give me credit for that much at least. I wouldn't take us into a Jeker fleet.'

Jawala nodded. They were all Hakrans, and Hakrans prided themselves on their self-control.

'I do give you credit, love,' she said. But her hands on her hips told him that she was angry, or afraid. Perhaps both.

'War is death to trade,' Miti sang from her place by the anchor stones. It was a truism in Rasna, their far-off homeland.

Aanat was still looking at the devastation. Men moved like ants through the rubble; the market square was blazing.

'We won't land,' he said, trying to keep his voice steady.

'We need water, food and trade, in that order,' Jawala said.

'I'm fully aware,' Aanat said. 'And we'll find none of that here.'

He clapped his hands, and his crew all looked at him, and he raised his voice.

'Let her fall off to port. Smartly now. There ...'

Mokshi, the cook, and Pavi, who usually handled the cargo, were working the twin steering oars. Jawala let the sail out and it caught the breeze; the little ship heeled into it, and turned gracefully north.

The *Untroubled Swan* was twenty paces long; she had a single tall mast rigged with a heavy boom and a massive cotton canvas sail with light wooden brails, currently just filling with wind. She had two cargo holds, one before the mast and another aft; her bow was shaped like the breast of a swan and her stern was shaped like a swan's tail. And she was fully laden and low in the water.

'Vote?' he asked Jawala.

She shook her head. 'No, north is fine with me.'

She looked aft, at her mates, but none of them seemed to require a vote.

Aanat nodded. 'We'll try Kyra. And if that's as messed up as Hekka, we'll pay the damn taxes and trade in Narmer.' Despite his efforts at self-restraint, he couldn't help but add, 'As you wanted to all along.'

Jawala smiled. 'So I did, love. And still do. But right now, we need water.'

Aanat fingered the amulet at his throat and nodded to her.

'Take command,' he said, and stepped down into the hold.

He was surrounded by bundles of cotton cloth from their own looms in Rasna, as well as more recent wools from Mykoax, and he was out of the wind.

He waved his hand in the still air and said a Word of Opening, and the zodiac lay before him in lines of blue fire. He rotated it, looking for something...

He touched his amulet and said the true word for water.

He felt the connection – the moment when he was one with the divine, the more-than-human. The Greater *Aura*.

He shuddered. His very simple water-finding spell should never have pulled him in this deep. He croaked a counter-word, and saw the hieroglyph of his Word vanish to be replaced by a fine-featured face in lapis blue.

He was slammed backwards; he bounced off the bales of fabric and fell to his knees.

His zodiacal working vanished with a pop leaving a slight marsh-gas smell, and he permitted himself a single expletive, in Mykoan. Hakran didn't have such words. Swearing disturbed a person's *Aura*, or so he was repeatedly told.

He got up, dusted off his tunic, and climbed the ladder back to the command platform.

'What happened?' Jawala asked.

'One of their so-called gods just ordered me to land,' he said.

Jawala smiled. 'They *are* gods,' she said. 'They just aren't *our* gods.'

He had to smile back. 'You are braver than I am.'

She shrugged. 'Your new god had better provide us with water.'

The amulet told him where to land, and he tried not to think about some foreign god manipulating it. A parasang along the coast from Hekka, he obeyed its tingling dictates and turned the ship landwards, into the evening land-breeze, and he and his mates took the sails down and rowed the swan-breasted little ship in towards the magnificent beach. It was a deep beach with red-brown sand that extended as far as the eye could see to the north, towards Kyra and Narmer. It was a place where the deep desert came right down to the sea.

And sure enough, there was a break in the sand dunes, and a flow of water over the gravel of the beach.

Jawala glanced at him. 'This smells of miracles and mage-craft,' she said.

'All I did was look for water!' Aanat complained. Then he took a breath, dropped easily into near-meditation, and rose to the surface of his thoughts. 'Apologies, love. I'm as troubled as you are. But it is water.'

The beach was empty, as far as they could see.

The whole of the marriage clan had chosen Aanat to be captain because he could lead, and in this case, leading took the form of dropping over the side in shallow water and trudging up the red-brown gravel, alone, and unarmed. Hakrans didn't carry weapons or use violence. Ever.

So he walked up the beach, the salt water drying on his legs and the sand sticking to his feet, and waited to see what the foreign god had left for him. For a while his heartbeat accelerated like a runaway horse, and then he controlled it, turned, and walked north towards the stream.

It ran clear over the sand, digging a little canyon as it went. Aanat didn't think it had even existed a few hours before. He knelt, raising the hem of his kilt to avoid getting it sandy, and cupped his hands.

The water was excellent. Clear and cold, which was impossible. But they needed it.

He rose to his feet to beckon the others...

Ten paces away, on a dry dune of the deep desert secure from sea and stream, a shrouded figure rose from the sand. Aanat totally mistook the threat and began a simple turning spell for the undead. Unquiet spirits were everywhere in the world of violence, and Aanat specialised in moving them along.

But as he finished the cantrip the *thing* spread its wings…

Aanat froze. His philosophy told him to expect death – that death was all around him, and he should always be ready to accept it.

In reality, terror ran like a lightning bolt down his spine.

It was a Dry One. One of the Bright People.

It stood a little taller than Aanat, folding its wings back against its body. It was thinner than a man, and brightly coloured in reds and yellows, except for the mouse-brown of its powder-dry wings. He'd never been so close to one before, and for the first time he took in the smell he'd heard of from other traders. Musk, or perfume, or spice, or all three together…

He bowed. 'Greetings,' he said, in a steady tone of voice.

Not bad, he thought.

It had a human face, almost; it was much longer, and had no jaw because the mouthparts didn't work like a human's, and the eyes were multifaceted and bulbous. And it had almost no nose; just a little ridge of… bone? And yet it had an aethereal beauty that was… not as alien as it might have been.

It had arms, with hands that ended in talons. It raised one now, and pointed at his ship.

Aanat was perfectly prepared to die where he stood. In fact, it was part of the Hakran creed. No one was indispensable. The marriage clan had eight members, and two were back at home with the children; even if all six aboard the *Untroubled Swan* died, their children would live on.

He might die. But no way was that monster getting on his ship.

'No,' he said.

He thought the Dry One slumped, like a person defeated.

Fastidiously, it used a long green tongue to remove a clot of sand from one of the joints where the great brown wings met the body. Then it raised its taloned hand and pointed a finger at the ship.

'No,' Aanat said.

The Dry One did an odd thing. It began to beat its hands together – not like clapping, but the individual digits snapping against each other as if they were very hard, almost like tree branches in a wind. Then it straightened its legs and gave an absurd hop, and the wings flapped, and it flew less than twenty paces, alighting with the grace of a moth or butterfly. He had hoped for a moment that it was going, but instead it raised a hand.

One digit traced fire in the air, and the dry sand opened like a cedar-wood box.

Now the taloned hand pointed down into the sand.

Aanat felt a chaotic tangle of reactions. First, as a magos of some skill, he was both entranced and appalled by the other creature's raw *power*. He saw the results, but he couldn't feel the expenditure, and that was…

Not … possible.

Except that it had happened right in front of him.

Second, he was a trader, and it was already obvious to him that the thing wanted a ride and was willing to pay for it, and they were negotiating.

He glanced down into the hole in the sand. He saw wax-sealed stone jars. He knew exactly what they contained, because the Dry Ones only traded in a few substances.

'Jawala?' he called.

'I see it!' she called back.

The ship was only forty paces away.

'It wants to come to the ship,' he said.

148

'I gathered that!'

'It has a fortune in resin to trade for passage,' he said. 'I see ten jars.'

He looked at the jewelled, multifaceted eyes, and that leathery face – if it was a face – seemed more like a mask than something that could carry an expression.

The wings fluttered and it crashed its hands together. Was that impatience?

'We're voting!' Jawala called.

'We're voting on it,' he said to the silent monster. 'You see, among our people, we decide any issue that is contentious by discussion and vote.' His voice was low and, he hoped, unstrained. He talked to wild dogs this way.

The Dry One's leather mask and crystalline eyes watched him.

Talking made Aanat feel better, so he continued.

'Sometimes it takes a while. I'm sorry.'

The mask-face tilted slightly to one side. Then the green tongue flicked out. It was at least two feet long, and that was fairly disconcerting.

'Let's see if we can communicate at all.'

Aanat tried all his languages: Trade Dardanian, because almost everyone who bordered Ocean spoke it; Narmerian, which got a wing flap; and Kashian, which any of the Hundred Cities would speak; and what little he knew of the 'Desert Trade' language. He didn't have any Jeker beyond 'I surrender' but he tried Mykoan Dardanian and then, without much hope, the one Dendrownan tongue in which he knew 'hello' and 'no deal'. There were five major languages in the region, and at least a dozen dialects…

His mind was spinning with terror and hope and he was thinking about language.

I really don't want to die here.

149

Nothing. No real response to any greeting.

He used the tip of his finger to draw in wet sand, and sketched a rough oval. Then he drew a line that connected to the oval.

'Narmer,' he said.

He drew a stylised tree at the top.

'Dendrowna,' he said.

Then he made a series of X's.

'The Hundred Cities,' he said. They were all below Narmer.

He began to draw a spike that appeared to be breaking his oval from the bottom. The hand reached forwards, and one very black talon touched the tip of the spike he'd just drawn.

Aanat forced himself to remain calm.

'Akash?' he asked.

The wings shuffled a little, and the talon dug a little deeper into the sand.

'We still need water,' he said.

He turned his back on the beautiful monster and called to the ship, 'It wants to go to Akash.'

Jawala came to the stern rail, wearing the look she saved for when she felt that he had done something really stupid.

'Akash,' she said. 'Where the Jekers are.'

Aanat shrugged, his back all but burning in the knowledge that it was bare to the monster.

She looked down at him. 'Ten jars of resin could make us all very rich indeed,' she said. 'Or very dead.'

He nodded. He couldn't help it; he sneaked a glance at the thing. It hadn't moved.

Jawala could be heard speaking to the rest of the family. And then she came back to the rail.

'What's your vote?' she asked.

He shrugged. 'I'm biased. I don't want to die. So I say, let's give it a go.'

Jawala's mouth twitched as if she'd tasted something bad.

'Well, then,' she said. 'It's unanimous. We're all fools together.'

Three of his mates came ashore, and the four of them worked to store water in jars, vases and amphorae that could be stacked in the hold, doubling as ballast in the lowest tier. It made for a long day, as much of the cargo had to be rousted out and set carefully ashore, and the little ship had to be run right up the beach. And it was clear that their new passenger was deeply impatient. But, well before sunset, they had it done. The resin was hidden with the water, and the water was clear and fresh and delicious, not at all the brackish stuff they usually got.

Aanat hoped that was a good sign.

The Dry One was ensconced against the sacks of woven cotton in the forward hold. The ship wasn't big; every member of the clan could see the thing from every part of the ship.

Jawala was with Aanat in the stern. The two had taken the steering oars from their junior spouses to have a little privacy.

'He wants to go to Akash,' Aanat said.

'What makes you think they are a "he"?' she asked.

He managed a grin. 'Good point.'

The Dry One wore no clothing or jewellery; there was nothing that might denote gender. It had a bulbous upper body like a man in full armour, and hips that appeared too narrow to support the thing's weight, and back-bent legs made for leaping.

'Mother of mysteries, what do we call—?'

'"It" will do,' Jawala said.

'It was trying to tell me something,' Aanat said. 'It wants to go somewhere else, either before or after Akash. Maybe both.'

'Akash is in the middle of the Jeker plague.'

Aanat looked out over the sparkling sea. 'No shit, my darling.'

Jawala wriggled. 'I don't particularly want to commit suicide.

I am still in my material phase. I'd like to be rich and enjoy perfumed baths.'

Aanat nodded. He managed a smile. 'Ten jars of resin will buy a great many perfumed baths.'

She smiled. 'Sweet, why do you think I voted to try? It's all about the perfumed baths.'

They grinned at each other like young lovers, and watched the sea over the bow.

Most of the warrior cultures didn't prey on the Hakrans. When they were taken, they offered no violence, but most of them committed suicide very quickly after capture. None of them would work or co-operate in any way with their attackers, and the Hakrans would cease trade altogether with any culture that preyed on them, with slow but steady results. The Mykoans had had a try, seizing dozens of Hakran ships; that had been three decades before, and a generation of Mykoan princes had since been wiped from the earth by their rivals after they were starved of tin and other commodities.

But the Jekers were more like a plague than a culture. They had no trade, and they seemed to enjoy taking Hakran ships, torturing the crews with relish, although it wasn't easy – Hakran ships were very difficult to catch. They had tricks in shipbuilding that hadn't been copied ... yet.

Aanat didn't relish sailing through Jeker-dominated waters. But he thought it could be done.

'Ten stone jars of Dry One resins,' he said to Jawala. 'A fortune.'

'Tell me about the magic,' she said. 'When you came aboard, you said ...'

He swallowed. The magic upset him more than the possibility of Jekers, and that was saying something.

'You know how magic works,' he said.

Every Hakran did. They prided themselves on the education of their children.

'So?' Jawala asked.

'So it cast twice in a few seconds and the Great *Aura* never altered.'

He looked forward, and the Dry One's jewelled eyes came up to meet his across the twenty paces of distance, and it was as if a little fire lit in his mind, the contact was so palpable.

'So?' Jawala asked.

'So I'm a competent weather-worker and I know a bunch of spells ...'

'You are the best *naumagos* in the fleet!'

Jawala praised him so seldom that he was taken aback. He shook his head, not in denial, but in confusion at her praise. She *never* praised him.

'Well, it is out of my league. It has powers I can't fathom. I can't even see it working. Do you understand? It's as if our ship moved without a breath of wind.'

Jawala looked back thoughtfully. 'But you *have* made the ship move without wind.'

Aanat thought about that a moment. 'By which you mean ...?'

'Maybe it is fate, beloved,' Jawala said. 'Study it. Learn about it, for all of us.'

Aanat looked back at the winged monster in the forward hold, leaning stiffly against a bale of cotton fabric, one deadly taloned hand resting idly on the top of the bale.

'We brought it aboard,' Aanat said. 'I don't really see any choice but to do what it says.'

Jawala smiled. 'It's not a Jeker. And it's made us rich.'

'We're not rich yet,' Aanat said.

The next morning, they were sailing south as the sky turned pink over the low hills of Hekka, shining red through the smoke of the burning city. The Dry One leapt into the air, flew aft, and landed like a predator pouncing on the stout timbers of the swan's tail where it rose to cover the helms. The Dry One was poised there, as if balancing on a slick surface was no effort at all, and pointed east, towards the low hills, sea pines and the rocky beaches of the Hekkan countryside just outside the charred and broken walls.

They were south of the burning city now. A fishing boat out of Kyra had confirmed the news: Hekka taken and sacked, the god-king killed; their own Kyran god-king triumphant and already marching home on the inland road. And a rumour: people said that a man had defied a god – had hurt or killed it in combat. All this shared over a net full of little mackerel.

'I'd buy some bigger fish!' Aanat had shouted over the side in Trade Dardanian.

The fishermen all shrugged. The loudest shouted back, 'Two years since we've seen anything bigger than that!'

Aanat had paid the man in copper and poled off, feeling reasonably secure from the god-king of Kyra's army, marching steadily north and two days' travel away.

Until the black talon pointed inexorably at the beaches south of the sacked town.

Aanat looked up at the Dry One.

'The city is on fire.'

It pointed again.

'Too dangerous!' he said, with more emphasis than his people's beliefs encouraged.

The black talon pointed more insistently; the jewelled eyes were unblinking. The wings twitched.

I have no idea how to communicate with this thing.

'The town has been destroyed.' Aanat made wide sweeping gestures with his arms. 'Fire! Swords.'

It was uncanny how the talon didn't move, despite the swaying of the ship.

He felt it first in the steering oar under his hand, and then he looked and saw that their ship was turning in towards the land.

The sails flapped, and he roared at his clan.

'Mainsail! Brail her up!'

The bow rose on a wave and slapped down, and they were now making a beeline for the spot on the beach that the talon still indicated.

Aanat swallowed his frustration and fear.

'Very well.'

He began to give the orders to move the ship under its own power. One of his many scattered, fearful thoughts was, *Did it hear me speak of a ship moving without sails? Can it read my mind?*

They crept closer to the beach. The headland of the city proper had two beautiful horseshoes of sand. Further along to the south, under the ancient pine trees that grew all along the shores of Ocean, the beach was more rock than sand, with pebbles in a gentle gradient of sizes, from largest up the shingle to smallest at the sea's edge. Aanat's magpie mind wondered, not for the first time, what force had made the stones sort themselves so neatly.

Closer in, and a charnel house smell of cooked meat and rot swept over them – burnt wood and baked mud with a meaty after-smell.

There were people alive and moving in the ruins. Aanat feared them, but he feared everything, which helped keep all of them alive. He got his clan on the sweeps and dropped big stones at both bow and stern while the bow was still in a man's height of water. The breeze was soft enough that the little ship shouldn't move much, but if the wind got up the stones would drag and the ship would spill her guts on the land.

He kissed Jawala and Miti, stripped naked and leapt over the side to swim ashore. Above him, the Dry One leapt into the air in a blur of hard-edged motion, too fast to be natural, and flashed through the sky to the beach, landing in a moment of instant stillness.

Bastard, Aanat thought, but he kept swimming until he could stand and splash ashore.

The reek assaulted him. He'd assumed it came from the ruined city, but as he came up the beach he had to confront another work of man: a forest of ancient sea-pines, each of which held one or more dead people. Many were bound to chariot wheels; most were just skeletons. Some were rotting.

And every tree had a god's eye painted on it, or a faience plaque, the deep blue cobalt eyes staring into him.

As quick as thought, Aanat seized a stick and began a warding spell against the unquiet dead. Sites of murder and depravity were very dangerous to the unprotected. He touched his amulet and powered his wards, feeling the dead already moving around him. Wisps of dark auratic matter began to accumulate to sustain the angry dead.

The Dry One waved one elongated hand, the fingers rattling like the bones of the dead, and every god's eye in sight shattered or warped.

Then it sprang into the air, for all the world like an enormous grasshopper or a locust with more handsome wings. It landed again, just as quickly, at his side, so that one of its terribly dry and dusty wings touched him lightly. The dust immediately dried his skin and made it itch.

The Dry One leant over to look at his powered working.

Its wings twitched – something Aanat had seen before, that particular twitch. Agreement? Interest?

A very faint exotic smell, like cinnamon, floated through the air, covering, at least for a moment, the smells of death. He waited, sigils powered, for the dead to move, but neither ghosts nor animated corpses came at him. They hovered at a distance, and his wards lay untested, and he let them lie, keeping his power close and safe.

The Dry One seemed to tremble, all its limbs moving together, and then it leapt away. In a single immense and instant bound, it leapt to one of the trees dangling its rotten fruit. It spread its wings, and pointed.

Shaking his head and sighing, Aanat crunched over the gravel to the base of the huge old tree and saw that one of the men bound to a chariot wheel was not dead. All four of his limbs had been broken, and he looked like a wounded spider. Aanat, whose Hakran beliefs prohibited any form of violence, felt bile rise in his throat, but he fought it down.

The insistent black talon pointed at the man.

'You want me to put him out of his misery?' Aanat said aloud.

'Water...' the man croaked.

Aanat jumped. And then, because his people were deeply altruistic, he conquered his revulsion and gave the man water from his clay canteen.

The man had been quite handsome. One of their arrogant aristocrats.

'Thanks,' he managed. 'Now kill me.' Even broken on a chariot wheel, the man made it sound like an order.

Aanat looked up at the great dark figure of the Dry One.

'I don't think that's what's happening,' he said.

The broken man could still turn his head, and he did, following Aanat's gaze.

He spat. 'You never think things can get worse,' he said.

The Dry One pointed at the lashings on the man's arms.

Aanat nodded, and went back to the beach. He called for his co-husband Bravah and two sharp stone knives.

When he went back, he gave the broken man more water.

'You could just kill me,' the man said, in a conversational

voice. He might have been a Hakran, for his imitation of unconcern.

'My passenger wants you cut down,' Aanat said.

The man spat again. There was blood in his spittle.

Carefully, with as much delicacy as the two strong men could manage, they cut the chariot wheel free and lowered it to the ground, and then cut the lashings. The man didn't even groan.

'My back's broken,' he said. 'I haven't felt anything from the neck down since I...'

Was that a chuckle? Aanat's respect for him increased.

'Since I smacked a god.' The man coughed up a little more blood. 'Who are you, anyway?'

'I'm Aanat. A Hakran merchant of far off Rasna. Currently serving the monster over there.'

'Zos,' said the broken man. 'Formerly a godborn sell-sword. Currently parting with life.'

Bravah got the last of the lashings off and they laid the man on the gravel.

Aanat glanced at the Dry One.

It shook itself – a new gesture. And then it stalked towards them, a predator ready to finish its prey.

Aanat turned his head away.

Perhaps I will choose suicide, he thought. *I won't serve evil knowingly.*

The Dry One didn't bend well, or at least, it didn't bend like a man. Instead, its back-bent knees flexed and it leant forwards until its head was nearly touching the broken man's head.

'Well, well,' the man called Zos said. 'You ...'

The Dry One's mandibles, which folded perfectly into the bottom of its head, opened, and the green tongue shot out. In a single moment, it passed between the man's teeth and vanished into his body, and Zos gave a convulsive shiver. His eyes rolled back.

And then he was still.

After a long instant, the tongue withdrew and the Dry One settled back on its version of haunches. It continued to regard the broken man closely.

Lights began to sparkle in the air around his body. Blue and golden lights.

Aanat cursed and began his own magic. He raised his zodiac and rotated it to his best guess of the day and hour and then attempted to view the scene through his projection.

The sparkling motes in the air were magnified, and he gave a grunt of amazement. Then closed his zodiacal orrery with a snap before the monster could lash out at him.

'Is it eating him?' Bravah asked.

'I don't think so,' Aanat said. 'I wouldn't put it to a vote yet.'

'We have a moral obligation...'

Young people had more moral obligations than their elders; Aanat was considerably more cynical than his junior husband, but he'd also seen more of the world.

'Maybe he's healing the man?' he said. 'Don't always assume the worst.'

Bravah shook his head. 'Maybe he's turning him to jelly for a better meal.' The other man shrugged. 'That's what spiders do.'

'I don't think...'

Aanat wasn't sure what he meant to say. The blue and gold motes were strange and they, unlike the Dry One's casting, left a shadow in the *Aura*. It still made no sense, but it offered him... something.

'You don't cast heavy-duty magic to eat something.'

Bravah shrugged. 'Who knows what the barbarians do?' he muttered. 'Maybe this is how they prepare victims for sacrifice. And *no one* could heal that poor bastard.'

The Dry One straightened up to its full height, bent, and

leapt again, this time whirring to a different tree. And again, it pointed at the bindings.

Aanat was in a quandary. His upbringing and his religion forbade him to serve evil in any way, and he could not be sure what was happening.

He examined the problem for ten breaths.

'These men are, to all intents, already dead,' he said.

'That's a prevarication,' his junior husband replied.

'It's not a vote situation,' Aanat said. 'We will go along with it until it is proved bad. That's my word.'

And that will keep you and me and Jawala and Miti and everyone alive a little longer.

Bravah was very unwilling to cut the next man down, the more so as the man began to croak a scream as soon as they touched his wheel. Giving him water only made it worse. This man was conscious and raving, and his back wasn't broken. He could obviously feel everything in his shattered long bones.

Suddenly, a long red and black arm passed between the two Hakrans, and a long black talon touched, and then pierced the chest of the screaming man.

The talon went in no further than a thorn might penetrate, but the man's body slumped.

The Dry One withdrew its arm and then backed away, the first clumsy movement Aanat had seen.

'He killed the guy!' Bravah insisted.

'I don't think so,' Aanat said. 'Get him down.'

'I really don't like this, Aanat.'

'So noted. Now help me.'

The second man was thin, and bald, and much easier to get down than the big godborn had been. Once he was down, the Dry One leant over him, and his tongue went deep into the man's throat ...

'I refuse—' Bravah began.

Aanat shook his head. 'Shut it. 'It's on me, all right? If I'm wrong, I'll never be reborn. But I think he's healing them. I think so for complicated scholarly reasons having to do with rules of magic and colours and the *Aura*. I ask you to obey.'

Bravah sucked in a breath. Greatly daring, he walked over to the first man – Zos.

'Breathing,' he admitted.

The second man gave the same galvanic twitch that Zos had made. But his head came up.

'Oh,' he said. 'Oh, by Enkul-Anu and Great Lady Sypa!'

Aanat leant over him. The man's broken limbs appeared frozen in place – an odd change.

'Oh, gods,' the man said. 'Save Atosa.'

'See?' Aanat said over the second man's body. 'He's healing them.'

'No one could heal that first one.' Bravah's belief was shaken.

Aanat was still hoping he was right.

There was only one more living man in the trees of the dead, and it was only a little more work to cut him down. He was deeply unconscious, and only his stentorian breathing indicated that there was still life in his body.

They laid him on the sand by the Dry One.

The monster didn't move for a long time, as if uninterested in the third man, or refusing to help. And then, quite suddenly, it bent low, and its tongue snapped out. This time, it lingered longer over its victim, or patient. This time, Aanat began to doubt his reasoning, because it really did look as if the thing was feeding. Its tongue gave obscene twitches and swellings.

Aanat reviewed all of his decisions. And felt guilty and …

The Dry One stood. It pointed out to sea with one taloned hand, and then leapt into the air.

'Do we leave them on the beach?' Aanat asked the empty air.

'We cannot,' Bravah insisted, and Aanat agreed.

But moving them to the ship was easier said than done, and it took them an hour, some fancy ship handling, and the cargo sling to get the three unconscious men onto the deck and laid out under the stern awning.

'More passengers?' Jawala asked. She smiled.

'You don't want to know,' Aanat told her.

'You know I do, darling,' she replied, and he told them all.

There was a vote, and they agreed to give the monster another day or two to prove its intentions, rather than to face it now and perhaps die.

They were still deep in the argument that often came *after* a vote when there was a crack, as if of thunder, and the Dry One in the bow leapt into the air.

Something *immense* shot through the sky like a meteor, and in seconds it was obvious that it was coming for them.

The Dry One shot towards it.

What followed was too fast for thought, and later proved difficult to remember. There was a mighty roar, like all the thunderbolts ever thrown, and an explosion in the sky. Small black clouds appeared around the Dry One, and it twisted and turned in flight, almost invisible with speed, and then a fireball seemed to envelop the flying meteor. It turned, and Aanat could feel the *Aura* being sucked into it like water running down the drain of a great bath in Rasna, all the magic flowing away from him...

The Dry One hung in the air for a long heartbeat, and lavender fire played over its talons.

The lavender fire met the white fire of the other. Aanat thought he saw a giant crustacean form with putrescent yellow-green skin and fiery eyes and fifty chitinous legs supported by massive dragonfly wings. It was a glimpse of pure alien horror, far, far worse than the Dry One.

Aanat pushed Miti to the deck and threw himself over her,

guessing that the intake of *Aura* was going to lead to something terrible.

But all that happened was a sort of *pop*. Or perhaps a *blink*. Later, none of them could agree whether there had actually been a sound, or a change in light.

The Dry One landed on the foredeck, all its grace gone, and stumbled forwards to collapse into the hold on the cotton bales.

The other monster was gone.

'What was that?' Miti whimpered.

Aanat shook his head and lifted himself off her.

'I have no idea,' he said.

The Dry One rallied long enough to rise and point south over the starboard bow.

They got the ship out to sea, and steered in the direction that the talon pointed.

The next day Pavi caught a big fish – a salmon out of the deep river Aka far to the south – and Mokshi lit a very carefully banked charcoal fire in a big clay brazier set on bricks in the hold. He rolled the fish in a dough made with salt water and flour, and baked it, and every one of them salivated at the smell. Eating fish was a violation of *himsha*, the law of non-violence, but traders received an absolution; long sea voyages made vegetarian eating difficult. And despite that, when the pastry was cracked open and the fish offered, all of the Hakrans sang the *Song of Sorrow* for the fish, and for Pavi who had killed him. And Miti, the strictest observer, confined herself to eating chickpeas and lentils, and had no fish.

The paralysed man was fed with a spoon.

'That was the most delicious thing I've ever eaten,' he said. 'No prayer to the gods?'

Aanat shrugged. 'No. We Hakrans worship the world. Some say we worship ourselves. A few believe there is some other immaterial being beyond the forces you call gods. Someone who creates and controls the spheres.'

'She's an evil bitch, if so.'

Aanat smiled. 'You are feeling better.'

The man raised his eyebrows. 'It's a low bar. But sure. I'm better. Now, if my broken back would heal and then my arms and legs, I'd be fine.'

He made little jokes when one of them had to clean him, too; he had no control over his bowels or anything else.

And yet, Aanat had an odd faith in his monster. Especially after watching it fight a god, or a demon, or whatever the flying horror had been. He had a hard time remembering the alien shape – that's how horrible it had been.

The other two were still in comas. They breathed regularly, but they didn't awaken. The Hakrans tended them as best they could, wrapping them in wool shawls meant for trade when the night was cool, and putting a shelter over them as the seas rose on the third day out of Hekka. They were well down the coast towards Ugor by then, and so far out to sea that only the presence of birds and a sort of yellow haze to the east suggested that they were near land at all.

Jawala lay down by Aanat after they said their evening prayers and each had meditated.

'Is there a storm coming?' she asked.

'A long blow,' he said. 'Not much rain, I think.'

She propped herself up on one elbow. 'We're sailing into Jeker waters. With a monster at the helm.'

Aanat nodded. 'We saved three men.'

'One of them is a very bad man. A killer. I can smell it on him.' Jawala raised an eyebrow. 'You're not really listening to me.'

Aanat sat up. 'I am. Listen – even when I cast a weather-reading spell, I see this foreign goddess meddling in our affairs.

We're bound to this, and we have to hope that the same force that drives us will protect us.'

She frowned. 'These foreign gods are all crazy. They're murderous children. None of them can be trusted.'

Aanat nodded. 'I know,' he said. 'But I think it is wise that we do not struggle against that which we cannot move.'

That was one of the thousand sayings. It was rare that he was the one quoting scripture, and he relished the moment in the endless spousal contest.

Jawala lay closer to him, and put her head on his chest.

'I want to believe you,' she said. 'I'm not ready to die.'

He shrugged. 'Let me get the monster out of our holds. We'll sail clear of the barbarians and the murderers, and I'll cook exciting curries for years. While you take perfumed baths.'

The wind came up after the second moonrise. The ship was ready for it: the hatch covers were lashed with so much cord that it looked as if they were carrying a cargo of rope; heavy cables had been run to the masthead, and the big cotton canvas lateen was replaced by a much smaller wool sail. Aanat rose from his sleeping mat on the deck and stood between Jawala and Pavi. They watched the rollers come in under the stern and lift the bow so high it seemed it would never go down – that they'd turn and slide off the waves and crash into the sea below.

But the *Untroubled Swan* was well built and had seen worse, and what she lacked in speed she made up for in sheer seaworthiness. The scrap of wool sail didn't split, and held them on course, and they ran due west through the darkness, headed into the great green of Ocean.

Morning came with no sign of the sun, just a grey-green expanse of clouds from horizon to horizon. Big rollers sometimes whipped up in gusts that were not always in line with the waves, which made the helm difficult to manage, but the clan had been long-haul merchants for hundreds of years, and the sea was not an enemy but a lover to be propitiated. Miti prepared a little glass perfume bottle, filled it with spices and topped it with a pearl for the sea, and flung it from the bow with a hymn.

And they ran on.

The third night was worse, as the east wind roared, weaving and changing a few degrees every heartbeat, and Aanat took a turn at the oars and was exhausted at the end of his watch. Some rain fell, a vicious blast of water that scoured the decks and drove the three injured men against the bulkheads; Bravah had to tie them down.

But they made it into a pink dawn, and by the time the sun was high in the sky they were turning back east with a westerly wind under the stern quarter. Mokshi relit his charcoal and served up a spicy meal of rice and reheated vegetables.

'Beloved,' Miti said, addressing Aanat.

She didn't usually speak to him in such an endearing fashion, because she disliked all authority, especially his, and she disliked work, which made him especially her opposition.

And she had a flair for the dramatic, which didn't make her an easy subordinate or a perfect mate, but then, life was never easy, and she was strong, athletic, and capable of delivering miracles when interested in her work.

So he didn't give a snarky response but rose from the rope he'd been mending.

'Dear? Can I help you?'

She motioned, and then led him forward towards the bow. She didn't have to take him far for him to see the problem.

There was an enormous ... tent. Of web, or spider silk. Something.

It covered a third of the forward hold, and it was a little scary. And it explained why they hadn't seen their passenger in days.

'I can't live with this thing on my ship,' Miti said. And then she immediately backed down. 'I'm scared.'

He nodded. 'We are to be hospitable and kind to foreigners, are we not?'

'I know,' she said pettishly. 'But…'

He shrugged.

Bravah climbed down from the mast.

'Nothing gave way,' he said. He looked forward. 'Yeah. The locust is building a tent. Gack.'

Aanat touched his amulet. 'Blessings,' he said.

His first, awful vision was that it was going to hatch a thousand little Dry Ones on his ship. He shuddered.

'What if it…' Miti was preparing to deliver a diatribe. Aanat shook his head.

'Let's just wait and see,' he said.

'That's all you ever say,' Miti spat back at him, and Bravah, her favourite, put a hand on her shoulder.

Aanat went back aft to his rope repair. But when he'd re-woven one of the main hawsers that held the mast to the bow, and put it back in its place with Miti and Bravah lashing it home, he climbed down off the bow's painted bird head, slipped carefully by the spider-silk tent, and went to the three injured men. Pavi was giving Zos some lentil soup; he could hear the man's bantering tone.

'He moved a toe!' Pavi said. She was grinning from ear to ear.

Zos rolled his head and looked up at him.

'I don't know whether to hope or not,' he confessed. For a moment, the pain of *not knowing*, the fear of a life as a cripple, was writ plain on his face, and then he was smiling again. 'But the toe moves. And hurts like the seven demons of Kur.'

Aanat nodded. 'This is good,' he said.

He all but slapped his head as he understood a whole set of things that he'd seen but not observed; the swollen skin of the arms and legs, and their apparently frozen state, had kept the limbs straight and splinted. It was as if they were already wrapped in bandages – cold, rigid bandages.

'He *is* healing you,' Aanat said.

'Or he has bizarre sexual tastes,' Zos said, and Pavi blushed.

The godborn man grinned, pleased to get a reaction, and said, 'Always a possibility.'

'You are a crude man,' she said. 'Do you have a name?'

He looked at her for a moment as if that was a difficult question, and then he said, 'Zos.'

His head gave a little jerk, as if the man was trying to shrug.

'I'm not always crude,' he continued. 'But current circumstances have robbed me of most of my ... civilisation.'

Pavi stuck out her tongue at him, and he laughed.

The next morning, both of the other men they'd rescued were awake. The swelling and cold in their limbs was much reduced, and Aanat's confidence in the Dry One was suitably enhanced, but their guest was now deep in a cocoon that covered most of the forward hold.

'I'm Pollon,' said the tall one with no hair.

'Atosa,' said the shorter, older man. 'I'm ... It's ...'

'Rest now,' Aanat said.

Pollon raised his head and rolled slightly, stretched his arm and gave a choked scream. Then he grunted.

'Still hurts,' he said.

'It's a slow miracle,' Aanat said.

Pollon smiled. 'You're a Hakran?'

Aanat nodded. 'Yes.'

The bald man shook his head. 'Amazing. Do you really not believe in gods? Do you eat only green leaves? Is it true—?'

Aanat smiled. 'Oh, I believe in the gods,' he said, with a wary glance at the Dry One's cocoon.

'But you don't sacrifice ...?'

'Sacrifice is violence.'

Pollon nodded, and a faraway look passed over his eyes.

'You have *that* right,' he said fervently.

Atosa tried to roll over, then grunted and gave up.

'I'd like to sit up,' he said.

'I think the pressure on your broken legs would be very painful,' Aanat said.

Atosa nodded. 'I suppose I'm fucking lucky to be alive. And I guess the god-king will never have us back now.'

'Your god-king is dead,' Aanat said. 'Or so I'm told. Your city was sacked.'

'Anzu's hairy arse, he's dead?' Atosa made a face. 'Well, I feel better already.'

Pollon looked at his arms. 'Am I right? I saw a ... a ... Dry One?' He looked around. 'I've only seen pictures.'

'Yes.'

Yes, it's about forty feet away from you and it's hatching a swarm of deadly nestlings. Or something.

'Sail ho!'

That was Pavi. Having fed and cleaned the men, she'd gone aloft, climbing to the leather basket in the mainmast.

Aanat looked up. 'Where away?'

'Off the bow!' she called back.

The swell from the two-day blow was still high enough that she crossed a fair amount of sky as the ship swayed, but Aanat was used to such acrobatics; he ran forwards and shaded his eyes to look across the sea.

Nothing.

Climbing the mainmast made him feel old, but he did it anyway because his eyes were sharper than Pavi's – sharper than anyone's but Miti. He held on to the stays with his toes and shin while he leant over Pavi in the leather basket to stare into the haze to the east. It was as intimate as lovemaking; he was stretched across her, and she was almost naked, and she grunted.

'Behave,' she said with mock seriousness.

He deliberately nuzzled past her neck and then froze, salacious thoughts banished.

'Fuck,' he said in Mykoan, the best language he knew for swearing.

The sails were there. There were three of them, and Jekers usually travelled in trios. And the notched mainsail was a Jeker sign visible out to the horizon, as if they wanted to be seen.

'Jekers,' he said.

Pavi shrank away. 'No.'

He leant back, then let himself slide down the back stay towards the helm.

'Keep a good eye on them, dear,' he said. *Foolish thing to say.*

Pavi's back was already to him, staring at those sails.

On the deck, he saw to it that the ship was turned south and a little west, and the big square sail's brails began to rattle and shake, and the sail flapped.

'Push her head to port until the sail is taut,' Aanat said. 'But any time you can cheat south and west, do it.'

Jawala, now at the weather helm, nodded.

'How bad is it?' she asked.

'They'll have seen us as soon as dawn caught our sail, an hour ago,' he said. 'We missed them because they are up-sun.'

'So ... bad.'

'Very bad,' he admitted.

Aanat went down into the aft hold, and began casting. He cast three weather workings as soon as he was in touch with the Greater *Aura*, and as soon as he cast the first, he felt the change in the ship's motion. Now they had a north wind in their square sail, and they'd be moving due south faster than the Jekers were headed west.

Second, he cast a fog between their ships and his.

And then, above the fog, he started to weave a squall. It was essential that he not harm the Jekers in any way – essential to his own notions of morality, and to his eventual hope of reincarnation. But he was able to deter them, if he could do it without violence. It was the way of his people, and they had a great deal of practice.

As soon as the fog was responding to him in the *Aura*, he cancelled his northerly, swarmed up the ladder, and raised his head above the deck-edge.

'Turn to starboard. All the way to due west. Then keep turning until you're headed due north.'

'You want me to turn head up into the wind and then fall off north?' Jawala asked.

'I'm going to put a wind in your sail and keep it full all the way through the turn.'

'Have I mentioned how much I love you?' Jawala asked.

'I love you, too,' Bravah said from the other helm.

And damn, I love them. Here we go.

Aanat was already tired, but he reached out, found the *Aura*, and began to play with it. A wind that turned was a complex spell – almost a masterwork; ordinarily, he'd fidget with his signs and glyphs for days.

That day, he wrote three in letters of red fire, and then chose the simplest solution.

'Call out your headings to me!' he roared.

'Aye, husband. South-south-east.'

He reached out a tendril of *Aura* and captured his three glyphs, and he began to turn them. To make it easier, he cast a cantrip that illuminated a compass rose.

Thirty deep breaths later, Jawala sang out, 'South by east'.

He rotated his glyphs.

'It's working!' Bravah said.

And it did work. Before the sun had crept another finger above the horizon, the *Untroubled Swan* was flying due north, and a wall of fog separated her from her pursuers, who had last seen her turn south.

By the time the wall of fog dissipated, the horizon was clear, and a very relieved Pavi called out from the masthead that she couldn't see a sail in all the circle of ocean.

Aanat slumped against a bale of colourful woven Dardanian wools from Mykoax.

'Drek,' he muttered, postponing his reincarnation a little more for the pleasure of a curse.

He crawled up on deck, and found that all three of the injured men were staring at him.

'You are a magos, I find,' Zos said.

Aanat went and sat with his back against the slight step where the stern cabin rose above the cargo holds.

'Aye,' he admitted. 'We're all a bit of everything, among my people.'

Zos nodded. 'And modest. How odd. All the magi I know are arsehats.' He shrugged. 'Jekers out there?'

Aanat saw no reason to lie. 'Yes,' he admitted.

'I can move both my fingers and my toes today,' the aristocrat said.

Pollon managed a smile. 'I can use both my arms,' he said. 'You were precise, sir. It's a slow miracle. I can't even remember the pain...'

Atosa pushed himself up on his elbows and supported his weight.

'It certainly is,' he said. 'Ara's balls. My legs feel like ice, but the rest of me feels...' He glanced at Pollon.

'Fantastic?' Pollon offered. 'Captain, I've reached the age

where most things hurt most mornings. Last night I slept on the bare boards of your ship. And nothing hurts but the cold burn in my legs. Yesterday, I had that burn in my arms.' He raised an arm, flexed a muscle. 'And now ...'

Aanat examined the arm, and then felt Pollon's legs. He could see clearly where they had been smashed; he could see the heavy bruising, the lacerations. And he could see that the wounds looked months old. And the limb was straight, and as cold as ice. The arm, by contrast, showed only traces of the abuse – like a year-old injury, perfectly healed, with some mottling at the point of the vicious break.

And the arm was warm and human.

Zos met his eye and nodded.

'It does seem that we're being healed. For which ...' He laughed, and the bitterness was suddenly obvious. 'I suppose I can go and be a healthy beggar somewhere. Where do you propose to leave us, Captain?'

'I'm no captain,' Aanat said. 'I'm the senior mate, of a family clan. Even that is implying more ... rank than I truly hold?' He was running through Trade Dardanian words and trying to explain.

Zos nodded. 'And where is our Dry One?'

Aanat had forgotten, or pushed down, thoughts of a thousand little Dry Ones hatching in his ship.

'He's woven a tent, and vanished into a cocoon,' he said.

'Ah!' Pollon said. 'We are at sea, after all.'

Aanat glanced at the writer. 'So?'

Pollon smiled. The smile was very slightly patronising, or perhaps just the joy of a man who enjoys imparting information.

'They like to be dry,' he said. 'Absolutely dry. They do not like water.'

Aanat sat back on his heels. 'Aha!' he said. 'Blessing on you, man of wisdom.'

173

Pollon smiled. 'Sometimes,' he said with utterly false humility, 'I know things.'

Aanat nodded. 'And it fought a god,' he added, considering what he thought he'd seen. 'Maybe it's hurt.'

'Who knows?' Zos asked. 'Maybe. alone among deadly aliens, it's built a safe haven?'

Pollon nodded towards the warrior. 'Interesting.'

Zos smiled.

That evening, over more lentils, Jawala pushed their fears into the light.

'We'll never get to Akash,' she said. 'And the monster is in a cocoon.'

Miti raised her head and nodded.

Bravah smiled. 'Just so,' he said, with as much calm as a young man can muster.

Pavi frowned, and Mokshi looked away.

Aanat looked at his senior spouse. 'What do you propose?'

'I propose nothing. I make some observations. By my calculations Noa is due west, perhaps ten days' sail. And when we fled the Jekers, we sailed north, *away* from Akash.'

Aanat nodded. Without the powers of the *Aura*, Jawala was a much better blue-water navigator than he; she read the stars with uncanny precision.

'I can take a reading,' he said. 'But yes. With a fair wind and luck, ten days.'

'Mykoax is about the same,' she said.

'Yes.'

'And the mouth of the mighty Iteru, in Narmer, I make it fifteen days.' Jawala leant forwards and used her wooden spoon to refill her bowl – a pretty thing from Noa, painted with an octopus. She pointed at the bowl. 'We know Noa, and we have credit there. I say we run west, pick up the southerly at mid-ocean and go to Noa. We need food – we will need water.'

Aanat sighed. 'Our monster said Akash.'

'Our monster put his talon in the sand and pointed at a messy triangle,' Jawala reminded him. 'And while it's in a cocoon, we can replenish our supplies and reconsider.'

'You want to go to Narmer,' he said.

It was an old argument. Their last port of call before the ruins of Hekka had been Pleion, port of Mykoax; the warlike westerners were nonetheless fair traders. The crew had wanted to make the safe run to Narmer afterwards, due east on the trades, and Aanat had convinced them to run south for better profits.

Jawala shrugged. 'I do.'

'And if the monster awakes?' Aanat asked. 'We can't even get at our forward hold. And surely you can't plan to invade its tent. That would be against *himsha*.'

'I think we can outsail the Jekers,' Mokshi said.

'I think we can put into Noa and sell the monster's resin, and leave our clan rich, no matter what befalls us after,' Jawala said.

Aanat blinked, looked up at the stars, and then nodded.

'I think you are right.' Among Hakrans, the first rule of command was to know when you were wrong, and change accordingly. 'Let's run for Noa.'

As it proved, they were only eight days running west and another on the southerlies that were often felt at mid-ocean, before the massive islands of Noa rose from the deep, their central mountains reaching for the sky. In those nine days, they saw sails twice. One was a possible Jeker far to the south, but they ran on, scarcely touching a sail or a stay – the kind of perfect sailing that seafarers remember for years and imagine as a sort of nautical heaven.

When the mountains of central Noa were filling the horizon to the south, they turned east, bought fresh vegetables from a pretty white village perched high on a cliff above the sea, and then ran south to one of Ocean's greatest cultures, their bellies full and their injured passengers almost fully recovered. Pollon and Atosa were walking now; Zos could sit up.

Jawala looked at them with concern.

'We'll have to hide them when we land. And no one can be allowed to look at the forward cargo hold. We need to put the spare mainsail over it.'

Aanat frowned. 'Perhaps we should just buy our food in the villages and—'

'We're merchants,' Jawala said. 'We need to trade. Lay aside some cut silver for bribes, that's all I'm saying.'

Noa was nothing much to look at from the sea; the principal city was several miles inland, and only at sunset could you see the smoke rising and the last of the day reflected from the golden statues and the gilded bulls' horns along her walls. The port itself was like every other port on the Ocean – two deep crescent beaches lined with warehouses built of wattle or old planks, with hasty roofs only good enough to keep off the rain, and built in no particular order. Aanat could smell it from a couple of stadia at sea, and close in, it was worse.

Boats and ships were beached in such profusion that it looked as if Enkul-Anu, the Storm God, or Timurti, Goddess of the Deep Sea, had thrown a hundred ships onto the beach with one mighty wave of their hand. Some were neatly beached on rollers, stern first; others looked as if they'd been washed ashore broadside, or hastily abandoned, although Aanat knew from experience that this was deceiving and that every ship's berthing was the results of some problem, repair or cargo necessity.

There were hundreds more ships and boats at anchor, with two or three or even five stones over the side to hold them in a wind. There were little fishing boats, long reed punts from Narmer, and the Noan paddle ships – incredibly inefficient, but still somehow essential to the Noan character. Noan ships had big crews of paddlers and didn't use oars; their sails were triangular and not square, and they tended to stick to coasts more than other ships, but they could get farther upstream when they ventured along rivers.

All this in a glance. The Noan temples were all within their city with their bulls' horns, their giant axes and their magnificent priestesses. The beachside was a permanent market, repair shop and gossip circle, and Aanat was rubbing his hands in eagerness to be at it. This was his favourite part of being a merchant – meeting new people, arranging trades.

The harbour had several partitions. There was a long breakwater made of huge stones, masterfully placed together so that it appeared almost seamless. It rose just a handspan above the water at high tide, and there were people fishing from it. The official harbour was inside the breakwater, with a handful of fast military vessels at the southern end, and a long sandy beach packed with elite merchants. As Aanat watched, a pilot boat came out from behind the breakwater, eight paddlers moving it very quickly. Jawala just had time to throw a big tarp over the forward hold and its spider-silk occupant, while Miti pushed the three rescued men into the aft cabin.

A practised merchant, Aanat pulled the cover off the aft hold as a tubby man in a spotless red and blue striped kilt leapt aboard with an agility that belied his weight.

'Last port?' he asked.

'Pleion and Mykoax,' Aanat said.

'Good answer,' the man allowed with a professional smile. 'We're to arrest anyone shipping off the Hundred Cities.' He looked hard at Aanat for a reaction. 'Order straight from the Great Bull, Enkul-Anu.'

Aanat's smile didn't waver. Harming others was strictly forbidden but a little lying was part of being a merchant.

'Mykoax,' he said, making up a story on the spot. Though it was true, and by good fortune they'd come from the north, down the Noan island chain, because of the storm and the Jeker chase.

He tossed back the corner of the wrapping on a bale of wool, so that the customs officer could see the Mykoan tartans and the baked-clay seal of the royal house of Mykoax – the badge of King Agon – with their two lions and central pillar.

The customs officer didn't want to go down into the hold, that was obvious. But he leant down, checked the seal, nodded, and made a note on a wooden tablet with wax pages.

'Seen any ships?' he asked.

Aanat thought it was a very strange, vague question, but he did his best.

'We had a storm – a heavy blow,' he said. 'Before it came up we saw three Jekers, and ran from 'em. Last few days, fishing boats and Noans on your coast.'

'You came down the west coast?' the man asked.

'East coast of the main island,' Jawala said. She smiled.

Behind her, Pavi was at the port-side steering oar, stripped to the waist, and suddenly the two women were the focus of the customs officer's attention.

'Touch anywhere, mistress?' he asked.

Women ran a lot of things in Noa, and Aanat was happy to let the man assume that Jawala was the captain.

'Just south of the Lion,' she said. 'Little village tucked up in the cliff.'

'Mathala,' the man said, nodding. He made a note. Then he looked at his tablet. 'The gods say you left Mykoax more than three weeks ago.'

'Aye,' Jawala said, volunteering nothing more.

178

The man looked at Pavi's breasts a little longer and then back at Aanat.

'I'll want you to come up to the customs house with your bills of lading,' he said.

'Of course, master,' Aanat said with a highly trained note of obsequiousness.

The customs officer nodded. 'Here's your spot on the beach,' he said, handing over a piece of bark with a set of Noan symbols inscribed. He pointed at an empty slot on the far beach. 'Apologies,' he said, risking one more glance at Pavi. 'Best I can do. Show it to the soldiers when they come.'

Aanat nodded. 'Yes, master.'

The man jumped down into the pilot boat, and was paddled away.

'Three cheers for Pavi's chest,' Jawala said softly.

It was not the first time they'd been used. Women at sea often worked in only a kilt or even less – but dockside officials were easily impressed, men and women alike.

'I feel stupid,' Aanat said.

'We're all fools,' Jawala said. 'We can't survive an inspection; we have an … *infestation*.' She looked at the forward hold.

'And three wounded men,' Aanat said. 'Let's land, get our food and water, and get back to sea by sunset.'

'Since when do customs officials come out for inspections?' Miti wrinkled her nose.

Pavi spat in the water, and she and Bravah turned the little ship in towards their spot on the beach. Aanat and Jawala stripped and leapt over the side with lines, handed out some copper wire to buy the services of local stevedores, and together they carefully pulled the bow into their landing place. Pavi nudged the ship ashore, and Bravah threw three anchor stones over the stern.

Aanat got a nice kilt out of the cabin – Narmerian-made,

brilliant white linen with a heavy fringe and a matching sash. It looked prosperous without being ostentatious, and it went well with his mahogany skin. He put a solid gold bangle on one wrist, and he had a good gold and carnelian earring in his right ear; no one would take him for a slave, or a person of no consequence, which was very important with these people. He combed his hair back and put a fillet around it, and then went down the ladder to the beach. Once he was above the sand line, he slipped on good sandals, and experienced a moment of vertigo as his legs and head got used to the land.

He went up the dusty road, passing hordes of small boys and a dozen beggars, and then turned up the main port road towards the citadel. The customs house was at the top of the road, where it met the main paved road for the palace and the city.

There was a line of captains and merchants waiting outside. He listened to their gossip, stuck to his story, and noted the two enamel god's eyes set into the building; a third was painted around the corner.

Everything they said was being heard, or so he suspected.

'Never seen the like,' he said cheerfully to the man ahead of him.

'Nammu's hairy balls, brother,' the man said. 'I was here three weeks ago and there was none of this crap. It was the usual — wander up, drop a silver hack on the officer, get the chop on your bill of lading and away you go to the market.'

'The goddess–queen must need the tax money,' Aanat said quietly.

'No, they're asking about the Hundred Cities. Someone's really pissed off the gods. Big trouble. Big threats, too.'

The man was Mykoan. Most traders were. The warlike Mykoans and the pacifist Hakrans had their differences, but they tended to get along like brothers when trading overseas. The man looked at him.

'Do I know you from somewhere?'

Aanat made himself smile. 'Hall of trade at Mykoax?'

'Maybe,' the man said, his oiled moustache gleaming.

Aanat nodded, and something clenched in his stomach.

When it was his turn, the officer's glance at his bill of lading was cursory, to say the least. The two clay tablets had several erasures and he had an additional wax tablet; Jawala kept a clean bill. They didn't smuggle.

'Tholon met your boat?' the man asked.

'Yes, sir,' Aanat said.

'Last port?'

'Mykoax.'

'You haven't been over to the Hundred Cities or Narmer this voyage?'

'No,' Aanat answered.

The man nodded. 'You haven't picked up any passengers? Anything... odd?'

I have a Dry One in my forward hold. Is that odd?

'No, sir.'

The man nodded. 'Boss says you saw Jekers. How many days ago?'

Aanat knew he had to be very careful here.

'It was before the blow,' he said. 'Seven days? Eight?'

'Huh,' the man said. 'Where were you?'

'Somewhere south of Sala,' Aanat answered, guessing that on a slow, cautious passage, that was where he'd have been.

The man nodded. 'Right,' he allowed slowly. 'That's fucking far north for Jekers. Scary.'

He handed back the clay tablets and the wax, and pointed to a writer sitting with a team of other scribes.

'Get these recopied fair, and I'll seal it.'

'Yes, sir,' Aanat said.

He couldn't relax, so he kept his back a little bent, very much the harmless man of business, and he tipped the writer well to recopy the whole bill of lading, clean, into new clay.

The man was very fast, but Aanat still had time to hear the next three sets of questions; two Dardanian merchants from Pylax, and a woman, a local, had just landed from Narmer with a cargo of flax. She was sharper, and she was clearly someone important; she drove the officer to explanations.

'It's the gods, mistress. They are demanding that we search every ship. Something bad – a plot against them, or something. I don't know any more.'

The woman wore a magnificent layered skirt and a tight, tailored jacket that emphasised her femininity and her authority. She was not young, and her dark hair had broad white locks over her ears.

'Where are you bound next?' the official asked.

'What business is it of yours?' she returned. 'I am a godborn lady and captain of my ship. I am Noan. Save your questions for foreigners.'

'I have to ask …'

'And my ship was searched,' she said. 'By what right?'

'The gods …' the man began.

'I'm not used to having my ship searched, warrior,' she said. 'My sister is a high priestess. My mother's sister is the goddess-queen's raptere.'

The officer cringed. 'I know, mistress, but the gods …' He looked at her.

The woman raised an eyebrow, but after a long pause she said, 'When I have a new cargo of wine, I'm bound for Vetluna in Rasna.'

The official made a mark. 'Thank you,' he said with ill grace.

She favoured him with a smile that might have frozen a younger official, and said no more. She did glance at Aanat; she winked, one captain to another, and then turned away.

The writer gave him his tablets, and he read them over, making sure all the amounts were accurate. Writers were remarkable for their attention to detail, but errors could be made.

He put down a second tip, and went back to the officer, who took a small ivory seal off his sword belt and stamped the clay.

'Have it fired outside,' he said. 'You're done. Next!'

Back on the ship, Aanat grabbed Jawala's hand and led her into the aft cabin.

Inside, the stern shutters were open to let in the brilliant sunlight of an evening in Noa. The harbour waters gleamed as the sun in the west lit a path of flame.

The three rescued men sat on the deck, playing something that looked like Senet from Narmer. Pollon was rattling the sticks, and Atosa was leaning forwards, while Zos looked out over the harbour.

'So?' Aanat asked. Jawala closed the hatch behind him. 'What exactly did you people do?'

He stepped over them and pulled the cabin shutters closed. Jawala lit a lamp.

'Do?' Pollon asked.

'No good deed ever goes unpunished,' Aanat said.

'Aanat!' Jawala said. She never liked his blasphemies.

He shrugged. 'There are soldiers and customs officers looking for three men who were taken off the coast of the Hundred Cities.'

Zos froze. Pollon sat back, his game forgotten.

Atosa said, 'We didn't do anything! I went to testify for Pollon here, and they took me and broke my hands.'

'And then they broke the rest of us,' Pollon said.

Zos took in a long breath through his nose, and then let it out.

'I injured a god,' he said.

Pollon's head turned.

Atosa smiled. 'Good for you, man,' he said. 'Fuck them.'

Pollon winced.

Jawala pursed her lips. 'Injury and violence only mar your soul.'

'How did you hurt a god?' Pollon asked.

Aanat had been about to ask the same. Weapons didn't harm them. Everyone knew that.

Zos was just able to sit up, and he was clearly in pain still. But he rolled his head to Pollon.

'I'm not entirely sure what happened,' he said. 'The memory… is cloudy. I hit the bastard in the knee. Probably shattered it.'

Aanat looked at Jawala. Jawala looked like she'd drunk bad water – but she held his eye.

'We rescued them, and they are our guests,' she said.

'And the monster in the forward hold?'

'We could just go ashore and disappear,' Zos said.

'You can't even walk,' Aanat noted. 'Also, this is Noa, the most organised and perhaps richest kingdom in the God-Lands after Narmer. They'd have you in three hours.'

'Not if we're beggars,' Zos said. 'I know a thing or two.'

Aanat looked at him, tempted.

Sail away, and no harm done. Not directly, at least.

Jawala shook her head. 'The Dry One is still here, and we are in its web.' She shrugged.

'Literally,' Aanat said. Jawala was quick with words. 'And it ordered us to rescue you.'

Zos winced. 'I have no idea why.'

Aanat nodded. 'All right, what do we do?'

Pollon spread his hands. The blue fire of a magos' *Aura* appeared between his hands and he began to manipulate the glyphs.

It wasn't anything like Aanat's *Aura*; no, on further observation, it was like but unlike.

'You never said you were a magos,' Aanat said.

'You never asked. Anyway, I'm just a writer. But I can do a little...' The man turned a little pale.

Zos glanced at him. 'What, brother?'

'Brother?' Pollon asked.

Zos smiled. He had a very engaging smile.

'We were broken on wheels together,' he said. 'Doesn't that make us brothers?'

'So they *caught you* and then tortured you?' Atosa asked.

Zos shrugged. 'I think I was wounded first – paralysed. Badly hurt.' He sighed.

Pollon rotated his *Aura* with his will and then activated a series of symbols. Suddenly all of them could see a whole row of images: people talking; a woman selling peas; a ship anchored out with two small boats alongside; a woman practising with a sword in a courtyard with magnificent pillars behind it.

Zos blinked.

Jawala spoke for them all.

'You can see through the god's eyes?' she asked.

Pollon made a face. 'I wasn't sure I could still do it...'

'Druku's twisted member,' Atosa said. 'Why didn't you just spy on the fucking raptere?'

Pollon shuddered. 'I'm a fool, perhaps. Regardless, none of the eyes are on us right now – there's not many on the waterfront, to be honest. A little surprising.'

Zos nodded. 'Most of the god-kings are hesitant to let the gods see everything,' he said. 'And the goddess-queen of Noa is reputed to be very effective.'

'Goddess-Queen Cyra is more than just effective,' Jawala said. 'I've heard that Great Goddess Sypa is jealous of her wealth and power. But I would bet she has her own ways...'

'We need to get out of here before we get searched again,' Aanat said.

'I've started a deal for one of the stone jars,' Jawala said. 'Give me a few hours and we'll make a good profit and get our food stores as well.'

A few hours became a night and then a new day, and every time one of the goddess-queen's godborn warriors walked under the bow of the *Untroubled Swan*, Aanat felt as if he'd aged a year. Bravah went ashore, dressed as well as Aanat and adding a fancy pleated linen shirt, and came back with a donkey cart laden with fresh vegetables, as well as bags of chickpeas and barley. He'd also purchased a whole cartload of the local pottery — bowls, spoons, and richly decorated amphorae and pots, most sporting beautifully painted fish and one with an octopus so real that Miti laughed aloud. Noan ceramics were valued as far away as Dendrowna.

The fresh vegetables allowed Mokshi to make them a splendid dinner, and Zos didn't even bemoan the lack of meat.

Jawala was late, but climbed up the side, plucked a bowl from her second husband's hand, and kissed him.

'Cooking is the most beautiful skill,' she said.

Aanat smiled. 'It is delicious.'

She squatted on her haunches despite her tight-fitting sari, and dropped a bag on the deck. It made a musical noise.

'Six cubes of gold,' she said.

Aanat was speechless.

'The buyer made the mistake of admitting she'd never seen resin of that purity.' Jawala pinned back her veil — something that she did expertly despite never wearing one anywhere but in the God-Lands. 'I'm of a mind to keep a flagon for ourselves, family.'

Miti made a moue. 'What for?'

Jawala looked at Aanat.

He shrugged. 'Good resin, real resin, is a life-giver. The Dry Ones make it, somehow. It's in almost every medicine, and most of the longevity treatments that the rich take and we're forbidden.'

Zos leant forwards, using his chin to ask Pollon to get him a second bowl of the vegetable curry.

'Eggplant?' he asked.

Mokshi smiled. 'Yes!'

'And cinnamon,' Zos added. 'You can't be a soldier without learning to cook. I mean, you can, but it makes life so much better.'

Jawala, who had had nothing good to say about Zos, gave him a look, as if she'd found silver in dung.

'You can cook?' she asked.

Zos shrugged. 'Not like this one,' he said, pointing at Mokshi. 'Why are you forbidden to use longevity drugs?' he asked. 'I mean, no one can afford the real thing anyway, except the greatest god-kings.'

'Cyra has been goddess-queen for one hundred and forty years,' Jawala said.

Zos nodded, his head going sideways – a Mykoan habit. Pollon spooned curry into his mouth.

Aanat shrugged. 'We have a lot of rules. But to us, life is about climbing a ladder to ... well, to being *better*. And that means not cheating. Life-extension is cheating.'

Zos laughed. 'If you ain't cheating, you ain't trying.'

Jawala looked at him with contempt. 'If you cheat, all you are is a cheater.'

Zos snorted. 'You are *merchants*, right?' He smiled smugly. 'And you never cheat?'

Aanat finished his bowl while the others fell silent. Contention was rare on a Hakran ship; confrontation led to anger, which was often a danger to the soul.

Jawala was sitting perfectly still, containing herself.

Zos raised an eyebrow, and then Pollon gave him more food – possibly to forestall any attempt to argue further.

Aanat rose to his feet.

'Well, we have food, and we've made a sale,' he said. 'No one's offering for our Mykoan wools – too much here already. Let's get to sea.'

Zos suddenly looked at Jawala.

'Wait a minute,' he said. 'Where'd you get the resin?'

She looked forwards. 'You know there is a Dry One aboard, yes?'

'Shit,' he said. 'Your buyer just got pure resin. It only comes from one source, and I was under the impression the gods held it all.'

Jawala closed both eyes in consternation.

'We *really* need to get to sea.'

'In the dark?' Miti asked.

'Not for the first time,' Bravah reassured her. 'You'll see.'

They rocked her off the cap of the beach, with Atosa joining Aanat and Bravah to push her bow. Aanat added a little force from his *Aura*, painfully aware that to any magos on the beach, he was lit up like a rainbow. But they couldn't risk any delay.

Her bow floated free and immediately Pavi sang out, and the women began hauling against the anchor stones, pulling her stern-first into the low surf. The men scrambled aboard and took sweeps as soon as they were clear of the hulls on either side. Before the moons were any higher in the sky, they'd backed her out of the surf and into the deep water, retrieved their anchor stones, and turned her to catch the land-breeze. Aanat got the big square sail down; Pavi, knowing their crisis, had left it in yarns, so that one person could cut them and drop the sail while she steered and others rowed.

The *Untroubled Swan* wallowed for a moment, broadside on to the low waves, and then the sail filled and they were turning, turning...

There was a beacon on the long, low mole that guarded the harbour. No one ran to light it. Aanat held his breath; they weren't fast enough to outrun a picket ship, or even the paddled pilot boat.

But the *Untroubled Swan* steadied, heeled a little in the light air, and swept majestically – if a small, tubby ship could have majesty – out past the mole and into the ocean.

Pollon came out of the cabin, his *Aura* lit between his hands. 'All of the waterfront god's eyes are watching us,' he said.

Aanat did his best to stifle a curse. He ran aft, his bare feet slapping on the deck.

'I'm going to fill our sail with a mage-wind.'

He slipped into his trance, and then raised his own *Aura*. Through it he could see the writer's *Aura*; the man was losing contact with the god's eyes, as the distance opened between them, but he was right – they were all watching the *Untroubled Swan* turning out to sea. Perhaps they were the only interesting thing on the waterfront; perhaps it was something more sinister.

'Can you turn those things off?' he asked.

Then he had a thought. Like most ports, Noa was at the end of a promontory.

'Cheat us to starboard,' he called.

Pavi obeyed, turning the ship as far to starboard as would keep the land-breeze in the sail. A moment later Aanat heard the battens rattle as they lost the wind, and then Pavi steadied them.

'Tell me when you can no longer see the harbour lights,' he said.

The turn should get them clear of prying eyes. Granted, the

city and the palace were out there, above them and several stadia inland, but that couldn't be helped.

'Gone,' Pavi sang.

Aanat raised a mage-wind with three glyphs, and held it.

'South by west,' he ordered.

Somewhere, Jawala let out a *hmmff*. But no one called a vote in a real emergency. Even if he was turning them away from Narmer, and towards the Jekers, and Akash.

He released his mage-wind, and the sail filled with a crack, and the brave *Untroubled Swan* leapt ahead.

Heaven

Sypa sat comfortably on her consort's couch in his private hall. Most of the gods had private halls, and they were fascinating in their diversity; Enkul-Anu's was almost severely plain, very much at odds with the opulence of the Hall of Hearing or the lowering darkness of the Hall of Judgement. The Storm God's hall was ... comfortable.

'My son Telipinu says that we lost a demon,' she said.

'Telipinu should be careful what he says,' Enkul-Anu growled, but he was pleasantly sated and the growl was no more dangerous than a lion full of meat out on the desert sand. 'But it's true.' He lay, face down, fully relaxed.

Sypa smiled to herself, and deepened the note of concern in her voice.

'I wouldn't have thought ... anything ... could destroy one of our demons,' she said.

He grunted. 'What you don't seem to get,' he muttered, 'is that this world is still very dangerous. We have a good thing here, but we all have to work to keep it. Maybe losing a demon to some unknown ambush will wake some of the old folk up.'

Sypa rubbed oil steeped with the sacred resin into her consort's back. He groaned again.

'But what could have killed a demon?' she asked, as if deeply afraid.

He raised his head. 'Anything. Fucking anything. A child with a fucking peashooter who got lucky. A hero with an artifact – there's a hundred of them out there and I try to get them back, and our various foes toss them to new meat. Or maybe a magos with a new spell – they're fucking hard to control. Maybe some monster from the spawn of the old gods that we've missed. It's a big world we rule. And yet, most of our idiot offspring think it's a sinecure.'

'But this dreadful mortal must die!' Sypa said. 'Send more demons!' Then, with sly suggestion, 'Or send Nisroch – you like to use him—'

'Sypa,' Enkul-Anu said with smouldering anger, 'you are absolutely transparent. I know exactly why you hate Nisroch, and I know you'd love to see him ripped apart by some fucking monster.'

Her hands never stopped rubbing his back.

'That creature's son will never serve you well, consort!' she said, with a little more heat than she'd intended.

He rolled over. 'Damn it to all seven hells, woman!'

She shrugged, all complacence. 'It's Temis, my darling. She's making all these things happen. You should ban her from the halls, or throw her into the Outer Darkness.'

He lay gazing up at her, by far and away the most beautiful of all the goddesses. His anger dissipated. But he got up on his elbows.

'No. Listen. I know you are smarter than you play, consort, so *listen*. Temis bleeds off the dissent. So does Druku, with his drunken orgies. You cannot rule strictly by fear, consort. We need the rebels to believe that they have a chance at rebellion, and we need the drunken fucks to have a place to blow their minds. So that we can keep milking the rest of the cattle. That's how it works. The Huntress is as much a part of our system as you or I.'

Sypa gazed at him with a facsimile of smiling adoration. And then, cooing, she said, 'And I see that Cyra of Noa has again declined to send tribute for me.'

The god under her hands let out a snort of derision. 'Sypa, she owes you no tribute.'

'She is too rich, too old, and too vain,' Sypa said. 'She is a *threat*.'

Enkul-Anu rolled so that he could see her. 'Cyra of Noa is the single richest woman in the world. She is refreshingly competent, runs her people with ruthless efficiency, pays all her tributes and taxes, and her very desire to live forever makes her utterly dependent on us. Only we can give her resin. Our *ambrosia* is the bridle on her ambition.'

'You think everything through so well, consort,' she said with touching humility.

'Not everything,' he said. 'There's still that idiot Resheph and his drooling father, the war god. I'm not ready to tell Ara that the mortal who struck his precious son has escaped. He shook his head. 'Ara was the best of us. What in Kur happened?'

Sypa made a humming sound.

Enkul-Anu shook his head. 'I do not want him to hear of this from anyone but me. Don't speak of it.'

'Oh,' she said, opening her long *heton* and joining him on the couch. 'Oh, I never would.'

Chapter Six

Era

Something told Era to avoid Weshwesh, and she did. She led Daos away from the beach road, and they walked from village to village in the fertile land inland of the great city. The peasants were little more than slaves, working from dawn until dusk to bring in enough grain that the god-king got his due, and they still had enough to eat. The girls were women at thirteen; the men were dead at thirty.

No one had ever told them that their lives were unhappy. In every village, she would take out the beautiful kithara and play, and the younger people would dance, despite a day in the fields, and the toothless old women of thirty-five would smile and touch her.

They'd play with Daos, and give him food they could ill afford to share, and she loved them all, and felt for them. None of them complained; usually they pressed gifts into her hands in the morning – pretty pebbles, twists of copper wire, and once, a bit of lapis. She sang love songs and dirges and epics and a battle song, and they liked it all.

Era was twenty-four, and she was older than most of them, and she looked as if she was from a different world – taller, stronger, with smooth skin and black hair.

I am not godborn, she said to herself, but she might as well have been, compared to the peasants of Weshwesh.

About halfway around the spokes of the wheel that was the layout of the farming villages supporting Weshwesh, she entered a village to find that the men were even smaller and thinner, the women were hags at twenty, and no one waved, no blessings were called.

She sat in their dusty little square. The village didn't have a donkey. It was by far the poorest village she had visited, and she could see why. The desert dunes were so close they looked like rollers from the sea about to overwhelm the low mud houses.

'Can't farm sand,' an ancient crone said.

Era looked under her hand. 'I know,' she said. 'It's terrible.'

The crone shrugged. She had a necklace of amulets, and they looked real.

'Desert is coming,' the crone said. 'Soon, the Dry Ones will take us all, and that's the end of it.'

'Can't you move?' she asked. 'Surely there's better land…'

The crone laughed, a scratchy cackle worthy of the crones of legend.

'Honey,' she said, 'this estate is owned by a rich man who needs his peasants to pay his taxes. He can't be expected to come and farm it himself, can he?' She laughed. 'And anyway, the Dry Ones are coming for all of us. In the end, the desert will win. I've lived a long time, and the desert always wins.'

'Don't pester the singer,' a man's voice said. 'Pardon us, mistress. The old woman says such things… and who can punish an old woman?'

Era turned to find a bent stick of a man leaning on a stick.

'And you are…?'

'Tesh. Village headman. Terrible job.' He smiled, and she admired his humour.

Daos sat at her feet, playing with his bear. He told the bear stories; that night, he told a story about a wave of sand that ended the world.

What a terrible time to be a child, Era thought, but then, the world had been a terrible place for children for a long time.

The next day, they walked on. The road was hard gravel, rutted where chariots had passed, and the sand dunes came right up to the road for stadia, and every breeze threw another finger of sand across the track.

'Is the desert really going to swallow the world?' Daos asked.

'The desert is part of the world,' Era replied.

The boy was silent for a while, and then said, 'Sure. The desert is part of the world, but it's not a part where people can live.'

He was watching the dunes as if he expected something to appear.

'That depends on how you define people,' Era said. 'Nomads live in the desert. And the Dry Ones. The Bright People.'

Daos glanced at her. 'I'm hoping to see one,' he said. 'My father saw one once. Said they were amazing.'

Era nodded and relented, too.

'The desert *is* swallowing the world,' she said. 'The world of men and women was much bigger, once. But the desert has been winning for many years. Generations, really.'

'So it is like the old nanna said?' the boy asked. 'In the end, the desert always wins?'

Era thought of her lover, dead with her knife in hand, and the town, destroyed by Jekers. She was tempted to say *I hope so*. Were Jekers even fully human? People said that they ate human flesh.

She shivered. 'I don't know.'

★

The next village had only three occupants, and two of them were dogs. The third was an old man with a wispy beard and one good eye. He fed Era a good meal of barley and mutton, and enjoyed her songs, and flirted harmlessly. The boy played with the dogs.

The man had a good house — four stone-built rooms, with a pleasant front porch held up by a single pillar. It was like a very small palace. His furniture was good, too, and he had an extensive garden, but the whole back wall of the house had a massive sand dune against it.

'This year or next,' he said. He shrugged. 'More honey?'

'You live by yourself?' she asked.

'Hard to keep dancing girls here,' he smiled. 'I'm an exile, and I'll die here. It's not bad.'

She waved a hand at the back wall.

'Oh, yes,' he said. 'The great sand sea will probably get me before the nomads or the Dry Ones do.' He grinned, and looked younger. 'I wager with myself. Roof collapse? Arrow in the gut while I work my garden? One last scent of cinnamon?'

'Cinnamon?' she asked.

'You look like a woman of broad experience. Have you smelt cinnamon?' he asked.

She smiled. 'Ah. Yes, I have.'

'The Dry Ones give it off — with some other remarkable smells.'

'You've met one?'

'I've met dozens. They're very careful around water, but they need it, and I have a well.' He smiled. 'I trade with them. I leave them water in covered amphorae, and they leave me resin, and bits of copper and silver. But one day ...' He shrugged. 'One day they'll just take the well.'

Era was sitting on a stool. She'd stopped playing to rest her

197

hand, but she began to play chords, trying to decide how to please the old man.

Daos looked up. 'Is it true that the desert is going to take over the world?' he asked.

The old man locked his hands over his knees and leant back, studying the boy.

'It may be,' he said. 'There's a lot wrong with the world.'

'I agree,' the boy said, as if they were peers.

The old man smiled. 'How far are you two going?'

Era shrugged. 'At least to Ma'rib. Perhaps further.'

'If I was a god-king, I'd stop the desert,' the boy said.

The old man swayed a little.

'Aye,' he said. 'That's how you'd start. But in a year or two, you'd realise that to stop the desert, you'd have to irrigate all the outer farms. That would take water and a lot of workers, which would cut down on farming, and mean that everyone had less to eat, and you'd have angry people – and you'd be poorer. If nomads attacked, or the bastards in the next city, you'd have no baked brick to build fortifications, because you'd be using it all on your irrigation ditches.' The old man smiled. 'You understand me, boy?'

The boy nodded, and even flourished one of his very rare smiles.

'I understand you perfectly, sir. You were a king.'

The old man spat onto his hearth. 'Never,' he said. 'I tried to be a raptere for a little while, and I made a lot of enemies.' He looked out towards the distant sea. 'The only way to stop the desert would be to unite everyone in the Hundred Cities. And that's never going to happen. They can't even combine to fight the fucking Jekers.'

Era nodded.

'Bah, I'm old and cranky, and you folks have a long way to

walk. Play me an epic, beautiful lady, and I'll serve you some palm wine.'

Later, when the boy was asleep, he gave her some very pure resin.

'What am I going to do with it?' he asked.

'I still won't sleep with you,' she said.

He shrugged. 'Bah. Probably for the best. You'd just fall in love with me and decide to stay, and my solitude would be ruined.'

He glanced at her, and just for a moment, his bitter sarcasm was somewhat appealing to her.

'We need to avoid that,' she agreed.

Era put a stool against her door, from habit, but the old man didn't trouble them, and in the morning, he offered both of them good cloaks – straw cloaks – against the rain.

'Misty,' he said. It was grey outside, making everything indistinct. 'You won't have trouble with the Dry Ones in this weather. Comes off the sea. They hate the sea.'

At the door, he made sure they had filled water bottles, and then he offered each of them a sword.

'I have a dozen of these,' he said. 'Relics of a misspent life.'

The boy's bronze sword was beautiful, if very small; it had an elaborate ivory handle and a fine bronze blade as long as the boy's forearm, and it was very sharp. The scabbard had a stone bound on with chords; upon examination, it was a sort of belt loop.

'Mine when I was a boy,' the man said. 'In Karna.'

'Karna!' Era said.

Situated on the south-western shore of the Ocean, Karna had been the first city conquered and destroyed by the Jekers.

'An early lesson,' the man said. 'One for you, too.'

He handed Era a long blade with a plain sheepskin scabbard,

the sheep's wool turned in to put oil against the blade. The hilt was wrapped in silver wire.

'I can't accept these,' Era said, half-heartedly.

The old man nodded. 'Yes you can,' he said. 'In a few months they'll be buried under sand. The Dry Ones can't use them, and the nomads would use them to murder more villagers.'

The boy drew his sword and began fighting the air with all the relish of boys with swords everywhere.

'A real sword!' he said. 'My mother and father had swords.'

Suddenly his face fell.

The old man's house was the last structure they saw in the countryside around Weshwesh, and they travelled three days on the food and water the old man had given them, reaching the sea and the old coast road. There they met a caravan – dusty, deeply tanned men and women with salt in their hair and the smell of camels and burning camel dung in the air. They got food and water in exchange for Era's songs.

They exchanged news, and tales. The caravan leader was a middle-aged woman of the Hundred Cities, broad-shouldered, with a dusty outer robe made of Mykoan wool worth a small fortune, and a necklace of gold beads. Years in the desert had turned her skin to walnut-dyed leather, but her eyes were bright.

'The gods are angry,' the woman said, and her drivers nodded sagely. 'The great mountain smokes, and the gods are coming and going like hornets in a nest dug up with a stick.'

Era nodded. She'd never seen Auza, the mountain of the gods. She wasn't fond of the gods and had no reason to go on such a pilgrimage, but she maintained the appearance of piety, bowing her head at the mention of the sacred mountain.

'And dangers?' she asked.

Mira, the caravan leader, shrugged. 'The world is nothing but dangers,' she said. 'There's nomads raiding all the way down to the road, and Dry Ones popping out of the sand at your feet, and the god-kings grow ever more…' She looked around, and subsided. 'The taxes are high,' she said slowly, glancing at one of her drovers, a small man with a ferret face. He appeared to be playing Senet with another man. Era thought he was listening intently.

She noted him.

'Tell me your news,' Mira said.

Era sang her news, slowly and clearly, composing the couplets as she went. She sang of Akar, destroyed by Jekers; she sang of Hekka, up north near Narmer, taken in war by her neighbour Kyra; and she sang the rumour that the god-king of Narmer was dead. She chose not to sing the rumour that a mere man, a godborn, had wounded one of the gods in the fighting at Hekka. She'd heard it twice on the road, and it didn't sound likely; besides, it was just the sort of titbit to get her into trouble with authority.

'By the thunderbolts of Enkul-Anu,' Mira swore. 'The fools kill cities, but no one builds new ones. Eventually, there will be no one to trade with.'

'And the sand is coming,' Daos said.

He'd been casting Senet sticks by himself in a corner of the great camelhair wool tent, and his voice had a different quality, almost as if a spirit was speaking from the dead.

Ferret-Face looked at Era and stretched.

'It is all in the hands of the gods,' he said smoothly. 'It's dangerous to suggest that anything is more powerful than the gods.'

Mira gave the very slightest inclination of her head, as if to say *There, you see what I put up with?*

Era slept with her sword clutched in both hands.

★

South, and further south.

The boy was getting stronger – just in time, because Era couldn't carry all of their supplies all the time, and now he had his own basket on his back. Era didn't want to feel like an old woman, but something in the villages around Weshwesh had scared her. Now, bending her back every day under a load of barley meal and dry sausage, she was afraid of ageing as never before.

Every morning she woke up and her hips and back hurt in ways that should not pain a dancer.

Greatly daring, she ate some of the resin that the old man had given her. The change was miraculous. Nothing hurt; nothing ached, and she felt as if she was filled with energy and purpose.

And the gods have a monopoly, and keep it from us.

She cursed, but they walked on, and the boy carried a little more. They met another caravan, not as welcoming but still willing to trade food for songs, and a pair of messengers in a chariot flew by them the other way, rushing from the north to Ma'rib in the south.

After two weeks of walking, they found a village that had been destroyed. Era crept into the wretched burnt hovels and took as much food as she could find; she didn't know enough to know whether the corpses were the result of nomads or Jekers, but in this case she suspected the Dry Ones, because most of the people looked as if the water had been sucked from them – or perhaps their blood.

The boy waited outside the village for her, and then they walked on.

The next day they found a camp such as the caravans and nomads used, a circle of huge rocks at the edge of the sea. There were people, all dead, and animals, also dead.

They'd been dead for a month, perhaps twice as long.

'Jekers?' the boy asked.

'Plague, I think,' she answered. She took a little more resin and gave the boy some as well.

The next day, the strap on her sandals broke and she spent an hour cobbling up a new one. Her temper was fraying, and her project of walking south to Ma'rib seemed insane, and she wasn't absolutely sure that she could remember her goddess directing her to do it.

And then a miracle occurred.

Right by the road, at the edge of the desert, there was a donkey cropping the wiry grass. He watched them from a long distance, and never made a move to run. Era walked up to him and sang him a little song – one of her many songs that had a little power in it. He waited for her as if expecting her, and an hour later, he was carrying their baskets and seemed every bit as stolid and annoyed as donkeys always seem to be.

They were saved. With a donkey to carry their packs, walking the coast road grew much easier, especially as the road left the desert and began to climb to high cliffs along the water.

Three days later, they rounded a long promontory, and there was Ma'rib, revealed in all her glory. She was built into the side of a mountain, so that it was a thousand feet from her beaches at sea level to the tip of the citadel and the great crouching hippogryph carved in stone and gilded on the topmost tower. The god-kings of Ma'rib controlled the trade in frankincense and myrrh and a dozen other valuable deep-desert commodities, as well as controlling contact with the Bright People.

Era looked at the lines of the walls, the towers at every angle, the hippogryph symbols visible to the naked eye even from ten stadia away, and smiled. She lived for new experiences, and she'd always wanted to see Ma'rib, and now here she was. She looked at the boy.

He was bigger. Every day.

He smiled at her. 'It's ... amazing!' he said.

The main gates were on the east side, facing the desert and set between massive limestone towers. The gates were open, leading to a narrow corridor, turning sharply to the right, lined with high crenellated walls and patrolled by guards who could watch everything from above. The smoky smell of hot olive oil might have come from cooking, but Era suspected that what she could smell was a weapon kept hot to deter surprise attacks. She could see the galleries built into the walls from which to pour the oil, and she cringed.

A pair of godborn guards in good bronze and leather armour stopped her at the inner gate. They gave the donkey a perfunctory search, and waved them through.

'Keep your boy close,' one guard called out. 'Children get lost in the big city.'

She frowned, and took Daos' hand. The donkey followed along up the steep ramp and through the inner gateway to the city beyond.

Inside the gate, it was the smell that hit her first. She'd been twenty days out in the wilderness where the desert met the sea; the smell of fifty thousand humans and their cooking and their waste all hit her at once. Spices, and incense, and latrines and unwashed people. It was overwhelming.

The cross-street at the top of the gate ramp was crowded with loud beggars and lined with stalls, each ingeniously set up with four bare poles and a scrap of fabric around a table. The street itself was beautifully shaded from the omnipresent sun by the ancient wisteria trees growing up the sides of the buildings and interlinked in a glorious organic lattice overhead.

Era was hungry, and the meat pies being sold off a cart with a brazier made her stomach rumble. Despite her innate sense of caution, she pushed through the crowd to the cart.

'Two pies,' she said.

'What've you got for them?' a woman asked. She was small and lithe, and wore a local wrap-garment that almost covered one arm and left the other bare. Her arms were marked in soot, but the woman was cheerful.

Era lifted the flap of her shoulder bag, revealing some copper wire and other scrap, as well as stones she'd collected as they walked.

'Oooh! Nice,' the woman said.

A hand reached for her belt, and something brushed her sword.

Daos grabbed at a boy his own size, and the boy slammed a fist into his head and ran. Daos fell back against the trunk of a wisteria and then shook his head.

'A thief!' he said.

No one even turned their heads.

'Guards know you have swords?' the pastry-woman asked. 'Not legal unless you're godborn.' She winked. 'I'd take that nice red stone for my pies.'

The stone was carnelian, and worth far more than pies, but Era was not in a position to argue with the woman who had seen her sword. Only then did she realise what a pair of marks she and the boy made, in their fine straw capes, swords, and good linen clothing. And her with a bag of metal scrap like a fool, and the dead woman's kithara on her shoulder.

And the donkey.

I should know better. This boy is making me less sharp.

Era decided not to examine the boy's injuries there and then. Instead, she hauled him along, checked the donkey and somehow, without losing anything but her temper, got them through the crowd and out the other side, where the press of people was lessened, and the thieves and beggars fewer.

'Turn here,' Daos said.

She looked down at him, a little shocked, first at his calm tone, despite his injury, and second, that he was guiding her.

'Bror says here.'

He took a pie from her and began to eat it, as if communicating with his bear was an everyday event.

Era obeyed, turning to the right and uphill, into the more expensive parts of the city. But she stopped when there was almost no foot traffic and faced the boy.

'When you say Bror... speaks to you...' she said. 'I need to know what that means.'

The boy turned to look at her, still chewing on a mouthful of pie. He looked at her as if she was mad.

'I don't know,' he said. 'His mouth opens and sound comes out?'

She looked at the toy bear in his arms.

'He's a stuffed bear,' she said in some frustration.

'You'd think so, wouldn't you?' the boy said. 'I know. But he talks.'

She looked down at the toy bear, a tattered relic that bore as much resemblance to a bear as to a donkey in many ways, with patches and various signs of hard usage – food and other stains... The bear, if he was a bear, had carefully painted eyes in black – elongated like god's eyes, and somewhat out of place on a child's toy.

One winked.

Era closed both eyes, took a deep breath, and let it out.

'All right,' she said, as much to the universe as the boy. She took his hand, greasy from the pie, and led them all uphill.

But they didn't go up for long; Daos, his cheek still bleeding, led them off to the left, across a long one-sided street. On the mountain side, there were good houses with big courtyards and trees, and on the land side, just a retaining wall that fell away to the gate-street below.

There were few people; the gates to the courtyards were all closed.

'And now here,' Daos said, and led them down a set of stairs that annoyed the donkey.

Era was beginning to believe they were being followed. She'd seen movement each time they turned a corner – hinting at someone hurrying to keep up.

At the bottom of the steps, a street ran both ways, and more steps led down – a lower level than the main gates, or so it appeared. She was already lost, but they'd come a quarter of the way around the mountain, and the sea glittered in the afternoon sunlight, filling the world to the horizon.

Daos surprised her by turning to the left, so that they continued going around the city-mountain. Now they were going towards the sea, and the levels were further apart and the stairs steeper.

'We can't get the donkey down here,' she said.

Daos took a last bite of his pie and shrugged, his usually sombre face quite cheerful.

'You can,' the boy said. 'You know how.'

Indeed, he led her through some very narrow streets, into an area of the mountainside where the street was so narrow that there was no wisteria overhead and the buildings almost touched. Houses had huge earthenware pots outside, that stank of old food and worse; she wondered who came down here and emptied them, but kept moving, holding her clothes away from the seepage. They went down a steep set of stairs, the donkey complaining at every step, but she withstood the animal's braying and sang to him as the stench increased. At last they came to the base of the steps, passed under an arch and were on the main road down to the port. It had a long series of switchbacks, and the donkey bore these with surprising patience, as if relieved there were no more stairs.

'Have you been here before?' Era asked the boy.

He shook his head. 'No, but Bror has.' He waved. 'Come on. We have to hurry.'

That gave her pause, as the constant directions had not.

'Hurry?' she asked.

'We have to save an old man,' the boy said. 'And a Dendrownan. Maybe some other people.'

Era glanced at him, shook her head, and tugged the donkey on.

They went down and down, turn after turn, and almost every turning had a tower and two gates that could be shut, one on each side, so that the whole town could easily be divided up. Era wasn't sure whether that was to deter attackers or political unrest within the city, but she noted it, and that there was always at least one godborn warrior at every gate. Ma'rib had a great many such warriors. And, as a city renowned for bronze-smithing, they were exceptionally well armoured. Even the rank-and-file soldiers had helmets of boiled leather stiffened with a bronze hoop, and most of them had bronze scales, at least under the sword arm where a shielded man was vulnerable in close fighting.

She'd heard all her adult life that Ma'rib was rich. But this was staggering, and the warriors were only part of the riches. The people strode about in fabrics traded from everywhere on Ocean; there was a man in Mykoan tartan, and beside him, his wife or daughter in a magnificent pleated linen dress from Narmer. Everywhere she looked, people had silver jewellery, not the usual copper, and there was the glint of gold here and there.

Of course, there were also slaves, and an incredible number of beggars, some displaying hideous deformities or wounds, and others sitting in sullen silence, refusing to do more than hold out a hand. They tended to congregate around the gatehouses.

Down, and down. Her left sandal, with the broken strap, was

not tight enough to stay on her foot on a steep incline, and each time she stopped to kick it back on, the donkey stopped and required coaxing forwards again.

And the boy had begun to roam ahead. She was afraid for him; he had a sword, which was apparently illegal, and he was not as adept as she was at concealing it, or anything else. He had a gold seal ring on his finger, and she knew she should have made him take it off before they entered a city as renowned for its thieves as for its metalworkers.

She caught sight of his hair, and then lost him at a turning, and tried to hurry. The sandal slipped from her foot, and the donkey butted her and she almost fell, despite her reflexes.

When she got to the gatehouse, the godborn in his gilded armour smiled at her. It wasn't particularly predatory; he just liked the look of her, in an almost harmless way. She looked down – the only possible response, in this city.

'Your boy's by the fountain,' the man said.

She had to smile now; a kind godborn was a remarkable occurrence.

She inclined her head – thanks and respect together – but remained silent because men could take anything for an invitation. By a miracle, the donkey followed her without a struggle.

'Good-looking woman, for a matron,' a soldier said.

'Eyes front, Thamud,' the godborn snapped.

Then Era saw Daos by a fountain. It was quite pretty, and distracted her for a moment, and then she realised they'd come all the way down the cliff and reached the port, hundreds of feet below the gate where they'd entered and halfway around the mountain.

She could smell the sea; it was a better smell than the streets above. Gulls cried and squabbled on the other side of the fountain square; in fact, the west side of the square was the waterfront itself, with a long row of pilings and a low stone wall.

The rest of the square was full of the little stalls she'd seen at the main gate, but more, and in most cases, better appointed. There were hundreds of them, in fine colours: reds; deep blues; pinks; magentas; strong yellows; lurid greens.

Era got a hand on the boy as she looked among the stalls. Past them she could see a row of wine shops. Sailors were rough, but better than soldiers, and she thought that a waterfront hostel might be the best place for them.

They were standing out, though – because of the donkey. It was the only animal in the square except a dozen feral cats and a sleepy dog.

'Bror says this is the place,' the boy said with the unshakable confidence of the young.

She nodded, looking around, trying to get her bearings. It *was* the kind of place where she'd usually perform; there were wealthy clients here, the kind of merchants who could take a street singer home to entertain rich guests. And it had the right feeling of familiarity – a proper market, like hundreds of others in which she'd been.

It was just *much* richer. Only in Narmer had she seen this level of riches. It seemed that every luxury she'd ever heard of was for sale somewhere in the closely packed market. Right next to the fountain, a hawk-nosed man in a magnificent long robe was selling ivory – real elephant ivory from far up the coast in Narmer. Tusks that big came from deep in the desert, or so people said. There was a woman with a table of sword blades, each finer than the last, and all different shapes – the sickles of Narmer, the leaf blades of Dendrowna, the rapiers of Noa, the long, wicked blades of Dardania. She saw a whole row of Hakrans, most of them selling cloth – wools, silks, cottons and linens. One woman had a table that held nothing but woollen tapestries, every one of which told some story about the gods. Fabulous cloth, only for the very rich. Right there under her eyes, Sypa, Goddess of Lust, killed Thyna, the former Goddess of Love, in the final Battle of the Gods. It was a popular subject for men – two voluptuous, naked women fighting.

'We need to stable our donkey, she said. 'And get beds, or at least space to sleep.'

'Come, Nannu,' Daos said.

The donkey made a coughing noise and followed the boy.

'I didn't know his name,' Era said lightly, hoping that the boy would laugh. Instead, he looked back at her.

'He's called Nannu,' he said.

They made their way carefully to the northern edge of the square, and then she followed her traveller's instinct, leading them along a narrow, cobbled street under yet more wisteria until she saw a fat orange cat sitting in the window of a taverna painted a brilliant yellow. The cat looked well-fed, and even as she watched, someone stroked the animal, and it stretched…

She didn't like cats, but she usually liked the people who kept them.

'Here,' she said.

Era pushed through the wooden gate into the courtyard beyond, dominated by a horse trough and a rose bush. The courtyard was lined on three sides by a low arcade; the walkways were decorated in shells worked into the ground, and a brilliant red flower she didn't know was trellised along the arcades to give privacy.

'Mistress?' a young woman said, the question a lilt in her voice.

She was inside a curtained room, weaving, and she waved Era inside.

As Era's eyes adjusted to the light, she was *amazed* by the quality of the woman's weaving, and also by its subject. It was intricate and almost lifelike, nothing like the stylised representations of Narmer; the figures seemed to move and breathe.

But more shocking still was the content – for here, Shemeg, the ancient sun god of the Hundred Cities, was shackling the World Dragon, a magnificent red-gold dragon sparkling with malevolence and a dark beauty. Not a legal subject for tapestry, almost anywhere. Shemeg had been replaced, first by Arrina, and then by the upstart Uthu.

'I need a room, and stabling for a donkey,' she said.

The girl put a finger to her lips, and nodded.

'The room is not a problem,' she said. 'The Sypa festival is over, may all the gods be thanked. Let me send a girl to see if old Hamku can take a donkey. It'll cost you.'

'How much?' Era asked.

The girl looked her over. 'What do you have?'

'How many days will this buy?'

Era put a fine silver bracelet, worked like a snake, into the woman's outstretched hand. Her hands were prettily decorated with henna, and she made Era feel dowdy and a little old; the girl was not beautiful, but had an indefinable air of neatness that bordered on beauty.

The bracelet had belonged to Daos' mother.

'I can also play. I am a singer.'

The girl looked as if she had singers visiting her house all the time.

'I suppose I'd let you have two nights for the bracelet, but you need to make your own deal for the donkey,' she said.

She clapped her hands and a younger girl, still just a child, appeared.

There was a rapid exchange in Saabian, and Era, who knew a number of languages, was left out.

The girl put a hand to her mouth and ran.

Era put out a hand to stop her.

'I'm sorry,' she said, her tone icy. 'I'm clearly in too fine a place. Have a good evening.'

She picked up her bracelet.

The young woman didn't let it go, so that they were each holding the bracelet. She smiled, and her smile was dazzling, and Era suddenly wondered why she'd thought the woman anything but beautiful.

'Perhaps three nights,' the young woman said lazily.

They were very close together, and the girl's breath was scented with something. Mint. Rose water.

Era smiled and tugged lightly at the bracelet.

'Four would be closer to the mark. Or three, with dinners.'

The girl frowned. 'Sing me a song?'

Her eyebrows were dense and rich and a beautiful black-brown.

Era squared her shoulders and threw back her head.

'Hear anew the golden voice!
O hear and listen! Come as in that island dawn thou camest
Billowing in thy yoked chariot to Era,
forth from thy mother's house to play in the waves.
Fleet and fair thy sparrows drew thee, so that
all rejoiced who saw thee, Goddess of Love.'

Throughout her song, Era's eyes never left the young woman's, and she had the good grace to blush.

'I suppose,' the young woman said, 'that I could have you for three nights.'

Era almost shuddered. Had she put an emphasis on *have you*? The silence went on far too long as the two women looked into each other's eyes.

'What's your name?' Era breathed.

'Zaya,' the younger woman said. 'I have a longer name, but my sisters call me Zaya.'

She blinked. She had large eyes, and black eyelashes, and Era

213

was tempted to fall into them, but she had a donkey, a boy, and some sort of god-touched plot, and it was with real regret that she bowed.

'I must go and stable my donkey,' she said.

Zaya smiled again.

Uh-oh, Era thought, already smitten.

She went out to the donkey, and a pair of slaves were taking their leather bags into the room provided, which was off the courtyard behind the screen of red flowers.

Daos was almost bouncing with impatience.

'This isn't the right place...'

Era thought of Zaya.

'It is for me,' she said, joking with herself – mostly – as she followed the slaves into the room.

Different places had different thoughts about men lying with men and women lying with women. In most of the Hundred Cities, it was the norm until marriage, and then strictly forbidden afterwards.

Because women might get ideas, like not having children, Era thought bitterly.

But Ma'rib was not really one of the Hundred Cities, and she'd have to watch her step.

'Mama!' the boy said.

Era blinked and smiled, and tossed her basket on the floor, which was fired brick and well-swept and had thick woven-rush rugs, doubled at the sleeping shelf.

'I have definitely seen worse,' she said.

The boy was looking out of the door.

'We have to go,' he said. 'We need to save them *now*. Bror says so.'

Era pulled her dusty road dress, which was sweaty and had been on her for days, over her head. She pulled off her linen undertunic and washed at the basin, which sat on a nice wooden side table that might have graced a good house.

The boy ran out into the courtyard, embarrassed to see her naked. She smiled, and used a towel to wash, and it felt wonderful.

She got dry, pulled a fresh, pale-yellow tunic over her head, and followed it with an enveloping mantle – a big linen gown with a thousand pleats in the neck and shoulders that gave it shape and made it easy to wear.

You are putting on your best clothes for that girl, she thought, but she didn't care.

She did buckle on her bronze sword, under the pleated gown. With her apron on, it was almost impossible to see. Then she picked up the dead woman's kithara, because a musical instrument was always the best cover.

She went to the door and saw Zaya and another girl coming with water and linens, and she smiled.

Zaya raised her head. 'Oh,' she said.

Again, they looked at each other for a moment too long.

And in that time, Era thought, *where is Daos?*

He wasn't among the flowers and he wasn't with the donkey, who was standing in the courtyard, eating anything that got within range.

She flashed a smile at the girls.

'Have you seen my ... son?' she asked.

Zaya shook her head, dropping her eyes fetchingly, but the other girl said, 'He ran into the street! I saw him, just a minute ago.'

Era cursed, slipped past them, hiked up her gown, and ran.

Behind her, Nannu brayed loudly enough to wake the dead, threw back its strong neck, snapped its lead and followed.

She ignored the donkey and got to the arch that led to the cobbled street. It was already darker; the wisteria, offering shade when the sun was high, now cut off much of the light of the late afternoon. Many shops and houses already had oil lamps lit.

She looked both ways and didn't see him or his bright hair. But she assumed he'd gone back to the square; he'd said something about it being the right place and she hadn't been listening.

There were people coming down the narrow street towards her – a great many of them – and some were panicked. Two women were looking over their shoulders.

There was a burst of shouting and raised voices. A man roared an order, and suddenly everyone was bursting past her. She was thrust into the recess of a doorway, pressed against the god's eye on the door; someone in this house was a government official or a minor priest.

She ducked, hiding her face automatically, because followers of the Huntress were never popular with the authorities.

The donkey shot past her with an incredible bray, headed for the seaside square and scattering the remaining people.

Era had no idea if the Huntress was the goddess of donkeys, but it looked like a sign and she followed it until she heard shouting.

One of the voices sounded like Daos. She ran, legs flashing; she was fast.

She burst into the square, and there was the boy, his white-gold hair marking him out from thirty paces away. He was by the fountain. There was a chariot down by the seaside where the wharves ran out from the sea wall, and a godborn officer in the chariot. He had a dozen soldiers and an armoured driver, and a smaller man, richly dressed in foreign wools, standing behind him.

There were three more soldiers watching the square. She'd heard one of them from the alley, and he was still bellowing in Saabian for everyone to remain calm. She understood that much.

But no one was calm. The richer merchants were having their apprentices pack their goods; some stalls were already empty.

She stopped running, so as not to catch anyone's eye, and began to move towards the fountain. But the boy was moving towards the chariot.

Cursing, she followed. She had the advantage of cover; she went down the lane made by the largest textile stalls, those of Hakran merchants. Several of them looked at her; one gave her a smile of understanding. She'd always meant to visit the Hakrans – with their famed love of baths, they sounded remarkable.

'Don't go over there, lady,' a Hakran woman called to her.

'My son,' she replied, moving a little faster.

Daos walked up to the soldiers and slipped through them. They didn't even stop him.

For a moment, Era considered leaving him.

Nannu brayed. The two chariot horses raised their heads, interested, and the men who were supposed to be holding them stepped back in surprise.

She shook her head. She was perhaps a horse-length from the chariot. It was utterly incongruous on the waterfront, and she couldn't imagine why the godborn officer thought it was a good idea, but then he seemed unsure of himself. He had a big, heavy godborn bow in his hand and was fitting an arrow to it. The smaller man behind him was literally pulling at the hem of his fighting tunic.

'I tell you, he tried to sell me star-stone. He's visited half the smiths in the town.'

The man wore a complex amulet at his neck – gold and lapis – and was clearly a person of consequence.

Star-stone. The words went through her like fire.

The godborn officer turned his head. 'Is this a formal accusation, warlock?'

The man with the amulet looked as if he thought he was deal-ing with a fool, and made the mistake of showing his contempt.

'I have been saying so for half a glass,' he spat.

The godborn officer raised an eyebrow. 'You *told me* that these men were causing a disturbance,' he said. 'Now you tell me it's an issue of the forbidden star-stone.'

Era decided to play it as a mother and trust to the Huntress. She ran, quite deliberately, at the back of the little crowd of soldiers.

'My son! My son!' she called out in Trade Dardanian.

A soldier in a big bronze conical helmet, with a nose-bar that hid his face and made him look menacing, turned and faced her.

'You have no business here,' he said.

'My son!' she called. 'He just pushed past you! You let him through!'

The soldier looked chagrined, even behind the nose-bar.

Era pushed past him.

Now she could see. Down on the wharves, there were half a dozen people, most of them the ruddy red-brown of the far north, where the Dendrownans lived in the great forests.

'My son!' she yelled again, for emphasis.

She started down the slippery stone steps to the wharves.

Daos looked up. He was out on a wharf, standing with an old man in a long wool robe; a godborn aristocrat, tall despite his age and with an arrogant air, gold jewellery and a colourful shawl. He and the Dendrownans were standing beside a small merchant ship, or perhaps a big fishing smack, judging from the smell.

The Dendrownans, smiths of some kind from the tools in their hands, stood in a line across the wharf facing the soldiers, and the situation was obviously very tense.

'There's my mother,' the boy said, in a voice that carried. 'I mean, she's not my mother, but she is now. Bror says—'

The tall old man looked at the godborn officer up above him.

'I was not creating a disturbance,' he insisted.

The officer shook his head, as if weary.

'My informant,' he said with distaste, 'tells me that you deal in forbidden things. Star-stone.'

'Preposterous,' the old man said. 'It's illegal and immoral.' He didn't sound convincing.

'You're a liar,' screamed the richly dressed man at the back of the chariot.

The old man squinted.

'Ah, it's Shafi,' the old man spat. 'Well, we *are* fucked.'

'These are the people,' Daos said. 'We must rescue them and go with them.'

The biggest of the Dendrownans, with arms like a bronze smith's and legs to match, covered in intricate tattoos, motioned at Era without turning his head.

'You'd best take your boy,' he said in a kind voice, accented with a Northern lilt. 'This is about to get ugly.'

Up above them, she heard the creaking sound of the wood and rawhide of the chariot as the godborn shifted his weight. Drawing his great bow, no doubt.

'Lie down and my men will tie your hands, and we'll search your goods.' The godborn's voice still held nothing but boredom.

The old man sighed. Then he thumped his staff on the ground, and smoke began to flow from it like hornets from a disturbed nest.

The godborn officer loosed an arrow. It struck one of the Dendrownans and went through his guts, and the barbs on the arrow did terrible damage. The man fell, screaming.

'Lie down!' the officer called. 'Or I will kill you all.'

'Mama!' the boy yelled, and Era cast.

It was a simple spell. Her little castings, which all had to do with nature and animals, were usually worthless amid violence, but they made few demands on the Great *Aura*, and in this one case, she had real power.

The two chariot horses leapt forwards, scattering the soldiers. Naturally, they turned away from the sea wall and the drop and the water – all things horses might fear – and ran into the market, toppling stalls as they went.

The chariot car slid sideways along the sea wall and the offside wheel slammed into the column at the head of the steps, spilling the driver to fall down the steps. The godborn officer, better on his feet and trained to chariots all his life, got a hand on the car's rail, but missed the reins, which went flying through their loops and fell to the ground. He had to drop his bow to stay in the chariot, and vanished from sight, pulled away from the wharf by the terrified horses.

Up in the market, there were screams of pain – and anger – as the chariot overturned stalls of priceless goods, sending tapestries worth a mina of gold into the dust.

Smoke continued to bellow from the old man's staff. The whole of the wharf was covered in it already, which was odd, with the early evening land breeze coming off the mountain.

'Onto the boat!' the man with the huge arm muscles called. He said it in almost flawless Narmerian, and the old man began to back away, his staff still spitting smoke.

He looked at Era. 'You did that,' he said – almost an accusation.

She shrugged. 'Someone had to.'

The old man nodded. 'You'd better come with us.' He made the sign of the antlers with his hand, and she managed a smile.

'Huntress,' she said.

'Whatever you call her,' said the old man.

'I told her,' the boy said. 'She didn't believe me.'

Era ignored them both and crooned at the donkey. It trotted through the smoke as if this was an everyday event.

'That's ...' The old man looked at the donkey, and then at her, and then crouched. 'Damn,' he said. 'That donkey looks very familiar.'

The donkey turned its head and regarded him with one black eye.

'Come on!' the bronze smith called.

'When you are my age, leaping from docks to boats gets a trifle harder,' the old man said. 'I can't make the jump.'

An arrow whipped through the smoke and through the sail that someone had just cut free.

The bronze smith leapt back onto the dock. He had a big board in his hand, and he dropped it. Immediately, the donkey gave a short bray and trotted down the board and onto the fishing boat, for all the world as if the board was meant for him.

A soldier came out of the smoke, his bronze armour lit by the sunset to look like liquid gold. He saw the old man, and cocked back his spear.

The old man turned at Era's shouts, and parried the spear with a turn of his walking staff. The almost casual parry told her that he was a trained fighter.

The smith, if he was a smith, picked up the gangplank and threw it at the soldier. It was a big, heavy board of oak – or something as solid – and it knocked the man flat. He didn't even twitch when he went down, but lay as if dead.

Era hoisted her overgown and drew her sword from under her skirts as the smith fetched the board and swung it back into place.

The old man hobbled across, and more soldiers emerged from the smoke. All three made the mistake of ignoring Era and going for the smith. The big man caught a spear thrust out of the air and pulled his opponent off balance, tore the spear from his grip, swept the man with a foot-lock and a strong arm across his throat, and stabbed him right through his bronze scales.

The spearhead slammed home with such force that Era heard the terrible sound of the bronze *thunking* into the wooden dock beneath them.

But the spear point stuck there, leaving him open, and the man closest to Era lunged, throwing his weight forwards...

Era hamstrung him. He was ignoring her, half-turned away, and she cut his unprotected right leg from the side even as he realised his mistake and tried to turn. The sword felt good in her hands, and she was tempted to go for the third man. Her victim thrashed, no longer able to walk or rise to his feet, and he screamed.

She ignored him – he no longer presented a threat – and leapt for the boat. The smith kicked the gangplank into the water and leapt, leaving the last man aghast and alone on the pier.

'They'll chase us,' Era said.

'Good luck to them,' the old man said.

He was casting; she could see him at it, and sense his power, which was many times greater than hers.

The smith picked up a long pole with a bronze hook – probably for bringing boats alongside. He hefted it once, and then threw it with incredible force at the man standing on the dock.

'Do they have a harbour chain?' the smith asked, as if he had not just thrown a huge pole ten horse-lengths and killed a man.

The old man shook his head. 'I don't know.'

The smith ran to the bow, making the little ship rock. Era grabbed a stay to keep herself from falling, and looked for Daos, who was sitting with his arms around the donkey's neck.

The old man cast his spell. For a moment, nothing seemed to happen, and then she felt the moisture in the air, and the chill. Thunder rumbled overhead, and the lateen on the mainmast amidships filled with a snap and a crack, and she could hear the long yard taking the strain.

'Isn't the harbour chain of Ma'rib famed the world over?' she asked. 'Two hundred links of pure bronze?'

'Now that you mention it,' he said, and turned.

But either the chain had not been raised, or the huge Dendrownan in the bow had done something, for the inner harbour lighthouse was passing to port and the long arm of the breakwater to starboard, and the sky was filling with clouds. Ahead, the sea was red with the sunset ahead of them, and beyond, the gods' mountain of Auza rose to the south from the coastline of Akash like a ghostly presence.

'It's not easy to launch a warship,' the old man said. He seemed to recollect good manners, and he bowed. 'Lady, I'm Gamash. Sometimes a seer and magos.'

'And sometimes a warrior,' she observed.

He smiled. 'A long, long time ago.'

He was old, and tall. Old men were supposed to be short and withered. This one stooped a little, so he'd once been even taller. He had dirty dark hair streaked with iron grey, a white beard with some black left in his moustache, and huge, out-of-control eyebrows against skin like old, deeply tanned leather.

She dropped a straight-backed curtsey right out of the ancient Narmerian *Book of the Correct Life*.

'Sir. I am Era. I'm a singer – I can tell all the epics back to the *Lament of Lamesh*. I can play any instrument you hand me, dance, compose—'

'And cast subtle spells to woo the hearts of donkeys and chariot horses,' the old man said. 'Or cut a hamstring with delicacy and tempo. And you're modest.'

'Men expect women to be modest,' she said, 'so that they themselves have more time to brag.'

Gamash nodded, his grey-black rag of hair blowing in the wind.

'Too fucking true.'

The big man had taken one steering oar and another of the Dendrownans, a tattooed woman with arm muscles like twined snakes took the other. Both of the Dendrownans seemed completely competent. They turned the boat north of west, into the setting sun which blazed a shining gold road on the surface of the waves. Above them, and between them and the city, sat a storm squall, a black cloud that allowed no light to penetrate, and against which the red rays of the setting sun made an unearthly black-red colour.

'Where are we going?' the big man asked. He didn't have to shout. He was loud all the time.

'Dendrowna!' Gamash shouted into the wind he'd created.

But the boy, who was in the hold with the donkey, looked up.

'No,' he said. 'Make for Noa.'

'Noa?' Gamash asked.

'Bror says Noa,' the boy said. 'We'll never get there. But it's the right path ... then we'll all go to Dendrowna together.' He shrugged. 'Eventually.'

Gamash played with the Great *Aura*; Era could feel it. He was adjusting the wind in the sails. The little boat ran through the evening waves like a racehorse on a flat track, and Era had never moved so fast in her life.

The mast hummed with the strain. She put a hand to it and looked aft at the magos.

'I'm not sure all this is good for a little fishing boat,' she said.

'She's not so little,' Gamash said. 'In my youth, I started with a boat this size.'

'Started what?' she asked.

'Piracy.' Gamash smiled again. 'Listen, a merchanter convoy went up the coast yesterday – mostly Noans and Dardanians. I want to join it. Word in the harbour is that the Jeker fleet is at sea.'

Heaven

The Dark Huntress, Temis, stood in the great Storm God's inner sanctum.

'I warned you,' Enkul-Anu said. 'I told you not to come back.' He sounded more weary than angry.

She shrugged. 'Did you know that Hazor fell to Jekers a month ago?' she asked.

Enkul-Anu sat back. He'd been reading a scroll. It was the most innocuous thing she'd ever seen him do. He looked like someone's grandfather – someone's enormous, scarlet grandfather. Now he rolled the scroll carefully and put it in a fine ivory tube.

'Hazor? As in the great city of the eastern coast?' He looked at her in surprise.

'The very same. Utterly destroyed. By Jekers.' The Black Goddess shrugged. 'I thought you'd want to know.'

Enkul-Anu sighed. 'How did Jekers get so close to a city so powerful?'

'Ask your spy,' the Black Goddess said. 'I'm your enemy. But as you said yourself, the Jekers are everyone's enemy.'

Enkul-Anu narrowed his eyes. 'What's your angle?' he asked her.

'Making sure you don't throw me in the Outer Darkness because you think I'm the one in league with the Jekers,' she said. 'But someone is.'

Enkul-Anu didn't even say 'Fucking idiots.' He just stared at his enormous scarlet feet for a moment. When he raised his head, she was gone.

★

'I told him about Hazor,' the Black Goddess told her ally.

Tyka, the Blue Goddess, nodded.

'And you wanted me to do that,' Temis asked. 'Because?'

They were in a temple in far-off Py, deep in the deserts east of Narmer – the furthermost human outpost in the sea of sand. They were sharing a meal of nuts and honey. The Blue Goddess favoured honey. Unlike the other gods, she never ate ambrosia or drank nectar.

The Black Goddess favoured red meat herself, but none had been offered in sacrifice and she had to make do.

Tyka filled a taloned hand with sand and spread it on her own altar. And then, with her golden claws, she drew a chart in fine lines: Dendrowna; Narmer; the Hundred Cities; Noa, Mykoax and the Dardanian lands; Akash and the south. She sketched with immortal speed and precision. The Huntress could not have matched her. Then she took almonds, still in their shells, and put them in critical places – Vetluna, Mykoax, Noa, Memis, Weshwesh, Dur Sarukin, Ma'rib. A few in the north; a few in the south.

'The world,' the Huntress said.

The Blue Goddess looked at her sister for a long time.

'Fine,' Temis conceded. 'Our world. The world of mortals.'

Tyka nodded. She drew what appeared to be tiny arrows in the fine sand. They were far out on the sea, south of Noa.

'Ships,' the Huntress said. She'd played this game for hundreds of years, and she still wasn't very good at it, because her sister wasn't really very interested in communication.

Silence.

'Many ships.'

Silence.

'Jekers!' she said, and the blue head nodded.

The Blue Goddess split an almond with precision, made a tiny ship of the shell and put it north of the Jekers. Then the golden talon drew a line from the heights of heaven on the great mountain of the south directly into the heart of the Jeker fleet.

Then the blue and gold taloned hands cupped themselves over Narmer, farther north. The fathomless golden eyes met her sister's.

'We direct his gaze on the Jekers and protect Narmer. But why?'

The inscrutable blue face looked at Temis, and she shook her head.

The Huntress pointed at the almond shell ship. 'And the band of mortals we've gathered? What about them, now?'

The golden talons cracked a shell and ate the meat within.

'I don't understand,' the Huntress said.

Tyka cracked another shell. Then she dribbled a tiny bit of honey from one claw into the boat-shell.

Almost as if summoned, a black and yellow wasp came out of the night to settle on the shell.

Faster than thought, the Blue Goddess caught the insect and cracked its carapace, killing it messily.

The Huntress licked her lips.

'Ah,' she said. 'The mortals are the bait.'

Chapter Seven

Pollon

The scribe was awake, staring at the beams over his head in the little airless aft cabin.

The warrior next to him stirred, moved both his arms, and cried out. Pollon put a hand on his shoulder and shook him gently.

'Peace,' he said.

A moment later, the warrior was snoring again.

It was interesting, being confined with a godborn. The man – and he was just a man – seemed so ... normal. Amusing, even. Neither as ignorant as most warriors nor particularly arrogant.

Pollon wondered if the man would still be so amusing when he had recovered. It was obvious now that he would recover; his limbs were straight and the cold had left them, and perhaps most important, his back was somehow no longer broken.

Pollon went back to staring at the beams overhead.

Gods. A Dry One. His raptere's betrayal. The torment of being broken on the wheel for a crime he did not commit, and the insane unlikeliness of his rescue. He thought of Mura and her hidden room, and wondered if she had been wise enough to survive the sack. Was it wisdom, if she had? How would she live now?

All of his life, he'd followed the straight path. He'd obeyed, learnt, practised. Memorised the hundreds of glyphs and wards and hieroglyphs and scribal signs; learnt to use them in ways both prosaic and magical. It gave order to the mind, and with that order, writers were taught, they could bring order to the world.

The last fifteen days suggested that there was no order to the world whatsoever.

He could never go back to Hekka. And indeed, there was no Hekka to which he might return.

Am I now a rebel? he asked himself in the marches of night. *Or am I yet a servant of Nisroch?*

In the morning, he went on deck and offered to do any work that needed doing. Aanat put him to sweeping the deck and tidying the aft hold with Mokshi, who sometimes appeared to be in charge and other times not. But he was easy to work for, polite, attentive to his fading injuries.

'Your hair is coming in,' he said.

Pollon rubbed his scalp and laughed. The laugh was bitter, but Mokshi had no way of knowing that.

'Hot stones are few and far between, here,' he said.

He had his first sight of the Dry One in the forward hold, and his stomach rolled, and he lost his breakfast over the side.

A startlingly beautiful young woman smiled at him from the helm.

'I know,' she said. 'I feel the same way – a pain in the gut every time I see it.'

'That's Miti,' Jawala said from the other steering oar. 'Our newest wife.'

'She's a beauty,' Pollon said.

Jawala raised an eyebrow. 'She's competent enough, anyway.' Her voice was mild, but Pollon got the notion that physical beauty wasn't as important to the Hakrans as it was in the Hundred Cities. He kept sweeping.

By midday he was pleasantly tired, and Atosa came on deck and took the broom from him and went to work in the aft hold with Mokshi, shifting cargo. The two holds connected under the deck, and Pollon watched as Mokshi and Bravah, coached by Aanat, moved cargo around to make a passage into the forward hold. They were apparently trying to get at a tier of water amphorae and were terrified, as anyone would be, of disturbing the monster walled up in the forward hold.

But they were successful, and big, heavy water amphorae were handed back and restacked, ready to hand in the aft hold. Pollon threw himself into it and worked until he was very tired, and then sat back as they repacked bales of cotton and wool fabric, contemplating the routine heroism of life at sea.

Evening came. Mokshi made dinner with the last of the fresh vegetables, and they all squatted or sat on the little afterdeck above the cabin. Zos even managed to hobble out onto the deck and was helped up to join them.

It was Miti's turn to say the evening prayer, and she put a scarf on – a sacral knot of beautiful fine wool, almost transparent, dyed a dark red like blood. She raised her arms and gave the prayer to Evening, and then the Hakrans sang a hymn to life and peace.

Zos rolled forwards, too clumsy yet to kneel, but he could take a wooden spoon and he fed himself for the first time, which was messy but oddly cheering.

Pollon was staring at his bowl.

'You miss the God's Prayer?' Zos asked with surprising courtesy.

Pollon made a face. 'Do I? I cannot decide.'

Zos lay back, his face worn with pain. But he flashed a smile.

'I'm not prepared to join the Hakrans,' he said quietly. 'But their prayers make a good deal more sense than ours, brother.'

One of the godborn just called me 'brother'.

The sun was setting gloriously in the west, and Pollon knew enough about navigation to know that they were sailing almost due south. Off to the west and south there was an island, a big one; Pollon could see the mountains. He pointed at it with his bowl.

Aanat, the senior of the family, nodded.

'Salamis,' he said. 'The northern tip of Akash. We're making good time.'

'In the last watch we'll turn due east and then look for the sea marks for Ma'rib tomorrow night,' Jawala said.

Pollon was used to thinking of Akash as immeasurably far away, and somewhat fantastical – the vast city of Dur Sarukin high on the central mountains, and the mythical home of the gods, Auza, towering above, the highest mountain in the world.

The gods. I guess I'm no longer their devotee.

'Where are we headed?' he asked.

Jawala glanced at Aanat. 'Ma'rib,' she said without tone.

Aanat nodded. 'We can trade at Ma'rib,' he said agreeably.

'Harusa and the rest of Akash are closed to Hakran traders,' Jawala said.

Zos scooped up more cabbage soup and beans.

'This is delicious,' he said with a nod to Mokshi. He glanced at Jawala, and then at Aanat. 'Why is Akash closed to you?'

Aanat made a little motion with his hand, as if holding a balance.

'Their customs officials claimed that some Hakran traders cheated them during Great Market last year,' he said. 'A whole family lineage was seized. We'll only trade with them when the family is released.'

'And if the family is killed?' Zos asked.

Jawala raised an eyebrow. 'Then they won't receive any tin from Vetluna for a long, long time.'

'Or cotton cloth, or northern wood, or Mykoan wool...' Aanat said.

Zos smiled, as if tolerating them. 'Oh, the Mykoans are with you?'

Aanat answered in the same bantering tone. 'The Akashans executed a dozen Mykoan traders and seized all their goods. One of them was a *basilios*.'

Zos winced. 'I'm surprised the war fleets haven't sailed.' He looked at Jawala. 'Why were they so stupid?'

'You are Mykoan?' Pollon asked.

Zos made a face. 'Mmm,' he said. 'Mykoax isn't the only city in Dardania. My father was the god-king in Trin.'

Everyone looked blank.

Pollon saw Zos make an effort. The man was hard to read; he used humour as armour, but in this case, something had stung him.

'Well...' he said in a Dardanian drawl. 'It's a small place. And Mykoax conquered us.'

Aanat looked down, and then at Jawala.

'Your father supported the Hakran traders?' he said cautiously.

Zos laughed without mirth. 'So he did,' he said.

Pollon looked at the godborn man. 'Trin supported the Hakrans—'

Aanat leant forwards. 'It is shameful that Jawala and I didn't remember the name. Some years ago—'

'Thirty-one,' Zos said.

'Thirty-one years ago, Mykoax and Sala, the two greatest states of Dardania—'

'Debatable,' Zos said.

Aanat smiled. 'The two most militarily powerful states—'

'Fair,' Zos agreed.

'...made a pact, and attacked Hakran traders. They launched a sea raid against us.' Aanat shrugged. 'A lot of us died. More were taken as slaves... and then died.'

Zos was looking out at the sunset.

'One of the Mykoan cities stood with us – even supported us militarily. I had... forgotten.' Aanat leant forwards and put his hand on Zos' hand. 'I am ashamed. I apologise.'

Jawala put her hand on Zos' other hand. 'I'm sorry. I had no idea...'

Zos smiled. 'You know,' he said, 'we call ourselves Dardanians. Not Mykoans.' He shrugged. 'I bear you no grudge. In fact, I am fairly certain that I owe you my life.' He leant back, as if the exchange had fatigued him, which Pollon thought was all too likely. 'At any rate, you're saying that Akash has put their foot in it and you're not trading there.'

He looked back at Jawala, and Pollon thought that some peace had just been made between them. Pollon looked at Zos, and then at Aanat.

'I remember... I mean, I was just born. But there was a mighty war fleet from the Hundred Cities. It sailed for Rasna.' He set his mind to recall the details. 'One of the Weshian war mages led the fleet to help the Hakrans.'

Aanat frowned. 'Gamash?'

Pollon nodded in appreciation. 'Gamash of Weshwesh.'

Zos smiled. It wasn't a nice smile.

'Too late to save my father and mother,' he said. 'But in time to save the Hakrans.'

Jawala looked at him, angry again. 'We did nothing to summon them.'

'You Hakrans won't make war,' Zos drawled. 'But you weren't above arranging for the ruler of Mykoax to lead his fleet into a trap.' He shrugged. 'I was too young to be a warrior, but I remember the god-king of Mykoax coming home, his fleet shattered.

His wife, the high priestess, murdered him for failing. His son took the throne...'

Aanat made that motion with his hands again, as if he was holding a balance.

'I believe it was merely fortune,' he said. 'I do not believe that our council would act in such a way as to cause deliberate harm.'

Zos rocked a little, as if nodding, and then settled back against the helm bench.

'Sure,' he said, in a way that indicated that he didn't believe Aanat at all.

Later, lying on their sleeping mats, Pollon heard Zos roll over, and he said, 'Are you awake?'

Pollon smiled. 'Mostly.'

Zos stirred. 'The thing is...' He hesitated. 'So... this makes no sense, unless I tell you that I was a child hostage at the court of Mykoax.'

'How...?'

'Long story – and the only reason I'm alive. But after the ambush at Vetluna, most of us knew that their ruler claimed he'd been told to make the attack by the gods themselves.' Zos wriggled. 'By the great god Enkul-Anu, in fact.'

Pollon sighed. 'Over the last three weeks, I've all but given up trying to understand it all.'

Zos grunted. 'You were a servant of Nisroch?'

'Yes,' Pollon said.

'Access to all the god's eyes, and all the reporting?'

Pollon shivered uncomfortably.

'If you two are going to talk, you can go on deck,' Miti said from her blankets.

Zos snorted but said nothing.

Pollon thought, *This from a woman who makes love twice a night.*

But he rolled over and eventually went to sleep.

234

Pollon woke early, almost with the sun. He'd seldom felt so good in all his life, and he cast off the borrowed cloaks that were his blankets and rolled up the sleeping mat without disturbing Atosa, who was snoring, or Zos, who lay on his side and muttered unintelligibly from time to time.

Two people were making love on the other side of the small cabin. There was very little privacy anywhere in the Hundred Cities, so Pollon did the polite thing and slipped out without a glance in their direction. He didn't even know who they were.

The deck was cold – surprising for the middle of the southern seas. It was dark, and stars twinkled in all directions, magnificent sheets of stars so bright they took his steaming breath away.

Pavi was at the helm.

'You could take the other oar, if you had a mind,' she said.

'I wouldn't know what to do,' Pollon said.

'I'll teach ya,' Pavi said, with a smile that flashed her teeth in the moonlit darkness.

He looked up again. Ara, the red planet, burned as if it was only a few hand's breadths above his head, and Kul, the Dark Moon, was in the Gate. Directly overhead, the Gift sailed through the heavens, the ring of emerald stars incredibly bright, so that the deck was very faintly tinged with green. Kul in the Gate – not good, at least for him.

He could imagine a seer saying, '*Take no risks, and whatever you do, don't take a sea voyage.*'

Pollon smiled.

I am no longer a Court Scribe.

He took the big steering oar where it was lashed to the hull, and released it under the direction of Pavi. He let it slowly into the water, afraid . . . afraid to do the wrong thing.

'Feel it bite?' she asked.

He did.

The oar had a long, bent handle, beautifully crafted, so that he could hold it steady against the thole pins with the weight of his body and have his hands free. In the time it took for the Sisters to transit the sky, from the Dark Moon to the Red Planet, he could keep the ship on something like a steady course.

Pavi nodded. 'You've got her,' he said. 'Mokshi is making love with Miti and I don't want to call him away.' She raised her oar.

Pollon fought down panic. 'You're leaving me to steer?'

Pavi nodded and slapped his back, as if they were both godborn warriors.

'Yep,' she said in the easy lingo of Trade Dardanian, and skipped away into the darkness of the holds.

Pollon controlled his panic and leant on his oar as if his life depended on it, which perhaps it did. He tried to imagine the family system of these people, and the lack of jealousy...

In a few moments, he saw Pavi climbing the mainmast, her legs locked around it. She climbed so quickly he couldn't really believe he was watching a human woman. She *swarmed* up the mast.

The sky in the east was pink, and they were headed almost due east. They must have changed course in the night, as Jawala had said.

'How are you doing down there?' Pavi shouted down.

'Fine,' he said, hoping that he didn't sound as tense as he felt. There was enough light now to see the sea and the wake they left in the unhurried ocean; he could see that when he turned his head to look up at Pavi, he left a little nick in his wake. And it looked to him as if he was steering a long curve.

He put a little more pressure on the oar.

Sure enough, the ship responded, now truly straight.

'Shit!' Pavi called.

Somewhere to the east, there was a bright flash, like summer lightning, that lit the whole sky for a moment.

236

'There's…' Pavi hesitated for a long time. 'There's…'

Another flash, this one clear from horizon to horizon.

'What in all the hells is that?' Pollon asked the sky. It was much lighter now.

He was trying to look forward for the flashes and keep the ship on course, and so he was perfectly placed to see a long, black talon pierce the great tent of superfine silk at the other end of the ship. The talon came through and then slit the top of the tent like a sharp bronze knife.

Pollon felt his abdominal muscles clench. He'd once seen *irkallu*, the evil dead, rising from the sand, and they had looked like this.

The Dry One's head popped through the slit web.

'Pavi!' Pollon called. His voice sounded appallingly normal.

'I think it's Jekers,' she called down.

'Pavi!' Pollon grabbed the wooden spoon that sat by the helm. 'I'm going to sound the alarm!'

'Sound the alarm!' Pavi shouted. Or was she asking?

Pollon slammed the wooden spoon into the ship's precious bronze bell with more force than he'd intended. At the same time he let the ship slip off to starboard several points, then leant too hard against the oar, and only then began a regular beat of the spoon against the bell.

Mokshi was the first on deck. He emerged from the cabin, looked forward, saw the Dry One, and leapt onto the aft deck anyway.

'Where's Pavi?' he asked.

'Masthead,' Pollon said, trying *not* to watch the Dry One.

'Jekers?' Mokshi asked.

Behind him, Jawala came up the ladder, looked east, and then took the starboard steering oar.

'You had the ship?' she asked, evenly.

'Pavi said…'

She smiled. 'You did well. Give the oar to Mokshi.'

The Dry One appeared at the mast, having clambered out of its cocoon and the forward hold. The taloned hand came up and pointed almost due east, into the rising sun.

Jawala looked stunned.

Aanat emerged, naked. In what Pollon saw as an act of incredible courage, the small man went forwards and stood within easy range of the Dry One's long arms.

'Welcome back,' he said.

The Dry One lifted a long arm again, and pointed east.

'You want us to go east,' he said.

Another flash, this one an azure that clashed with the pink of dawn. The light on the sail was blinding for half a heartbeat.

Zos appeared. 'Oh, fuck,' he muttered, when he saw the Dry One. But he was on his feet, and he was moving.

Pollon had no idea what to do.

'It wants us to go east, towards whatever is happening,' Aanat said.

Zos fingered his new beard. 'It's taken on all comers so far,' he said. 'I'd hate to see it angry at us.'

'They can't all be this powerful,' Pollon said to Zos.

Zos shrugged. 'How the fuck would we know? Is there a sword on this boat?'

'You can't fight,' Pollon said.

Zos looked aft, at Jawala, and forward, at the Dry One.

'I might just want the power to not be a slave,' he said.

Jawala nodded approval. 'We have knives for just this purpose,' she said. 'Have Miti hand them out.'

Aanat looked at his wife with eyes full of sorrow.

'I brought us to this.'

The Dry One's wings flapped. Pollon could smell something exotic. Like ... myrrh. But richer.

'Fine.' Jawala looked at Mokshi, and at a word of command they turned the ship a few points, more north of due east.

There was another flash, and something on the horizon was on fire, and the smoke was rising into the new sun.

Aanat took the oar from Mokshi and sent him aft, as Pollon took a short, very sharp bronze knife from Miti. It didn't have a scabbard.

'You just keep it in your hand,' she said, a little unsteady. 'And use it when you need to.'

Pollon looked at Zos. 'Is suicide our only option?'

Zos shrugged. 'Honestly? As long as the bug is on our side I'm not so worried about Jekers, but ...' He waved one arm. 'I'm not much for fighting right now, as you noted, and Jekers are mean mother-eaters.'

There were now six ships on the horizon. All six appeared to be sailing, broad reaching, on the same wind that they were using, and in the opposite direction, so that they had quite a closing speed.

On closer examination, Pollon thought one of the ships was damaged and on fire and falling rapidly behind.

'Sail's going to catch,' muttered Zos with professional interest. 'Yep.'

The whole damaged ship seemed to catch fire all at once.

Two of the other ships were trying to close on the third from either side. They were obviously Jeker longships – black pitched hulls and rusty brown sails that some said were dyed in blood, with their characteristic notch.

The other two were harder to identify. They looked like two more Jekers ...

Zos grabbed a stay and leant out.

'Dardanian. He's fighting one of the Jekers. Look, the Jeker ship has the notched sail. The Dardanian—'

'I see it,' Pollon said.

Now that he looked, the Dardanian was different in a dozen ways; her bow was almost blunt, at right angles to the waves; she was longer and lower, and carried her sail high on her tall mast.

'You cannot mean to fight,' Jawala said to Aanat, behind them.

'I am obeying the dictates of my passenger,' Aanat said.

'You must be aware that it intends to cause harm...'

Aanat turned his head and his tone changed.

'Jekers are *less than beasts*. But perhaps our monster can save some people... perhaps they are *our people*.'

Jawala shook her mane of dark hair.

'I know all of these arguments,' she said. 'We should stop acting for our *passenger* right now and refuse to participate.'

Miti said, 'I agree!'

Mokshi looked at Aanat.

Pavi, at the masthead, called 'Agree!'

Bravah, in the forward hold, called 'Agree!'

Jawala stepped away from her steering oar. The ship immediately swayed off course.

Zos, with more agility than any of them might have imagined, crossed the aft deck in two long strides and took the oar.

Jawala glared at him with a look of anger, or worse.

Zos smiled. 'It's too late to run,' he said. 'It's too late to pretend you aren't involved. But it's never too late to capsize.'

Pollon thought *Ahh, there's the arrogance.*

'We voted!' Bravah called.

Aanat was still at his oar, and the *Untroubled Swan* was still racing down the wind. In fact, Pollon noted that the wind was now more astern than abeam, and freshening, and he felt the power in it; Aanat had cast a spell.

The monster moved into the shrouds and forestay of the bow, clinging with dagger-like feet and fluttering its wings. A fine spray was coming off the bow as the ship lifted into the swell and came down.

'Don't do this,' Jawala said.

'It's already done,' Aanat said. 'I'm sorry, my love, but we're already committed.'

Ahead, two or three stadia away, a Jeker ship made a run at the smallest of the three – more like a big fishing boat than a merchant. Spears flew, and perhaps an arrow or two. Aboard the Jeker ship, the wet oars flashed in the brilliant sunlight. The ship was long and low, black with pitch, more like an oversized harbour boat than a true ship. A man was impaled on the bow, alive, screaming his despair.

But just before it could crash alongside there was a flash, and the whole Jeker ship seemed to *bounce*, and skid across the surface of the water.

It tried to turn away, and the Dardanian slammed into it, bow-on. It had been hidden for a moment by the fishing boat and the Jekers had been focused on their prey.

The Jeker ship broke in half, the two ends rising either side of the onrushing Dardanian. The northern ship had her oars out now and the sail already down – a fabulous piece of seamanship.

The Dry One leapt into the air and was gone. Pollon thought he could see it at the apex of its incredible, impossible leap.

And then one of the Jeker ships turned and made for them.

'Well, well,' said Zos.

Aanat's face was pale – almost grey – with anguish.

'We're going to turn to port on my command.' Aanat didn't sound calm. He sounded terrible. 'I'll need the sail dropped the moment I give the order.' Whatever he was feeling, his voice was steady.

He didn't look at Jawala or at Pavi, who was up on the masthead.

Zos did, and Pollon looked, too. Pollon looked out over the starboard side. The rammed Jeker was *gone*. The Dardanian was turning...

'Hard to port!' Aanat called, as the Jeker ship closed. It, too, was low in the water. This close, Zos could see the slaves rowing under the lash, and smell the carrion smell that Jekers wore like a perfume.

It was perhaps ten spear-lengths away when Aanat gave the order.

Pavi leant out and used her suicide knife to cut the lashings on the big square sail, dropping the main yard into the crutches waiting to hold them. Suddenly there was canvas everywhere, but the design kept the sail off the deck and out of the crew's way. Pavi immediately began to re-thread a line to raise it again.

Zos and Aanat leant *hard* on their oars.

The small merchant pivoted almost as nimbly as an alley cat taking a rat, and the Jeker ship shot past their stern, rowers pulling flat out, small bow-sail full of wind. Pollon saw that Aanat had done something remarkable, tossing his mage-wind into the *other* ship's sails so that it gained speed and went by all the faster. The crew was taken aback; Pollon saw one bloody-mouthed, red-bearded brute throw a heavy spear, and it came aboard with a *thunk*, but the rest of their volley fell into the sea. So many boarders were packed along the side that they caused their ship to list. The ship passed harmlessly, four spear-lengths astern.

'Take the steering oar,' Zos said to Pollon.

'I'm ...' He was on the verge of declining, but that made no sense, and he took the oar.

The big man stepped forwards, grasped the heavy spear carefully, and began to rock it carefully along the axis of its cutting head until it popped free of the planking.

'That's more like it,' he said.

Jawala was a few feet away, helping Bravah to raise the main yard again. She looked at Zos very seriously.

'If you kill a single man, I will drop this sail,' she said.

Zos

Zos paused for a moment.

Not the time to fight her, or the place.

With a curt nod, he stowed the spear in the rack of boat-poles.

Jawala nodded, too, and Pavi began to haul on her line.

'I could use some help here,' she said, and Zos joined her, feeling like a tired old man.

The sail went up. The *Untroubled Swan* had never lost steerage way, and now she was moving like a gazelle. A fat gazelle.

To the south, the second Jeker ship was on fire, and drifting. To the east, the Dardanian was running parallel to the *Untroubled Swan*, slowly falling behind because she was under oars. Zos' full attention was on the ship to the east, but Pavi was looking south. She began to climb the mast again.

'Are all Dardanian merchants so good at fighting?' Pollon asked.

Zos was leaning heavily on the rail. He raised his head.

'Yes,' he said. 'When trade is bad, piracy is always an option.'

Pavi made a choking sound from high above. 'Shit,' she said clearly. 'Oh, Mother.'

Zos looked up. 'What do you see?'

Pavi leant down. 'The horizon to the south is...' She shook her head. 'The Jeker fleet is right there. I can see a hundred masts. Mother of Earth. A thousand.'

Zos could climb a mast. Or, at least, he'd been able to before his back was broken by a god. He put his hands on it, broad as the trunk of a tree, and jumped as high as he could.

Almost everything hurt as he began to swarm up. His arms felt weak, and his legs shook...

I used to be quite good at this.

He refused to give up. He looked up, to gauge the distance,

and made another hand's breadth, and another, and another. He wasn't a bit ashamed when Pavi reached an iron-hard hand down and gave him a boost to the masthead. The leather bucket was too small for two adults, and above it a veritable tent of stays that held the mast in place forced both of them into a crouch, their legs nested together. The mast bent under their combined weight.

Zos had to breathe for a little while.

'I'm out of shape,' he said.

'You were *almost* dead,' Pavi replied.

Zos looked past her to the horizon, and what little breath he had was sucked out of him. South and east, the horizon was *filled* with masts and sails, the notches in the mainsails clear as they came up over the rim of the world; a few sails were black, but most were the dirty brown of old blood.

'Demons of Kul,' he muttered. 'I didn't know there were that many Jekers in the world.'

'Tell Aanat we have to run,' Pavi said.

Zos was still watching. 'They're not going east,' he said. 'They're sailing north.'

Pavi looked for a long time.

'Yes,' she agreed. 'North. A little west of north.'

Zos looked around.

'Do you know how to slide down a stay?' Pavi asked.

Zos raised an eyebrow. 'I've heard it can be done,' he said, and jumped recklessly for the backstay that ran to the *Untroubled Swan*'s tail at the stern.

His arms just held him to the deck, and his hands burned against the untarred rope that the Hakrans used, but he landed on the deck with a semblance of grace.

The Dry One was perched in the rigging of the big fishing boat. Even as Pollon watched, someone very large on the deck of the third Jeker threw a spear at it.

It leapt.

Zos took the steering oar back, watching the Dry One fly through the air towards them.

'Coming back aboard,' he said.

Aanat looked over. 'I'm about to make another turn to port,' he said. 'With a little luck and some wind manipulation, I can bring us alongside the big fishing boat.'

'The whole fucking Jeker nation is just south of us on the horizon. While we dick about, they're coming up on us hand over fist.'

The Jeker behind them was a stadion away now, the sail burning, and it was slowing, and the stiff breeze was turning it broadside to the wind.

'They're done,' Zos said. Then, louder, 'Aanat. Did you hear me?'

Aanat didn't turn his head. 'One crisis at a time.'

He flashed Zos a smile, and he recognised a kindred spirit, for all that the man was dead set against violence.

The Dry One landed. Somehow, Zos had assumed that they were as light as insects, but the Dry One *just* made the ship, and the whole bow dipped, and water crashed over the foredeck, drenching Bravah ... and the Dry One, too.

'Uh-oh,' Zos said.

A third Jeker was already well to the west, but turning north to give chase.

This time, before they turned, Aanat filled their sail and held the wind through the turn, so that, as the fishing boat passed them, they fell in, at first behind, and then gradually gaining.

In the stern of the fishing boat, they could see a tall child jumping up and down and waving.

There was a dead man amidships, a big spear through his guts, and a wounded woman sitting with her back to the mast. A huge man, almost the size of a god, stood at the tiller, and a

245

ragged elder like a vagabond stood with a slim woman by the low rail.

Zos watched them for several hundred beats of his heart, and decided that the low rail was low because the fishing boat was sinking.

Aanat glanced at Zos, and then forwards at Jawala.

'This will be close,' he admitted.

But Jawala smiled. 'I was wrong,' she said. 'This is a correct action.'

Aanat's whole face lit up. There was so much emotion there that Zos had to look away.

Zos grunted. 'Let's get this done.'

Aanat looked over at him. 'We're going to lay alongside. Zos, I assume you can use a boat-pole? Hook them on. Jawala, take the other steering oar. Pollon, I need you to talk them aboard. Make sure they understand that the Dry One is our ... friend.'

Crisp. Decisive. Zos almost smiled.

Who knew that pacifist heretics were so good in a crisis?

Pollon responded as he might have to the raptere, with a short bow, and went to the side. Zos handed the steering oar to Jawala; something passed between them.

They made a fine adjustment and began to overtake the smaller boat.

Pollon

Ahead, to the west, the Jeker had dropped its sail and completed its turn. They might be animalistic brutes, but they were good seamen. Off to the east, the Dardanian was well behind now, under oars.

Forward, the Dry One was lying atop the wreck of its cocoon, its wings spread, pulsing feebly. Bravah was trying to avoid it.

'What do I do?' he called.

'Nothing.' Zos looked at Pollon.

Pollon was trying to think of what to say to the other boat. He looked forward.

'It needs to dry off,' he said. 'That's a guess, not a fact.'

Zos nodded. He had a long boathook in his hand.

'They're going to have almost no time to get aboard,' he said. 'I'm not really strong enough for this.'

Bravah came and joined him. He fetched another boathook. Atosa, who had stood by throughout the action, grabbed another boathook and stepped up to the rail.

'Three are better than one,' he said.

They glided closer.

'Come aboard!' Pollon shouted. 'Your boat is sinking!'

'Really?' shouted the slim woman, with what sounded like derision.

'Steady,' muttered Zos.

The helms shifted a fraction, and the *Untroubled Swan* swung in to touch the side of the fishing boat. The moment they did, the huge man at the tiller picked up a pole and ran forward, leaving the tiller.

A donkey brayed.

'We can't take a donkey!' Bravah yelled.

Atosa got his hook into the other boat's shrouds and pulled hard; Zos got the boat's side, and Pollon caught a stay, and the three of them pulled as hard as they could to bring the two ships together.

A boy leapt aboard as the two ships went broadside to broadside, and the donkey got its forefeet on the higher deck and sprang over the bulwarks with surprising agility. Another long-limbed man scrambled aboard, as graceless as the donkey.

In perfect contrast, the thin woman picked up the wounded woman and leapt, balanced despite her heavy load, onto the bulwark's top edge, and then jumped down into the aft deck, making the *Untroubled Swan* rock as her bow bit into a wave.

Zos knew the thin woman immediately from the land of dreams, where he'd driven her in a chariot. He stood, stunned, on the deck. But he didn't relinquish his hold on the boathook.

'I have to turn!' Aanat called.

The Jeker ship was coming at them like a sea monster now, oars out either side, boat sail flapping.

Zos and Bravah had the other boat; they'd both hooked into the stays that held the fishing boat's mast amidships, but Zos was clearly losing the battle to keep the two together.

The old man got his arms over the bulwark, and then the huge man jumped, and his jump drove the two ships apart, so that the old man was hanging on by his arms.

Pollon grabbed the only thing he could reach – the man's head. Then, because he'd done a little wrestling, he got his strong right arm under the other man's arm, tangled in his cloak, and managed to get his hands clasped behind the old man's back, like a wrestling hold.

Aanat turned. It was another hard turn; somehow he was holding on to his wind spell, and the *Untroubled Swan* went so far over to starboard that for a dizzying second the old man was almost horizontal on the hull. He used that moment to his advantage, swarming over the bulwark even as Pollon hauled him aboard and stumbled back as the deck seemed to drop out from under him.

The Jeker ship unleashed another volley of spears and javelins.

The *Untroubled Swan* slammed down on her keel, righting herself at the end of her turn and splattering spray over the port side.

The Jeker ship, intending to ram, instead passed down the starboard side, fouled the sinking fishing boat, and came to a near stop with a horrid *snap* as her mainmast broke off a man's height above the deck. The fishing boat was caught under the bow of the onrushing Jeker, and was pushed steadily down into the water until she sank.

The Dardanian swept by, and arrows flew as she raked the Jeker's deck. But she didn't ram. Pollon thought her captain wise; ramming would cost time, and if the Dardanian's lookouts had seen the Jekers downwind, they'd know that time was something they did not have.

Pollon turned back to find Bravah lying on the deck with a throwing spear in his side, and Miti crouched by him. She was also bleeding. The last volley had taken its toll; there were a dozen throwing spears lodged in the deck, an arrow was buried in the mainmast, and the slim, long-limbed man was bleeding out on the deck. A heavy spear had struck his throat and almost severed his head.

On the command deck of the Jeker, a red-cloaked figure seized a boy and cut his throat. The men around him raised their arms in prayer. Pollon caught this terrible scene in a flash as the ships passed, and felt the burst of dark power in the *Aura*.

He did what he could to parry the attack, but then the old man in his arms stiffened and a brilliant blue-white flash lit the ship.

Pollon lowered the old man to the deck. The donkey jumped fastidiously down into the aft hold where the bales of cotton cloth were. The boy looked at him, then turned to his mother, who was herself putting the badly injured woman on the deck.

'These are the people,' the boy said. 'Bror says so.'

Pollon noted that the boy was clutching a soaking wet toy bear.

The huge man had a weapon – a sword – and he was looking at the Dry One, still lying, twitching feebly, on the ruins of its cocoon.

'Leave him alone,' Pollon said.

'He attacked our ship,' the huge man said.

'No, he didn't,' the old man said. 'He landed on us and attacked the Jekers.'

The huge man shook his head. 'Fuck,' he said. 'I got that all wrong.'

Pollon was looking at Bravah, who was badly wounded, at Miti, who had a deep gash on her left arm and had lost far too much blood, and at the woman who'd been carried aboard.

He looked at Zos, who had sagged against the side of the ship. The warrior was almost as grey as Aanat had been – exhausted, probably.

But godborn warriors were often quick at healing.

'Zos,' Pollon said.

'On it,' the warrior said.

He moved as if his sinews had been cut, but he got to the bleeding pair.

Astern, the Jeker ship was trying to get underway under oars while they fished their mast out of the sea. The mast had carried the sail with it, which was acting like some huge jellyfish of canvas.

Pavi slid down a stay to the deck, and opened a wooden box set into the step where the low aft cabin met the main deck.

'Bandages!' she shouted. 'Clean linen! Honey!'

Zos started issuing orders. He did it well; his words were clear, and his tone brooked no argument. He dismissed Bravah as effectively dead; Pollon saw his minute head-shake. Then he put a thumb on Miti's arm, finding the pressure point and stopping the bleeding.

'Keep the pressure right here,' Zos said to Pollon, with a flash of a tired smile. 'Don't let go. Pavi, do you know how to wrap it?'

'Yes,' the middle-aged woman said. 'And how to use a spoon on the pressure point.'

'Perfect,' Zos said, and his whole attention moved on to the injured woman who'd been carried aboard. She had a deep slash in her right forearm, right to the bone.

'Huh.' Zos looked forward at the fluttering of the Dry One's wings. He looked up at Mokshi. 'You know how to make a tourniquet?'

'I do,' Mokshi admitted.

'Tourniquet that ... right there,' he said, and turned away.

'Where are you going?' Miti asked. 'Bravah needs ...'

Zos tottered forwards, ignoring her, and climbed out onto the tent of spider silk.

Pollon tried to watch him and hold Miti's arm at the same time. The tent-stuff apparently wasn't sticky; Zos moved clumsily, but he moved.

'Get me a towel,' he said. 'Something absorbent.'

'Cotton,' Pavi said.

'I know what cotton is,' the thin woman said.

'Aft hold,' Pavi said.

The thin woman jumped down, passing the donkey, and was back with a shawl worth a silver talent. Two shawls.

'Toss them to me,' Zos called. He was all the way out on the tent now, kneeling by the prone Dry One, whose wings brushed him every time they fluttered.

'Almost there,' Pavi said by Pollon's side, and she smiled at him.

Zos caught the fluttering shawls. Pollon had guessed what he intended, but it was incredible to watch him do it.

He was drying the Dry One.

He was meticulous, and the process wasn't fast. At this close range, Pollon could see that the Dry One's body was covered with tiny spines, and the shawls caught them whenever he dried against their grain.

Zos lifted one of the legs and began to dry it. The strain was

251

telling on him; Pollon knew the man well enough to see that he was losing a battle with the leg.

Then the huge man was beside him – so huge that he made Zos, a big, dangerous man himself, look almost like an adolescent next to a hardened warrior. The huge man was Dendrownan, almost certainly: red-gold skin, and a curious topknot of hair with a long bone spike through it, and he was more muscular than anyone Pollon had ever seen and covered in tattoos. He lifted the leg carefully, almost delicately, and Zos continued drying.

The thin woman looked at Pollon.

'Why?' she asked.

He was still holding the pressure point and his thumb was growing numb.

'Some of us were terribly injured,' he said. 'The Dry One saved us. It has … amazing … powers.'

'And it doesn't seem to like being wet,' Jawala called from the helm.

'Done,' Pavi said, slipping a wooden spoon under Pollon's thumb. 'You can let go.'

He made himself go forward. Partly it was that he'd already come to like Zos, and partly that he loved to learn things. He'd never have this chance to be so close to a Dry One.

He took the second shawl.

Its skin was hard but yielding, like very good, very well-tanned leather. Not like insect chiton at all. The spines were very small, and he suspected very dangerous, and he said so.

He worked on the other leg. The huge man was supporting both.

'I'm Pollon,' he said.

'Hefa-Asus,' the Dendrownan said. He was holding the not inconsiderable weight of a Dry One over his head without apparent effort.

Zos, on the other hand, was almost unable to raise his arms, and was not helped by the long burn marks where the wet dust from the Dry One's wings had smeared down his chest. Whatever it was, it was potent and terrible. Atosa took the cotton shawl from him and continued his work.

Pollon considered what he knew about butterflies.

'Let's try standing him up in the wind,' he said – which was when he saw the bronze arrowhead lodged in the Dry One's thorax. A blue fluid was leaking out around the penetration and crystallising. It smelt...

It smelt like resin. Frankincense and myrrh and cinnamon together.

'That's not good,' Pollon said.

Zos gave a grey-faced nod.

Hefa-Asus lifted, hard, his arms around the big monster's waist. He placed it so that it was looking into the wind over the bow and its wings got the full force of it, stuttering as if they were independently alive.

Pollon was suddenly pushed away; a taloned hand was against his chest, the needle-like talons just pricking his skin.

'I'm backing away,' Hefa-Asus said.

Zos was behind it, trapped between its body and its wings, and he let out a choked scream as a damp wing touched him.

The monster moved with its usual rapidity. In a flash, it was grasping the windward sidestays of the mast. Zos was rolling on the remnants of its cocoon in pain.

A bright blue spurt of something – blood, Pollon assumed – spurted from the wound. Where it touched the wood of the deck, it hardened very quickly. Hefa-Asus bent over it, eyes brimful of curiosity. The Dry One seemed unconcerned, and its jewelled eyes turned on Pollon, who looked back with something like divine revelation.

'Come and help,' Pollon said. 'We need you to heal.' He said it in court Narmerian, for whatever reason, and then again, in Trade Dardanian.

Pollon turned and went aft to Bravah, who was moaning. The spear had torn at his intestines and had barbs set into the shaft. Miti, arm bound against her breasts, was weeping.

Pollon opened his mouth to speak, and suddenly the Dry One was there. It fitted itself into a very small space, and leant over the wounded Hakran, wings folded tightly against itself.

'No!' Miti said.

'Let him!' Aanat screamed from the helm.

Pollon, with a curse, grabbed the young woman around the waist and hauled her off her lover, heedless of damaging her wounded arm.

The green tongue flickered and went deep into the dying man's throat.

He gave a convulsion, and his eyes closed.

Miti pounded one sharp fist against Pollon's shoulder, but he trusted their Dry One and didn't let her go.

The tongue withdrew, and the monster staggered. Pollon had never seen it stagger before and worried that it was hurt badly.

But it turned, tottered to the woman with the nearly severed arm, and lifted the hand to the wrist. Then, faster than Pollon could track, it bound the hand with some sort of... web, its taloned hands moving almost too fast to see, the web emerging from the spines...

It was so ... *alien*.

Almost as if it understood him, the Dry One looked up, turned its head at an impossible angle, and slashed through the tourniquet.

Why did it look at me when it did that? Pollon thought.

No blood flowed out of the dense web wrapping.

Pollon let Miti go; she'd understood, or surrendered.

Zos was dragging himself by the arms along the deck.

The Dry One stood erect, all eight or nine feet of its height, and looked astern, towards Aanat. A long arm went out, and it pointed due north.

The boy smiled up at the monster.

'It says, we're going to Dendrowna now.'

And then the Dry One fell backwards into the forward hold. It bounced on the remnants of its cocoon, and then slid into an ungainly heap of brightly coloured limbs and thorax, and its wings looked ruined.

'Shit,' muttered Zos, and collapsed to the deck.

The next two days were, in many ways, harder than the sharp moments of conflict with the Jekers.

First, the crises never seemed to end. The lone Jeker ship that they could see got underway, cleared the wreckage before the *Untroubled Swan* could get over the horizon, raised a new mast, and gave chase. Her sleek war hull was faster, but Aanat was as wily as a rabbit chased by a wolf; he turned as soon as it was dark, emptied himself casting fogs and weather diversions, none of which quite seemed to lose the Jekers, and changed his sail settings and even the load of the holds for an extra knot of speed.

They lost the Dardanian without ever having exchanged a word.

But while the work of the ship never ended, there were other perils. Bravah was out – immobile, his body icy cold. Miti was in shock; the pain, the cast on her arm, and her first experience of that sort of terror had left her almost unaware of her surroundings. The Dendrownan woman with the injured arm was similarly shocked, and Pollon and Atosa found themselves fully employed as nurses.

Zos slept for ten hours and rose, if anything, stronger than the day before. Aanat put him to work as a steersman immediately, something for which he seemed to have great experience. The thin woman, Era, and her adopted son, Daos, both worked as untrained sail hands, and Daos seemed especially at home climbing the mast like someone's pet monkey.

Gamash had crawled to a sleeping mat and collapsed. Pollon suspected he had over-cast – something that powerful magi were all too prone to doing, especially when their lives were threatened. The man seemed to be able to sleep forever.

But the Dry One lay where it had fallen. Hefa-Asus and Pollon did their best to arrange it more neatly. While Hefa-Asus held the big body clear of the hold, Atosa and Pollon carefully folded the thing's wings away, using woollen textiles that smoked and burned, and handling the wings as little as possible.

'Is he dying?' Hefa-Asus asked.

Pollon shrugged. 'See the arrow?'

The shaft had broken, leaving little more than the arrowhead behind. It was probably barbed – they would be lodged inside the thing's abdomen – and it might be poisoned, although Pollon suspected that poisons meant for men would have little effect on the blue ichor of the Dry Ones.

'Pull it out?' Hefa-Asus asked.

Pollon ran his fingers around the wound. It had the icy cold feeling of the other wounds doctored by the Dry One.

'No,' he said. 'It's a better healer than I'll ever be. We have to believe it can heal itself.'

Hefa-Asus set the Dry One's body down very gently, and took off a leather hood he'd fashioned from a tanned hide in the cargo. He'd worn it to protect him from the spines and the wings, and, despite being heavy enough to make a battle shield, it had scorch marks.

'I'd love to understand why this powder burns,' Hefa-Asus said.

'You are an alchemist?' Pollon asked.

Hefa-Asus smiled. 'I am a smith, and I like to understand everything.'

Pollon returned the smile. 'I am a scribe,' he said. 'But I also seek to understand everything.'

'Well, then, I propose that we take a little of the powder and find something that it does not burn, as a start.'

Hefa-Asus pointed to the fired bricks and slate where Mokshi cooked when the weather allowed. Pollon looked down at the folded wings.

'I worry that these textiles could catch fire,' he said.

Hefa-Asus nodded. 'As do I, which makes our efforts seem more important, does it not?'

The powder did not burn the fired brick, nor the slate, nor fired ceramic. The two men ascertained that the Dry One's wing-powder appeared organic, and that it had a very definite *Aura* and was probably magical.

'I'm probably keeping you from your work,' Hefa-Asus said after they had rearranged the Dry One so that it lay on the upper tier of water amphorae, where he was safe from burning anything. Sure enough, the wrappings on the bales of wool were scorched. By that time, Era, the thin woman, had joined them. Her son was high above, in the leather crow's nest, watching for any Jekers.

Pollon looked aft, where Aanat was explaining something to Jawala and Zos.

'I don't know enough about ships to do more than sweep,' he said. 'But if you have something better to do, be my guest.'

Hefa-Asus smiled, but the smile was bitter. 'I risked my life to forge star-stone for the magos, and now all of it is sunk into the sea.'

Pollon said, 'Star-stone?'

Era gave a knowing smile. 'You might look in the baskets on the donkey,' she said. 'My ... son is quite clever.'

Hefa-Asus leapt to his feet.

'Star-stone?' Pollon asked.

The thin woman wore a long knife at her waist, hanging somewhat incongruously from a beautifully woven *zone*. She drew it. The pale grey blade glittered coldly in the sun like an unmelting icicle, lacking the richness of bronze. Pollon flinched.

'It's perfectly safe,' she said.

'Perfectly safe for us,' Gamash said. He'd finally risen from a full day of sleep, and stared down into the forward hold at the carefully folded body of the Dry One.

'What does that mean, respected elder, sir?' Era asked carefully.

The old man smiled. 'Respected elder? Are you planning to sell me some used pots?'

Era smiled back. She wasn't so much thin as well-muscled, he could see at close range; her arms were like whipcords, and, from what he could see of them, she had dancer's legs.

'I mean,' Gamash said, 'that star-stone is just a metal to us. But it seems antithetical to the so-called gods.'

Hefa-Asus shouted for joy, though, and jumped up onto the afterdeck. Aanat was still explaining his next manoeuvre, and Pollon saw him turn, clearly annoyed at the interruption.

Hefa-Asus was looking up at the boy on the masthead.

'You are brilliant, boy! I thought it was all lost!'

Daos looked down from on high and gave a boyish laugh.

'I thought you might want them,' he said.

Even thirty feet away, Pollon saw the change in Zos' face – the flush of emotion, the change in colour.

'Star-stone?' he said in Trade Dardanian. 'Cursed metal?'

'You know it?' Gamash said.

The magos climbed up out of the hold where he had joined Era and Pollon, and went to the afterdeck. Pollon followed him, and then Era, so that they were all gathered under an awning stretched from the little aft mast to the graceful swan's tail of the stern.

Zos was up and steering, but his eyes flashed as he looked at Gamash.

'Oh, I know it,' he said. 'I know it, and I suddenly understand where all this is leading. We're *tools*.'

Era looked at him as if seeing him for the first time.

'Tools?'

Zos shrugged, managing not to disturb the course of the ship.

'The Enemy. The Huntress and her sister. We're doing their bidding. Although I don't understand the Dry One's role.'

'The Huntress isn't the enemy...' Era said.

Zos made a face. 'You mean, all the gods are evil, and the Huntress and her sister alone are good?' He leant on his oar a little. 'Just a touch of inversion, don't you think?'

Gamash settled against the bulkhead. 'What if I told you that all the gods are, in fact, entirely evil?'

Zos glanced at him for a moment.

'I won't pretend I've never thought it,' he admitted. 'I think they all suck.'

Era looked at the warrior. 'You swear by the Huntress?'

Zos smiled. 'Aye, and much good it's done me. My mother followed her, and my father, too. And look what it got them? My father burned in his palace, and my mother...' He turned away, anger painting his face. 'My mother...'

Pollon looked at the old man. 'With respect, sir. The gods are evil? This sounds ... insane.'

The old man leant back and crossed his long legs. 'You were a scribe?'

'A Writer,' Pollon said, capitalising his role with pride.

Gamash nodded. 'Tell me, writer, have you ever seen any of the gods do anything to *help* any mortal?'

'Many prayers are answered,' Pollon said. 'I have documented—'

'Let me put that a different way,' Gamash said. 'You have *seen* the gods?'

'Several times,' Pollon admitted. 'The great god Enkul-Anu, and the war god Ara, mostly. And of course my patron, the herald, Nisroch.'

'I'm going to wager that people were sacrificed to summon them,' Gamash said.

Pollon winced at the latest memory. 'Yes.'

'And when they appeared, did they do anything to help? Drive off the Dry Ones? Repair shattered irrigation ditches? Sink Jeker ships?'

'Never,' Pollon admitted. 'But with the power of the gods, we do all these things as their willing—'

'Tools,' Zos said, and spat over the side.

Gamash nodded. 'Why do you think the power is from the gods?'

Jawala laughed. 'We don't think any such foolish thing!' she said. 'In Rasna, you won't find many worshippers of your gods.'

'Nor in Dendrowna,' the big smith said.

Pollon squatted on the deck, his world reeling.

'We know that power comes from people's wishes and desires...'

Aanat said, 'No. We *think* that. It's not proved.'

Pollon looked back and forth between them. Until that moment, he hadn't really contemplated the absurdity of his position – a loyal servant of the gods, rescued by people who didn't respect them or concede they *were* gods. And they had betrayed him... but surely...

'If the gods created the *Aura*,' Gamash said, 'why can the Dry Ones cast magic so effectively?'

'They don't really use the *Aura*,' Aanat put in.

Gamash's head turned so fast it might have snapped off. Aanat shrugged apologetically.

260

'I can *see* the *Aura* when people cast, even if I don't have mine up. The Dry One doesn't even ripple the Great *Aura* when it casts.' Then Aanat made a face. 'Except when healing. The healing leaves marks.'

Gamash leant back, settling his shoulders into the curve of the hull.

'That is the most interesting thing I've heard today.'

'And I'm having real trouble casting, all of a sudden,' Aanat said.

Gamash made a face. 'As did I, when I was facing the Jekers, or I'd have sunk their ships.' He looked pained. 'The best I could manage was a shield and a good light show.'

Any further discussion was interrupted by the shout of 'Sail ho!' from the boy at the masthead.

'Our Jeker, coming over the horizon,' the sharp-eyed boy called. 'And the Dardanian, well off to the east. I think it's him.'

'Fuck,' muttered Aanat, and they were at it again. Sails were wetted; Aanat got Gamash to support him in casting a squall. The two worked well together – a rarity among adepts.

Zos looked aft, shading his eyes. He had Atosa and Era and Jawala around him, weaving rope under the awning. Pavi was at the other oar.

'This makes no sense,' he said.

'How so, warrior?' Era asked.

The Dardanian smiled at her. 'Because those Jeker ships are packed with men, not food. And because, dangerous as they are, they're not great sailors. It's as if they're hunting us.'

'Hunting us?' Pollon asked. 'Of course they are. And as for food, they eat their captives.'

Jawala nodded. 'We hold that to be true.'

'Yes,' Zos said. 'But I mean, hunting *us* specifically.' He turned back. 'Star-stone, the Huntress …' He looked forwards. 'A Dry

One and a famous warrior magos … we're part of some god's plot. And the counter-plot is coming up behind us.'

'Counter-plot?' Era asked.

'Famous warrior magos?' Pollon asked.

Zos looked aft, and then over at Pavi, and they shared some small communication about the helm.

'Gamash of Weshwesh,' Zos said, pointing at the man with his chin. 'He led the war fleets of the Hundred Cities against Mykoax and won the battle of Vetluna.' He smiled without mirth. 'Thirty-one years ago.'

Pollon looked again, to the old man standing with Aanat, holding an auratic zodiac.

Era grinned. 'Perfect,' she said.

Now it was Zos' turn to be puzzled. 'Perfect?'

She nodded. 'A month ago I saw Jekers sack a city – Hazor.'

'Druku's twisted dick!' Zos said. 'You were *there*?'

'I was,' she said. 'I found the boy there.'

Zos glanced up. 'Wait one,' he said to Era, and then he bellowed 'Report, mast!'

'Hull up!' the boy piped.

Zos nodded to Era. 'I suspected you were clever,' he said.

'I hid in pig shit.'

His smile was winning. 'I'm putting that in my bag of tricks,' he said. 'No one ever died of pig shit.'

'I wasn't sure of that at the time,' Era said. 'That's not my point. My point is that after the sack, while the fuckers were still eating their captives, *one of the gods came.*'

Zos looked at her, and so did Pollon.

'I'm guessing he didn't scatter them like chaff and burn their ships?' Zos said.

'If he had, this would be a very different conversation,' Era said. 'I didn't hear what he said, but he spoke to them, and then they packed their slaves and left.'

'Which god?' Pollon asked.

'Nisroch the Herald,' Era said, and Pollon winced.

Pavi whistled. 'You mean one of your fucked-up gods is backing the Jekers?'

Jawala glanced at the other woman. 'Your language is deteriorating around all these foreigners,' she said sharply. 'Cursing is not good.'

Pavi shrugged.

Pollon shook his head. 'I've ... interacted ... with Nisroch. It is his duty, as Herald of the Gods, to gather information. He is the writer of the gods! You must have misunderstood what you saw.'

Zos was stroking his beard. 'Jekers,' he said quietly. 'I think it makes sense.'

'The Jekers worship no gods!' Pollon said.

'Do you *know* that, writer?' Zos asked.

'Squall is hitting the Jeker!' called the masthead. 'I can't see him!'

'Prepare to turn hard to starboard. I'm bringing up the wind,' Aanat said. And then, worriedly, 'It's getting harder and harder to do this. What's wrong with me?' He looked at Zos. 'I'm turning towards that Dardanian. Can we trust him?'

'Trust him to make the greatest profit he can,' Zos said. 'Another time, he'd take you and sell us into slavery. Today, he can't spare the time because there's a Jeker fleet just over the horizon. He'll be an ally.'

When the sun rose the next morning, glorious and pink, on a pure blue sea, the Jekers were nowhere to be seen in the circle of the world – neither the single ship nor the vast fleet. But the Dardanian lay off to the east, almost in formation with the *Untroubled Swan*, her big mainsail high on her tall mast.

Aanat looked bad, with dark circles under his eyes. He'd been on deck for two straight days, and Pollon knew he'd had

263

a long, difficult quarrel with his people about the crisis and the violence of it. And that he was burning himself out with repeated weather castings.

But the news that there were no enemy sails on any horizon seemed a tonic. Aanat handed over the deck to Pavi, and she commanded while Mokshi and Zos took the steering oars. Instead of being exhausted, the Dardanian seemed stronger every day, and by noon, Aanat had convinced Pavi to try Hefa-Asus in the other oar.

After noon, Jawala and Aanat came on deck, both of them looking better.

'We need to talk,' Aanat said.

'Mokshi should cook,' Jawala said.

Zos laughed. 'Mokshi should always cook,' he said. 'Best chef I've ever met. Please add some pork to mine.'

Jawala rolled her eyes. 'Must you?'

Zos pretended to be surprised. 'Must I insist on meat?'

'Peace,' Gamash said. His age carried some authority; they were all from cultures that revered elders.

Jawala looked at the deck, and Zos bobbed his head as if acknowledging his error.

They sat in a circle under the awning in the stern, and they weighed enough to lift the bow a little out of the water, but that was all. It was a fine day, the sea was blue, the sun hot but pleasant, the wind blowing south-west to north-east, so that with the square sail set they were making good time north.

Zos and Hefa-Asus were on the steering oars, and Pavi sat so that she could watch the mainsail. Everyone had a bowl of a sweet soup – barley and beans flavoured with dried dates – and a jug of beer went round.

'Delicious,' Zos said. He was eating his third bowl, as was Hefa-Asus.

'And yet, there is no pork,' Jawala said with a mocking smile.

'Ah, some pork spiced with chillies!' Hefa-Asus said. 'Your southern food is dull to the palate.'

He glanced at his female apprentice, a big-boned woman who shared his sculpted cheekbones and red-brown skin. She was awake for the first time in days, and Pollon sat by her, feeding her. He'd learnt that her name was Nicté.

The woman grinned. 'It would be good to eat some civilised food,' she said, and then, with a bow, 'but this is delicious, master cook!'

Mokshi smiled. 'We've had passengers before. We usually win them over after a few meals.' He leant over. 'Tell me about these chillies.'

Hefa-Asus waved a hand. 'I believe we're headed for my homeland,' he said. 'At some point, I'll introduce you.'

Gamash held up a hand. 'Exactly why we are all together,' he said. 'We need to decide what we're doing.'

'And where we're going,' Aanat said. 'Jawala and I have certain ... strictures.'

'They're everyone's strictures,' Jawala said.

Mokshi smiled at her. 'We're almost out of olive oil, and we're using the last tier of water amphorae again,' he said. 'This sweet Narmerian beer was supposed to be a name-day treat for Miti but it's the last drinkable stuff in the hold.'

Gamash nodded. 'We need a port.'

'We need a port, and we suspect that the ports are watched by the gods,' Jawala said, nodding to Pollon.

Zos smiled a wicked smile. 'Let's take that Jeker ship behind us. Don't pretend all you mages couldn't take it. Dump the crew over the side—'

Aanat was shaking his head vehemently. 'No!' he said, and Miti and Jawala joined him.

Zos leant back against the bulkhead and took another mouthful of beans and barley.

'I know,' he said. 'I know. Stupid plan. But it felt so good to say it.'

Mokshi put a gentle elbow into his side. 'Anyway, no one would trade with a Jeker ship.'

Jawala smiled at Zos. 'I don't think he's serious.' She stretched. 'He's trying to shock us.'

Era snorted. 'Warriors make war,' she said with a mixture of derision and acceptance. 'Where do you propose to land?'

'If we're really careful with what we have,' Aanat said, 'we can make Narmer without getting too hungry. Ten days with a good wind.'

'I hear a "but",' Zos said.

Era glanced at him.

Aanat nodded. 'I'm finding it harder and harder to cast weather spells.'

Hefa-Asus stroked his chin with one big hand. 'I suspect...' He paused. But no one else spoke up. 'I suspect that the star-metal does something to block access to the Great *Aura*. Pollon and I share a certain mindset – perhaps we could perform experiments.'

'Perhaps we could just drop the stuff over the side,' Jawala said.

Gamash shook his head. 'People died to get that star-stone, and people died to save the refined metal.'

Pollon thought of Era's knife and shuddered. He glanced at Atosa, but the jeweler merely looked interested.

'I don't like it either,' Pollon admitted.

'It's just a metal like other metals,' Atosa said. 'It seems to corrode easily though. Not as pretty as bronze.'

Era sat up. 'I think we need to go deeper than this,' she said. 'I think we need to decide what we're really doing here.'

They all looked at her. Hitherto, she'd been among the quietest; despite her fierce good looks, she had a tendency to stillness

266

that made her almost invisible at times. But now she was almost vibrant with charisma.

Zos looked at her, and gave a nod, almost as if the two of them had agreed on something in advance, which seemed odd to Pollon.

'Yesterday, Zos said that we were part of conspiracy,' she said. 'And we are. We are the kernels of a rebellion. The seeds of a new planting.'

Gamash nodded.

Hefa-Asus smiled.

Nicté grinned.

Atosa looked interested.

Jawala shook her head. 'We Hakrans are no part of your rebellion. We do not rebel, because we do not serve.'

Aanat looked at her, and Pavi looked up at the sail settings. Mokshi glanced away.

They're not all in accord, Pollon thought.

'I'm not sure I'm a rebel,' he admitted.

'I'm in,' Atosa said. 'I spent my life making beautiful things for those fuckers, and they broke my hands. Your Dry One didn't just fix me, he made me young. No pain in my hips, no pain in my hands.' He looked around. 'No god-king ever did *shit* for me that rivalled that. If that makes me a rebel, let's go.'

Pollon leant forwards. 'The god-king fed and maintained you—'

'Slaves grew the food and fed it to me, Pollon. Open your eyes! The whole thing's broken. *They were going to torture us to death.* Remember?'

Zos leant out from his steering oar and put a hand on Pollon's shoulder.

'Hold hard there, Atosa. Pollon is brave for saying his truth.' He looked around. 'We from the God-Lands, at least, have grown up with dissident ideas about the gods. And their rule over men. About our place in the world.'

Atosa drank a mouthful of beer. 'I always had my doubts, but I thought, "keep your head down, do your work, don't make waves."' He glared at Pollon. 'Until a brute with a bronze rod crushes your fingers, and you realise it is all a lie.'

Zos looked at Era. 'I have fought for various god-kings all my life,' he said. 'All various degrees of wilful, incompetent, venal and mad. But...' He was looking at Era, and Pollon had the feeling again that the two had had a private conversation. 'But my parents died fighting for the Huntress, or whatever we call her.'

'You don't know that,' Era said.

'I don't know that she's any better, or any different,' he snapped back. 'I know that she's a plotter – I know that the other gods call her and the Blue Goddess "the Enemies".' He looked around. 'I'd like to hear Gamash tell us how he served this Black Goddess thirty years ago.'

Era said, 'I thought you were in?'

Zos nodded. 'I'm in. I'm an ageing warrior with no armour, no sword, no horses and absolutely nothing to live for. You can have me. I'd like to have time to train and think and arm myself to bring one of the fuckers down. Dead.' He looked around. 'At this point, I'd hold my life well-lived if I could put one of them down. But Era, some of these people have lives, unlike thee and me. Pollon is a scribe and can get real work anywhere. Atosa is a master craftsman, as are Master Hefa-Asus and Nicté. Our hosts on this vessel are merchants with a ship, a family, children, and no stake whatsoever in our gods or our problems.'

Era raised an eyebrow. 'They don't have to be involved!'

Jawala closed her eyes and opened them. 'We are already involved.'

Pollon nodded. 'I can look through the god's eyes. Or at least, I could a week ago, when we left the beach at Noa. When this ship had the full attention of the Watchers in the Nexus.'

'Watchers?' Era asked.

'The god's eyes have professionals, usually scribes and writers, who watch and prepare reports for ... the gods.' Pollon looked around, aware that he was the centre of attention and not sure he liked it. 'The gods – usually Nisroch but sometimes other gods – give us lists of things to watch for. And we respond by noting when those things are seen, and where.'

'That's terrible,' Era said.

'Sounds like a system that could be fooled,' Hefa-Asus said. 'Very inefficient.'

Pollon was briefly and irrationally tempted to defend the system. It took an effort of will to place himself *outside* it and admit that it had flaws.

'To be honest,' he said slowly, 'there were the same people and things on the list every day ...' He looked at Hefa-Asus. 'So either they weren't getting reports ...'

'Or those things remained of interest.' Hefa-Asus said.

Era cut through their thoughts. 'Jawala, I fear your ship may be compromised.'

'Do you?' Jawala asked. 'I fear that this ship and her cargo represent the vast bulk of the possessions of my clan. That this is, truly, the food for my children and the house of my people, and it is now in danger.'

Era swallowed, as Zos had earlier.

Zos nodded. 'This is my point, Era. And I promise you, we are being manipulated to do someone else's bidding.' To Jawala he said, 'I think you should put us ashore somewhere, distance yourself from us, and tell the authorities that we forced you to aid us.'

Aanat shook his head. 'First, you do us no justice when

269

you suggest that we're not involved. We live here, too. We're involved. Second, your authorities are not well known for their moderation or sense of justice. They won't stop at asking us a few questions.'

Gamash nodded. 'Well,' he said. 'I, for one, am sorry. I had no idea what imposition I was putting on you when I came aboard.' He looked at Zos. 'It is true. I was young, and full of power, and I offered the Black Goddess my loyalty in exchange for more power. She sent me across the sea with a war fleet, to save Vetluna.' His eyes met Zos'.

Zos nodded. 'So when the great god Enkul-Anu sent the god-king of Mykoax against Rasna, the Dark Huntress countered by sending you.'

Gamash nodded. 'Yes. And several thousand Poche warriors from Dendrowna.' He shrugged. 'They did most of the fighting.' He looked out over the sea. 'I thought Enkul-Anu had forgiven me – my sacrifices were accepted. But then I was not chosen god-king in Weshwesh, in favour of an idiot, and then, suddenly ... as if he'd forgotten me and suddenly remembered ...' The old man's eyes were full of tears. '*Not* being chosen god-king was the best thing that ever happened to me. Until he killed my daughter.'

Zos looked at Era, and there was a long silence. And then, cautiously, Zos said, 'So this started thirty years ago. Or more, eh? Who knows what a labyrinth of lies we're in right now?' He glanced at Jawala. 'Do you see why you cannot afford to have anything more to do with us?'

Aanat looked at Jawala and then at everyone else.

'We do not hold any of you responsible,' he said. 'The Dry One led us to make the decisions we have – that I have made. We Hakrans believe in individual responsibility.'

'I didn't make that decision,' Miti spat. 'You did.'

Jawala smiled like tolerant parents everywhere and said,

'Perhaps collective responsibility would have been a better phrase.'

'The point is,' Aanat said, 'that we can't escape. We can't abandon you, according to our own ethics, and anyway, we don't want to.'

Miti crossed her good arm over her injured one and snorted. 'They almost got Bravah killed.'

'Most of us want to help,' Jawala said. She looked at Zos. 'I don't want to eat pork, and I don't want to hurt people or kill them. But I do believe that we could make a better world without these so-called gods.'

'People are going to die,' Zos said. 'I don't think that can be avoided.'

'Gods are going to die,' Era said.

Jawala looked at Aanat, and then Mokshi. And then Pollon.

'What do you think?' she asked.

Pollon had begun to grow a beard, like a warrior, and he rubbed at it.

'Like Zos, I have lost everything.' He paused. 'But like Atosa, I begin to see that I never *had anything*.'

Atosa put a warm hand on his back.

'Maybe it's time to bring it all down,' he said. 'And yet ... my relationship to my gods ...' He looked at Zos. 'Easy for you, Godborn. You are ... utterly yourself. But I am a mere man. Who am I without my gods?'

Atosa shrugged. 'Whoever the fuck you want to be. I'm pretty sure I can find buyers for gems I carve, whatever I worship.'

Gamash nodded. 'Pollon, there is merit in what you say – and many will feel the same way. But as Atosa says, you have a talent, a rare and valuable one – you can write both in the physical world and in the *Aura*. You will be a valuable member of any community, gods or no gods.'

'No gods.' Era blinked. 'Even when we talk about it, I have a hard time getting my head around it.'

Gamash smiled, and rose to his feet, with a groan as his hips engaged.

'Perhaps I should get wounded so that your Dry One will make me young,' he said.

Atosa shook his head. 'Not worth it. Or maybe… maybe it is. Those moments were the worst of my fucking life. They didn't just break my hands, Magos. They broke *me*. I dream it every night.'

'Listen,' Gamash said. 'I am like Pollon, and Zos, and you. I thought that it was… the way of the world. I've done it all – I've sacked a city, and I've had slaves. I had doubts and I crushed them as weakness. I did the bidding of the gods, and thought… I thought myself righteous.' He shook his head and his voice quavered.

'But age brings its own wisdom. And in age I began to have doubts, and then I found… love. A woman, not a slave. A child…' He paused. 'And one of the gods killed her, in a rage. Out of spite.' He nodded at Zos and at Era. 'I share Zos' reservations. But I agree that the remedy is not abandoning the struggle. The remedy is bringing them all down. Burn heaven. Destroy the gods. That's the vengeance that I, this puny mortal, have promised myself. I won't live to see it, but Daos might.'

He looked around. 'I have done many bad things. I'll do more, for this. But I, too, want to bring them all down.'

Jawala looked up at him. 'And the Jekers? The Dry Ones? The encroachment of the desert?'

Gamash nodded. 'One evil at a time. One day at a time. Let's agree what to do. If we survive that, let's go to Dendrowna. If we get there, we find the star-stone…'

'More star-stone?' Zos asked.

'Enough to make ten thousand swords,' Gamash said.

'Ten thousand star-stone swords,' Zos said. 'With that many, perhaps we *could* storm heaven.'

Era nodded. 'And that may be what we do, in the end.'

Zos lay back, his handsome head studying the sky.

'I think I know where to find an army,' he said.

'So,' Jawala said, 'we go to Narmer?'

Era looked around. 'We really mean to bring them all down?' she asked.

Everyone nodded, even Pollon.

Zos flicked his eyes to Era, and then to Jawala. 'Then we need a plan. A good, tight plan. In the end – or rather, in the middle – we'll need armies, and magic.'

He smiled his gracious godborn smile; Pollon responded warmly, and Era bridled.

Zos went on, 'If we win... Gamash is right. The Dry Ones and the desert and the Jekers are all problems as large as the gods.' He shrugged. 'But first, the war.'

Jawala frowned. 'None of that is anything to do with us,' she said.

'We'll need people,' Zos said. 'Lots of people.'

Pollon was feeling the enthusiasm of a convert. In his head, he was still imagining a world without gods. And it was as if a blindfold had been lifted from his eyes.

A world without gods.

Era nodded, as if seeing the practicality of Zos' words.

'We will need people.'

'Even to gather this star-stone,' Zos said. 'Hefa-Asus, will the ajaw of Dendrowna allow us to gather it?'

Hefa-Asus made a face. 'There is not just one ajaw, may their names be blessed. I have had dealings with the great ajaw of Poche, but he and I are hardly close companions and I have been away for years. But if I were to speculate, I would guess Era would be taken for his harem, and you, Godborn, would be sacrificed. Although it seems possible to me that you might be allowed to play the water lily game.' He made a gesture with his hands. 'The Hakrans would have no trouble. I am from the People of the North, and the ajaw's people would be cautious with me and with Nicté, whose mother is an important woman.'

'That's a *no*, then?' Zos said.

'I have wondered since the respected elder mentioned it,' Hefa-Asus began, 'how exactly we were going to land in Dendrowna and get this star-stone without real trouble.'

Era wore a look of deep frustration. 'I thought...' She rounded on Zos, as if blaming him. 'Damn it!' she said. 'Are you just throwing up barriers?'

He smiled.

He fancies her, Pollon thought, with revelation. *He's debating with her, but at the same time courting her. And she is so uninterested in him that she can't read his signals.*

He shook his head. 'Even in Hekka,' he said, 'one hears tales of the legendary greed of the ajaws.'

Nicté took another bowl of soup with her good arm and settled against Hefa-Asus. Pollon noticed that her canines were filed to points.

'All you southerners talk of Dendrowna as if it is one vast empire like Narmer,' she said. 'Dendrowna is a whole world. By Nanuk's white fur! You'll see! There are three ajaws along the coast, all roughly equal, always at war. But further inland, things change. People are different. And across the mountains—'

'Mountains?' Pollon asked. 'I have never heard of mountains in Dendrowna.'

'I am from these mountains,' Nicté said. 'They are the most beautiful place on the face of the world.'

She patted Hefa-Asus' knee, not like a lover, but like a daughter.

'This one is deeply impressed by the people and the ajaws

on the coast. Yes, they have huge cities. But they have never conquered us, and they only control the flatlands. In the woods and waters, their war parties stumble and die. There are ways to reach the mountains…'

Hefa-Asus nodded. 'There are ways, but the easiest would be to pay a fee, a great hoard of gold, and not to creep like thieves in the night.'

Era sat up again, legs crossed – not a position Pollon had ever seen a woman take, except among nomads.

'Hefa-Asus, I begin to understand what Zos is telling me. So… how many people do we need to harvest the star-stone, and to forge it?'

He gazed into the middle distance, trying to calculate it.

Zos looked at her. 'After we have the stone, we will need an army,' he said. 'If we're storming heaven. And an army means food and water, ships, donkeys, chariots, horses. It takes time to make just one chariot. It takes years to train a good chariot horse. Without chariots, we cannot defeat people, much less gods.'

Pollon had thought Era's intense look was angry; now he realised that her angry face was in fact an expression of examination and intellect.

Perhaps I fancy her too, he thought. *But at least I'm not so arrogant as to think a woman who prefers other women would cleave to me.*

Hefa-Asus raised an eyebrow. 'For the star-stone – perhaps three hundred people to extract it, and twenty more, trained by me, to manufacture weapons.'

'I'm in,' Atosa said. 'And while I'm not a smith, I know my metals.'

'Three hundred!' Gamash exclaimed.

Zos looked at Era again. 'I think we need every human who

is not a slave to the gods,' he said. 'I think we can only win if we enlist everyone.'

Era smiled at him. 'I had not expected you to be a revolutionary, Godborn.'

Zos smiled back. 'I have a suggestion.'

'Somehow I knew you did,' Era said.

Zos spread his hands. 'We want to base our entire plan on slaves.'

'You cannot trust slaves,' Nicté said. 'They'll sell you out for a meal!'

'Not if they have nothing to sell out,' Zos said.

Era was nodding. 'I already like it,' she said. 'It strikes a blow immediately. Freeing slaves is a good thing all by itself.'

Hefa-Asus looked less enthusiastic. 'And because you've freed them, they'll work for you?'

Now Era looked around – and at Zos.

'I think it has to be more subtle than that,' she said. 'We need them to revolt all by themselves. We sow the seeds, and let the gods reap the crop.'

Pollon rubbed his new beard. 'Give me an example.'

Era pointed at Zos. 'He *hurt a god*. People must be talking about it. Slaves must be talking about it. We write a song, and we sing it in Narmer, and see where it goes.'

'By itself—'

Era shook her head. 'By itself it is nothing. But if we create symbols …'

Jawala leant forwards, as if unable to restrain herself. 'Freeing slaves is a great good,' she said. 'A magnificent achievement to place against our sins. Or so we teach. This is *dharma*.'

Pollon said, 'Dekhu.' He looked first at Gamash, and then at Zos. Nicté glanced at him and smiled.

'Is Dekhu one of your gods?'

'Dekhu is the slave market of the world,' Gamash said. 'It's an island at almost precisely mid-ocean. The navel of the world.' He shook his head as if he was weary. 'It used to be the abode of the gods. The old gods.'

Nicté snorted. 'How many slaves are there?'

'Several hundred a day. We bought them in parcels.' Pollon looked apologetic. 'I didn't invent the system! But we ran short of war captives years ago. And anyway, everyone knows foreigners make the best slaves.'

'Nowhere to run,' Era said bitterly. 'Not all slaves pass through Dekhu. But many do.' She glanced at Pollon. 'Why there?'

'It's not defended,' he said.

Era wrinkled her nose as if she'd smelt something bad and Zos leant back again.

'Well, well,' he said.

'No, that's insane,' Era said. 'You're just looking for a fight. There must be half a hundred slave-dealers, each with a dozen guards—'

'And a thousand slaves with very little to lose,' Zos said. 'On any given day.'

'You are talking about the deliberate use of violence,' Jawala said.

Era cut Zos off before he could interject.

'Lady,' she said with quiet respect, 'anything we do to free slaves is going to result in violence. Our whole world is based on violence. Whatever we do, we're going to swim in a river of blood to get there.'

Aanat winced at her imagery. But when he spoke, his voice was strangely commanding.

'Family,' he said, 'if we agree to help these people, we are turning our backs on some of the things we hold most dear. Let us admit that.'

Jawala sighed.

Zos said, 'It will not come to violence immediately. And you need not be involved.'

Jawala smiled, a smile that held all the bitterness of a lived life in the world.

'Sometimes you argue so well, Zos,' she said. 'And other times you are like a child. If I carry you to your battlefield, I might as well swing an axe. I would be participating.'

Era nodded. 'You see it clearly.'

Jawala turned to her, her face as impassive as iron.

'I am not offering to swing an axe – I'm merely pointing out that I'm not a fool. I will think on this.'

Gamash nodded. 'Jawala, you make me very happy that I sailed for Vetluna as a young man. Even though I did it for vainglory.'

Zos nodded again at Pollon and then turned to Aanat.

'Can you trade at Dekhu?' he asked.

Jawala and Pavi glanced at each other.

'Perhaps,' Jawala said. 'We neither buy nor sell slaves, but there is a market and Hakrans trade there. We have to be careful – in the past, Hakrans have been accused of helping slaves to escape.' She smiled. Aanat smiled, too. Even the usually silent Mokshi was grinning.

'You know how to get slaves out of Dekhu...?' Era said.

Jawala smiled and scraped her bowl. After a long pause, she said, 'Yes.'

'It's a big market,' Aanat added. 'We can do business there.'

'And it is close enough to Narmer that if we can't make a profit, we can be in Narmer in a few days,' Jawala said. 'But no violence!'

'This is more like a reconnaissance,' Zos said. 'We look it over... with an eye to eventual violence.' He smiled beneficently at the circle. 'I like to look things over before I commit.'

'Does killing slave traders even count as violence?' Era asked.

'Yes,' the Hakrans replied in chorus.

Era shook her head.

They altered course that evening.

In the morning, when they were all on deck, the Dardanian ship began to edge up on them.

Zos watched the manoeuvre closely.

'No one on deck is in armour,' he said. 'His benches are half empty. I don't think he's an immediate threat.'

Aanat was at the steering oars. 'What does he want, then?' he asked.

It proved that what he wanted was water.

A Dardanian leant out over his stern rail. The two ships were under easy sail, headed north.

'Where are you bound?' he shouted in Trade Dardanian.

Aanat and Jawala nodded to Zos. The warrior leant well out. 'Dekhu!' he roared.

'We need water!' the man shouted.

Zos looked at Aanat and at Jawala, who had a very crisp four-sentence discussion in Hakran.

'We can give him thirty water amphorae,' Jawala said. 'If there's a way you can tell him that we're giving him water and we're perfectly aware that in other circumstances he'd kill us all, please do.'

From the hold, Daos shouted, 'The donkey is gone!'

Jawala looked at Zos. 'Can you deal with the Dardanians?'

Zos nodded. 'Let me handle this.'

The Dardanian ship was still separated from them by a stretch of ocean wider than a house when Zos made his leap. He leapt at the top of the roll, when the stern was high on a wave, and

279

landed as the other ship was diving down the other side, and tumbled forwards to rise to his feet by the helmsman.

Every part of his body screamed in pain.

He managed a collected bow.

'My lord,' he said.

The Dardanian shook his head. 'You're a fucking bull-leaper,' he said. And then he bowed respectfully. 'Gods favour you, warrior.'

Zos returned a respectful hand gesture. 'And you, lord of the sea. That is a Hakran vessel, and she will give you thirty amphorae of water.'

The Dardanian captain raised an eyebrow.

'I could just take it.'

He pointed forward, where his half-empty rowing benches still held twenty men. None of them were slaves, and they all had helmets and war gear.

Zos nodded. 'You could, but there would be a lot of blood.'

The Dardanian hadn't offered his name, which was a very bad sign.

'I disagree, bull-leaper. They are Hakrans. They will choose suicide, and I'll have their ship, their food and their water.'

Zos sighed. 'We helped you fight the Jekers, so you know we have a magos of some capability.'

The Dardanian fingered his beard. Dardanians were all crazy; they believed that taking extreme risks was a way of honouring their gods. And they were touchy and violent.

'And second?' he asked, as if they were actually in a negotiation.

Zos hadn't moved since he'd tumbled to the base of the helm. Now he moved like a striking snake, and had the helmsman's sword from its scabbard before the man could react. He raised his right hand, now holding the sword across the helmsman's body, put his right foot behind the other man's and flipped him, uninjured, to the deck. Zos took the steering oar in one hand.

'If you make trouble,' he said, 'I'll kill everyone aboard.'

The Dardanian captain didn't show any anger – or remorse. He crossed his arms slowly and put his right hand to his beard, obviously far from his sword hilt.

'You make a good point,' he said with a smile. 'In fact, *both* of your points are good. I will accept the beneficence of thirty amphorae of water, and I'll escort you to Dekhu.'

Over the horizon and then some, the Jeker ship had the mainmast back up and the sail drawing, and the heads of a dozen sacrificed captives leering their death's grins over the bow. The warriors were feasting amidships while the surviving captives rowed. The shaman poured the power of the blood into the ship's sail to make it faster, and the warriors jeered at the vast fleet behind them, calling them laggards and cowards.

They were too busy gorging on uncooked flesh to notice the darkening of the sea beneath the ship. It happened quickly, as if a single cloud was blotting out the sun. Then an oarsman cursed, pulling uselessly at his oar, and suddenly it was ripped from his hands.

A spathulate tentacle came over the side. It took the gunwale of the ship firmly, and tipped it over in a single titanic pull.

The screams didn't last, and the whole ship was pulled down, disappearing with terrifying speed into the depths, leaving nothing but a few pieces of drifting wood, a stoppered vase that floated for a long time, and someone's spare cloak billowing purple on the surface of the sea like a brilliant jellyfish.

The cloak floated for hours, until the Jeker fleet swept up from the south like a moving forest of rotting wood and decaying canvas.

A bearded man in a green cloak decorated with human hair hooked it from the sea with a spear and tossed it on the deck.

'Blood and murder,' he sang, and his warriors echoed him, and the shaman in the stern smiled a cruel little smile.

Hyatta-Azi, champion of the Jekers, pointed north with his barbed spear.

'Dehku!' he roared. 'A feast of blood lies ahead.'

Heaven

The ruddy bronze light of late evening fell on the stainless black marble of the halls of heaven, tinting them a shade of war. Nerkalush, junior god of the underworld, was standing with Resheph, God of Pestilence During War. They were quite loud – posturing, bragging. Both of them were displaying an array of human remains: Resheph, fresh from the western deserts of Narmer, had severed heads hanging from his belt, the blood of his victims staining his beautiful jade-green tunic; Nerkalush had the tongues of his victims around his neck, and fresh and putrid skulls on a spear. Enkul-Anu had sent them to punish Narmer for something; clearly, some punishing had happened.

Neither seemed to be having the hoped-for effect on Lady Sypa's nymphs.

Gul, Warlord of the Hosts of the Dead, stood staring into space, his intent in entering the hall lost, his interest having wandered away with his thoughts. Nerkalush glanced at him nervously.

Nisroch the herald had no time for the senility of the great gods, but he was alarmed to see that Resheph was bigger, stronger than before, and his skin had taken on the ruddy-gold colour of some of the older gods.

Where is he getting that power? Nisroch asked himself. *Not from massacring farmers in Narmer.*

Nerkalush looked equally robust. Nisroch was used to thinking of the two as powerless. Now, they seemed to have imbibed something.

Resheph glanced his way, and his face took on that stupid, jeering look that Nisroch hated most.

'Ooh,' he said. 'The servant god.' He brayed his silly laugh. 'Do all the *servants* worship you?'

'No, no,' laughed Nerkalush. 'No, he's the peeping tom god, and all the little men who can't get off worship him.'

Nisroch had never seen the two of them behave with such open insolence, and he went red with rage before he could control it.

Resheph enjoyed seeing his reaction. 'We're having a contest to see how many mortals we can slay,' he said. 'I'd invite you to join, but it's strictly for male gods.'

Nerkalush slapped his bloody thigh.

I need to know why these two have suddenly been enhanced, Nisroch thought. *And then I think I need rid of them.*

'I like your pretty peacock cloak,' Nerkalush said. 'If I were a eunuch I'd wear one, too.'

Nisroch pasted a smile on his face, bowed, and allowed his cloak to snap behind him with the speed of his turn. He'd deal with them eventually, but first he had to do Enkul-Anu's bidding, even at the risk of impropriety and his own skeins of deceit. Gods who failed the Storm God didn't last long.

He reached through a portal and stepped into the private apartments deep in the mountain beneath the hall.

Druku's private chambers.

Druku lay on a couch, his erection just beginning to deflate; his partner, drunk to the point of somnolence, was lying on her stomach. Nisroch, who was surprisingly prudish for a god, looked away but remained towering over the elder god's bed. A curtain of auratic power hid the god and his nymph from prying eyes, but allowed them to watch the goings-on in the hall. Nisroch had arrived *inside* the curtain, which he now regretted.

'Disgusting,' Druku said. 'Idiots need a lesson. Not how you impress a girl. Eh, Laila?'

The immortal woman purred.

'Or a man, for that matter. Useless adolescent. Resheph is just trying to make up lost ground.'

Nisroch nodded. 'Uncle, I wanted to speak to you—'

'I hear some human twit hit him so hard he's still limping – that's *after* resin.'

Druku rolled his partner over and began to caress her. He was in full male form today. Very male. Already. Nisroch looked away again.

'It is an important matter,' he began again.

'Have you found the creature that hurt him?' Druku asked. 'I watched it happen, you know. Impressive fellow. I hear he's still alive.'

Resheph had been told that the human warrior had been tortured to death, broken on the wheel and left to die in the sun. He hadn't been told that his assailant had subsequently vanished, but it was an open secret among the senior gods.

'I'm looking, Uncle. And that's why I wanted to talk to you. I fear that there is … a plot afoot.'

The drunken lecher god glanced at him. 'And why are those two posturing ninnies killing people in Narmer, eh?'

Druku's caresses had grown more serious. Laila's eyes had rolled back in her head. She was clearly enraptured – unashamed. And Nisroch felt a taint of jealousy. She'd never worn that look …

The Herald of the Gods wondered to find them together, but neither of them seemed to be hiding their passion from him. It was possible they were both too drunk.

He felt a pang of jealousy, as he rather fancied Laila himself, and they had a little history. But …

'There's always a fucking plot, boy. Look to the Sisters – they do all the plotting. And your useless cousins, nephews and nieces. Also plotters. Don't look at me – I don't plot. I drink and fuck.'

He demonstrated his resolve by rising a little, bestriding Laila from behind, and taking up a big gold cup of sweet wine. He drank some, thrusting away, and then held the cup for Laila, pulling her up against him so she seemed to sit in his lap. She drank greedily, her eyes wild. She wasn't drunk; she was lost in the ecstasy of a complex high.

'You really are the greatest god,' she said, quite distinctly.

Resheph and Nerkalush were out there in the Hall of the Gods, watching the nymphs around Sypa, clearly unable to tear their eyes away. In fact, most of the courtiers in the Hall of the Gods were watching the dancing nymphs.

Druku obviously didn't care, and neither, apparently, did Laila.

'Uncle, I need your help.'

'I'm a trifle busy, lad.'

'You have more worshippers than anyone ...'

Laila started to make a noise halfway between a moan and a whistle. It was quite rhythmic, and strangely beautiful. She was leaning back against her god, the tattoos on her arms seeming to have lives of their own, her long black hair whipping across her face.

'Three guesses why, lad.'

His hands came up to caress her breasts. He was careful – meticulous, even. Possibly even sober.

'I need access to your temples, Uncle.'

The Herald of the Gods went back to watching the hall, seeing Resheph's attempt to impress the Lady Attaru. He swaggered, said something to her, and his effort went in flames as she turned away uninterested. Beside him, Laila's rhythmic moans quickened. He glanced back without thinking.

Laila's completion was surprisingly quiet; Druku's made his

face purple for a moment, the way he appeared in some of his temple art.

'If you are finished?' Nisroch said.

'No,' Druku said. 'Fuck off. People go to my temples to get away from all that. And I'm not finished, boy, and you are interrupting.' He smiled down at Laila. 'Mostly, I'm never finished.'

'I need more god's eyes,' Nisroch said firmly.

'No,' Druku said. 'Why don't you go chase one of Sypa's boys or girls? Do you a world of good. Stop dancing to Enkul-Anu's tune. He sees conspiracy behind every column.'

'No thanks, Uncle.'

'Fuck off, then.'

'I really must insist,' Nisroch said.

There was a pause, and Nisroch felt as if all time and space had come to a stop. Even in the Hall of the Gods, several hundred feet of bedrock away, the Immortals were silent, mostly to watch Resheph squirm.

'I'm an elder god, boy,' Druku said, and he really didn't sound particularly drunk. 'You don't *insist* to me.'

'I have Enkul-Anu's authority, great god Druku. I need access to your temples.'

Suddenly Nisroch was feeling unwell. In fact, he had a growing feeling of unease – a sort of spinning feeling. His knees were weak. His head ached.

Laila shook her head just slightly at him, as if she was admonishing him for being foolish.

Suddenly he wanted her as he had never wanted another being, mortal or immortal. Only his head was starting to spin.

Druku rolled off his couch. Naked, unarmoured, and obviously sober, he was a head taller than Nisroch and broad enough to make two of the Herald of the Gods. Nisroch found the great god's bouncing erection particularly distasteful, and moved back.

A smell of musky sex pervaded the air, and the scent of good wine.

'No,' Druku said, so that the floor shook.

His disagreement seemed jocular, except that Nisroch was blinking away the need to sleep while feeling immensely, erotically charged. The herald stood his ground, but he was already weaving shields. Or rather, waving his hands, clumsily trying to conjure what should have been second nature...

Druku put a finger under his chin — delicately. He ran it down the herald's neck to his chest.

'I'm a very powerful god,' Druku said. 'And I'm not even exerting my full power yet.'

Nisroch found himself responding powerfully to the wine god's roving hand. The wine god's lips were so...

In the Hall of the Gods above, the golden door behind the throne appeared and opened, and Enkul-Anu entered. His shining scarlet skin seemed to give off heat. His golden eyes emitted light, and his hair was like a cascade of darkness.

He strode into the hall and the courtiers fell on their faces — those who were not already cowering in fear. He raised a hand and suddenly he vanished, to reappear beside Nisroch. He raised an eyebrow at Druku.

'Brother,' he said.

'Enkul-Anu!' The God of Drunkenness and Orgies pointed at the Herald of the Gods. 'Your jackal here says you want to put god's eyes in my temples!'

Nisroch stumbled back, lust forgotten, his temples throbbing in pain.

'It's necessary,' Enkul-Anu said.

'Not what we fucking agreed!' Druku spat. 'People don't want to be *watched* while they drink and fuck? While they lie, or cheat? I *am* the fucking counterculture. I let them vent their petty rebellions so we won't have a worse one.' He waved a big hand. 'That's what we agreed. Remember?'

Nisroch smiled uncertainly. 'Something's come up ...' he began. But he could barely speak.

Druku's face was the same purple he'd worn at orgasm, but the expression was now one of rage.

'Something always fucking comes up!' he roared.

Enkul-Anu crossed his arms. 'You wouldn't understand ...'

'Don't fucking patronise me, brother,' Druku said.

'Bah, you're drunk,' Enkul-Anu said.

'Not so drunk I don't know when a brother god is overstepping,' Druku shot back.

Enkul-Anu crossed his arms. 'I have spoken,' he said. 'Beware my wrath.'

Druku spared Lady Laila a glance and looked back.

'That's your stance?'

'Just obey,' Enkul-Anu said. 'Or I'll ram a lightning bolt up your arse and let you contemplate the difference in our powers.'

Druku nodded. 'Fuck you,' he said. And *vanished*.

Time stretched. No one moved, although Laila buried her head in a pillow.

'Well, fuck,' Enkul-Anu spat.

Nisroch could barely think, his head was spinning so hard. He sat down. Enkul-Anu gave him a hard glance.

'What's wrong with you? You look drunk,' he said. 'And Druku, for all his failings, is one of the few gods of my generation still functioning, so enraging him had better be worth it. When you have all your god's eyes installed, I want you to use them to find him. Understand me? And send someone to bring him home. Laila, for example.'

He looked at the nymph. She favoured him with a winning smile.

'I need to sober up, first,' she sighed.

Time passed oddly in the home of the gods. Later, Nisroch was in his most secret place, the black marble room where he watched the god's eyes. Other gods called it 'the message room' because they assumed that he ran a sort of postal service, proving that most of the gods were fools. There was a comfortable chair and a gold-inlaid floor with a summoning triangle and four layers of outer wards.

On the polished walls, he could summon hundreds – thousands – of mage-lit pictographs, each one representing one of his eyes. He had eyes the other gods probably wouldn't expect; one hung on the mainmast of a Jeker ship, for example, pointing aft at the ongoing ritual cannibalism. Six covered every angle in the Hall of Hearing. He'd placed those himself, and they were cunning, hidden in the latest redecoration of the hall. No one even knew they were there, including his father.

Nisroch enjoyed being cunning.

He had a bank of new eyes now – the product of Druku's self-exile and of an edict to the priests and priestesses of Druku in all of his aspects, who tended to be a debauched lot anyway. They had submitted tamely enough; none of them had emulated Druku's resistance or flight.

Nisroch opened the new eyes one by one with mounting annoyance. Many were misplaced: one, on careful inspection, seemed to point straight up at a coffered temple ceiling; another was so hazy as to be useless. Resistance? Or just bleary-eyed incompetence?

He made a note on his tablet and moved on, watching the ports in Narmer, looking at ships, looking at people. He fell easily into his routine, reviewing Watcher reports; a hierarchy of priests sifted them, judged which were worthy, and passed the most important on to him. The most interesting was an older report that had previously been ignored – a fault in his bureaucracy, but at least the senior priests had brought it up now.

It was from a mid-level Watcher in Hekka. Nisroch glanced at his immortal tablet, looking through his notes. The Watcher was a palace writer with an excellent reporting record and the highest accuracy score on reports.

The doings of mortals seldom interested the Herald of the Gods beyond their immediate threats or utility in his plots, but this Pollon had been a useful tool, like a well-made sword. Probably killed in the sacking of the palace, although the god-kings had explicit rules forbidding such stuff; the gods defended their slaves. Usually.

But fucking Resheph had wrecked Hekka and everything had been sacked.

Drat.

The probably dead Watcher's report was thorough, and suggested that at least four pieces of star-stone had struck the western desert. The nomad he'd spoken to, and her family, had located two and given their locations with enough local references. They appeared reliable.

Nisroch immediately summoned Azag, Enkul-Anu's Captain of the Demons.

Azag appeared in the narrow confines of the summoning triangle, his head and shoulders squeezed uncomfortably against the ceiling. He was huge, and wearing *auros*-reinforced armour of bronze and gold.

'I need a demon on each of these locations,' Nisroch said, sharing the information from his tablet.

Azag snorted. 'Deep desert. We attacking the Dry Ones, boss?'

'Perish the thought.'

Nisroch smiled inwardly at the notion that the Dry Ones were enemies of the gods.

Milk cows, more like. Honey bees.

'I need these sites watched, and any interlopers brought to me.'

Azag nodded. 'Not killed and eaten, then?'

'Expressly brought to me, and *not killed and eaten.*' Nisroch shook his head in despair.

Azag grunted. 'I've got a few sluggards who need a touch of discipline. I know who to send.'

'Immediately,' Nisroch said.

'Your wish is my command,' Azag said, and vanished.

The presence of the huge demon had been like a pressure in his mind, stifling like a pillow over the face, and Nisroch didn't like things that made him uncomfortable. Sometimes he thought of raising an armed force of humans to replace the demons, who were violent at the best of times. But he hated dealing with mortals.

He hated dealing with Immortals, too. He still felt queasy from dealing with Druku. And Sypa's handmaidens all hissed every time he passed them now.

He sighed, calmed himself by watching his Jekers eating a few of their captives, and then turned his attention to Narmer. He had plans for Narmer; he had plans for everything. But he had to at least appear to carry out Enkul-Anu's plans, in which Narmer figured as well.

Druku was one of the more popular gods in Narmer, manifesting there as Nebet, goddess of beer, drunkenness and excess. The priestesses of Nebet had installed Nisroch's god's eyes at once, but he averted his eyes from the orgiastic display of temple ecstasy in every conceivable form and gender pairing.

Nisroch pursed his lips. At least the Nebet temples had obeyed him. Now he had to recruit a new cohort of Watchers to sort the wheat from the chaff. He pushed that down to his chief of Watchers in Narmer and found a report on the new great goddess-queen, Maritaten, who had somehow taken power in record time and was immediately building a fleet.

A fleet?

A fleet in Narmer ran directly against his own machinations and had to be stopped.

Why is she building a fleet? Nisroch asked himself.

He made a note for the Watcher and then reached through the *Aura* and pulled at the man's amulet.

'My lord god?' The Chief Watcher of Narmer was a priest of Enkul-Anu in Lukor – a rich, powerful man.

'Tell me about your new queen and her fleet,' Nisroch said.

'Lord god, yesterday in closed council she proposed to use the surplus on this year's wheat crop from the royal estates to buy a fleet.'

'For what purpose?' Nisroch asked. And then, considering Enkul-Anu's demands on the mortal kingdoms, he said, 'What surplus?'

'That's in my report,' the Watcher said.

'If I wanted to read the entire report, I wouldn't be wasting my time talking to you, would I?' Nisroch snapped.

The man paled. 'Lord god, Herald of the Gods, despite the failures in western irrigation, the Iteru had a near record soil delivery this year, and crops were … extravagantly good.'

Nisroch was impatient. 'I know that. I also know we're taxing Narmer to the point of rebellion to keep her poor. Too poor to make more trouble in the Hundred Cities, for example.'

'Yes, lord god. But the great queen seized all of the estates of the … err … former royal family and now owns vast areas of tillable land. The royal estates have their own slaves. They, too, had a bumper crop.'

The complexities of mortal administration bored most of the gods. They bored Nisroch, too, but his power was based on understanding them.

'You mean to say that Maritaten is going to use her *own* riches to buy a fleet?'

'Yes, lord god. That is exactly—'

'*Why* is she building a fleet?'

'She says that the Sun God Arrina told her to.'

'The Sun God Arrina has been cast into the outer darkness.' Nisroch spat.

My mother.

'I want to know exactly *why* Maritaten of Narmer is using her own wheat and gold to buy a fleet of warships. And I want her stopped.'

He thought longingly of summoning Azag and ordering the Captain of the Demons to sweep into Maritaten's magnificent delta-palace north of Memis and kill everyone in it. Maybe then the endlessly rebellious Narmerians would get the message. Come to think of it…

'How did this Maritaten come to power so swiftly?' he asked.

The Watcher coughed. 'The… uh… demons…' He paused.

'Yes?' Nisroch was looking at other eyes, his attention already moving.

'The demons destroyed the entire royal clan, root and branch. They ate the children.' The Watcher coughed.

'Yes. As ordered. So?' Nisroch asked.

The priest took a deep breath. 'It's a long story,' he began.

'Make it very brief.'

The Watcher shrugged. 'Very well. Maritaten's family were once kings. But they remained loyal to the Sun Goddess Arrina when Enkul-Anu declared the worship of the Sun illegal, and they were deposed. Maritaten's grandmother was made a slave.'

'Sure,' Nisroch waved dismissively. 'And?'

'And when the demon guard of the great god Enkul-Anu slew all of the family of the king he had himself appointed,' the

Watcher said carefully, 'the people thought that the Storm God meant us to restore—'

'You're fucking kidding me,' Nisroch said.

When I am Storm God ..., he thought, and then carefully walled that thought off.

He thought about the Jekers. He needed a new aspect – a violent, bloody one. The Jekers would never push their *Aura* to him unless they recognised him as their own ...

Dangerous business.

Maybe he should manifest a beard ...

He snapped back to the priest.

'Watch everything she does. Recruit spies throughout her palace.'

'Yes, lord god.'

'And quickly!'

Nisroch interrupted as the terrified man spoke. 'My lord god, I will do your bidding—'

'Yes you will,' Nisroch said. 'Another matter – I need forty new Watchers for the eyes I've placed in Nebet temples. Probably best they be eunuchs.'

'I don't have forty eunuchs—'

'Make some,' Nisroch said. 'Or I'll make *you* one. Go!'

He sat back, contemplating his eyes, watching his Jekers, and pondering the immediate future. His intention was to drive Narmer to open revolt and then to coax Enkul-Anu to crush them. He'd looked at this plan from every angle and found it perfect. When the Jekers rolled over the remnants of Narmer, the world of men would be doomed.

But what if the Jekers assaulted Narmer without any prompting from the Storm God ...?

He smiled. He could do it. He could do it *now*, on a much shorter timetable. He'd need a bolt-hole. Otherwise ...

He listened to sixteen Watcher reports that had been tagged

for his attention. It was only the second from last that changed his expression.

A Watcher on Noa had made a report about a merchant ship from Mykoax. It seemed routine until he saw mention of a stone jar of near perfectly pure resin being sold in the market.

He stiffened in his chair. Telipinu, Enkul-Anu's son by Sypa, ran the resin production for the palace of heaven; it was the most important of his duties as chamberlain, the *ra-pte-re* of heaven. He also oversaw the creation of godly ambrosia from the resin.

Telipinu was a friendly fellow, for a rival god, but Nisroch's distrust was immediate and deep. Instead of contacting Telipinu, he used his god's eyes to go to a senior human underling – the Chief Herder, as he was called.

'Get me the palace resin log,' he said. 'Orders from Enkul-Anu. Tell no one of this enquiry, and that includes Telipinu.'

The terrified man obeyed immediately.

Nisroch hated this routine work, but by doing it, he stayed ahead of the lazier gods, who were virtually all of them. He ordered the Chief Herder to count all of the resin jars in the Palace of Heaven.

'Count them yourself,' he spat at the terrified mortal.

The man had managed to extend his life for hundreds of years by being the officer in charge of resin extraction. Behind him, Nisroch could see the mosaic of cells that housed the captive Dry Ones. Thousands of them. They were set into the floor of a vast cavern floodlit by mage-light, and slaves moved about them, extracting the resin from the cells.

'Count them *now*,' Nisroch said.

This all had a nightmare quality; after all, Nisroch's mother had attempted to toy with the production of resin and had been banished to the void. The resin was at the very heart of the Palace of Heaven and the rule of mortals. And *someone* had a jar of the pure stuff out there.

The report included an image of the ship: Hakran. Nisroch cast a minor working and froze the image, then left it to hang in the air.

Nisroch hissed. He *hated* the Hakrans, but then all the gods did. Enkul-Anu had tried to exterminate them several times, and various other gods had protected them by turns, for their own reasons. Nisroch looked through the reports and ordered more; he ordered a Watcher in Noa to go in person to the port captain and get the ship's bills of lading and authentications.

'I have to do everything myself,' he muttered.

An hour later the Chief Herder appeared and said, with great reverence, that there were no jars missing.

Nisroch cursed. In almost every way, this was worse than the resin representing theft from the Palace of Heaven. This meant that someone was trading with the Bright People, and that way madness lay.

Before the gods began their evening meal in the great hall above his head, he had the port captain's report, giving the sailing route and a very suspicious gap of ten days. Plenty of time to sail to the west coast and make contact with the Dry Ones. The wild Dry Ones. The Bright People.

It was a staggering thought. There were Dry Ones out there ... producing a rival product? On purpose? It suggested a level of conspiracy that was vastly more threatening than some meat-sack who'd managed to hurt Resheph, or even a star-stone fallen in the eastern desert.

Nisroch occasionally daydreamed of hurting Resheph and his sidekick, Nerkalush, himself. But as he daydreamed he came back to the thought: *Why is Resheph growing in power?*

He chewed on that for a while, and then went back to

the matter at hand – the Dry Ones. And some sort of cursed smuggling trade.

How can they even communicate?

He looked at his eyes thoughtfully, and then summoned Azag again, despite his misgivings.

'Great lord?' Azag asked.

Was that sarcasm?

'Find this ship.'

Nisroch indicated the hovering image, and sent it into the demon's thoughts with a casual motion.

The Captain of the Demons nodded. 'Me, personally?'

'No, no, send demons. Search ... the Hakran coast, and Dardania. And Akash, I suppose.'

'Half the earth, you mean?'

Nisroch took an immortal breath. 'And get me a minor demon to watch the glyphs. One that can handle pattern recognition.'

Azag smiled, showing barbed teeth with a terrible pink-brown discoloration.

'Of course.'

Nisroch reached up to the ceiling, where the floor's summoning triangles were repeated, and pulled one down into the centre of the room – not physically, but in the *Aura*.

A monkey appeared inside the first triangle. Nisroch moved the second to imprison it and then hung it in the centre of the black room, where its oversized eyes could see every sigil and hieroglyph.

'Name?' Nisroch asked.

'Oh, we don't like to share our names,' the monkey said.

'I command you by the power of Enkul-Anu and the triangle in which you are bound.' Nisroch waved a hand. 'Don't fuck with me, monkey.'

'I am Wukung,' the monkey said, and screeched.

Nisroch added the name to his tablet, and looked at the creature.

'Notify me if this ship appears in any of these sigils,' he said.

'I had no idea you were so fascinated by weapons,' Nisroch said.

The magnificent Lady Laila leant in from behind him, her bare breasts emphasised by the fitted jacket that covered the rest of her upper body. Her mass of black hair was held up with jewelled pins, and her scent was heady, disturbing, and everywhere.

But her grasp on his finest sword was skilled and un-erotic, and she spun away from him, her bare feet dancing, her tiered skirts flying as she turned, the sword cutting the air.

'Beautiful,' she said. 'Made by mortals?'

'Yes,' Nisroch admitted.

'Their lives may be brief but their artifacts are anything but ephemeral.' Her eyes flicked to the electrum inlay on the bronze-bladed *khopesh*. 'I've never made anything as beautiful.'

'But you yourself are the epitome of beauty,' Nisroch said, stepping closer.

She gave a pirouette, stretching her arms to the heavens. The axe-blade of the *khopesh* sailed past his nose and he flinched back.

'Do you have any … *magical* weapons?' she asked. 'The old gods made so many wonderful things.'

She was still cutting the air with his favourite *khopesh*.

He sighed. 'You know perfectly well that my father has them all locked away.'

'In the treasury.' She licked her lips. Her eyes met his. 'Have you ever *seen* any of the old weapons?'

He stepped cautiously towards her. Was she leading him on? But he saw the passion of the collector in her eyes.

I have something in common with Lady Laila.

'I have seen Ara's *Terror*,' he said.

'What if I could show you *Godkiller*?' she breathed.

His pulse began to hammer. 'How?'

She put the sword back in its rack. 'You can see everything, can you not?'

He nodded.

'Is the gate clear?'

'You're not even supposed to know about the gate,' he blurted.

She leant very close, and just touched her lips to his.

'People tell me things.'

After a glance at his sigils to confirm that the coast was clear, they slipped, hand in hand, through the treasury gate.

While Lady Laila continued to show uncommon interest in Nisroch's weapon collection, the Black Goddess entered his most secret room. She used her golden sword to slice through his wards as if they were spider-webs, and she sat in his beautiful chair as if she owned it.

The monkey screamed.

She plucked it from its perch and patted it until it was quiet. And then she touched one of the glyphs, cast an intricate series of workings, and the glyph she touched suddenly displayed a different image. She repeated this with several glyphs.

She smiled, patted the monkey, and then hung its lifeless body over the perch.

'Fucking idiots,' she said, fondly.

Book Two

First Blood

Chapter Eight

Zos

Zos began his life as a warrior again. Despite his aches.

He'd been down for nearly three weeks. He was old enough that he knew he'd lost muscle; he was bored and excited at the same time. His leap aboard the Dardanian ship had cost him more than he'd expected; on the other hand, in some ways he felt better than he had in years.

He rose early, alongside the Hakrans, and joined them for their morning meditation to the sun, a series of stretching exercises that were not very different from those of the godborn warriors, at least those who took such things seriously. After they stretched and prayed, they all went to look for the donkey, who'd been missing for two hours and then had reappeared.

'There's no place to hide an animal that size on this ship,' Jawala said.

Aanat made a face that indicated that he thought that the world was full of unexplained donkeys, and Jawala frowned, and they all went to their daylight tasks.

Zos joined Atosa in sweeping the decks and raising water buckets, which Aanat and Pollon purified of their salt to fill some water amphorae, setting the cakes of sea salt aside for future use; the Hakrans wasted nothing. It was a process that depleted their *Aura* at a prodigious rate, but apparently it had to be done. As a man with no contact with the *Aura* whatsoever, Zos simply did what he was told.

But by the time the water was purified, the ship was in order; it was another beautiful summer day, the sky a magnificent blue, the sea a matching azure, a line of wispy clouds at the eastern horizon marking the existence of the Hundred Cities far out over the horizon. The sails were set and drawing so well they looked like they'd been carved from wood. Aanat and Jawala were at the steering oars, and Zos had several hours before his watch would be called.

Zos took a boathook about the same length and weight as the spear he'd claimed during the brush with the Jekers and began to fight the mainmast.

He was aware that Daos, the boy, was watching him from the crow's nest high above the deck. Era was watching him – and Aanat and Jawala, too, and probably Pavi.

He did care. He was a vain man, and he knew it, and he wanted to look beautiful, but the hard fact was that if he didn't start practising, some bastard would kill him. So he moved about the deck, slowly at first, going through the rituals as his father's enemies' weapons-master had taught him when he was a young hostage. He made parries and thrusts, sweeps with the hook, stop-thrusts with the butt, turning the pole as if paddling a boat, or dancing. He missed some easy thrusts, aiming at a particular pitch-spot on the mast; he tripped over the deck edge of the forward hold, sprawled into a bale of deck cargo and rose, embarrassed. But after a dozen such mistakes, he lost all thought of himself and it began to flow.

Then he began to attack the mainmast in earnest, ducking, cutting, thrusting against the rope-wound mainmast's lower trunk.

Pollon began to beat a time on the deck and Zos nodded his thanks. He was beginning to warm to the scribe, despite some initial hesitation. His automatic reaction to writers was contempt, and he knew better, but they were often silly men with silly goals and he had grown up in a world that valued them for taxes and otherwise ignored them.

But Pollon was deeply honest, a rarity in his breed, and seemed inclined to please. And he had a tendency to *think* that Zos admired. He was also obviously brave,

And the beat helped him focus. There was music to the war dances, which helped a warrior remember.

He leapt in the air, slammed the pole into the mast, and landed gracefully, sweeping an immediate parry against an invisible thrust, and suddenly there was true music.

The beat of Pollon's hand on the deck was now accompanied by a kithara, and the instrument, almost lost in the sounds of a ship at sea, played one of the epics. It wasn't the music to which Zos had trained... but he loved the epics. He loved the Hero Twins, and the Warrior, of course, but his favourite was wily Magwesh, cunning as a fox, clever and funny, sometimes brilliantly heroic and sometimes abjectly wrong, and it was one of Magwesh's tales that Era was playing. She began to sing. It was a simple tune, repetitive, but she adorned it and Zos almost lost his pattern of cuts and parries in sheer admiration. Her voice was beautifully pitched, and somehow at odds with her speaking voice, which could be quite harsh.

Is there nothing this woman cannot do?

He admired her too much already. She had exactly the kind of muscular looks he liked best in a woman, and she compounded that with her lack of subservience.

He stepped long to the left, rotated his spear and struck *back* like a reverse dagger strike – the most difficult blow. His point thudded home into the spot of black pitch, and he began to feel *it*.

Just watching her made him feel more alive.

He wasn't watching her now, and he leapt...

She sang of Magwesh stealing the cattle of the Sun God Shemeg, an incredibly ancient tale – and an illegal one, as that Sun God had been destroyed a thousand years before.

Zos landed, already tired. His leap hadn't been perfectly in time to the music, and he dropped to the deck.

'I can't laugh and fight at the same time,' he said to Pollon and Era.

Era sang the closing lines, where Magwesh has to try and hide the glowing cattle of the Sun God, and anywhere he goes at night, everyone can see them. She stilled the strings with her hand and sat back.

'I haven't really played in weeks,' she said. 'I am out of practice.'

'As am I.' Zos realised that he had just implied that she *was* out of practice. He saw her reaction and cursed inwardly.

Pollon gazed at her with something akin to adoration.

'May I ...' He was very hesitant. 'May I try your instrument?'

'You play?' she asked, and handed it over.

'It is incredibly beautiful,' Pollon said. 'Such workmanship ...'

Nicté had been watching Zos, but she, too, looked at the kithara.

'This is marvellous,' she said. 'The inlay is as good or better than any I could do.'

'Or I,' said Atosa. 'Druku's lame dick, lady, where'd you get this?'

'It was my mother's,' Daos said. He'd slid down a stay as if he'd been born to sea.

Atosa looked embarrassed. 'Sorry, Era,' he said. 'Didn't mean to swear in front of the boy.'

Pollon began to play. His notes were soft and hesitant; he stilled the strings and fussed over them, tuning them, and played again. His music was different from Era's – almost discordant, but sweeping and exciting and containing complex rhythms.

'Ah, Narmer,' Era said. 'I like it, but it's not the music I learnt from my mother.'

Pollon looked down. Zos thought the man was blushing.

'Teach me to fight,' Daos said. 'I'll be your *papista*.'

Zos had an image of Aiois, his last *papista*, being sliced in half by the plague god's sword.

'I don't think I need one just now,' Zos said. 'I don't even have a shield for you to carry.'

'If you don't teach me to fight, I'll die,' Daos said. '*And I will drive your chariot of fire.*'

'What?' Zos asked.

Daos shrugged. 'It just came out,' he said.

'Perhaps not,' Zos said, looking to Era for help.

'Oh, no, I'm quite sure,' the boy said. 'It will happen in a couple of months. I go ashore with you in Dardania, and a man kills me. Or I kill him.' He shrugged. 'If he kills me, you all die.' He smiled a normal child's smile. 'And otherwise, I drive your chariot of fire. So … I think you should teach me.'

Pollon was as pale as death and Atosa was trying to look away.

Era nodded. 'He sees things.' She tried to smile, but she was clearly as awed as Zos felt. 'I take him seriously.' She looked at the boy. 'Dardania?'

The boy shrugged. 'I know! Although it might be Narmer. Why would we go to Narmer?'

Zos looked at the boy. He was tall and well-made, for a boy before his manhood-growth.

'My last *papista* died fighting,' he said, a little harsher than he'd intended. 'And so did the one before that, and the one before that.'

The boy smiled. 'You'd better train me well, then,' he said.

'And anyway, I'll be your charioteer.' He smiled more widely. 'For a little while.'

It was as if a cloud had covered the sun. Zos felt a chill.

'Until I die?'

Daos shook his head. 'No,' he said. 'I don't see you dying, not if we do this right. It's hard to explain.'

Zos made himself smile. 'Well, that's heartening. All right, boy. I suppose I'll train you.'

'Good,' the boy said.

Training someone else is, he thought, *a good way to train*.

So he began with the simple dances he'd learnt as a boy – forwards and back, side to side, arm motions that would in time be lethal, but for now were just movements.

Zos had taught war dances to many men, and a few women. It was one of the reasons god-kings hired him. Daos was unlike most students; he asked no questions, and simply repeated what he was shown, over and over, with a patience that was at times as chilling as the boy's prophecy.

After an hour, Zos declared a rest, and drank some water, while the boy flowed through two of the simple dances. He wasn't flawless, but he was already showing an understanding of his own weight.

Pollon came and touched the warrior's arm.

'Really,' he said, 'you should probably teach us all.'

The next four days were surprisingly pleasant. The food was cut back to a mere subsistence, and there was neither wine nor beer, and the water was on short rations because they'd shared with the Dardanians. But despite that, the dances on the main deck became a focus, and they all participated except the Hakrans, who remained curious but aloof, and Gamash, though on the fourth day he and Zos fought with poles and improvised shields of rawhide from the cargo. The magos was too old to last long, but he was graceful, almost liquid in his movements, and he landed a killing blow in the first seconds, a thrust that seemed impossibly slow, and yet penetrated Zos' guard to touch him right over the heart.

'You are a master,' Zos said quietly.

Gamash smiled. 'I am an old man,' he said. 'But I once knew how to wield a spear.'

When he bowed and sat, Era picked up his weapons and bowed to Zos.

'I wish to fight,' she said.

He bowed in return, and they went at it.

She was flexible, graceful, and very fast. In the first clash, Zos' spear went past her as she made an almost impossible dodge. He closed to sweep her from her feet with his spear-arm against her neck, but she flowed with his movement, never quite losing her balance, stepped through his searching out-thrust leg and vanished under his arm.

He froze in astonishment and she poked him with her spear.

'Hit,' he admitted, and he didn't sound happy.

She grinned mockingly.

'Not what you expected, eh, Godborn?' she said over her shield.

They circled for a moment. He was giving her a wider berth, looking for an opening, and then she thrust at him under her shield, aiming at his forward leg. His spear licked across his shield, caught her spear and drove it to the side. He twisted so that the butt of his spear came up under her shield and into her neck.

'Oh!' she said, backing away. 'Hit.' Now it was her turn to sound annoyed.

She *was* annoyed. She began to move faster, and her strikes had a pecking quality, as if she was an angry bird. He was bigger, taller, and just as fast, and in the centre of the deck, they exchanged a flurry of blows. He made three strikes and she caught them all on her shield, and returned two with counter-strikes that he dodged or defended. She leapt back and he flipped back like an acrobat.

Gamash applauded.

Zos circled, and she pounced, a movement so fast that Pollon, who'd looked away, missed the whole engagement. Zos backed, tripped over the heavy hawser that ran the length of the ship, connecting bow and stern and keeping the ship rigid, and fell backwards. Era leapt forwards, but Zos rolled with his fall, flipped over in a somersault, came up on his feet, and made a thrust which she parried. Before she could respond he thrust again, and this time he turned an overhand thrust at her neck into a strike against her outstretched bare foot, catching her instep hard enough that she roared.

Instantly Zos stepped back.

'Damn you,' she spat. 'That was too hard.'

'My apologies,' he said. 'I struck in haste. You are very fast, but sacrificing control for speed is a fool's game.'

'I'm a fool?'

'I meant me,' Zos said. 'I should not have struck so hard.'

Era's dark face was red with pain and anger.

'Why not?' Daos asked. 'Isn't the purpose of fighting to kill?'

Zos glanced at him, keeping Era in his peripheral vision.

'Yes,' he said. 'But it takes very little strength to wound a person in the foot with a spear. If, however, I drive it into the deck, or the ground, or my opponent's shield, or even just too deep in my victim's body ... why, I lose control of my spear.' He nodded at Era, who was starting to relax. 'And injuring your sparring partner is hardly good for training, is it?'

Zos wanted to apologise again, but Era avoided him, even in the close confines of a small ship at sea.

The next day, after they'd danced until their muscles flowed well, Hefa-Asus took up the wooden pole and rawhide shield. He was huge, and very strong.

Zos seemed to hit him at will, and after a few exchanges, the big man raised a hand.

'I am not fond of war,' he said. 'And yet, I have been very successful killing men, when required.'

'If you let me train you, you will be better,' Zos said.

That afternoon, Era took up the practice shield again. Zos smiled.

Perhaps not the best response, he thought later.

Era leapt at him.

Zos matched her leap with one of his own, a flexible move that carried him clear of the aft hold and into the narrow space between the two holds – a piece of deck only about a pace wide, and with the mainmast right in the middle.

She came on again, leaping...

His bare pole caught her in the midriff and dropped her into the aft hold, onto the bales of cotton shawls.

She rose, favouring her hip. And came at him again. She hit him hard in the shin, a brilliant stop-thrust into his complex overhand attack, and he saluted, and she attacked again.

He bounced back and dropped his shield.

She paused. 'Now you mock me?'

He smiled. 'Oh, no. I salute you. Now I'll fight you as I really fight, not the way I train shield-bearers.'

They both struck. There was a flurry, as she thrust and he covered, both hands on the spear, and using both ends, which drove her to play closer. She stepped in and he went almost past her, with his free hand on her shield. He used it and her strength to throw her over his leg and she was flat on her back, his point at her throat.

'Ahhh,' Gamash said, off to his left. 'He really is very good.'

Era spluttered for a moment.

'Shields are for stopping arrows,' Zos said in his teacher voice. 'And for keeping untrained people alive.'

'You are *so fucking pompous*.' She rolled back over her head to her feet like the acrobat she was. 'But I admit that was ... excellent.'

Gamash sat back. 'You were a bull-leaper?' he asked.

'Yes.' Zos grimaced.

Era picked herself up. She looked as if she was on the edge of saying something, but she turned and settled against the rail instead.

'Teach me to do that,' Hefa-Asus said.

Zos nodded, but he was watching Era. He'd embarrassed her, as he'd meant to, and now he felt like a fool.

'Sure,' he said to Hefa-Asus.

Later, when Zos was at one steering oar with Jawala at the other, Era came and sat on the steering bench.

'I was wrong to be angry,' she said.

'I was wrong to hurt your foot yesterday. How is it?' He sounded wrong, even in his own head – stiff, formal.

'Fine,' she said. 'Listen to me when I apologise, please.'

Zos bowed his head.

'You made me angry because you hit me easily, not because you hit me hard. I know how to fight. I expected to do better.' She didn't meet his eye. 'I've never been thrown before.'

Zos nodded. 'You expected to beat me?'

His incredulity flared her anger – he could see it – but he had the hardest time imagining a *woman* who could beat him. Or a man. Anenome, perhaps. He was reputed the best spearman in the Hundred Cities, and he'd killed more men than the plague. But not some dancer ...

Some dancer. I'm an idiot. That's exactly why she's angry.

Era nodded, as if his question answered something. 'Fuck you,' she said.

Zos choked down his own anger. 'You wanted to beat me,' he said. 'You, a dancer, wanted to beat me, a professional warrior.' He raised a hand like a man surrendering in a wrestling match. 'No, never mind. Of course you wanted to beat me.'

'I've beaten a few men, here and there,' she said.

Zos willed himself to be silent.

'And I'm tired of you looking at me,' she said with a sudden renewal of anger. 'Keep your eyes to yourself.'

Zos felt his eyes narrowing and the anger rising.

'You could have just told me that,' he said. 'Instead of fighting when you are supposed to be sparring.'

'Oh, did I *try too hard*, godborn warrior?'

They were both silent. Zos thought about Jawala at the other oar. Hearing it all.

'And you have begun to act as if you are the leader of this enterprise. You are not. If you continue to give orders...' She paused.

'I have given no orders.' Zos was being defensive and that annoyed him, but he wasn't sure how to react.

'Every body posture, every intonation, every little bit of rhetoric is the rhetoric of godborn command,' she said. 'My father was godborn. I hate all that shit. Stop it.'

She rose and walked forward towards the bow, back straight.

Zos looked at Jawala. She didn't betray any amusement, which was probably good, he thought.

'Do you wish me to comment?' Jawala asked.

'No?' Zos said, trying to force a smile. 'Yes?'

'You do tend to look at all of us women,' she said, 'the way a child looks at sweets laid out for a feast.'

Zos felt himself flush. 'I've never heard any complaints before.'

'You wouldn't, would you – *Godborn*?' Jawala said. 'And you are so evidently used to command.'

Zos felt the anger rise within him as the shot went home.

I'm trying to be what you want me to be! he thought. *I could just kill some of you and take whatever I want.*

He considered that last thought and smiled ruefully.

'When I was among godborn,' he said, 'I was contemptuous of their arrogance and privilege. I told myself I was never really one of them.'

Jawala raised both eyebrows.

'Now that I am among you, I begin to see just how very godborn I really am.' He shrugged.

'That is well said.' Jawala nodded. 'I'm a merchant, Zos. Wherever I go, I'm foreign. I don't eat meat, I look different, and no one in the world has family relationships that work like ours.'

Zos didn't understand where she was going.

'My point is that we never really fit in. We all carry our Hakran beliefs around with us. You were brought up at a court ... Mykoax?'

'I was a hostage,' he said. 'We were all the sons of princes and kings, and we all trained together and played together and did stupid shit together. And then one day the king was murdered by his wife and his son became king, and he took out his anger on me. He could have executed me. Instead, he made me watch as they took my mother to be a slave.'

'That's terrible.' Jawala said.

'Oh, it's still all godborn. I wasn't killed or enslaved or sold off as a chattel, because I'm godborn and male. The king came to my tent – I had my own tent, of course. And he said, "Welcome to the world." He gave me a nice dagger and suggested that I could end myself, if I wished. Or understand that this is the world, and continue to serve him. I could be a ruler or a slave, he said. No other choices.'

Jawala looked at him. 'You killed him?'

Zos laughed bitterly. 'Killed him? He was a full-grown man

surrounded by guards. I was seven. No. I served him until I reached manhood. He taught me to fight. Sent me to be a bull-leaper – he didn't care if I lived or died. Never offered to restore my kingdom, though. And then, when I was old enough, I left. I bought my mother free and got on a ship and sailed for Lazba.' His voice was quavering now. 'You see, I believed him. Agon of Mykoax, son of the great Atrios. I still hate him.' His voice cracked. 'And thanks to him, I thought, this *is* how the world works.'

A heavy silence hung between them, broken only by the sound of someone going up to the bow to piss over the side, and the creak of the hull, and the wind in the rigging.

When he had control of his voice again, Zos said, 'At some point I realised I'd been sold a rotten squash. This *doesn't* have to be how the world works.'

Jawala sighed. 'Well,' she said, 'perhaps you will find a new road. But not through Era. She doesn't incline to men, and you represent almost everything she hates.'

Zos nodded to himself. 'Lucky me.'

The Dry One in the forward hold lay where he'd been arranged. Zos checked on him every day, with Pollon and Atosa. Both of them smelt the body for rot; checked the deep puncture wound for leakage. The wound no longer leaked, and the blue-green ichor had first crystallised and then formed a tarry substance on the surface of the wound – sticky and pleasant-smelling.

Pollon sniffed at it and shook his head.

'I lack the experience to know,' he said. 'But based on descriptions, this is the pure resin that we make drugs from.'

'That's a terrible thought you have there,' Zos said. 'But he's not dead.'

'No, I think he's recovering. But we can't leave him here.'

Zos nodded. 'I have an idea.'

Together, he, Hefa-Asus and Pollon wrapped the Dry One in the oldest, worst clothes left on the ship – mostly things they'd been wearing when the ship picked them up. When finished, and leaving a copper tube for the creature to breathe, the Dry One looked like a badly wrapped corpse ready to be buried. They moved the Dry One into the small forward space under the forward deck.

'Did you see its blood, when the wound was fresh?' Pollon asked.

Hefa-Asus nodded, reached into his belt-pouch, and took out a lump of a blue-green, tarry substance.

'I saved some,' he said.

'It is the *resin*, isn't it?' Pollon asked.

Hefa-Asus paused, sniffed the lump, and then shook his head. 'What a fool I am. Of course it's resin.' He bit off a small piece, chewed it, and nodded. 'Full of power. Gods and demons, Pollon. It's fucking *resin*.'

In addition to martial training and tending the Dry One, there was another activity in the aft hold, every morning and evening: Gamash, Aanat and Pollon would read the astrological signs of the day, try to work out the portents, and then would conduct experiments with bits of star-stone and casting.

Zos left them to it, although there were moments of crisis, as when Gamash set the partition between the hulls afire, and moments of comedy, as when a miscast working by Aanat caused water to appear over his head and fall on him.

Zos watched from the steering bench. Pavi was teaching Era to steer, and both women were obviously just as interested in the events in the aft hold as he was.

'Do you understand what they're doing?' he asked Era.

She nodded, as if they'd never had a spat. And as if she hadn't been avoiding him for a full day.

'Gamash believes that the star-stone inhibits casting. Aanat believes the star-stone directly affects the ability of the caster to reach the Great *Aura*, and Pollon is recording the results.' She glanced at Zos. 'My silver is on Pollon. He'll work it out.'

'How does it work?' he asked. 'The … magic? I have none.'

Era looked at him a moment, and he had the sense that she was considering a biting remark. Instead, she met his eyes and held up a hand. Suddenly, a pale blue fire blazed at her fingertips. 'Mage light,' she said. 'Made from my own *Aura*. Easy, quick, but a very finite resource, like muscle; you wear out.' She made it vanish. And then, after a moment of stillness, she had a fire again, this time a pale golden light. 'This is my connection to the Great *Aura* that is everywhere around us. I am not particularly good at it. Gamash is very powerful indeed, and can access it instantly and channel huge amounts of it.'

'Is that training or talent?' he asked.

She made a face. 'I'm not sure anyone really knows,' she said. 'I've heard that use of resin enhances you, but I haven't experienced that.'

He nodded. 'Thanks. I've always wondered, but I've only met a handful of *magi* who weren't fakes, and none of them were very … approachable.'

She nodded. 'You are a curious man for a godborn.'

He couldn't stop himself. He raised an eyebrow. 'You are as godborn as I am,' he said.

She got up without another word and walked away.

Zos stood at his oar, managing to do his part in keeping their course, and wondering why he'd had to say that.

Why am I such a fool?

He reminded himself that three weeks before, he'd been a broken man bound to a wheel waiting to die.

★

They smelt Dekhu before they saw it. The smell was just an annoying trace at first – a feeling in the back of the sinus that something smelt wrong.

By the time the island's central volcano-mountain was clearly visible, it was more than a feeling. It was a scent on the air. And that scent was human faeces.

Atosa, whose sea legs hadn't been the best, lost his very small breakfast over the side.

'Fuck me,' he moaned.

Zos held the man's long hair. 'The smell of despair,' he said.

'Oh, you've been a slave?' Era asked him.

'I've owned a few.' Zos had decided in the night that if he couldn't join her, he'd beat her.

She spat over the side. 'Godborn arse.'

Hefa-Asus loomed over him and elbowed him in a manner that was probably meant to be playful.

'You two need to let your charcoal cool,' he said. 'You burn too hot.'

Zos made himself *not* look at Era.

'I know,' he said.

I'm not used to being disliked, he almost said, but that was too weak to be spoken.

An hour later, and the smell was pervasive, and instead of growing used to it, they were all struggling not to gag.

'Tiny island, thousand slaves,' Pavi said.

'You've been before?' Zos asked.

'Twice,' Pavi said, with what looked like pride.

'Can you give us the layout?' he asked.

Pavi took a piece of charcoal out of Mokshi's long-dead firebox and squatted. The rest of them gathered around as she drew a rough, thin rectangle with a long point like a barbed arrowhead pointing due south, with a pair of deep, moon-shaped

318

bays on either side, and a barbed line for steep hills down the middle.

'Here's the two ports,' she said, pointing at the bays. 'One beach faces Narmer, the other Sala and Noa. Here's the ruins—'

'Ruins?' Nicté asked.

Everyone looked at her.

'Dekhu was the seat of the old gods,' Era said. 'The Sun God, the God of Music, the Goddess of Dance ...'

'You're not a *restorationist*, are you?' Gamash asked Era, and she flushed.

'I know all the old epics,' she said. 'Perhaps I have a certain ... nostalgia for them.'

Gamash smiled. 'I have a suspicion that the old gods were every bit as useless as the current crop.'

Pavi waited politely. Era looked as if she was going to say more, but decided against it. Zos forced himself *not* to make the gesture that would command the woman to go on. Because he waited, Era indicated Pavi should go on.

'The ruins of all the old temples are here, as well as the houses of the gods, with the Street of the Gods running this way. The slave-dealers mostly set up in the porticoes of the old temples.'

Gamash nodded. 'The ultimate revenge,' he muttered.

'What?' Nicté asked.

Gamash spread his hands and looked at Pollon. 'I've never really thought about it that much. But it occurs to me that the gods are still fighting this old war. The old gods are utterly defeated, and yet ...' He shook his head. 'All of the propaganda is still meant to discredit them.'

Pollon looked thoughtful.

Era gestured at Pavi again, who smiled at Pollon.

'The slave market is right here, on the Street of the Gods and around what used to be the great square. It's a huge expanse of

319

dirty white marble, the size of… I don't know, the size of the port in most towns. There's shacks and booths along the edges, in the rubble. But that's it. There's not much in the hills but volcanic rock and beetles.'

Zos leant over her map. 'Any other landings?'

'Another beach down over here, on the west side. Otherwise that side of the island is one giant rock.'

Aanat nodded at Zos. 'Our people have rescued a number of slaves over the years – usually runaways who get to the far side of the island. If they are strong swimmers, they can get clear of the surf and out to a waiting boat.'

'Most drown,' Pavi said grimly. 'Slaves are not heavily guarded. When one escapes, the slavers all gather with dogs to hunt the escapee. If they catch one, they torture them and then crucify them in the agora. Very few run any more.'

Zos nodded.

Era squinted at him. 'What are you thinking?'

He shook his head. 'I don't know yet.'

The Dardanian ship left them a few stadia from the headland with its ruined statue. The statue must once have been colossal, as the feet alone stood high enough to be a sea landmark. The Hakrans steered to starboard, to land at the eastern harbour. The Dardanian captain waved and steered to port, to land at the western beach.

They still weren't used to the smell when they landed. There was no customs boat, because Dekhu wasn't a city state or a country. It was more of a pirate haven, except that the slavers clearly had rules as, shortly after they landed, a handsome man in a brilliant scarlet cloak hailed them from the beach. Aanat went to the peak of the stern; they'd landed stern first and had half a dozen anchor stones out from the bow.

'Welcome to Dekhu,' Scarlet Man called. 'I'm Amethu.'

'Hail, and the gods favour you, Amethu.'

The man nodded. 'You are Hakran?' he called up.

'We are,' Aanat answered. 'We have a few passengers as well.'

Amethu nodded again. 'If you wish to trade here, we are pleased to inform you that you and your goods are welcome, so long as we may search your ship now, and again before you sail.'

Aanat looked forward. Jawala nodded, and Amethu came up the ladder with a pair of heavily muscled bravos. They had big oak clubs and small round leather shields.

'I could kill them both,' Era said quietly.

Zos nodded. 'Me too. Which one would you like?'

'Oh, you are such a gentleman.'

The man in the red cloak bowed slightly to the passengers. 'Purpose of your visit?' he asked.

Gamash had been chosen as spokesman, and had been offered the pick of the crew's jewellery as well as the textiles from the cargo. He was splendidly dressed in a salmon-red-orange tunic with embroidery at the throat and hem, and a light cotton cloak, a chlamys from Rasna that spoke subtly of status and power. He wore three gold rings, one of them borrowed from Daos. He had Aanat's visibly magical amulet around his neck, with another of his own.

'I am Lord Gamash of Weshwesh,' he said.

Amethu's head snapped back as if he'd been struck.

'Ahh,' he said. 'My lord.'

'These are my people,' Gamash said. 'I am on a mission for my king, and it is none of your business.'

Amethu cringed, and went from pompous to obsequious in a single heartbeat.

'But my lord,' he said, 'I am required to ask—'

'Nonsense,' Gamash snapped. 'You are a slave-dealer. You aren't required to ask me anything.'

Zos, standing next to him in another fine tunic, looking

as obviously godborn as he could, smiled to hear the man's authority.

'Nonsense,' Gamash repeated. 'You aren't the law. You have no authority that I recognise.'

'I can—'

'I can have my warrior kill you and your two useless slave-soldiers and we'll all go about our days,' Gamash said.

'No killing on my ship,' Jawala growled.

Is she play-acting?

Amethu blinked. 'My lord...' he began. 'Is it fair to say you are here to buy slaves?'

'Master Amethu,' Zos said, 'my lord does not like being questioned by inferiors. So let us agree between us that it is fair to say that my lord is here to buy slaves. Or a slave.'

He let that red herring slip in like one of Gamash's slow spear thrusts.

'Ahh,' Amethu said. 'And these are all your people?'

'Yes,' Zos said.

'This is a sizeable entourage for a lord purchasing a slave.' The man was looking at Era.

Gamash snapped his fingers and Zos stepped closer to the man.

'This is verging on an interrogation and my lord is becoming impatient.'

Amethu shook his head. 'Hakrans steal slaves,' he said, as if to Zos, but loud enough to carry. 'I'm only doing my—'

Jawala stepped up. 'Perhaps you want to see our cargo?' she asked.

Amethu seemed eager to leave.

'Arse,' Era said, not very quietly. 'I hate his kind.'

'Slave traders who are also jetty bureaucrats?' Hefa-Asus asked. 'What's not to hate?'

The scarlet cloak moved briskly through the forward hold, saw the shrouded corpse, and shivered.

'We were attacked by Jekers,' Jawala said.

'Your people don't fight,' Amethu shook his head.

'We didn't fight,' Jawala said. 'We ran.'

Amethu saw the nine stone jars sitting deep in the hold.

'Wine?' he asked.

'Resin,' Jawala replied. 'Pure.'

Amethu glanced up at the two slave-guards.

'For sale?' he asked.

Jawala nodded.

Amethu looked down. 'I'll have to test it.'

'No,' Jawala said. 'I'm sorry, but I won't break the seals unless paid. You can see they are intact – you can see that they're not... human.'

Amethu looked at her and climbed out of the holds.

'Six minae of silver,' he said with a rich smile.

'That's about one tenth of my opening price,' Jawala said pleasantly. 'Or are you attempting to get a fifty-five mina bribe?'

'I can be a powerful friend here,' Amethu said.

'I can buy many powerful friends for sixty minae of silver,' Jawala said pleasantly. 'I'm sorry, sir. I know this market. I know the value of my goods.'

Amethu's eyes narrowed. 'I don't have that kind of silver, but I have a heavy stock of unsold slaves.'

'We don't deal in slaves,' she said.

'Perhaps you could take them in trade and then free them, according to your fine principles,' he suggested. 'Or do your kind only steal other men's property?'

'I think we're done here,' Jawala said.

Zos caught one of the armed slaves by the arm. The man tried to shake him off and failed.

'Is he really allowed to try and cut trade deals while acting as the customs inspector?' Zos asked, and the slave grunted.

Zos put a small silver ring into the man's meaty hand.

'We're not the enemy,' he whispered.

The man didn't even turn his head, but he took the ring and made it vanish into his loincloth, which Zos found amusing.

Amethu climbed out of the hold. 'I could perhaps come up with twelve minae of silver,' he said.

Gamash ended the conversation.

'I'm going ashore,' he said. 'I do not endure the rays of the sun for this sort of thing.'

His transformation was incredible. The tired old man had been replaced by an energetic warrior whose arrogance was exuded like a bitter perfume from his pores. He swept his light cloak back over his shoulder, exposing the gold and lapis amulet he wore, and walked with dignity to the top of the ladder to the beach.

Zos followed him, with Era close by.

The slaves glanced at each other ... and let them go. Amethu caught them up before they'd walked a hundred paces.

'You cannot leave the ship without my permission!' he said. He'd have seemed more imposing if he hadn't been breathing heavily from the short run.

Gamash raised his staff, and rudely put the bronze-shod point in the centre of the other man's chest.

'And yet,' he said with contempt, 'I *have* left the ship, and you could not stop me. I have had enough of the pretence that I am some merchant and you are some sort of official. Begone.'

'I will ...' Amethu began, and realised that neither of his slave-soldiers had kept up with him. 'You will regret this, *my lord*,' he spat.

But he got out of their way.

'There's trouble,' Zos said.

Gamash glanced at him. 'Did I overplay it?'

Zos shook his head.

Era agreed, for once. 'No, you were perfect. He's a fool, and it is a pity that we got a fool.'

Zos took a moment to step aside with the slave-soldier to whom he'd given the ring.

'Will you report him?' he asked.

The man gave him perhaps a hair's breadth of smile. 'Fuck no,' he said. 'What do I look like – a public slave in Narmer?'

Zos nodded. 'Thanks, anyway. Are they all like this?'

The slave grunted, and the man crunched away on the sand with his partner.

'What now?' Era asked.

Zos looked at her. 'You hate it when I give orders.'

'I don't hate it when you have ideas,' she said. 'I hate it when you sound as if you're the only person with ideas.'

Zos took a deep breath. 'I think we should go shopping. I need a sword.'

'We have nothing to trade,' Era said.

'Jawala is sharing the profits from the stone jars,' Zos said.

'Jawala is too good to be true,' Era said.

'On that, we can agree,' Zos said. 'Great lord?'

'Let's shop, by all means,' Gamash said. 'I have a few minae of gold myself. We can buy you a sword.'

'And Pollon a lyre?' she asked. 'And perhaps a bow?'

'Remember there will be god's eyes,' Gamash said. 'Let's not attract attention.'

Zos pulled his chlamys up over his head, as men did to shield themselves from the sun. Era did the same, fixing a shawl as a veil. But they had already attracted attention. Before they left the beach to walk up what had once been the Street of the Gods, a big brown man with a forked beard and a very short kilt in a magnificent tartan came up from his ship. Zos knew him immediately, although the man was now dressed in all the finery of his kind; he had a necklace of gold and lapis around his neck and a mane of dark hair very like Zos' own, and his right ear was full of gold earrings.

He swept a good bow to Gamash – godborn to godborn.

'Great lord!' he said. 'Your unworthy servant wishes to express his thanks for the water. Because of you, I didn't lose a man.' He gave a shorter bow to Zos. 'I am Trayos, son of Liktor,' the man said. 'My god-ancestor was Nanuk, the old God of the Sea, and I have sailed the seas since I was a boy.'

Gamash gave a civil inclination of his head, godborn senior to godborn junior.

'Lord Trayos,' he said. 'I am Gamash of Weshwesh. And I am at the service of any courteous, well-born man.' He looked at the now distant figure of the scarlet-cloaked merchant. 'And I, in turn, thank you for your splendid efforts against the Jekers.'

'Not a bad fight, I admit,' Trayos said. The Dardanian captain ran his fingers down his sleek, waxed beard. 'My lord, I'm fully aware that advice is worth what you pay for it, but in this case, I feel I need to offer some. That's a bad man. And he has many friends.'

Zos raised an eyebrow. 'Lord Trayos, we're on an island well known for its violence and depravity, where slaves are bought and sold. I'm tempted to assume everyone here is *bad*.'

Trayos nodded agreement instead of taking offence. 'Myself…' he said. 'I'm here to make the best possible profit. And when I see that arse trying to fleece a lord…'

'My deepest thanks for your warning,' Gamash said, with another civil inclination of his head. 'I appreciate your courtesy. But I think our course with the man is set.'

Trayos bowed again. 'So be it. May I ask what you are here to buy?'

'You may, noble captain.' Gamash smiled. 'You are a captain, are you not?'

In Dardanian, the man said, 'I am *Vasilios* to the hunter-merchant *Trident*.'

Zos translated.

Lord Trayos turned to Zos. 'I know you from somewhere,' he said.

Zos smiled. 'I was on your ship ...' he began, and the Dardanian smiled in a way that showed far too many teeth.

'I know that, bull-leaper. I mean, I have seen you before. You are Mykoan?'

Gamash was showing real impatience now, and Zos kept his face impassive.

'I grew up at the court of the god-king,' he said.

Trayos fingered his beard. 'You know that Agon is sick?' he said. 'I should be bartering, for news like this. Were you one of his dogs?'

Zos spat. 'I am no friend to Agon.'

Trayos stepped closer. 'Then all the better that we should be friends,' he said.

Dekhu was an island of degradation and torment. They witnessed hundreds of acts of cruelty under every decaying portico. On one ruined mosaic floor, two slaves fought with staves, both of them covered in blood; on another, two women danced with chillingly unsensual lasciviousness. Whips cracked, fists pounded, and for the most part, the victims were blank-faced, unresponsive, less inclined to rebellion than donkeys or mules.

And the smell of human faeces was omnipresent. It was clear why; there was no organised latrine. The ancient white marble was shit-stained everywhere.

Zos had seen the sack of cities and the murder of innocents, but something about the businesslike bustle and determination of the human horror of Dekhu made him feel physically unwell. He wanted very badly to hit something, or someone. He'd owned slaves himself – more than a dozen – but never like this.

Or is it always exactly like this, in their minds?

They went all the way up the Street of the Gods, all the way to the centre, the navel of the world, where people had once gathered to see their gods made manifest. Most of the temples around the vast square had been thrown down, but a few still had columns standing. Very different from the squat modern columns favoured by Enkul-Anu, these ancient pillars stood straight, sometimes fluted or twisted, and appeared both slim and sturdy.

Across the huge open space there stood the Temple of All Gods, in magnificently polished black basalt, like a toad amid the white rubble of its former foes.

Zos looked at it too long. He found it odd that in a three-week voyage with a Dry One and some very strange shipmates, he'd become a convert to a revolution.

Except that I always was a convert.

The stench was overwhelming, and was made worse by the incense being burned by many of the slavers and some of the lesser merchants.

They found the section of the open-air market dedicated to weapons and armour, and Zos was immediately disappointed.

'This is all crap!' he blurted.

Era gave him a look. 'You expected to find fine craftsmen forging the best for slaves?'

But it was she who found the bow. It was old, a composite bow from Narmer, with a hardwood core and ibex antler arms. The belly was delaminating with age.

Zos played with it for long enough to raise the price, and Gamash bought it anyway, as all the other bows were short, cheaply made, and weak. More like stage props than real weapons.

Slave-soldiers were a reality. Most of them were better treated than their companions and in return gave good service. They were relatively cheap compared to godborn – and had no political consequences, the way arming the free men and women of a city did. After visiting half a dozen tables, Zos was convinced that only fools would buy the thin-bladed swords or wooden clubs. Even the shields were too light and too small. But many of the men and women he saw were competent, or more. He saw a Dardanian with muscles like ropes, and three nomad women, unbroken by their ordeals and standing together over someone they'd killed; he saw Narmerians and Dendrownans and men and women of a dozen cultures. He even spoke to a young man who claimed to be a charioteer from Atussa.

They were halfway around the agora, and Aanat and Pavi had caught them up, when Era touched Zos' arm.

'Those are Dendrownans,' she said. 'And there's a god's eye behind them on the pillar.'

Zos followed her gaze, and saw it, too – three men in chains sitting on their haunches. And the god's eye.

'So?' Zos asked.

Era shrugged. 'I've never seen Dendrownan slaves.'

'Not uncommon in Dardania,' Zos said. 'They capture one another and sell abroad.'

'Gods,' Era muttered.

Gamash nodded. 'Ask Nicté,' he said. 'Her people are regularly enslaved by the coastal peoples.'

'You say the old gods were the same—'

'This is not the place,' Gamash said in a low voice. 'There's another god's eye.'

'But look at us!' Era said.

Zos was listening, but his eye had been caught by the stall

next to the one where the three Dendrownans crouched in stoic misery.

By a woman.

She was tall, and as black as jet. Her eyes seemed huge, even at a distance. Her waist was small, and the rest of her was athletic ... and ample, too.

Her eyes met his.

Era was saying, '...it's the example they set.'

'This is not something to discuss here,' Gamash snapped.

Era suddenly stopped walking.

'That is the most beautiful woman I've ever seen,' Era said. 'Mother Bear, she's looking right at me.'

She's looking right at me, Zos thought.

Without conscious thought, Zos took a step towards the woman, and found that Era was by his side.

She kept walking forwards.

A big man stepped in from their left; the side Zos was on.

'Ah,' he said. 'You like my Dite, do you?' He bowed to Gamash. 'Perhaps a great lord like yourself would be pleased to own her.'

The slave trader was modestly dressed, but Zos could see the heavy gold chain around his neck and the excellent short sword by his hip, hilted in elephant ivory from Narmer, studded with silver nails for a better grip.

The trader ignored both Zos and Era and leant towards Gamash.

'Endlessly lascivious,' he said, his breath heavily scented with cardamom. 'Literally tireless. Born to fuck.'

The woman looked at Zos. She looked under her eyelids, and her huge eyes showed more white than pupil. She was dark-skinned, almost ebony, her body lithe and well-muscled, like a dancer or a warrior, but she had a look of impish sensuality on her beautiful face.

And she winked at him.

'Buy me,' she said. Her voice wasn't breathy or intoxicating. It was deeper than he'd expected. She sounded... kind. And commanding. Not like a slave at all.

She looked right into his eyes, and she made a sign with one hand.

Antlers.

'I will buy you,' Era said, at his side.

Behind them, the slaver was gesturing.

'I want a private sale, If I put her to auction, I lose a fee to the auctioneer and a market tax. So... fifteen minae of silver.' He nodded. 'Cheap, really. She'll keep you... vigorous. Three rides a day, eh, sir?'

Gamash didn't look outraged. He looked bored, and when his bronze-shod staff slammed into the man's shin the slaver was unprepared for it, and he went down like a sacrificed lamb.

'Guards!' he roared, and reached for the hilt of his sword.

Zos wasn't sure what Gamash was playing at, but he went with it. He stepped on the downed slaver's chest, then drew the man's own sword and put it to his left eye.

The four guards, all slaves themselves, shuffled to a halt.

'I thought we weren't attracting attention,' Era muttered. She was covering the old man's back.

Gamash leant over and spat in the slaver's face. 'I am a god-born lord,' he said carefully. 'You are a merchant. Know your place, or my people will teach it to you. And none of your slave-soldiers will protect you for a minute.'

Zos thought the slaver might be about to burst with rage.

'You do not speak familiarly about sex to a godborn, little man,' Gamash said. 'Or about anything else. Do you understand?'

The slaver was a pale southerner, and the flush showed bright red on his skin.

'Blind him,' Gamash said.

'No!' The slaver broke. 'No, please.' The rage was replaced with a whine.

'Do you understand?' Zos asked, taking his cue from the magos.

'Yes,' the man said.

'Yes what?' Zos asked.

'Great lord.'

Zos nodded. 'There, was that so difficult?'

He untied the ribbon of leather that held the man's scabbard to his broad belt.

'That's my sword . . .' the man had the courage to mutter.

Zos knew how to behave like a godborn.

'Mine now,' he said.

As Gamash began to walk away, Zos said, 'You give a shockingly good performance of a godborn great lord.'

Gamash smiled wickedly. 'I have some experience. Isn't it curious how easily we fall into the luxuries of evil?'

Zos turned back to make sure that the slaver wasn't coming for them. The sword felt good at his side.

The woman was blowing him a kiss.

He closed his eyes. She was *glorious*.

'We have to rescue her,' Era said at his side.

Zos glanced at her. 'We've found something on which we agree,' he said.

Later, at the leading edge of twilight, Zos slipped over the side, leaving Hefa-Asus and Atosa rebuilding the old bow with a stinking glue pot and some magic from the old man while Nicté slit some sinew she'd bought in the market.

Zos went dressed in a long dark *hymation* that reached to the ground, and a matching shawl which covered his head and face. He made it away from the *Untroubled Swan* without being noticed, and walked up the beach into the lamplit darkness of the beachside slave pens and small tavernas.

The Dardanian captain was waiting for him at a table under an eight-spout oil lamp. He was plainly dressed again, short, broad and powerful.

'Lord Trayos Liktores,' Zos said.

'Lord Zos of Trin,' the Dardanian said.

Zos paused. 'Do we have a problem?'

Trayos sat back down. 'Far from it, my long-lost prince. What we have is an opportunity.'

'Not interested.'

'Agon is doomed,' Trayos said. 'He's sick and he's lost the confidence of the gods. You know he lost a war in Hanigalbat, eh? Losing is a fine way to forfeit the confidence of your people, I promise you. His alliance with Sala is rocky.' The man paused, leaning forward. 'Do you know that Narmer has a new Great Lady? She's called Maritaten, and she's trying to restore the worship of Arrina.'

Zos sat. A blank-eyed slave woman came.

'Your best wine,' Trayos said. 'Really, your best.'

The woman was naked, except for a cord around her waist with a few beads on it. Trayos caught and then released it. He'd deftly wrapped a scrap of silver around the cord.

She glanced at it, and raised an eyebrow.

Trayos nodded. 'The best.'

She slipped away.

'So?' Zos asked. 'What's Narmer to do with anything?'

'So there are opportunities. Agon is weak and has no friends at home or overseas.' He raised a hand as if saluting before a duel.

'Huh,' Zos said.

The Dardanian looked at Zos. 'I knew you the moment I

333

saw you,' he said. 'I saw you make your leap with the bull at Mykoax.'

Zos laughed. It was a perfectly genuine sound and it shocked the other man. Heads turned.

Zos was still smiling like a fool when he leant forwards.

'Where were you a year ago?' he asked. 'I don't care any more. I've let go of all that, my lord. Sorry.'

'You've let go of revenge? Against the man who killed your father and sold your mother as a slave?' Trayos shook his head.

Zos thought, *He was just a tool. And his father did the worst of the horror, anyway. And the gods ... It's all the fucking gods.*

But the anger *was* still there, boiling away inside him. For his mother, more than anything.

Zos got to his feet. 'I'm not interested,' he said.

Trayos shrugged. 'Sure you aren't,' he said. '*Listen to me.*' He leant forwards and spoke quietly. 'I went to the oracle – the real one, at Phi. You know what the old woman said? She said, *When the Man-Eaters roam the waves, your fate will leap your wooden walls.* He leant closer. 'You are my fate, bull-leaper. The fucking Huntress told me so.'

Zos took a breath, as if he had to break the effect of a spell cast on himself, or a sudden bout of weakness.

'I'm not your fate,' he said.

He walked away into the night, leaving the captain to drink his wine.

He wandered all the way back to the great square, looking for the god's eyes and their faint blue glow. They were harder to see by day; by night, their unearthly mage-lit blue gave them away, and he prowled along, walking behind tents and between stalls, carefully avoiding the human dung that seemed to be spread everywhere, trying to avoid rolling his ankle on the splintered marble of the old gods' temples that looked as if they'd exploded from within.

Then he climbed up the hillside behind the old ruins. It wasn't a difficult climb, but in half-darkness it was challenging enough, and it took longer as the pink light faded in the sky.

I'm looking at the defences, he thought. *I'm not going after that beautiful woman. Not at all.*

Except that in addition to being beautiful, she'd given the sign of the Huntress.

Zos had his doubts about Temis, but he was human enough to silence them when following her dictates suited his agenda.

He reached his goal – not the top, but the peak of a ridge that overlooked the slave market and the ruined city beneath it. He pulled his shawl tighter against the chill, heard the unmistakable sound of metal on rock, and froze.

He waited, barely breathing.

Nothing.

He waited longer. He'd played this game before, out waiting an enemy, and he…

'So,' Era said, practically in his ear. 'What are you doing here?'

He flinched.

She laughed quietly.

'You are very quiet.'

'Eh. I had some trouble with the climb. But I came up the back side, which is much easier than the overhang.' She leant out. 'I saw you leave the boat. And I saw you sit down with the other godborn arse. I was planning to come up here myself.' She glanced at him. 'And I wondered what you were up to.'

'Scouting,' he said. 'I've counted all the god's eyes. I know where the priests of the temple live. And where the armed slaves are kept.'

'Ah,' she said. 'You didn't come out to talk to your friends from Dardania?'

335

He looked at her. 'Did you overhear?'

'Enough to know you aren't just some sell-sword.'

He shrugged. 'I am, though.'

She shook her head. 'I saw you walk away,' she said. 'Why? He was offering you a kingdom.'

Zos looked at her. 'No. He was willing to use me as a bargaining chip in some vast and terrible game of power. That's how Dardania works. I'm not going to play.'

Her face was very close to his. 'And you didn't choose to visit a certain slave?'

He was looking down, 'Thinking about it,' he said. 'She made the sign of the Huntress.'

'To me,' Era said. 'She made the sign to me.'

Zos thought about that, weighed it.

'Sure,' he said agreeably.

Era was looking down to where the lit oil lamps in the slave camps glittered like stars in reverse – bright yellow pinpoints in the unrelieved darkness of the ruins.

'I want to rescue her.'

'It's possible,' Zos said. 'The guard slaves are locked up at night.'

'That's stupid.'

'They're slavers, not soldiers, and they think they are unassailable.' Zos was watching the camp like a bird of prey watching its territory. 'They all have someone on watch. I count more than twenty slave traders.'

'And the customers are all on their ships in the harbours?' Era asked. 'I swam around.'

Zos smiled at her. 'Of course you did.' He looked at her. 'We could take this place.'

'That's the plan,' she said.

'No, I mean, now. Tomorrow.' He found her face hard to read by starlight.

'How?' she asked quietly.

'Buy all the slave-soldiers,' he said. 'And arm them in the market.'

'You're kidding. It can't be that easy.'

'Strike just after the guard slaves are locked up for the night. Kill the slavers, and then use the guard slaves and the soldiers to maintain order.'

'That's either insane or brilliant,' she said.

'Depends on whether it works,' he said. 'The real challenge is afterwards. What's your guess about the number of slaves here right now?'

'Seven or eight hundred,' she said.

'We'd have to get them out of here. A lot of angry people would be looking for them. And maybe a god or two.' Zos was watching the temple now. 'And if we lose control, and they start fight over the food or killing and raping each other, then we've only worsened this little hell instead of rescuing someone.'

Era grunted. 'Nasty thought.'

'I've had plans go bad before,' he said.

'So have I,' she agreed. 'But I like it. I want to do something. I want to strike out at our enemy, and slavers seem like a reachable target.'

'My version of this, it's more like a massacre than a fight,' he said. 'Jawala won't forgive me.'

'Jawala doesn't think that much of you now, godborn man.' Era said. 'But we can't do this without Gamash and Jawala. We need him to front it and her gold to pay for it.'

He was watching the lamps, and some moving torches.

'Yes. A pity. I think it would work.' He turned to her. 'I don't trust your Huntress. I want to say that to you in private. I know she saved my life. But she's a plotter, and we're her tools.'

'You said that before,' Era said. 'I heard you then, too.'

He looked away. 'My parents trusted the Huntress. And she sacrificed them like lambs to save Vetluna.'

He heard her breathing, easy and slow, like the athlete she was.

'Were you ever a bull-leaper?' he asked.

'No,' she said. 'I was in Narmer as a child. I admit I'm jealous.'

'In another world, you'd be the queen of the leapers,' he said. 'I've seen you move. But that's not where I was going with this. When you are bull-leaping, you can wait for your bull and your moment. But once you step forwards, you have to go all the way through. The bull puts its head down and charges you, once you make your move. The bull court is only so big – you have only space and time for three steps. And you need all three to get up speed. And you cannot hesitate. You must run right at the bull, all three steps. He's impossibly big and yet, by paradox, impossibly far away. And when you leap, you need the bull to keep running right at you. And you need to be high enough that when he tosses his head, you are clear of the horns. You come down on his shoulders, or his back, with your hands, and tumble off, and you're behind him.'

She nodded. 'It sounds marvellous.'

'I have a point. In this rebellion, we're going against the gods.'

'That's what I hear,' Era said.

'Once we step forwards, we have to leap. That's all I'm saying. I think the Huntress is aiding our cause, but don't trust there's not some plan under the plan where we end up tied to an altar with our throats slit.'

They were very close, and speaking very quietly.

'My father was godborn,' she said. 'He put me in my mother and left her to enjoy life as a pregnant dancer. I started dancing when I was three. When I was eight, I would dance with my mother for bread, or for gold. I have danced for the great king of Narmer, and for most of the god-kings in the Hundred

Cities – danced, and sung.' She smiled. 'My mother worshipped the Huntress and she has never let us down. I've survived more shit than you can imagine, warrior. And the Huntress has always been there.'

He opened his mouth to speak, and she said, 'And I'm a dancer. I know how to leap.'

He nodded. 'Good, then. I propose we go and try to convince Jawala and Gamash to try.'

'I agree,' she said. 'I think I might even know what to do with eight hundred people.'

He nodded. 'Are you carrying your star-stone knife?'

She tapped her leg. 'Yes.'

'I want to try something very dangerous.'

Era put a hand on his arm and followed him.

The two of them moved quietly into the market square, and eventually, to the god's eye set on a pole where the two streets of slave-pens met. The god's eye was at head height, and glowed with a soft blue, like the sky on a perfect autumn day.

Zos walked up, veiled in his shawl, and thrust the star-stone dagger overhand into the eye, as fast as lightning on a summer day.

There was a sharp crack, and the light went out.

A dog began to bark.

'Let's be gone.' Zos sounded triumphant. 'I think we've just started our revolution.'

Heaven

'Lord god?'

Nisroch looked at the watcher in Narmer.

'You dare interrupt me?' he asked.

He was still trying to work out how his monkey-demon had come to die and rot so very quickly. The stink had filled the room; heaven didn't contain a great many rotting corpses.

'Lord god…' The man was clearly terrified. 'All of the god's eyes on Dekhu have gone out, except one in the temple.'

Nisroch froze amid the preparation for a tirade.

'Gone out?'

'None of them are reporting, lord god. It's as if they've been unmade.'

Nisroch took a deep breath and then realised that he knew exactly what was going on.

'Fucking Druku,' he said. 'All right. Your interruption was justified. Carry on.'

Nisroch hastily summoned Azag.

'Again?' the Captain of the Demons asked.

Nisroch reached up to the diagram on the ceiling, gathered its power, and slammed the guard captain in the head with a triangle so that he roared with anger and pain.

'You are my humble slave,' Nisroch said. 'Say it.'

'Master, I am your humble slave,' the demon snarled.

'Good. I need two – no, three demons to go to the island of Dekhu immediately. I believe they will find the great god Druku there, sleeping off a hangover. Please have them report to you when they find him.'

Azag smiled so that all his hundreds of teeth showed.

'Your wish is my command,' he said.

Nisroch banished him, and only then realised that he hadn't given any strict commands about anything else the demons found. He had not fulfilled the formula of denying the demons a feast of human flesh and fire.

Oh, well.

In a few days, a fleet of his Jekers would land at Dekhu anyway. It was the next move in the game before his penultimate genius strike – the Jeker assault on Narmer. They could gorge on the slaves, and they'd make enough of a mess to cover any massacre the demons perpetrated.

He passed a hand over a glyph and located the Jekers on the ocean.

So close to Dekhu.

He smiled at his own cleverness.

In the glyph, a shaman was torturing a man – the usual pointless barbarity, as only the man's death would actually feed the *Aura*. Some of the gods wrongly believed that the torture enhanced the darkness of the auratic sacrifice. Nisroch wasn't one of them, but he wouldn't interfere, although he secretly felt it was a lot of mess for no purpose. It was clear enough to him that the *Aura* was powered by various tensions and dichotomies built into the fabric of the universe. But he leant forwards suddenly as the obsidian knife slashed and mutilated the screaming victim, who was spiked to the bloody deck. Two acolytes with bloody hands like long red gloves leant in, dug their hands into the man's body and ripped his lungs out through his back.

The shaman waved, and the acolytes raised the corpse, lung-wings fluttering in the world's wind.

Wings. Like *Resheph's* wings.

Nisroch froze, fingers raised in his casting.

You disgusting bastard. You are siphoning off the worship of my *Jekers.*

He sat back, contemplating the evidence: the new powers: the ruddy skin: the necklace of skulls. It was obvious, now that he looked.

He began to weave his counter. And he said aloud, 'All this will work to my advantage.'

All in a day's work.

Chapter Nine

Era

Night had come, a magnificent sheet of stars covering the heavens, the emerald Gift constellation rising in the west and the Crab wheeling high above. The Dark Moon was a black disk on the horizon and the Red Moon was just pushing its rim out of the sea. Most of them were sitting on deck drinking wine, which Mokshi had purchased, to everyone's relief. Zos asked them all to gather in the stern, and gave a sketch of his plan. Daos came and put his head in Era's lap and went to sleep.

Jawala stood with her hands on her hips, and if Era hadn't known her so well, she might have described her stance as aggressive.

'You said we were here to scout,' she said. 'You said there would be no violence.'

Era glanced around at the others. Zos, damn him, was silent. He glanced at her, as if willing her to speak, and Era admitted it was probably better from her than from a man, and a godborn at that.

'Jawala, we'll never get anywhere without violence,' she said. 'If we agree that the world is in great danger and that the gods are oppressors, and that we have a duty to act –' she smiled – 'then you need to admit that being *very sad* about the fate of all the slaves will not free them.'

'I'm glad to see that you can be just as patronising as our godborn warrior,' Jawala said. 'I have, in fact, considered all these things. My society has been coping with them for hundreds of years.' She, too, glanced around the circle of faces. 'I think I can sum up our beliefs by saying that when you dip your hands in shit, whatever you are hoping for, you end up smelling of shit.'

'So your counsel is to do nothing?' Era felt her anger flare.

'My counsel is to resist quietly, live the best life you can, and refuse to take part in their excess.' Jawala gestured at the heavens. 'If you fight, you will die, probably soon, by violence. Is that what you want?' She looked around. 'And who gives you the right to kill – the right to decide that some slaver is so much your lesser that he deserves death?'

'I have already decided that,' Era said. 'I can decide because I choose to. I *am* justice.'

'You aren't justice!' Jawala said sternly. 'You are angry.'

Gamash stood up, and Jawala bowed her head to him. Gamash looked them all over.

'First, I'm not sure that I believe that this plan has merit,' he said, and raised his hand, forcing Zos by weight of age and dignity to remain silent. 'But ... Jawala, perhaps it is time for us to part company. Because Era is correct, and her anger does not hide the essential truth. We choose to act. We have been brought together by one of the gods to act against the others.'

'That knowledge alone should give you pause,' Jawala spat. 'Zos said so himself.'

'And we have been brought together to *act*. We did not start the fire – in fact, we seek to put it out.'

'But you will fight fire with fire?' Aanat said. 'Try that when your ship is afire and see how it works!'

'I'm not willing to engage in an argument by analogy,' Gamash said. 'The gods need to be brought down. We're going to try and make that happen.'

Jawala seemed to shrink. 'You started this argument by analogy,' she said. 'And if you insist on your anger and your selfishness, then I need to ask you to leave my ship.'

'*Our* ship,' Miti said. 'I think we should vote.'

Jawala looked at the younger woman with surprise.

'You don't agree?'

'You always tell me to be wary of absolutes,' Miti said. 'I don't plan to put a sword in anyone, but I'm pretty happy to have these folks win. And I'm wondering if my ethical duty isn't to moderate their vengeance, rather than decrying the whole thing.'

Jawala was looking at Miti as if she'd suddenly grown a second head.

'Vote,' Bravah said.

Jawala was clearly angry. 'I don't think this is a voting matter—'

'Vote,' Mokshi said.

Aanat raised a hand. 'What are we voting on?'

Miti took a deep breath; this was a different role for her. She had surprised Jawala and she continued to surprise Era.

'I put it to a vote that our clan continue to support these people, using trade and persuasion and our ship, despite their violent actions.'

Jawala raised her hand. 'Acting as a base for them to kill and destroy?' she asked, and her sarcasm bit deep at Miti, who set her face.

'If necessary,' she snapped. 'All in favour?'

Bravah raised his hand immediately. And then Mokshi.

And then Pavi.

Jawala pursed her lips. 'We could lose our reincarnations for this,' she said. 'We could set our cycles back a thousand years.'

Down in the aft hold, the donkey brayed.

Zos smiled. 'No idea what that means,' he said.

'Means it's time to feed the donkey,' Daos said and got sleepily to his feet.

Pavi leant forwards. 'Jawala, I love you, but this isn't about us. I'm willing to miss a reincarnation cycle so that everyone else can have a life. This world is a *terrible place* and it's going to get worse. Standing aside seems the less moral option to me.'

The two women looked at each other.

Jawala finally nodded. Without another word, she stripped her working *heton* over her head, walked naked to the bow, and jumped overboard.

Gamash looked at Pavi.

Pavi shrugged. 'When we're angry, we swim. Don't read too much into it.' She looked at Miti. 'Swim with her?'

Miti nodded, and shrugged out of her tunic. Atosa ogled, and Pollon looked away. Era ogled a little herself. Miti was beautiful...

Banish that thought.

She looked at Gamash instead. The elder was still standing. He was looking at Era as if seeing her for the first time.

'You want to do this?' he said.

She nodded.

He looked at Zos. 'And you?'

Zos confirmed it.

'Atosa?'

The craftsman shrugged. 'I'm only here for the free travel and the wine,' he said. But then, looking down, he added, 'But I'd like to be doing something meaningful. Freeing slaves sounds... good.'

Pollon ran his fingers through his unimpressive beard.

'Four days of exercises with Zos, no matter how well taught, have not made me a fighter,' he said. 'But I am an archer.'

Hefa-Asus smiled. 'I like it,' he said. 'It's bold. And there will be slave metalworkers. Let me recruit them.'

Nicté drew her star-stone knife and licked it. 'I think Jawala is wrong,' she said. 'Death in war is not a bad thing. Who thinks it is?'

'I'm so glad Jawala didn't hear you say that,' Pavi said.

Gamash was about to speak when the boy came up from feeding the donkey.

'I don't see this,' he said.

Era turned and smoothed his hair. She had never expected to feel maternal, and now...

Banish that thought, too.

'What does that mean, my love?' she asked.

'I see these threads...' Daos said. 'It's like a loom. My mother had a loom, you know – and she would weave a cloth. It took her a long time just to set it up, and sometimes she'd have another woman to help.' He smiled, and then, as if understanding his own loss, swallowed heavily. And then he said, almost weeping, 'And then they'd weave together, and sing.'

Zos looked as if he was going to speak, but Gamash gently placed his staff on Zos' out-thrust ankle.

'Ouch,' Zos muttered.

'So I see threads, and... sometimes, they weave together. I see... Zos sitting on a throne, with a lion at his feet, and Era by his side in golden armour, and they're sitting at a great table... I see this like a tapestry, with the threads that lead to it.'

Zos grinned at Era.

Era chuckled. 'I like the sound of excellent armour,' she said. 'Not so much of Zos on a throne.'

'But I don't see this slave thing,' the boy said. 'It doesn't happen.'

Gamash was silent, and Zos thumped the deck.

'That's exactly why we have to do it,' he said. 'We are not the servants of the Sisters. We're planning a revolution against the gods.'

'Against *all* gods,' Era agreed.

'If Daos cannot see it, that's because the Huntress hasn't put it in his head because it's not part of her plan,' Era said. 'I love the Huntress, but I'm inclined to agree with Zos in this matter.'

Gamash smiled, a trifle ironically. 'Well,' he said, 'I'm willing to die here, and that's what we're discussing, isn't it? We have to win, in one fight. No holds barred.' The old man sat back down. 'So. We need Jawala's gold and my own. We need to buy slaves tomorrow, and win their loyalty in a day.'

'We need to know who locks up the public slave guards, and where the keys are,' Era said. 'I'll look into that.'

Aanat got up and dropped his loincloth to the deck, but before he headed for the bow, he shook his head.

'I'll have all the anchor stones up and the ship on a short tether,' he said. 'Because I sense you'll want to run once this is done. Care to tell me where I'm going next?'

Era looked at Gamash, and Gamash looked at Zos.

Hefa-Asus said, 'Dendrowna.'

But Zos caught her arm as the others went to their sleeping mats.

'Remember that the boy said we go to Dardania or Noa?' he asked.

She looked at him. 'Yes,' she said.

He was looking out to sea. 'The gods are probably already looking for the star-stone. And it takes time to raise an army.'

'So?'

'Maritaten of Narmer is already quarrelling with the gods,' he said. 'Or so it is said.'

Era shook her head. 'Are you going somewhere with this?'

Zos frowned. 'I'm not sure. But I have a hunch that we need a diversion. Something to fix the eyes of the Gods on ... on something else.'

Era suddenly saw it. 'Like Narmer,' she said.

'I've thought of a way ...' Zos paused. 'It's not an idea yet. But remember what I said about the three steps? I don't think we can just raid some slaves and then blithely sail for Dendrowna.'

Era nodded again despite herself. 'How would you do it?' she asked.

'No idea yet,' the man said. 'But if Daos is right, we do ... something.'

'You're the one who doesn't trust the goddess,' she said.

'I know,' he said ruefully.

Era slept late, rose, swam and then bathed in fresh water that Hefa-Asus had thoughtfully brought up from the beach.

The giant of a man was laying weapons out on the deck under the awning, relatively safe from prying eyes. He had spearheads and arrowheads and a dozen arrows already shafted and fletched, and he was cleaning them.

'They rust,' he said, shaking his head. 'Let me see your knife.'

There weren't a great many men who would look at her naked and only want to see her knife. She grinned and fetched it, and then put on the sort of nondescript wrap that she'd worn as a performer – the sort of thing that hides your figure and keeps the male attention at bay. She threw a shawl around her head and borrowed the donkey, placing her fine sword under her gown and hiding several other tricks in the wicker baskets on its sides.

Hefa-Asus returned her knife.

'It's oiled,' he said. 'And very sharp.'

She smiled. 'We're going to do this?'

He smiled back. 'Of course we are,' he said. 'But I want to get the rust off.'

Over by the mainmast, there was a bale of rags with three arrow shafts in it; someone had been practising.

'The Dry One has been restless,' Hefa-Asus said.

349

Era had no idea what that might mean, but it wasn't good.

She went ashore with the boy at her heels. She bought a flatbread full of spicy meat from a stall and they ate it with eye-watering delight, and then she drank some really bad red wine from another stall. The wine server, a slave, shuffled like a dead thing; Era made the mistake of looking at his feet, and she had to look away, and her resolve hardened yet more.

'A moment of your time, *despoina*,' Trayos said.

She turned to look at the Dardanian captain. He was clean and oiled today, and he'd waxed his moustache and pointed his beard. He had a magnificent red cloak embroidered with ravens over his arm, and an eye-watering tartan belted in gold. Real gold – a row of rosettes. The full display of a Mykoan lord... or a pirate.

'My lord,' she said, and dropped him her Narmerian curtsey.

He smiled. 'The prince is your friend?' he asked.

She had no trouble meeting his eyes, which were those of a cunning man.

'Yes.' She was a little surprised herself at the answer.

'Would you take him a message from me?' he asked.

She wondered if she should be afraid of Trayos. He didn't seem the type, but then she was reasonably certain he'd kill without mercy when it suited him.

'I might,' she said.

'Tell him that I want to meet him again. Please. Tell him...' The man looked away. 'Tell him it is my fate to help him.'

Era smiled. 'I'll tell him.'

'He's buying soldiers,' the captain said. 'And he's with Gamash of Weshwesh. Is he planning to take Mykoax himself?'

Era kept her eyes fixed on his.

'You would have to ask him. I'm merely a dancing girl.'

The Dardanian bowed his head, the greeting from one god-born to another.

350

'Now, my lady, I really doubt that.' His gold earrings winked and his eyes sparkled. 'If he is god-king, perhaps you will be queen?'

'That seems very unlikely to me,' she said.

Trayos cupped his jaw in his right hand, which he seemed to do every time he needed to think.

'I need him,' he said.

'I'll carry your message,' she said. 'Now excuse me.'

She walked through the agora, buying provisions. She bought a few other things: a nice perfumed oil in a faience bottle from Narmer, at what seemed a very reasonable price in hack silver and copper; a straw hat for the boy.

Then, without appearing to do so, she followed a pair of guard slaves back along one of the cross-streets, passing what had once been the brilliantly painted front of the Temple of All Gods, some thousand years before. At her feet, snakes coiled in a beautiful woman's hair. She didn't even know which goddess that had been, but the remaining paint on the fine white marble was carved with a perfection unequalled in the modern age.

Perhaps that is the measure of the success or failure of our gods, she thought. *The quality of art.*

The two slave guards passed the ancient ruin and she saw the barracks, and then she saw what she was looking for – the slave guard who'd come to the ship the first day. He was close to the barracks, which were built from cut stone, stolen from the old temples to build an ugly shed for slaves. It was low, squat and practical, and filled the end of a street.

Like slave guards everywhere, he wasn't working particularly hard. He and another mate were leaning against the remnants of the pediment to a colossal statue of Ranos, the All-Father of the old pantheon.

'Good morning,' she said, as if she meant it.

The man looked at her as if she'd grown a second head.

'Oh, shit,' the other guard said, and slipped away around the monument.

Era looked at the guard. 'What does that mean?'

'It means you're a free woman and any time the likes o' you wants to talk to us, it's trouble,' the man said. 'I don't want no trouble.'

That's uncannily accurate, she thought wryly.

'I'm not going to give you any trouble.' More hesitantly than she had meant, she said, 'I was just wondering what you do for entertainment?'

'Really?' he asked, and his voice lost its fawning edge and betrayed his cynicism. 'You really want to know what the slave guards do after hours? You looking to get laid, lady?'

'What? No!' She remembered her role. 'Maybe?' she asked with what she hoped was coquettish grace. 'You are so ... bold.'

'Oh.' The man grunted. He looked both ways. 'Listen, lady, I'd fuckin' love to and you look ...' He tried to make out her figure and shrugged. 'But I'd be killed for it. So, no dice.'

He had the grace to sound sorry.

She found that she couldn't hate him, and realised she had never spent so much time talking to a slave.

Do women do this? she asked herself. *Ask men for sex? Does that really ever happen?*

Lots to learn, sisters.

'When do you get locked up?' she asked, breathlessly. She tried to pretend he was a woman.

The slave woman in the agora. Pretend he's her.

Era tried to use her face and tone to suggest that she might break in to find him.

He shook his head, but then, as if humouring her, he said, 'When the Red Moon rises.'

She took a bit of silver scrap from her bag and pressed it into his hand.

'Well,' she said, 'think of me.'

She walked back to the donkey, which stood placidly while Daos fed him fresh hay. Nicté stood by, dressed as a craftswoman.

'Gamash said I should watch you,' Nicté said. 'And you suck at *that*.'

Era bridled. 'At what?'

'Flirtation. Seduction. Manipulation.' Nicté rolled her eyes. 'Next time you want something out of a man ask me, all right?'

'We're late – this all took too long.' Era was a little too dismissive, and Nicté sneered.

'Not my fault you took too long... What did the Dardanian want, anyway?'

'Where's Daos?' Era asked suddenly, concerned.

'I thought he was with you.'

Era felt the desperation that only a parent can know as she looked around the ruins.

'He *never* wanders off. And he *never* leaves the donkey.'

She put her hands on her hips, feeling the hilts of the bronze sword and the star-stone knife under her gown. She'd slashed the wool just ahead of her hips on both sides, and bound the edges to make the weapons easier to access. She'd seen older women do this for pockets strapped under their clothes; they had some sense.

She came out into the brilliant noontime light of the Great Square, and there was Daos, ahead of her.

'Daos!' she screamed, and the boy turned.

'I'm going to the temple,' he said.

'Get back here and do not wander off like that again.'

'I was going to the temple!' he insisted, as if it was important.

She was overwhelmingly tempted to slap him. Her mother had boxed her ears for less.

She dragged him back to the donkey, and now Nicté was gone. Era assumed that was on purpose, and she shook her head.

'We're late,' she said. 'Help me look for Gamash.'

'He's late, too,' Daos said. 'And I need to go to that temple.' He gave her a level, adult look. 'Now I know what to do. I didn't before, but now I know. And it's...'

Era looked down the Street of the Gods, where the major dealers were. She expected to recognise Gamash as a distance; he'd gone ashore early and hired a palanquin, but she didn't see him, or Zos, or Hefa-Asus, who should have towered over every man and woman on the street.

She turned up one of the alleys, and she found herself in the side street off the Street of the Gods where the beautiful woman-slave had been.

I always meant to come here, she admitted to herself.

She walked down the narrow street between two fallen temples, although from the rubble she couldn't guess which two.

There's a hawk's head over there ... which god was that?

She looked at the slaves. It was midday, and they were all on display. Every dealer had much the same arrangement: a roofed or tented viewing area, with stools and a carpet, and behind it a fenced-off pen, watched by guards, where the stock waited. They were kept too much like cattle for her to be comfortable with her own thoughts; in every fenced-in booth, it was clear that the stronger, more dangerous slaves had taken the best of the shade and the food and water. The poorer, weaker slaves, most of them women, sat abjectly in little huddles in the sun, or in the fast-dwindling shade of fallen columns.

And there she was. Dite sat on the leg of a colossal fallen statue, her legs tucked up in an easy posture, as if she was the queen of the island and not a victim. Several women sat below her, and one small man.

She sat in the full sun, as if basking in it. Her beautiful eyes were closed, her face turned to the sun.

When Era was twenty paces away, at the fence, the eyes

opened. They took Era's breath away. She'd already forgotten the impact of those eyes.

You fall in love with every pretty woman you see.

No, this is completely different.

You always say that. Think of the henna-handed woman in Ma'rib.

No, this is completely different.

The woman was looking directly at her, and smiling, her lips just slightly parted.

'If you ain't buying, then keep moving,' the dealer said.

Daos laughed at the man. 'You're so rude!' he said, and Era put a hand on his shoulder.

'Fuck off, brat,' the dealer said.

'You should be more polite,' Daos said. 'You have so little time left.'

The man started towards them, and Era dragged Daos away and got the donkey to follow her, too, as the dealer stepped out into the narrow alley, either to make his point or perhaps to strike the boy.

The donkey lashed out with its back feet. The move was sudden, unexpected, and explosive.

And like that, the dealer was dead. One of the donkey's hooves caught his jaw and drove his teeth up into his skull, killing him instantly.

'Shit,' Era said.

There were several other dealers on the alley, and at least a hundred slaves.

'Your beast just killed a very important man,' said a voice behind her. She turned as the man reached for her. 'You're going to—'

Era's experience of men and violence was wider and more horrible than she admitted even to herself. So there was never a decision to make. Her sword rose through the pocket slit

355

she'd cut in her mantle, and in the same moment he grabbed the fabric of her gown and she spilled his guts on the ground.

He fell forwards, too shocked to scream.

She whirled, stepping nimbly on his neck, pushing his mouth into the dirt and cutting off his last breath and any possible scream. Luck, and the position of the donkey and the narrow space between the stalls, had covered the killing. She stood a moment, blood dripping from the point of her beautiful bronze sword.

She considered dropping it and claiming the two men had killed each other.

She waited for the outcry.

So she was facing the wrong way when one of the dead man's slave-guards threw a javelin at her.

And then, like some final act in a cheap street drama, Nicté cut the javelin out of the air. The Dendrownan woman did a handspring, rolling forwards with incredible rapidity, and her angled stone knife licked out like a dewclaw, and the javelin thrower was very messily dead, his throat severed through to the backbone.

'Gamash told me to follow you,' Nicté said.

Era was still a little shocked, but she mastered herself.

'We need to get away.' She looked around. 'Where's Daos?'

Nicté was watching the back flap of the slave-dealer's 'sales area'.

'Don't know,' she said. 'My eyes were on you.'

Era stepped to her left, put her back against the donkey, and looked up the alley. It was almost high noon; most dealers were closing up, waiting for the auctions in the cool of the evening. But it seemed remarkable to her that there were two dead men in the alley and no hue and cry.

Then she thought of the woman.

'Other guards?' she asked.

The tent flap at the back of the sales area opened, and even as Nicté's sword came up, the woman stepped through. She wore a sleeveless tunic of dirty white linen, and every line of her showed through it.

'No,' she said. 'I killed the last one.'

Her left hand was red with blood, all the way to the elbow, like a scarlet glove. The blood on her ebony skin had a terrible blue-black shimmer, as if she was something unnatural, and just for a moment, fear conquered Era's essentially erotic response to her.

Which only made her the more appealing.

Era looked at Nicté. 'She's with us,' she said. 'Let's get out of here.'

'And the other slaves?' Nicté asked.

Era's first impulse was to tell them all that they were free. But her second impulse was darker and wiser.

'Leave them,' she said. 'They'll all be free in an hour.'

She went back into the alley. Flies were already gathering on the gutted slave-dealer. She could smell his intestines over the reek of the island.

The copper–pork smell of the other man's brains was a terrible counterpoint. And *still* no one cried out.

'Where is Daos?' she asked the world.

His stuffed bear was also gone.

'We're late, dammit. Gamash will be waiting for us!' she said in a fluster.

'He'll come back for food!' Nicté said. 'My brothers always did.'

Era hiked up her skirts and ran to the corner. 'We don't have time!' she called.

Then she turned the corner and…

There was Daos, standing with a long pole in his hand in the shade of the partially intact roof of a temple to Isvar, the old

357

Goddess of Motherhood. He was twenty paces away across the white-hot square. In the centre of the square a dozen desperate slaves were being crucified in the sun while others began to erect the platforms for the evening auctions.

'Where have you been?' she spat at him as she ran to him.

'Right here,' he said, and then she hugged him so hard he squeaked.

'Bror said to go this way, and I did. You were killing the bad men and Nannu was fine.'

She put her face at his level, squatting and scraping the scabbard on the marble behind her.

'Listen to me, Daos. We're about to do something dangerous...'

'I know!' the boy said. 'And now Bror knows, too, and the Blue Lady. And Nannu.'

He was grinning. She blinked.

'Nannu told me where to find this. And told me what to do. And...' He paused. He picked up his stuffed bear and kissed it on the head. 'I was told to give Bror to you – Bror will save your life.'

Era took the stuffed bear with a mixed sense of wonder and a fatigue at meddling with the extreme supernatural.

The boy was holding a trident. It was quite beautiful: the bronze of the tripartite head had been cast by a master; the blades were each formed into the tail of a horse; the three horses' heads merged together into the haft. The haft was carved, too, from a dark wood she didn't know.

'The *donkey* gave you a *trident*?'

'Yes.' The boy He nodded. 'Well, he's not really a donkey, is he?' Daos asked this as if it was an obvious question. 'Anyway, he told me to use it when the demons come. But not before.'

'Demons?' Era asked, as Nicté came around the corner leading the donkey. The beautiful woman followed her, wrapped to the eyes in a borrowed mantle.

'Those demons,' Nicté said, pointing at the sky. 'Three of them.'

Zos

'I don't have any more knives,' Hefa-Asus said. 'I can give you this.' He handed over a long, needle-like javelin head.

Zos smiled, and used the smith's glue pot to attach it to one of the boat poles, hastily cut short. He made it the length of a walking stick. He held it out to old Gamash, who worked his peculiar ageing magic and made the fish-hide glue dry in heartbeats.

Zos took it and then wrapped the head with a rag and walked forwards, to look in on the Dry One.

He squatted in the airless heat of the hold. He could see that the thing had moved since he'd wrapped it up – good news indeed, as that meant it was alive. He had a brief, terrifying notion of an undead Dry One, a *gidimu* of unfathomable power, and put a hand on his amulet. Of course, it was gone. Anenome had taken it, when they'd handed him over to the god-king's warriors for torture. That seemed like another lifetime.

He sighed, one hand on the Dry One in its casing, and the thing stirred. He rolled it over to look at its wound, or rather, the bandages over the wound, and it twitched.

Pain? Does it feel pain?

Zos undid the head bandage, which he'd put on as lightly as possible, and its terrible, beautiful long face and jewelled eyes emerged.

'You're lucky I'm brave,' Zos said.

The eyes lit from within. They had no lids to hide them, and Zos, cradling the monster in his arms, was a close as a lover.

The four-part mouth opened faster than Zos – a very quick man – could react, and the green tongue came out...

And just brushed his nose.

Terror went through Zos like a bolt of lightning, but he was a bull-leaper, and he had a thousand tricks to keep terror at bay.

'I like you, but not that way,' he muttered.

The head vibrated slightly.

Zos laid the creature down carefully. The thing was heavier than a man, but not as heavy as it should have been, as if it was hollow.

'You want the rest of these off?' he asked.

The unblinking eyes glittered at him.

'Don't you think this would all be easier if we could talk?' Zos asked. 'I'm about to attack a bunch of slavers. Do you know that?'

The Dry One quivered, and he started unwrapping.

'Is it possible that you understand me, but can't talk?' Zos asked.

Nothing. Just those unblinking eyes.

'Fine, I can take a hint,' he said, and unwrapped faster.

Pollon

Pollon had risen early and gone on deck, where Hefa-Asus was sitting cross-legged, surrounded by pots of glue, tools and scraps of fifty materials – a little fish hide, a pile of sticks, a large cow bone...

The big man looked up, saw him, and reached for something leaning against the steering bench.

'I hear you are an archer,' he said.

'I used to be,' Pollon admitted, still not awake. But he was fascinated by the bow they had been working on. It was heavier than any bow he'd ever pulled, and it bent differently.

'There you are, deadly archer,' Hefa-Asus said, passing it over. 'I made the string this morning.'

'Thank you!' Pollon paused, caught up in knowledge. 'Deadly archer is the ... the old name.'

Hefa-Asus smiled thinly. 'Perhaps,' he said. 'I'm from Dendrowna. We don't follow your gods much. We have our own.'

Pollon ran his hands over the belly of the bow like a man caressing a lover.

'She's beautiful.'

'Thank the magos. He caused the hide and the glue to dry – six months' drying done in a single night.'

Gamash spread his hands. 'Not exactly.'

'Thanks to both of you. If pirates attack us again ...' Pollon was gently flexing the heavy thing, testing it and flexing the muscles in his back.

Jawala, who was at the stern watching the beach, frowned at him.

'Just because my crew is willing to support your violent tendencies does not give you permission to shoot people from my ship,' she said.

'Our ship,' Miti said. 'But I agree, Pollon. Freeing slaves is one thing.'

'Shooting Jekers?' Pollon asked.

'No,' Miti said.

Pollon glanced at Hefa-Asus, but the big man was absorbed in cleaning his star-stone.

'I made you some arrows,' he said, holding up a long cane arrow with a star-stone head. It had fletchings of whale gill, a white, papyrus-thin bony material found in gill-sharks.

361

Then he glanced up at Pollon. 'I mean, I made them before I knew you. The shafts may be too light for that bow.'

Pollon shrugged. 'I'm not such a wonderful archer. I was in the militia at home.'

For the first time in days he thought of Mura, and blinked.

Hefa-Asus shrugged. 'But at least we have *an* archer,' he said. 'You and I are supposed to stay with the ship and defend it.' He looked up from the spearhead he was binding to a shaft. 'I thought you'd be happier with a bow.'

Pollon smiled. 'Very much so.'

'All the arrows with bone nocks have flint heads,' Hefa-Asus said. 'Only the three with red nocks have star-stone heads. I have more heads but...'

'I see.'

'Don't waste them. We're only fighting slavers today.'

Pollon got Miti to help him lift a water-damaged bale of ruined linens out of the hold. It was the same bale they'd opened to wrap the poor monster. He made a target which he placed at the foot of the mast, and stood just ten paces away. He put a star-stone arrow on the string and felt the malevolence of the thing. He could feel it eating his *Aura*.

Terrible.

He flexed the bow, drew it, and let the tension off. He hadn't even been close to a full draw.

He pointed the arrow at the deck, flexed his shoulder and back muscles, and rolled the bow up, high, then settled the glittering grey head on the target and loosed. His draw hand had been a whole hand's width from his mouth.

The star-stone head went deep into the ruined linen.

Hefa-Asus chuckled. 'Not a very challenging range, master archer.'

Pollon nodded. 'I assume you don't want me to lose one of

your precious evil arrows over the side,' he said. 'And this isn't like any bow I've ever shot. It's a monster.'

'Speaking of monsters,' Zos said, appearing out of the forepeak, 'ours is awake and I think it's hungry.'

Miti, who was sometimes the laziest member of the crew, seemed to be full of energy.

'Mokshi brought it honey,' she said. 'Enough that, if the damned thing doesn't like honey, we may have to go into the business.'

'Sort of a wild guess at its food,' Pollon agreed. 'That's a lot of honey.'

'Definitely worth a try,' Zos said.

He took the clay pot of honey and untied the oiled linen scrap that acted as a cover, and went back to the Dry One.

What followed was fairly disturbing. The monster looked at the jar for a long time. Its antenna twitched, and then it put a single black talon *in* the honey, and the mouthparts opened, all six of them hinging back to expose a very pink, very mammalian – and very unsettling – throat inside its complex insectoid mouth.

And then, of course, the green tongue flicked out, and was thrust unceremoniously into the honey. It had an air of desperation, panic, greed ... hunger.

And then the obscene swelling, as something obviously passed *through* the tongue.

Zos made himself watch. It was almost like one of his childhood meditations on violence – training to teach the mind *not* to look away.

Then the head came up. The tongue made a ridiculously unrefined slurping noise, and its eyes sparkled as the mouthparts closed again.

One taloned hand touched the clay pot and pushed it firmly towards Zos, and then pulled it sharply back. Pushed. Pulled.

Zos nodded. 'You want more?' he said.

Pushed.

The scent of cinnamon was overwhelming, and so was the vibration of the head.

Zos went and fetched a second pot, and a little later, a third.

And then the Dry One used its razor-sharp talons to shred the rest of the wrappings. Zos helped, pulling the clinging cloth carefully away from the spines and thorns of the thing's leathery skin.

When he was done, the thing put one taloned hand on his arm and Zos had to use all his self-control to remain calm. Faceted jewel eyes met his own. The talons on his arm were gentle, firm.

The monster nodded, once, like a man making an important decision.

Then, in one leap, the Dry One was in the air.

'What?' Zos spat, his concentration ruined.

The Dry One went almost straight up, just avoiding the rigging. It lit on the very tip of the mainmast.

'You can't!' he roared.

It hurled itself into the crystal-blue sky, passing over the whole of the slaver camp and the ruins of the ancient city of the old gods in a single incredible flying leap.

Zos closed both eyes for a moment.

Pollon was sewing himself a leather finger-tab. He looked up. 'What?' he asked. 'You seem disturbed.'

'Our pet monster just flew up to the mountains,' he said.

Pollon nodded, as if this was an everyday thing.

'He probably needs to dry off more than we can offer, wrapped in damp cloths on a ship,' he said.

'He probably just alerted every fucking slaver in this *actually* gods-forsaken place that there's a Dry One here. We're three, maybe four hours from ...'

Pollon nodded. 'No one will notice.'

Zos was listening for sounds of alarm and riot, and heard none.

'When do you go ashore?' Pollon asked.

'Any time now,' Zos admitted. 'May I use your target?'

'Be my guest,' Pollon said.

Zos unwrapped his javelin and threw it into the bale. It went so deep it stuck into the mast and had to be pulled out.

'You are a mighty smith,' Zos said to Hefa-Asus.

'I'm pleased with these,' the Dendrownan said. 'The star-stone is difficult to work with and even more difficult to make into a hard metal.' He smiled. 'Would you like to know how I did it?'

Zos grinned. 'Not really,' he said, though he loved the shape of the head, long and elegant, with a tiny whorl worked into the bottom of the leaf shape, like the best bronze pieces. 'But it's almost too good to throw.'

Hefa-Asus shrugged. 'It's made to be used.'

Gamash came on deck in his full godborn lord regalia.

'I think we need Hefa-Asus,' he said.

Zos looked at the smith. 'That leaves Pollon alone here.'

Gamash spoke quietly. 'Jawala is unlikely to allow them to fight, whatever the consequences. I failed to convince her that these were extraordinary circumstances.'

Zos looked forward. 'Then we should take Pollon as well.'

'No,' Gamash said. 'I like having an archer here. In this vantage point.'

'Where Jawala can break a pot over his head.'

'That would be violence,' Gamash said with a smile.

Pollon said, 'I can wrap the bow up like a staff. I'd like to come.'

Gamash shrugged. 'Let's get moving.'

Hefa-Asus shook his head. 'It will take me another half an hour to be done here.'

Gamash looked unhappy. 'They don't all have to be polished!' he said.

Hefa-Asus bridled. 'Are you teaching me my craft, old sir?'

The two men glared at each other, and for once, Zos was the peacemaker.

'Pollon can come now, and Hefa-Asus as soon as he can,' he said. 'We won't be hard to find.'

'Hurry,' Gamash said. 'I have a terrible feeling in my gut.'

Era was not at the agreed rendezvous.

Gamash leant out of his hired palanquin and shrugged.

'We don't really need her yet,' he said. 'Let's go.'

His bearers lifted him and he led the way, carried by eight men. Zos was close behind, lifting the heel of his fighting sandal to look at what he'd stepped in.

'Two days and I'm almost used to the smell of the shit,' he said.

Pollon raised an eyebrow. 'I could never grow used to this. Worse than anything in Hekka.' Suddenly he had an overwhelming moment of missing Hekka: the smell of Mura's spices; the tang of charcoal smoke ... 'This is the most disgusting place I've ever been.' He pulled a shawl over his head. 'It's terrible.'

Zos was watching and listening, still on edge after the flight of the Dry One, expecting to see an accusing finger pointed, or a mob, at any moment.

There was none.

They re-entered the Street of the Gods and stopped at the first dealer with a large parcel of fighting slaves. He had sixteen men and unusually, three women – all nomads. They were naked and heavily tattooed, with long parallel lines defining their limbs and complex baroque whirls on their hands and faces and breasts. Unusually, the women stood by themselves, hands on hips, as if they were the buyers, not the slaves.

'Nomads,' Zos said.

Pollon nudged him. 'I speak a little Nomad.'

Zos blinked. 'You are a man of many surprises.'

Gamash opened the curtains of his palanquin and Zos summoned the dealer.

Pollon stepped up to the three women. 'Greetings,' he said. He said it in Banye, which was Mura's dialect of the desert trade language.

The tallest woman jutted her chin at him, a slight movement but one he knew.

'I am Pollon,' he said.

The woman pointed at herself. 'Makeda,' she said. She sounded surprised, and nomads didn't usually reveal surprise; but then, she wasn't veiled.

'We buy you free,' he said.

At least, that's what he hoped he was saying. He was thinking of Mura – thinking that if these women understood Banye they almost certainly were from what had once been her clan. His eyes filled with tears, and he felt as if he had to sit down, he was so suddenly overcome.

'Pollon man,' the nomad woman said. 'Buy free what?'

Pollon saw no reason to be secretive. The likelihood that a slaver could speak Banye was very small.

'We kill all slavers,' he said.

To his left, the owner was dickering with Zos while Gamash remained above the discussion by virtue of the eight men holding his palanquin.

The second woman, the one with lips that looked as if they'd been carved from jet, turned to her friend and spoke very rapidly in a language that might or might not have been Banye.

Hefa-Asus stood at Pollon's shoulder. 'What are they saying?' he asked.

'I have no idea,' Pollon answered as the three women spoke, ignoring him.

'Done,' the slaver said.

Gamash handed Zos some ingots of gold. He handed them on to the dealer.

'You don't mind if I have this assayed, great lord?' The slaver was virtually cringing with obsequious subordination.

Zos waved. 'As you will. I'm taking this lot to the agora to buy them arms. You can find us there.'

The man licked a gold bar. He held it out to one of his guard dogs, which bit it, leaving faint marks.

The three women wore ankle chains, and the cuffs were left on, but the slaver pulled the bronze chain out of each cuff. He was surprisingly careful around the three nomad women, and the one sandy-haired Dardanian man who stood alone, nearly naked beneath a long, filthy Mykoan cloak.

The three women surrounded Pollon.

'Free?' asked Makeda.

'Free when sun down,' Pollon said, and then realised that he knew the Banye word for *evening*; it was in a song that Mura taught him.

'Free at evening,' he said. 'I give my word.'

Makeda shrugged. 'Sure,' she said with obvious doubt. Then she pointed at the Dardanian. 'Crazy,' she said. 'Be careful.'

Zos looked at the dealer with distaste. 'You've sold me a broken slave?'

'All slaves are broken,' the dealer said. 'This one is a fantastic killer. He is incredible. Look at his muscles.' The dealer ran his hand familiarly down the slave's flank. 'And he has other uses.'

Zos blinked, suffused with a strong desire to kill the man.

But he didn't. He turned and walked away.

The next trader who had slave-soldiers had six of the usual big, mostly overweight Hundred Cities bravos. Zos was tempted to turn them down, but that wasn't the plan. They were bought with a minimum of haggling. They had little spirit – less than the first group, by far.

The Dardanian madman from the first sale was covered in scars, some emphasised by tattoos. He looked as if he was not very bright, and also insane.

He kept looking at Zos.

Finally he said, 'Lord.'

Zos nodded. 'Do I know you?'

The man shook his head. 'No,' he said, in a tone that might have meant *yes*. 'Are we going to fight?' he asked, the way a person might ask about the weather, or dinner.

'Yes,' Zos said.

The man wore a sort of rag that might once have been a tablecloth, or a chiton. It went over his head, was tied around his waist, and covered his chest and pelvis. Now he smiled – a terrible grin that made his face a demonic sigil – and he stripped the rag over his head and threw it on the ground so that he was entirely naked.

The man had a bull's head tattooed on his chest.

The man nodded.

'Have you leapt a bull?' Zos asked.

'No, lord,' the man said. 'I ... failed. I never made my leap.'

Zos grabbed the man by the shoulders and stared at him. 'Truly now.'

'Truly, lord,' the man said.

He had scars all across his chest.

Makeda spoke in Trade Dardanian to Zos. 'We fight here?'

The other slaves all looked at her. Zos hadn't let go of the man with the bull on his chest, but he looked around.

'We will fight soon.' He did something with his voice that Pollon had heard the godborn do before. It carried with power

369

and emotional intensity, as if Zos was speaking to the powers of the universe. 'All of you who survive will be freed.'

He glanced at the man with the bull tattoo.

'What's your name?' he asked.

'Persay.' The man giggled a little when he said his name.

He's the right age. My age – a little younger. Gods. It's not possible.

They shuffled to a stop by a third trader who had the largest consignment of fighting slaves, but for the most part, they were captured soldiers who were intended to be forced to fight at funerals and such. Not really soldier-slaves, more like unwilling gladiators. A few of them were Dendrownans, and the rest were from the Hundred Cities.

They were sullen and hostile and loaded with chains. Most had bloody sores under their chains, and there were flies everywhere.

Zos realised that he was looking at one of his picked peasant-warriors from the last assault at Hekka.

And the man recognised him, looked away, looked back.

Gamash was sitting above him, fondling a gold bar.

'I think that man knows me,' Zos said.

'That's probably not going to help us,' Gamash said. 'Should we walk on? No one listens to a slave.'

'He was a pretty good man,' Zos said. 'And he might be helpful ...'

Without another word, he stepped out of the line of slave soldiers following the palanquin and turned to the waiting huddle of captives.

'You know who I am?' he said to the man.

Lefuz. That was his name.

'You know who I am, Lefuz?'

The former peasant, former warrior, raised his head.

Zos said, 'You can be free tonight if you do what I say.'

'You were fucking dead.' The man looked around. 'I saw the god break your back.'

Zos shrugged. 'And now I'm alive and offering you freedom.'

The man managed half a smile – a good show, given what he'd probably been through, Zos thought.

'Best offer today, boss,' he said.

'And these?' Zos asked.

'Mostly the bastards we were fighting,' Lefuz said. 'The survivors of Hekka.'

One man was quite old. The rest were younger, and none of them were warriors, really.

'I want Lefuz,' he said to Gamash. 'The rest aren't worth…'

Pollon pointed at the old man. 'And him,' he said. 'He's a master archer. And a veteran of fifty battles.'

Zos turned, reappraising the old man.

'Might as well take the lot, then,' Gamash said in his 'great lord' voice. 'Two gold minae.'

'They're all warriors!' the dealer said. 'I think ten minae is more the price.'

'See that man?' Zos said. 'Not worth a shit. See the way every one of them has wrist sores? That's days of training lost. See this skin-and-bones kid? He'll wet himself when he sees a spear, and that old jackass isn't worth my piss.'

The dealer blinked.

'I'll go two and a half,' Zos said.

They settled at three and a half.

And then the whole little army shuffled along to the Great Square. It was high noon; the agora was closing up, leaving a dozen slaves crucified in the sun, dying with relative quiet. At their feet, another hundred moved about, wearily setting up the auction block.

'We're late,' Gamash said.

Far off, across the square, a woman chased a child.

Zos led his charges directly to the weapons tables.

'Form up!' he roared. 'Eight wide, six deep. You – Lefuz – front rank, right marker.'

'Use the old man,' Pollon urged.

'You, old one. Pollon says you know how to do this.' Zos' voice held the deadly authority of the godborn.

The old man looked at Pollon. It was a very intelligent, considering glance – a remarkable glance for a beaten slave.

'Yes, lord,' he said to Zos. It wasn't an automatic response. It was a considered answer.

'Eight wide, six deep. Make it happen.'

The old man was fast. And he used his hands sparingly but quickly, slapping the slow ones, without rancour.

Zos had to admire the man.

'Perfect,' he said. 'Each file will go to the third table.' Zos had selected it because the weapons were marginally better and the proprietor looked marginally less evil... though, in truth, the kind of man who sold weapons to slaves was not the kind to ever rise much in Zos' estimation. 'You will choose an axe or a sword. You will choose a shield. You will come back immediately and stand in your place.'

The three nomad women, all in the front rank, licked their lips.

'We want veils,' the black-lipped woman said.

Close up, he could see she had tiny black designs tattooed over her lips.

Zos considered not answering. The first moments of command were when you established your role; his hated foster-father had taught him that.

Fuck him, Zos thought.

'Give me an hour,' he said. 'I promise veils, loincloths, cloaks.'

Black-Lips nodded smartly. 'Lord,' she said.

She was not accepting. More like measuring. But any crisis was averted.

That worked. For now.

The old man walked to the front of the right file as if this was Mykoax and they were going to dance for the king. The left-file leader was the Dardanian. He gazed on the weapons with lust.

'Watch that one,' Zos said. He motioned to the old man. 'Go.'

The first file went. It consisted of Lefuz, led by the old man, and followed by three overweight brutes from the Hundred Cities. The last man in the file was as red as portrayals of Enkul-Anu, tall and thin. From Dendrowna. He had high cheekbones and a broad, bony forehead and he looked to be tougher than an old bull.

I'll get to know the survivors, Zos thought.

He was relieved to see Hefa-Asus coming up the Street of the Gods, a head taller than anyone else. He was easy to spot since the noontime sun had closed most of the stalls.

He had Atosa with him, the smaller man almost running to keep up.

'You are arming these slaves,' a man said.

It wasn't any man — it was the arse from the harbour. He still had the scarlet cloak, and he had half a dozen armed men at his back.

Zos turned to give the man his full attention.

'It is illegal to arm slaves,' the man said.

Amethu. That was his name.

Gamash lifted the curtain on his palanquin.

'There is no law here,' he said.

Amethu smiled thinly. 'Let's say it's against our custom, then,' he said. 'But I'll be happy to dump you out of your chair and make you stop.'

Gamash smiled. The sheer patronising arrogance of the old man was worse than any accusation or insult.

'Oh, dear me,' he said, raising his hands.

Amethu grinned and drew his sword. At his back, his people did likewise. There were seven men at his back, and they were not slaves.

Amethu's hatred was focused on Gamash, and he drew and moved with decision, but Zos had plenty of time. He caught the other man's wrist as the draw came up, stepped in close, put his knee into the other man's groin with vicious intent, and simultaneously put the crown of his head into the other man's nose. There was an audible crack, and he took the man's sword as he fell.

Zos looked at Persay. The man's eyes begged him to be allowed to fight, and in an instant he tossed the sword to Persay.

'Kill them all,' he said.

The madman's eyes glittered like rubies in the sun. He crouched, and made the bull's horns sign, and then he leapt.

Zos had already tumbled back, a reverse handstand that allowed him to kick out as he went. He didn't make contact, but he did clear a space for himself and landed on his feet, and the short sword he wore – strapped on in two places so that he could wear it for such manoeuvres – all but floated into his hand.

Amethu's men were stunned by the speed of the action, but their eyes tracked Zos. Men drew and stepped forwards; one flipped his cloak over his arm in a very professional way.

One of the men at the back of the pack was suddenly de-capitated in a bright spray of blood.

The same swing apparently, somehow, hamstrung another. Persay was in among them, flowing like a dancer, tumbling, cutting their ankles and knees and groins. Then, in an incredible feat of athleticism, he seemed to leap from a forward roll, the bronze sword glittering in the sun as he burst from their loose front and his back-cut sliced across another victim's eyes.

Five of the seven men were on the ground.

He bowed. 'Lord,' he said.

Zos smiled. 'Still two left,' he said, with a burst of military humour.

Persay turned like an actor about to deliver a line. One of the two remaining men was looking down at his intestines, spilled out to the ground from a razor slash across his abdomen. The other had just discovered he'd been emasculated, and he shrieked.

Persay beheaded him.

Zos blinked. The man's skill was incredible, even by the standards of a bull-leaper. But he gathered himself, bowed, and then turned. The words 'Kill all the slavers' were forming in his mouth when Pollon pointed.

'What are those?' His flat tone carried enough urgency to draw Zos' eye.

Above them, descending on streaks of fire, were three...

Three...

Demons.

Zos had only ever seen statues, but they *definitely* looked like demons, with their flame-coloured skin, and wings of fire, and swords of red-hot bronze. Their eyes burned like the red stone in the heart of a volcano.

Gamash's eyes followed Pollon's hand as the seventh dead man hit the ground.

'Why?' he asked heavily.

But then he rolled out of the palanquin and dropped his outer robe of gold-embroidered wool.

Behind him, there was screaming in the agora.

Zos flicked a glance at his slave-soldiers. Two files were armed, and the third was at the merchant's table.

Above him, a demon extended a sword of fire, and a line of flame connected him to the slaves who had been crucified.

There was a wave of heat, and a ball of flame the size of a temple.

Zos' belief that he was master of the situation had melted away, leaving him rooted to the sand and powdered marble like a surprised child.

Gamash took his staff and began to sketch a design in the dust of the agora.

Merchants were running in every direction.

The first of the three demons began to slay them with fire. They were demons; it was instantly clear to every mortal present that the demons would be indiscriminate in their slaying. It was their nature. They'd killed whole cities.

The screaming intensified, although some slaves raised their faces in hope of a clean death.

A second demon landed on the dirty white marble, just a few hundred paces away from Zos, and he felt the impact through his feet. The thing was twice his height, or more, and it caught a running slave, tore him in half, and ate one part.

Gamash kept writing in the dust.

The third demon turned in the air and headed out over the ships in the harbour. It, too, began to rain fire on the earth and sea.

'Don't move,' Gamash said, his eyes still on his inscription in the dust.

Above them, the first demon made an impossible manoeuvre in the air, wings of fire beating slowly, and its fire-gold eyes seemed to rest on Gamash.

Zos struggled for control of his own muscles. He knew he was in shock; he knew he had to fight...

The bull lowered his head, the horns gleaming gold in the sunlight.

High above, the demon's sword spat fire.

Zos ignored Gamash's shouts, and leapt.

He leapt onto a raised pathway and then forwards into a rolling tumble, down off the path, over a fallen column...

The fire bolt struck as he rolled to his haunches, and the fallen marble column took most of it. On the other side of the column, he saw a shining half-sphere that glittered like a faceted gemstone, all the colours of crystalline light, protecting the others. The bolt struck it and splashed away, and fire filled the air. Zos ducked his head, his hair singed from the wave of heat.

He lay in the heat shadow of his column for long enough to take a breath and cover his face, and the heat began to recede.

Light flashed from the dome of gems.

Off to his right, in the air high above, a second demon flung gouts of fire, an endless paean of destruction, an insane grin on its hideous face. And to his left, the third, just rising in the air clutching a man in his talons.

Zos' mind was working better now. The demons had broad bat-wings, but otherwise had the shape of a man from the waist up, and then below the waist were more like monkeys. One was bright red, another pale yellow like molten gold, and the third a dark yellow like old urine.

Why are they here? Zos wondered. *Can they already know what we plan?*

But the heat was dissipating as fast as it had grown, and he began to move back towards Gamash. He assumed that the gemstone dome on the agora below him was the old man's doing.

I need to get back inside that dome, Zos realised.

Era watched the demons in shock until the first blasts of fire killed the crucified men and women in the agora.

'Come with me,' Daos said.

He slipped from her outstretched hand and began to run along the front of the shattered stoa that had once connected the Temple of All Gods to the ruins of the old Temple of Ranos. The ancient collapse of two hundred columns had made the area a white marble maze.

Era released the donkey's halter, picked up the skirts of her overgown, and ran. Behind her, she could hear Nicté sprint to catch up, her tough bare feet crunching on marble gravel.

To her right, a ball of fire lit the centre of the agora with a *whoosh* that sucked the air from her lungs and punched her in the belly at the same time, and then she was down, her face against the white cool of a fallen pillar, Nicté was against her back.

'You alive?' she asked.

'So far,' the northern woman said.

She had a cut across her forehead, and another on her cheek and shoulder from flying stone fragments. Era wiped it away with the hem of her overgown and then stripped the garment over her head so that she stood in a short *heton* usually worn by men.

'What the fuck do we do now?' Nicté asked.

'Follow Daos,' Era said. 'Keep him alive.'

She balled her gown up, and was going to throw the stuffed bear aside, but one did not lightly ignore the dictates of whatever god was helping them. Grimly, Era tucked the stuffed bear under her arm.

'Come on,' she said.

Nicté got heavily to her feet.

'The only thing worse than following a headstrong man,' she muttered. 'Following a crazy boy.'

They sprinted down a lane of fallen columns, up a long set of steps, and paused on what had once been the temple floor. Above, the red demon was hurtling bolt after bolt into the agora, and between bolts, Era could see a sparkling dome. It was quite large – as big as a megaron, or a small temple – and each fiery assault enveloped it, then receded like the tide, leaving the glittering structure undamaged.

Daos was off to her right, clambering over the fallen walls of the old Temple of Ranos that surrounded the black basalt structure of the modern Temple of All Gods.

'He's insane,' Nicté said.

Out over the sea, perhaps two stadia away, the dark yellow demon threw fire into the ships, and a dozen of them were afire. On the Street of the Gods, thirty or more people burned like torches, their screams shrill and awful. The pale demon was choosing her targets with care and setting them afire individually, a feline cruelty to her deliberation and observation, turning the screams into a chorus.

Before she left the relative height of the ruined temple floor, she saw Daos on the steps of the squat black temple, as if he meant to enter.

Out in the vast marble expanse of the agora, the jewelled surface of the hemisphere opened like a flower between gusts of fire.

Pollon

The slave-soldiers mostly screamed.

Gamash completed his working in the dirty sand of the agora, and said a word, and a canopy rose around them at the speed of thought, like a tent of crystal, or a palace of rubies and emeralds. A brilliantly coloured light came through …

Fire fell on the surface, and the temperature of the interior rose notably. But nothing penetrated.

Pollon glanced at where Zos had been, but the man had made a heroic leap, and vanished in the eye-blink before the darkly translucent shield rose around them. He was gone into the fire.

Gamash stood in the centre of his pattern, and Pollon watched as the old man struggled with the power of his own casting. He was simultaneously using the Great *Aura* and something else. Pollon guessed he was drawing on his own life force, his personal *Aura*. It was quite horrifying to watch; the man's hair whitened and some fell to the ground as another wave of fire struck, and another.

'I can't do this forever,' Gamash said. He seemed five years older already.

Pollon could feel the level of his auratic expenditure. It was like watching a dam collapse – that much magic expended with every beat of the heart, to stop a demon's fire striking them.

'Arrow!' Hefa-Asus called.

The two of them had performed a hundred experiments. Pollon needed no explanation. He had, in fact, been reaching for an arrow when the big man called.

Behind them, most of the slave-soldiers had left their ranks. A few had burst from the dome of power and vanished, but most lay on the ground, some with their shields over their heads.

But the old man stood his ground. He glanced at Pollon; their eyes met even as Pollon got the nock between his fingers. The old man gave him a nod.

I can do this, he thought.

Just behind Pollon, Persay and the three nomad women were on their feet. As he nocked his first star-stone arrow, a disgusted nomad stripped the shield and spear from a cowering man behind her.

He had the star-stone arrow, and everything seemed to move very slowly. Gamash's remaining hair was now dead white, only a fringe around his skull remaining, and he leant heavily on his staff. But he was watching Pollon.

The black-lipped nomad woman flung a hand out.

'There!'

Even through the veil of translucent, jewelled fractal light, she'd seen the demon high above. Now that he was revealed, Pollon watched his shape move across the rippling shield even as the nock slid over the string. The bow dipped and rose, his anger and his fear and his desperation transmitted into his back muscles. Above him, the top of the massive working opened like a flower, Gamash reading his readiness to loose.

He loosed.

He thought of the old man standing off to his right. Of the practice ground.

He didn't watch the arrow with his eyes. He plucked the second star-stone arrow from his quiver and nocked it, hands smooth in the rhythm of the work, dipped, drew so that his thumb flicked his cheek...

The flower was closing; the demon had turned, wings spread wide as he banked to the right. Two of the opalescent panels of the great working were folded together, and Pollon loosed before they closed.

Zos

Zos saw the second arrow strike.

The demon had just banked steeply, trading speed for manoeuvrability to dodge the first arrow with avian contempt, but that left him too low and slow to dodge the second arrow. The archer hadn't released perfectly, and the arrow seemed to flex in the air, almost to tumble, but it struck between the demon's widely spread wings...

And the thing *transformed*.

As if a veil had been ripped aside, Zos saw the demon's features vanish, the wings morphing and changing as it fell. He flipped himself back over the pillar, back to the circle of safety he should never have left.

But the sparkling walls were falling. Zos reached the high walkway of some long-forgotten priest in two bounds, and looked down into the great square. Close by him, almost at his feet, the million-jewel-shell of Gamash's working smashed like a crashing wave.

Pollon stood on the far side of a huddle of his now useless slave-soldiers, an arrow to his bow.

The demon had tumbled in the air, its thorax now glistening and crustacean-like, multiple rippling legs spasming, vast transparent insectoid wings beating futilely above them in a fruitless effort to stay above the ground.

It crashed into the burning auction platform the slaves had been erecting even as Zos jumped, rolling forwards to land not far from where he'd originally leapt.

A frail old man stood where Gamash had been, so old that he looked as if his rich clothes weighed too much for him to stand straight, leaning on his staff.

'Told you not to move,' he croaked.

Zos scooped up the javelin he'd left by the palanquin and stripped off the rags covering the grey-glitter of the head. He turned to see the mad Dardanian running across the ash and blazing white marble of the agora as the demon rose from the curtain of sparks like a veritable phoenix. Its segmented tail thrashed, raising smoke and ash, and it moved far faster than Zos would have thought possible.

Zos ran at it, and Persay was ten paces ahead of him.

Just like before.

Zos knew what the madman was going to do. He'd been planning to do it himself. But given the weapon in his hand and the other man's willingness...

Let him have his leap.

The demon blasted fire at them, and the Dardanian didn't hesitate, leaping through it, arms scissoring over his head, as if to cover his eyes, and then opening, as if the man was diving into deep water.

The demon, unlike a great bull, rose, its hideous deep-sea head and tiny, beady eyes following the flight of the mortal man, its two long antennae flickering, one clearly broken or damaged.

The man slammed into the head. His cheap bronze sword broke against its indomitable hide, failing even to scratch an eyestalk.

The horror reared back, two pairs of its insectoid limbs leaving the ground, its segmented torso gleaming pale pink in the swirling ash, trying to reach the man who had vaulted on to its head.

Zos was at a full run, and he had no intention of leaping, although in his heart he envied the other man. His soul applauded that leap which had been without fear – his timing superb, his effort magnificent, through fear and fire to his victory.

And that was what the bull-leapers lived for.

Zos felt something inside him – some memory of a greater version of himself. Of the moment when, as a very young man, he'd made the leap.

The sound of the bull's hooves.

The sound of his own heart...

Persay's leap had caused the monster to rear back like an

angry stallion, exposing its breast and the joints in its carapace. Zos took two more running steps and threw the star-stone javelin with everything he had.

Era

Era saw the charge of the young madman; saw the failure of his attack with a sinking heart, the pointlessness of his sacrifice…

And then she saw Zos throw. She knew him immediately; as a dancer, you don't share a boat with a man for a month and recognise his motion. She knew his run, and she knew his throw.

The star-stone bolt slammed into the thinly armoured chest, and where it punched through a white milk burst forth like magma from the earth, gouts of the stuff striking the marble of the square. A charring blackness began to spread out from the wound.

The thing thrashed, came down heavily, and Persay rolled over its antenniferous head, slid down the segmented back and tumbled over its tail to the ground behind it, landing with a flourish. The mad Dardanian *bowed* to the world.

Despite everything – fear for her adopted child, for her life, for the future of her world – Era grinned like a fool, and then she stripped her star-stone blade clear of her scabbard and sprinted at the sprawling horror.

By chance or design, it rolled on its shell and suddenly the legs were reaching for her, and she was *dancing*.

She swayed under the first leg and snipped at a joint as she passed, the star-stone severing the limb like a young branch, and then rolled *over* the second and cut up into it from below. Her blade went into the soft crinkles where the appendage met the armour of the thorax, ripped a hole the width of her shoulders, and she was gone before the third leg could catch her, kicking the fourth limb with everything she had, blocking its blow.

She had *never* danced so well. The joy raced through her – the pure feeling – and she felt a song rise in her throat.

Her right foot was burning where the white ichor had caught her. She turned her hips, powering the blade again, severing another limb.

Something caught her under the shoulders as she leant into the blow, and she was thrown, rolling clear of the fallen demon. Her head hit the ground; she caught something with an elbow and blinked away tears of pain, rolling to her feet, feeling her right foot give under her.

Nicté was between her and the monster, but the thing was spasming.

'It's fucking dead,' Nicté said. 'It just doesn't know that yet.'

Zos

Zos was standing weaponless at almost the centre of the vast stone agora when the pale demon turned inland again. She had toyed with her kills, as if savouring their pain; now she was drawn by her thrashing comrade.

She looks like a divine woman with the legs of a goat ... while it looks like a deep-sea monster spawned with a dragonfly.

He drew the bronze short-sword at his waist. He was aware that it was probably useless against the demon-soldiers of the gods, but any sword was probably better than none.

The creature hovered for a moment, and he was between her and her stricken ally.

'I will suck the marrow from your bones while you still live,' she said.

She was not pretty, despite her massive breasts and narrow

pelvis. She had skin like sour milk and an expression of determined fury.

She raised her right arm.

Zos stood his ground with an entirely false smile of contempt.
A life of facing terror left him able, one more time, to smile in
the face of death.

'I put your Resheph down,' he bragged. 'You aren't...'

But then she strode forwards, her long, supernatural goat-legs
giving her swaying hips the parody of a woman's walk.

Pollon, just visible in Zos' peripheral vision, shot her under
her raised arm.

This time the transformation seemed slower; or perhaps it
was the same, but Zos was better able to understand it, even as
he rolled to his right to avoid the demon's collapse forwards
onto all ten emerging limbs.

It smelt like lye and cardamom, and the heady odour caught
deep in his throat.

Zos slashed with his sword as he flipped back away from it.
His back muscles protested the years he hadn't been training
for this; backflips were for the young.

He did land on his feet, the bronze sword bent in his hand,
having done the creature no damage whatsoever.

But luck, and an excellent backflip, had put him just out
of its reach. He dropped his sword, caught one chitinous leg
after it failed to punch its point through his throat, and made
a spinning leap to the right, kicking his legs up and over the
limb he held. The whole weight of his leap and of his body
struck the thing's joints.

It would have shattered a man's shoulder.

Instead, Zos tore the forelimb right off the body of the thing
like a man ripping a leg off a cooked crab, and used the limb
to block another strike. The demon tried to push him to the
ground, and something rolled between his outspread legs.

He used the severed limb as a staff to push the demon away, and then Era, who had rolled between his legs, was cutting at it.

It spat fire, and Zos was burnt, though he was not the target. Then the thing, head down to target Era, stumbled and fell.

Hefa-Asus stood at its head with an enormous axe.

Now the third demon, the dirty yellow one, was coming. But it was not coming down to them; it went up, higher in the air, raining fire.

'Gamash!' Zos called.

The bent old man raised his hands. To his left, Hefa-Asus hit the female demon in the head again. Zos could feel the power of the smith's blow through his feet.

And then, hundreds of paces above the shattered marble of the agora, the Dry One hit the demon. Zos saw it for a hundredth of a heartbeat, clear as anything at the very apex of its flying leap from the mountain above them. In an eye-blink, there was a ball of white fire, and then a shower of burning monster pelted the agora.

Zos was hurt: a bad burn on his left side, and something was broken – a rib, or ribs. And he had muscles that were pulled or worse; one in his groin that worried him. His body knew how to fight like a bull-leaper, but he wasn't in training for it, and he was going to pay for days.

But his mind seemed to be clear.

'Hefa-Asus!' he called. 'Era is under the carcass!'

The huge man reached down at the same time that the beautiful dark-skinned woman from the slave market grabbed the body from the other side. Together they *threw* the demon's shattered remains clear.

'They're not that heavy,' Hefa-Asus said. 'But I suspect I can make something wonderful from the skin.' He looked at the woman. 'You are strong, lady.'

Dite blinked both her long-lashed black eyes. 'So I am, smith.'

Hefa-Asus drew his knife – a broad-bladed bronze tool, not a weapon – and began to cut into the fallen demon.

'The blood is—!' Era tried to yell, with blood in her hair and all down one hip.

'Yah!' Hefa-Asus sprang back from the corpse. He held up his hands. 'I'll need tools from the ship.'

One of the nomads handed Zos a pitcher of water, which he poured over the smith's right hand, and then over his own leg, and then over any part of Era that had the white milky blood spattered across it. It left marks like a sunburn, even on Zos' dark skin.

The mad bull-leaper was coming back across the agora, and Gamash was holding his head in his hands.

Zos glanced at the carcass.

'What the *fuck* are they?' he asked.

Pollon hadn't let go of his bow. He used a horn tip to prod one of the many legs, and the articulations. And then the leg Zos had ripped away.

Gamash laughed mirthlessly. He shook his head.

'Everything you know is a lie,' he said hollowly, as if that made sense of anything.

The slave-soldiers, at least some of them, were pressing in around Zos. A few had already run; a dozen were meticulously looting the market. Others were on their feet; some were under their shields in shock or terror. Zos understood both states; his mind was not grasping either the death of the demons, or their transformations, too well.

Everything you know is a lie.

But he was grasping what the next steps ought to be.

Zos turned to the slave-soldiers. The old man had a wicked spear and a Narmerian *khopesh* and he was in among the abandoned merchants' tables, throwing equipment to the able slaves. More than a dozen were dead or terribly maimed; a gout of fire had gone over the back ranks, sparing only the Dendrownan, and a burning piece of demon had killed two more.

The three nomad women were fully armed, and all of them, still naked, had veils over their faces.

Priorities, Zos thought.

He took a deep breath and realised that he still had the silver-studded ivory hilt of the dead slaver's broken sword in his hand, clutched in a death grip.

Never grow attached to a sword, he thought.

He made his hand open, and dropped it in the rubbish.

He turned to the slaves.

'All of you are free,' he said. 'Now we have a great deal to do, and I need you all to obey. Not as slaves. But as free people engaged in a bitter and important conflict.'

The old man smiled at him, showing a mouth full of rotted teeth.

'Or you could just start issuing orders and tell 'em why later.'

'Right,' Zos said. 'You two, attend Hefa-Asus. Fetch him whatever he wants from the ships. Old man. What's your name?'

'Jawat, lord.'

'Lord me no lords, Jawat. Take the right four files and go and seize as many ships as you can. From both ports. We need at least six. Twenty would be better. The *Untroubled Swan* is already ours. Understand?'

The old man viewed Zos with a cynical detachment that he found hard not to like.

'Take the ships. For us. Now. Whatever means necessary.'

Jawat ran a finger along the edge of his bronze sword. Then he barked an order. Half a dozen of his soldiers ignored him, but the rest turned smartly.

'Follow me, you lot,' he said.

'Exactly,' Zos said.

He turned to the three nomad women.

'Attend Era.' He pointed at the wounded woman. 'And guard her.'

The nomad woman nearest him licked her lips, and nodded.

The Dry One landed; its sudden appearance was like a bolt from the blue, except that Zos was more used to its ways. He pointed at Era, kneeling with her hands on the ground.

'Can you heal her?' he asked.

The jewelled eyes never blinked, but there was a slight purr, a vibration, and its long head tilted to one side.

It pointed south. And then it pointed more insistently.

'What now?' Era muttered from her place on the ground.

Gamash raised a hand and tottered forwards, and the Dry One turned to him.

A black-taloned hand shot out and grabbed Gamash by the throat. One talon pricked deep, so that a single dot of blood flowed.

Gamash's mouth opened, and in a strange voice, he said, '*You must flee.*'

Zos stepped back, and then made himself settle.

'You can understand us?'

'*You must flee. Jekers come. Gods come.*'

Era got to her feet. She took a step forwards and Zos could tell it hurt.

'We have a great many injured people,' she said. 'And it will take time to get all of them onto the ships.'

Zos took a hesitant step forwards.

'Can you help us? Can you heal …' He wanted to say 'Can you heal me?' but he was too proud. Instead he said, 'Can you heal Gamash and Era?'

The Dry One bent forwards slightly. Then it raised one hand.

A tiny blue spark emerged.

'It's drained,' Pollon said. 'I can feel it. The poor thing has used so much power for us, and now it is drained.'

Zos looked at Era.

Era shook her head. 'Huntress, but I'm tired. Zos, we have resin in the *Swan*'s hold.'

'*Heal*,' the Dry One said with Gamash's mouth. Then it opened its own mouthparts and Gamash didn't even have time to scream.

They watched, transfixed, as the Dry One did whatever it did, and Gamash gave a cathartic shiver and his eyes rolled back.

The Dry One laid him on the ground.

'Huntress,' Era said softly. And then, without hesitation, she walked to the Dry One. 'Heal me,' she said.

It wrapped her in its spindly, thorny limbs.

Pollon stepped close to Zos.

'Stop,' he said. 'We're killing it.'

'What?' Zos said.

Pollon looked at Hefa-Asus, who nodded.

'It's blood,' he said. 'The Dry One gives its blood.'

'That's what the resin is, Zos,' Pollon said. 'The Dry Ones' blood. That's why he's exhausted when he's finished. He builds a cocoon so that he can heal...'

'Fuck,' Zos said.

'It will die,' Pollon said. 'It's used all its power and it will heal us until it dies.'

Zos blinked. 'Fuck,' he said again.

The Dry One laid Era on the ground.

Zos nodded. 'That's enough,' he said. 'I'm going to the ship to get *resin*. To get ... the stone jars you gave us. Do you understand anything I'm saying?'

The Dry One swayed.

Pollon put a hand on Zos' arm. 'If you have the energy, run.'

Zos nodded, dropped his sword, and ran.

Heaven

Nisroch watched the glyphs on his black marble wall as a small man, or perhaps a boy, came into the temple. Among the many disadvantages of this god's eye was that it was located inside a dark temple, so that the outside was like a rectangle of white light, punctuated from time to time by inexplicable flashes from outside. He could only see one small patch of the outside world.

So the boy emerged from the brightly lit outside, carrying what appeared to be a long pole. He walked to the very centre of the floor.

It was a trident. He was far enough from the doorway for Nisroch to see that now.

The boy smiled straight at him, raised the trident, and slammed it into the floor.

The last working god's eye on Dekhu went out, and Nisroch felt a splitting headache flash through his immortal head. He shot backwards off his couch.

He could hear Enkul-Anu in his mind, roaring for him, and he stepped through the wall of reality into the hall.

Sypa was in her usual place; Ara stood like an armoured statue with his son Resheph and his sometime ally Nerkalush. The Great Lord of the Hosts of the Dead, Gul, stood with the Captain of the Demons, Azag. The Goddess of the Deep Sea, Timurti, was drooling, her face to the wall.

'What the fuck just happened?' The Storm God's usually carmine face was scarlet, and there were lines on his brow that portended thunderbolts.

'Something happened in Dekhu, where I'm looking for Druku.' Nisroch shook his head. He really didn't want the Storm

God looking too closely at Dekhu, but lying to Enkul-Anu was a very dangerous game. He hadn't meant to whine, but that's how it came out. 'You told me to find Druku.'

'He's using demons to look for Druku,' Azag growled. 'My demons.'

Enkul-Anu made a gesture for silence.

'In Dekhu?' he said.

'I think Druku is hiding there,' Nisroch said.

With terrible calm, Enkul-Anu turned to look at the Herald of the Gods.

'You know that Dekhu is a very special place, correct?'

Nisroch swallowed. 'No?'

He tried to know everything. But he didn't. Sometimes his inexperience showed.

Enkul-Anu backhanded the herald so hard he was thrown against the gleaming wall inlaid with the storming of heaven by the gods.

Being immortal, Nisroch picked himself up, more humiliated than hurt.

'What, exactly, is happening on Dekhu?' Enkul-Anu asked.

'Something put out the god's eyes there,' Nisroch said, hating his own cringing tone and his supposed father too.

His anger and resentment burned. He would have his revenge. The old ones stood by, senile and useless, and he was enraged by their ancient idiocy. And Enkul-Anu ruled by the power of his fists and his thunderbolts.

'And you didn't tell me!' the Storm God roared.

The heavens shook with his wrath.

'I thought it was Druku, irritated by your decree!'

He pointed at Azag. 'Call your demons.'

Nisroch pondered admitting that the boy with the trident had managed to do something very powerful in one of the temples. But he still didn't want Enkul-Anu looking too closely at Dekhu – not with his Jekers on the way there.

I am so close.

'There's *nothing*,' Azag growled. 'It's as if they're fucking dead.'

Resheph brightened. 'I'll go,' he said.

'Not alone,' Nerkalush said.

Nisroch realised that his prayers were answered.

'Yes!' he said. 'Let the three of us go.'

Enkul-Anu looked at his herald with deep suspicion.

'What are you up to, boy?' he asked.

Silence filled the hall.

Then Enkul-Anu looked at the three – young, and full of power.

'Go,' he said. 'But not a hair on Druku's head is to be disturbed, you understand me? Go, replace the god's eyes and find the missing demons. And return with a report.'

Nisroch bowed with false obsequiousness, and took himself to his own chamber far below, where he put a sigil lock over all of his eyes, and picked up his long, slim sword, one of a few things he'd stolen from Enkul-Anu's treasury when Lady Laila took him there. It had been a beautiful day – and just touching the sword excited him for her.

That had been the day he'd made his final decision. His father had to be overthrown. And when his work at Dekhu was done, he wasn't coming back, so he didn't need to worry about his father seeing the sword at his side. He'd know what was afoot, soon enough.

Nisroch put on his cloak of peacock feathers, and placed himself on the high portico outside the hall, where the winds howled. He stood among the great pillars, atop a cliff a thousand feet high. Far below, the sea beat against the base of the cliff.

The useless death gods were nowhere to be seen. He waited, and waited.

Immortality does *not* breed patience.

When they arrived he couldn't restrain himself.

'Great god Enkul-Anu awaits our efforts! Where were you two?'

Resheph grinned his adolescent grin. 'I couldn't decide what sword to bring,' he said.

Nerkalush laughed his silly laugh. 'And then...' he said, 'Resheph did the best thing.'

The two crashed their fists together.

'And what was worth making us late to save the world from chaos?' Nisroch asked.

Resheph couldn't hide his grin. 'I stole my father's war sword.'

'The sword of *Terror*?' Nisroch said, stepping back.

'Finding Druku could be dull,' Resheph said. 'I want to use it!'

Nisroch nodded. 'We'll find plenty of mortals to fall under your blade.'

Resheph, God of Pestilence During War, smiled.

'That's more like it,' he said. 'I want to kill so many mortals!' He glanced at Nisroch, and a little contempt showed, just for a moment. 'Not that you'd understand.'

Nisroch touched his own sword hilt and smiled.

'I'm sure it will be memorable,' he said.

Chapter Ten

Era

Era awoke feeling better than she'd felt in weeks, though her ribs were tender. She sat up, winced, and looked around.

Pollon was close by, with a stone jar in his hands. There were thirty people laid out by the tables of the market. Two big hide tents had been rigged to protect them from the merciless sun, and the agora stank. Era found that she'd tied the boy's toy bear to the woven *zone* at her waist, and that the stuffed bear had saved her life, or at least her hips, when the monster fell on her. And the rest of her...

The Dry One had healed her. It took her a moment to understand that, while she absently stroked the stuffed bear.

'You're awake,' Hefa-Asus said. 'Good. We have a problem.'

'We have quite a few problems,' Pollon said. 'Era, can you fight?'

She breathed in and out, touched her side hesitantly, and then nodded. 'I think so.'

'The Jeker fleet is on the horizon – maybe four hours away. And your boy says the gods are coming.' Pollon shrugged. 'At least some. A handful.'

'Just a handful of gods,' Era repeated with a smile.

'Resheph.' Gamash looked better, younger; she tried to adjust to that grey beard on an almost unwrinkled face. He said the name with a stark anger. 'Resheph is coming here.'

Pollon waited for the old man to say more, but he didn't. Finally, Pollon said, 'We're loading the ships, but half of them have already cut their cables and run, and others burned when the demons attacked. And your boy says we need to hold on here for another three hours…'

He looked at Hefa-Asus, but the Dendrownan smith was already back at work with Nicté, flaying the monsters.

Zos was drawing a map in the sand, but he paused.

'I'm not sure we should do what the Huntress wants. I'd like to know *why* we need to hold on for three hours. I think it has to do with the Jekers, and it doesn't seem wise, for us.'

'I want to take Resheph down,' Gamash said.

Era glanced at him. He looked younger than she'd ever seen him.

'I wouldn't mind that myself,' Zos admitted. 'But what are the chances?'

'Are we buying time for the ships to escape?' Era asked. 'Because I agree — waiting sounds insane to me. We won't last a minute against the gods.'

Zos helped her to her feet.

'Daos says we will.'

'And the Jekers?' Era asked.

Without thinking about it, she put her hand to her eyes and looked south, but of course, sails visible from the mast top on the *Untroubled Swan* wouldn't be visible from here, even if she could see over the ruins.

Hefa-Asus shrugged.

Zos looked them over. And then looked at Era.

'My notion is that we stay and fight, while Hefa-Asus, Nicté, Pollon and Atosa leave with the Dry One.'

Era blinked. That was not what she'd expected.

'Because they can make the star-stone weapons?' she asked.

'And plan the next step. And perhaps negotiate a way past the ajaws and into the mountains. If we die here, the rebellion goes on. If Hefa-Asus dies here ...'

'Gamash should go,' Era said. She nodded to Zos. 'Otherwise, for once, I like your plan.'

'It's not a plan yet,' he said. 'More like a casualty list.'

'I'll be staying,' Gamash said. 'You won't last a minute without me against the gods. And anyway, I want Resheph.'

'Only you know how to find the star-stone,' Zos said.

Hesitantly, as if he didn't like it himself, Hefa-Asus said, 'No. I know as well as he.'

'Take all the craftsmen, get on a ship, and run,' Zos said.

'I stay,' Pollon said. 'First, I'm your archer. Second, I'm not a craftsman. I'm a writer. They won't need a bureaucracy in the mountains.' As if it clinched his argument, he held up a single arrow, the cane shaft unbroken, the star-stone head glittering malevolently in the sun. 'And I still have one arrow.'

'Insane,' Era murmured.

Zos shrugged. 'We're a group of mortals trying to make war on heaven,' he said.

Era laughed. 'Point taken, brother. So ... we stand and fight?'

Zos waved his hand over the agora. 'I was thinking more of an ambush.'

Heaven

Nisroch led them, flying through the upper air. His cloak of feathers fluttered behind him in the thin air, and the peacock eyes tracked the two death gods in his wake because he didn't trust either of them.

But they seemed content, now that they'd arrayed themselves in blood and finery, to follow his lead. He wasted a little time flying along the coast of the Hundred Cities; it was *vital* that they come up to Dekhu from the east, as he didn't want the two little death gods to see his Jekers coming up from the south.

My Jekers, you adolescent fools. How dare you try to suborn their worship from me?

They swept along the coast, too high up to really feel the speed of their approach.

After an hour, Resheph came up alongside him to complain. 'This is taking a long time.'

Nisroch wanted to roll his eyes at the other god's immaturity, but instead he said, 'We're almost there. There's the delta of the Iteru. We turn west into the setting sun, and we'll be there in half an hour.'

Resheph fell back.

Nisroch watched him as he and his friend whispered, their words carried away in the speed of flight. They doubtless had some sort of force-bubble to allow them to talk; likewise, unless they were incredibly stupid, they knew he was watching them, so the exclusion was deliberate, a calculated insult.

They're jealous because I have a real role in heaven and they're children playing at death.

Useless bastards are trying to steal my Jekers.

Nisroch turned west. Far out over the sea, he could just make out the peaks of Dekhu, and away to the south, a smudge on the surface of the water that he thought might be his Jeker fleet – a thousand ships that would tear Narmer off the face of the earth and start the path to Enkul-Anu's fall. Such a simple plan.

Rid the world of humans, except the Jekers. And all the auratic power would be his alone.

I will be the only god, Nisroch thought. *Maybe I'll recall my mother from the void. But first, I need to deal with these two.*

He pondered that and decided that they needed to go before he found Druku; he didn't need a witness.

Unless I do for Druku, too.

In the sheath at his hip was the sword that Enkul-Anu called *God-Killer*. It was the sword that Ara had worn when storming heaven, and it was so dangerous that even *Terror* paled by comparison.

I could do for all three. Risky, but it could be brilliant. We split up to search, and I take them one at a time.

Coming in, Nisroch noted that the harbour was almost empty and ships were sailing off to the north and west. He marked them down for later destruction and wondered if it was possible that the island had some warning of the approaching Jeker fleet.

And then he was eyeing the ground of the ancient agora. It was the clearest space; there'd once been a city here, and the old gods had been defeated here. He knew that much, though it was all ancient history.

He landed, his cloak swirling about him, and his thousand eyes searched the ruins; he didn't like what he saw and his attention wandered. From above he'd seen a few dozen mortals. There had clearly been a fight, as the centre of the agora was scorched, and there was another scorch mark to the east, as if something huge had been burnt. But it was the centre of the agora that held his attention; twenty or so mortals had been crucified and then burnt, and the result was both horrible and somehow beautiful. A fitting greeting for the Jekers.

But he'd expected – he'd *needed* – to find the slave markets full…

The death gods landed behind him, and he turned.

'We need to find Druku—'

Both death gods were grinning from ear to ear.

'We'll find Druku,' Resheph said. 'But we're going to have a little fun with *you* first.'

'So tired of you, you arrogant little prick,' Nerkalush said, and Resheph drew his father's sword.

Instantly, Nisroch felt bile in his mouth.

Enkul-Anu stood over him, hands on hips.

'Do my bidding or I will put you in the Outer Darkness the way I did your mother,' the great god roared. 'You think you are truly immortal? I can end you in a breath.'

Through his terror, Nisroch felt real panic as he realised why the others had accompanied him. Though he tried to calm himself, he was on his knees, and the sword broadcast *terror* – sheer, unrestrained fear.

'We're going to slice you up,' Resheph said. 'And we're going to bind what's left of you and hide you deep, and we'll come and visit you sometimes to make sure you stay that way for a long, long time.'

Nisroch's hand was moving to his sword hilt but, as if he was a child, Resheph caught it.

'It's going to be part of our aspect.' Resheph was leaning over Nisroch now, close enough to grasp, except that Nisroch was utterly incapable of movement, lost in a wretched nightmare of fear. 'We're going to sacrifice you as an example to the Jekers, and you will become *The Sacrifice*, always bleeding, always weak.'

Nerkalush kicked him. 'Pretty clever, eh?'

Nisroch couldn't even think.

All he could do was scream.

Chapter Eleven

Pollon

Pollon lay under a table in the agora. The table was itself covered in cinders, and he lay on ash and blown sand. Zos had daubed him with ash to make him even less visible.

He lay alone, and shook with fear.

I'm not that good an archer. This is not a plan, this is a desperate hope.

All I needed to do was say that I wanted to go with Hefa-Asus. I'm not a warrior. No one expects me to die here.

But when Zos and Era agreed on something they were like a force of nature, and they had agreed on this. And so Pollon lay, alone and exposed, as the sun set in the west; the marble around him had gone from golden to pink and now orange. He was within easy bowshot of the Temple of All Gods; its black steps rose just fifty paces away, and Era insisted that the gods would come to the temple. Or rather, the boy did.

How long will I have to wait?

The sun was already setting in the west, and soon it would sink behind the mountains.

And then he felt them come. He felt them in the *Aura* before they landed; first a prickle of discomfort, and then something like a scent which he knew from the temple in Hekka.

Gods. Here.

So the boy was right. No surprise there.

And, looking out between the legs of a table that had once held cheap bark-cloth for slave clothes and now hid weapons, he saw them – three huge figures in the awesome space of the ancient agora.

Not in the temple. Right out in the middle.

He was seventy paces from the closest of the three, and perhaps a hundred from—

Oh godsohgodsohgodsohgodsgodsgodsgodsooooooooooooooooooooooooo ooooooooooo!

Terror struck him as one of the distant gods drew a sword, and nothing could have prepared him for the force of it.

Almost nothing. Except having been bound on a chariot wheel with an executioner breaking his limbs slowly with a bronze rod ...

Pollon felt the terror, and the first impact of it made him lose control of his bladder. He had no idea how long he was engulfed by it, before it faded to a distant fury, like the howl of wolves far enough into the desert that they were no longer an immediate threat.

Terrifying. And yet ...

Definitely not as bad as watching your limbs broken.

And someone else wasn't paralysed by it, because a silver mirror flashed off to his left.

Pollon got to his feet. It wasn't pretty, but he did it.

He picked up the bow buried among the rags on the table, and the single arrow – the only star-stone arrow that wasn't shattered. His bow hand shook so badly that he had to stop and breathe and calm himself.

Somewhere off to his left, a donkey brayed – a homey sound. He took another deep breath, drew the long cane shaft all the way to his ear, and brought the arrow up as he drew, over the target and then settling back down ...

403

A gentle hand on his elbow, and his bow tracked the width of an eyelash to the left.

Huntress, he thought, and loosed.

Era

Era had organised people to look for food, and to load carts in the central marketplace and deliver them to the ships. She and Jawat and Persay had seen the ships loaded, the wounded going up the gangplanks from the beach. They'd kept just two ships: the *Untroubled Swan*, because Jawala and Aanat insisted, despite the violence, and a long, low Dardanian pirate whom Jawat had convinced to stay.

And even while preparing the ambush she remembered the donkey, which had her scrap metal bag and her other weapons. She'd been loading the donkey when the first tremor hit.

Era had experienced earthquakes before, and she knew this one would be bad.

'Where's Daos?' she asked Dite.

The woman was handing a basket of fresh greens up to Jawala.

'I have not seen him in some time,' she said. 'He was trying to tell you something, and then he just walked off.'

'Huntress,' Era cursed.

She turned, glanced south to where the first jagged sails were just visible on the horizon, and then dashed up the beach.

Even as she ran across the huge open space of the white marble agora, the earth trembled again, and she stumbled.

Dite did not. The taller woman ran effortlessly.

'He'll be in the temple,' she said.

Era wanted to ask her how she knew that, but she didn't have the capacity to ask and sprint.

404

Dite was up the black steps of the Temple of All Gods even as one of the great statues teetered and fell off the pediment to explode into a thousand fragments. Era was hit twice; the blow to her right hip was excruciating, and Dite came back for her, apparently untouched.

'Fucking Sypa,' Dite said, looking at an enormous breast lying on the steps. Then she smiled at Era, and Era felt her heart beat very hard.

'I have to find Daos,' she said.

'He's inside, no doubt,' Dite said. 'Things are about to get complicated. There are more players here than I expected,'

'What on earth is he doing here,' Era asked. '*Daos!*' she shouted. 'Come out!'

Another tremor hit them.

Out in the fire-charred middle of the agora, she could see Pollon waving, and Zos and Gamash headed for the burnt area in the middle.

She picked herself up, passed a wary eye over the pediment, and then entered the Temple of All Gods.

There was Daos. He was easily visible on the black and white marble floor, and he had the trident in his hand.

'Mama.' He smiled from ear to ear. 'Two down, one to go.'

Era blinked, because the boy was a foot taller. Broader. But he had the same look of innocent delight.

'Mama!' he called again.

She was favouring her hip as she walked. Broken? Something was wrong.

Daos pointed down. 'I struck the floor when he told me,' he said. 'One more time and I release—'

'He?' Era asked. 'We follow the Huntress.'

Daos shrugged. 'Nannu told me to strike here. And look!'

A section of the floor had fallen in, the black and white

405

marble slabs collapsing to reveal an ancient stone stairway going down.

'We need to get out of here,' Era said, the insistent parent.

Daos shook his head. 'We need to find the eggs, and save them.'

'Eggs?' Dite asked.

She smiled, put a hand on the boy, and started down the steep steps. The treads were terribly worn and very narrow, and the whole enterprise looked very dangerous.

The woman's curiosity was as seductive as she was, and Era followed her down the steps.

They went on for a way, until it was pitch black. A kind of stygian darkness Era didn't like. And it was hot.

And just when she was thinking of proposing a retreat, the earth shook again. Dust moved; something settled into her hair, and she screamed.

Just dust, she told herself as she brushed a hand through her hair. And then there was a hand around her waist, and another at her shoulders.

'Almost there,' Dite said in her ear, and kissed her.

Era had trouble standing for a moment, and a wave of lust swept through her, conquering the fear and leaving her alert and alive.

Era still hated being underground. But she needed to be in front, to lead, so she slipped past, her fingers lingering on Dite's back. Then she began to descend sideways, left leg, right leg, left leg...

'Almost there.' Dite's voice was ghostly above her.

Her left leg found the next step, and then she was at the bottom.

It was absolutely dark. A heavy dark, that seemed full of menace, oppressing her; nothing like night outside; an utter absence of light.

She knelt, very slowly – one of the bravest things she'd ever done – and ran her hands over the ground.

And sure enough, there was an egg. It was very large – larger than an ostrich egg. And cold. As cold as winter ice. And heavy, like lead or gold.

She swore.

'Eggs,' she said.

'Fascinating,' Dite said.

The woman was next to her in the darkness, moving with a surety that suggested that she could see.

Who are you? Era wanted to ask.

'There are five eggs,' Dite said. 'Fuck. What is going on?'

'I can carry them,' Era said.

'No, my dear,' Dite said. 'It would hurt you. I have them.'

Era blinked. 'You do not act like a slave,' she said.

You are the queen of enigmatic statements, Era thought to herself.

Dite brushed against her on the dark and narrow steps.

'I'm not a slave,' she said. 'Except to my own inclinations.'

She smiled roguishly, and together, the two women began to climb out of the darkness. As soon as Era could see, she felt better; and as soon as she could see the eggs, that feeling wavered.

It was a day of supernatural extremes.

The eggs were made of a milky crystal, a pale violet in colour. And they exuded cold.

'You knew they were there,' Era said.

Dite shrugged her lovely shoulders. 'No, I didn't. Anyway, I haven't thanked you for rescuing me,' she said, and leant over and put her mouth on Era's.

Era stopped thinking, stopped fearing, stopped strategising. Her whole being went into that kiss.

Dite broke away with a secret smile on her lips.

'Oh my,' she said, and climbed to the top.

Era felt as if she was drunk. She could almost taste the wine on her lips. She blinked, shook her head, and put a hand on the solidity of the boy. But after a deep breath, she looked across the agora.

'I need to keep people moving to the ships. I can't keep chasing after you, Daos. Please stay close.'

The boy looked away.

'Will you come with me, now?' she asked.

Daos set his mouth. 'I need—'

'You need to stay where I can see you,' Era said. 'I have things I need to do.'

'But—'

'Move!' she spat at him, and ignored his hurt look.

She started across the floor, looked back, and the boy was leaning on the trident.

'Do you want me to carry that?' Era asked.

'Oh, no,' the boy said. 'When the gods come, I'm to strike the earth one more time.'

'Gods?' Era asked.

'Here they come,' Daos said.

Era ran to the gargantuan entrance to the Temple of All Gods – the new structure, flattened against one of the squat pillars – and immediately saw the three gods. One was on his knees; the titanic figure, twice the height of a man, showed every sign of being overcome with fear.

One stood behind him, holding one arm while the third giant figure held the other arm. That one had vulture wings, and Era knew him at once.

'Resheph,' she said. But the scene made no sense to her at all. 'What the fuck?' she muttered.

Dite turned her face. She was against the opposite pillar.

'They fight among themselves,' she said. 'It's what they do.'

She looked as if she was under a heavy strain, or looking into a strong wind.

Off by the beach, the donkey brayed.

'What do *we* do?' Era's heart was pumping, her body ready to fight, her usual reaction to the waves of fear striking her like a heavy wind.

The god with vulture wings held a glittering sword. He swept it down, and one of the kneeling god's hands fell to the marble, his immortal ichor splashing around it like wine.

As if in answer, a single arrow appeared from the agora, hung for a moment at the top of its flight, and fell with the speed of a striking eagle.

Resheph screamed, and stumbled back, the arrowhead protruding from his chest. He screamed again, and the sword in his hand fell to the ground with a *clang* that seemed to shake the earth.

For a moment, Resheph's form flickered, and he lost his semblance of human shape, and looked like … like …

Like something from a nightmare. Something made of chitin and gristle, and with too many appendages.

Era had her long star-stone knife in her hand.

'This isn't the plan,' she said.

Dite shook her long dark hair and stepped out from behind her pillar.

'This is no longer anyone's plan,' she said. 'Certainly not mine.'

Era moved forwards cautiously. The three gods were perhaps a hundred paces away, and she was tempted to run, because she generally ran at things she feared. They were huge – taller than Hefa-Asus, bigger than Zos. And two of them were flickering between their human-god form and something altogether alien.

I hate big things, she thought.

'Don't get ahead of me,' Dite said. 'You wouldn't enjoy it.'

Her beauty was slightly marred by the look of concentration

on her face. But she walked forwards with erotic, drunken dignity, and Era paced behind her, watching the three. Resheph – if it was Resheph – had stumbled back two steps and then gone down on one knee. The other god, the one with a diadem of skulls, still held one of the kneeling god's arms, and his severed hand lay on the marble, and the arm spat ichor.

And then the wounded god turned, and sprayed his undying blood in the face of the god with the circlet of skulls.

Nerkalush, Era thought, dredging the name out of her catalogue of useless gods.

Nerkalush stumbled back but didn't release the arm.

And Nisroch the Herald, Era thought.

'How fitting,' Dite said aloud. 'Oh, mighty Tyka, they have underestimated you, my darling.'

'What?' Era asked.

Dite made a dismissive gesture with her hand. 'Never mind me.'

Resheph was staggering to his feet, a hand reaching for his father's sword, when a beam of concentrated blue fire struck him from his right.

He turned, and sickly green plague-fire flashed back along the same line, and he screamed. And his godlike semblance flickered, as if reality was shattered; he had antennae sprouting from an elongated, insectile head … no …

His hyper-handsome face stabilised.

'*I am Resheph!*'

Another bolt of blue fire caught him, and he staggered back. Gamash rose from his cover and began to walk towards the young god with the vulture's wings, a single thread of burning icy blue connecting them.

Resheph threw back his now entirely alien head and screamed, '*I am Resheph!*'

The screams hit Era like blows.

Gamash took another step forwards, and another. The blue fire was relentless. So was the effect it had on its wielder; he was ageing before her eyes, his hair falling away, his limbs withering.

'No!' she called, but her cry was lost in the cacophony of the great agora.

Behind Resheph, Nerkalush had Nisroch's remaining hand in his own, and now he was fumbling to draw his own sword left-handed. But the three gods were changing, as if sloughing off their acceptable human forms.

Dite strode forwards, and Era matched her stride for stride.

Zos

He tried to watch the bull. The great beast's tiny eyes watched him.

About halfway along the sand was the man who'd gone first. He'd hesitated, fractionally, and now he lay with his ribs broken, the bull tattoo on his chest covered in blood. He was alive, for now. He'd either die, or recover and be sold as a slave.

One of the priestesses was shouting, and Zos knew that his failure was a terrible omen.

Zos had trouble taking his eyes off the man. And his failure.

The magnificent bull, black as night, glossy with perfumed oil and sweat, stood across the central court, and his right hoof pawed the flagstones. His horns were gilded, and a wreath of roses was woven between them.

He bowed to the bull, extending his front foot . . .

And the magnificent beast charged, the personification of the god.

He ran at the bull. Training overcame terror. And when Zos was afraid, he generally attacked.

The bull ran at him, hooves like thunder on the stone.

His fear rose to choke him and he hesitated between one step and the next, and the thunder was the bull, and he was nothing.

The great head lowered, the golden horns aimed at his waist.

His knees had no power, his legs trembled, and he was barely moving...

He stumbled...

The gilded horns punched through his abdomen, ripping his guts out through his back in an explosion of blood he'd never see...

This is a dream born of terror! Get out of it! You made your fucking leap!

You fought a god and lost once already. They broke your back and you're still here.

Get up and fight.

'I don't see you dying, not if we do this right,' the boy had said, and he knows something.

And fuck it, I never wanted to live forever anyway.

Zos didn't so much overcome the fear as subsume it in other things, and he rolled from his place among the charred corpses of the crucified slaves where he had lain covered in charcoal and black ash.

The terror was not real, but it was incredibly powerful. Walking towards it was like walking into a hurricane of wretchedness.

He could see the three gods ahead. He knew them all instantly: Nisroch was on his knees, his severed right hand on the marble before him; Nerkalush held his left arm and Resheph had Pollon's arrow in his chest. He knew them even in the confusion of their rippling changes of appearance between godlike and monster.

Resheph, my old friend.

Resheph looked at him. Ignoring the star-stone arrow in his gut, the god spat 'You!'

But as Zos moved forwards into the storm of fear, Gamash appeared from his left. He hit Resheph with everything he had, a line of blue fire that Resheph ignored for an instant too long, so great was his focus on Zos.

Even as Zos watched, Resheph went back to his knees, one taloned claw searching the ground, as if the God of Pestilence During War was blind. Now he was a worm or a maggot; now a thing with fifty legs, now the handsome human form, nearly melted with the cold blue fire Gamash continued to pour on.

Nisroch was wounded, and Resheph was down. Zos switched his combat focus to the one god still standing – Nerkalush.

Nerkalush was struggling with Nisroch, trying to drag the other god off his knees, trying to draw his own sword left-handed, both of them struggling to maintain their godlike forms. As Zos watched, the death god managed a reverse draw so that the wickedly barbed sword was held reversed, like a sacrificial dagger.

Zos leant forwards into the winds of panic and made himself run.

Nerkalush stabbed Nisroch. His reversed sword scored the other god's armoured body deeply, opening a long gash in the auratic bronze and slashing the god's vitals even as Nisroch caught a piece of the blow with his maimed arm. Nisroch abandoned his attempts to cling to the godlike form and rolled, revealing a mammoth thing like a tall lobster. Desperate, Nisroch swung a handless arm like a club, but Nerkalush maintained control, pulling the other god off balance despite its eight legs. Nerkalush, still in human form, raised his sword across his body, for a back-handed killing blow.

Zos saw Resheph's sword on the ground – the fabulous sword of gold and silver, bronze and ivory, and with a kind of radiance that magical things possessed. He took this in with a single glance. His sense of the combat shifted, Resheph's searching claw was explained, and between one stride and another

Zos evaluated and leapt into the very maw of his own fears. At the top of his leap he threw.

His thrown star-stone javelin struck Nerkalush low in the back, where a man would have his kidneys. It went in past the head and to the wood. Zos had thrown it from the top of his leap which now became a tumble, the marble hard under his shoulders, the ash burning the abrasions on his back. He rolled forwards over his outstretched arms and came to his feet holding the sword that had been lying on the cracked white marble paving stones. The sword Resheph had been reaching for. It came into his hand so easily that it might have sought him out.

It was longer than the longest rapier he'd ever wielded, but comfortable to his hand.

And the moment he touched it, all the fear was *gone*. That is, all his own fear.

Inside his head, the sword said, **wield me and rule!**

And just by him, Resheph quailed, and Zos' smile widened.

Era

Gamash stumbled forwards, hunched now, legs like sticks under his robes, but the blue fire never hesitated. Resheph fell back to his knees, his insectoid face stained with a deep blue, screaming incoherently at the heavens. He raised his left claw, and released his rage blind. His pus-yellow bolt of auratic fire blackened marble and destroyed the corpses in the middle of the agora, but Gamash was relentless.

Ten paces away, Zos struck, his javelin slamming into the death god Nerkalush from behind, and then executing one of his bull-leap-rolls to Era's left. He came to his feet with a long sword in his hands.

Almost at Era's side now, Gamash took another step forwards.

He was so close that he could almost touch Resheph's out-stretched hand; he was so bent with age that his skin seemed to wither on his bones as she watched.

Resheph's attention was still locked on Zos, who held the sword, *Terror*, and Resheph was paralysed with fear, unable to conjure or escape.

Gamash never faltered. He forced his ageing form to its full height, and took a final step forwards so that in his decrepitude, nonetheless his eyes were at the same height at Resheph's.

'*For Irene!*' he called to the heavens.

Era didn't follow what happened next, because she was moving to her right, behind Gamash, to slash her star-stone blade across the exposed hamstrings of the death god Nerkalush. He towered above her, the slim javelin head in his back smoking as if he'd been stabbed with a burning brand. And he was losing his immortal form, the plates of a massive armoured back increasingly visible instead of his marble-white human skin.

He screamed, the skulls bound around his head and neck opening their dead jaws in sympathy to his roar of pain. And then, for the first time, he seemed to take in that there was a wider combat than his feud with Nisroch, and he pivoted on his feet, slamming his right fist at Era even as he toppled.

She rolled with it, turning through her blow, pivoting, and his massive fist brushed her and tossed her. She rolled over her sword and came to her feet, swayed under the god's reaching hand and stabbed up into it with the star-stone knife.

The god screamed, and the hand wrenched away, her precious blade a spike through his palm. His hand caught fire, actual blue flames rising.

And now she was unarmed, and face to face with a god.

'Zos!' she called.

The jagged sword came at her, overhand, even as the god fell to both knees. His gold-flecked black eyes were locked on her, and even as he sought to tear the dagger from his hand with his teeth, the jagged sword reached for her with overwhelming speed and power. She leapt back, rolled to the side. The god followed her, his blade digging a trench in the marble, his fist knocking her flat despite her desperate series of dancer evasions.

'Uh!' she managed. 'Zos!'

But Zos couldn't get there in time.

The toy bear ended up under her hand, where it was warm and soft and solid; the fabric as tangible link to the woman who had woven it.

And then it felt like a handful of fur. She heard the snuffle of a bear, and just for a moment, she imagined the feel of a wet/dry muzzle against her ear.

Zos

They were too late.

Zos had the monster that had been the Herald of the Gods between him and Era. He saw her strike; saw the immortal death god's knee fail him, and her incredible leap, her dancing turn away, and her blow to the god's hand. And he saw the blow that finally knocked her flat.

They were all going to be too late.

Nerkalush fell to his knee, and turned, the jagged sword still held like an assassin's dagger, and the arm went up for the killing blow.

Zos lunged. It was too late; he knew it was too late. But he had to try. She called his name, and he knew she'd hate that – and he understood that, too.

He struck the herald, who was trying to regain control of his flickering immortal form. A slash into Nisroch's leg and he

416

was past, the sword moving like part of him, back behind his hips as he moved forwards...

The jagged sword came down at Era, and she rolled...

And then the bear rose over her.

The bear bloomed like a furry flower, rising off the ground, expanding as she rose, so that by the time she was on her hind legs, she was taller than any of the gods had been when they landed. And her claws were like swords, and her great teeth like axe-hammers of war.

One great paw batted the jagged sword away as if the god's best strength was the effort of a wilful child. The other paw raked the god's face, so that Nerkalush's skull shone in the last red sunlight, the red bones an ironic comment on the necklace of skulls he wore...

The young god fell forwards on his hands and knees. Zos, rising from his leap, brought the magnificent long sword up, placed his left hand on the pommel as he had learnt all those years before in the court of a king he'd hated, and cut.

The terrible sword flashed through the god's neck as if it was made of air, and Nerkalush's headless carcass crashed down. There was a pulse of power, and the form solidified and fell, a hideous tangle of beautiful human limbs and a long, multi-armed alien torso like a scorpion's. But the head that rolled clear was that of Nerkalush, beautiful in immortal youth, and all the more horrible for the contrast.

Zos whirled to face the bear, but the bear was already a normal bear, and she was licking Era's face.

She threw her arms around it.

'Zos!' Gamash shouted.

Zos turned to see the wreckage of the magos. Resheph lay full length on the marble. His eyes were black husks in a ravaged, alien face, but the god's body was twitching, and his wings were trying futilely to beat.

417

Zos managed three steps to join the withered magos. His muscles didn't want to work.

'Give it to me, please,' Gamash asked in the voice of a man with centuries on him.

Zos bowed and handed him the great sword.

Gamash tottered, and then pulled himself up, more skeleton than man. He raised the sword reversed in his hands, and plunged it into the god's right eye. The point slid through the skull, leaving the blade standing erect.

And then Gamash released the hilt. Zos could see that his ankles were like twigs, every curve of his bones revealed, as if he'd not only aged but been starved for fifty days.

His lips moved, and he said, 'Irene.'

And then he fell bonelessly to his knees, and then forwards across the dead god, and before Zos could reach him, he was nothing but a bleached skeleton inside his beautiful godborn robes, and his skull rolled away from his body. And still the bones aged, turning white, then brown, then black, and gradually falling away to powder.

'What...?' Nisroch managed.

Zos had cut one of his legs out from under him, a deep cut behind the ankle that should have severed all the tendons. He was missing his right hand, and his face and side were scored by Nerkalush's barbed blade, and he was no longer in immortal form, but a wounded, tentacled thing.

The bear moved towards the monster, and Era got to one knee, gripped the star-stone knife still piercing the dead god's outflung hand, and ripped it free.

'Hold,' Dite said, and put a hand on Zos' shoulder. She reached past him for the hilt of the sword, *Terror*.

'Who are you?' Nisroch said. 'Mortals? I need your aid!'

He flickered back into his immortal form, beautiful and terribly wounded.

Dite picked up the sword. Zos was again assaulted by waves of his own fears.

'This is not for you,' Dite said, with a loving smile.

Nisroch was trying to get the ichor out of his eyes.

'You will be suitably rewarded for your help,' Nisroch said, trying to draw his own sword.

Dite's smile held Zos in place more effectively than the waves of terror, but then Era got an arm around her neck, and with her free hand, she stripped *Terror* from Dite's outraged hand and it fell, to ring like gold on the marble.

Zos snatched it up again, backing away, and Era still held Dite close, a star-stone dagger at her throat.

'Who the fuck are you?' she asked.

Zos began to circle Nisroch. Behind him, Pollon moved forwards cautiously.

Dite raised her arms like a worshipping priestess.

'I mean you no harm,' she said. 'But that sword is too powerful for a mortal, and Enkul-Anu will come for it, or Ara will.' She blinked her beautiful eyes at Zos. 'Please put it away, at least. In the scabbard. It is shouting for its owners and I can't imagine why it is here.'

Nisroch was backing away.

'Who are you?' he asked Dite.

He was on his feet, taller than the columns in the temple, and while Era held Dite, Zos watched the Herald of the Gods.

'Who are you?' Nisroch repeated. His voice was terrible – as if a dozen were all speaking together, badly joined.

Zos moved to cover Era.

'Mortal, I am a god. Do my bidding. Give me that sword.'

Nisroch reached his left hand towards Zos. The sheer power of his command might have been greater if he hadn't been cringing away from the sword's terror at the same time, while bleeding ichor from three great wounds.

'Don't give it to him,' Dite said clearly.

Nisroch, wounded three times, missing his right hand, managed the left-handed draw of the sword at his hip.

Dite said 'Oh, shit.'

Left-handed, Nisroch swung *Godkiller* at Zos.

Zos stepped to the side against the titanic swing, and used *Terror* to parry, and *Godkiller* rolled off *Terror* like rain off a roof.

Nisroch bellowed his frustration to the heavens, and then saw Pollon drawing his star-stone arrow, unbroken, from the corpse of Resheph.

And then he flickered. He put a hand to an amulet at his neck, under the peacock cloak, and began to rise into the air, bleeding immortal ichor that smoked when it struck the ground.

'Druku!' he shouted. 'You fool! I will finish you and your mortal tools will suffer for eternity!'

The peacock cloak flapped like wings, and it was rising into the heavens, more monster than god.

'My Jekers will destroy the lot of you!' he called.

Zos took another step, and another, gliding to the side of the corpse of Resheph, which was visibly and horribly decaying, as if death were a disease it had caught from Gamash. Pollon had the star-stone arrow on his bow, and his face was set – a man overcoming all his fears.

And Zos thought, *There is courage.*

Zos caught at the scabbard that lay half under the corpse, and sheathed the great sword.

Then, disgusting as the job was, Zos took the sheathed sword, pulling the magnificent gold and ivory plaque-belt through the corpse and fastidiously using a scrap of the dead god's magnificently woven vulture tunic to wipe it clean.

'You really shouldn't have that,' Dite said, and her beautiful eyes were luminous. She seemed unmoved by the star-stone dagger at her throat. 'It's evil. Look what it did to Ara.'

Zos slipped the belt over his shoulder, and it *changed*, flowing to the size of its new owner.

'I won't debate it with you,' he said.

'You'll regret it,' Dite said.

'I regret many things,' Zos said. 'Possession of the sword of the God of War is not the top of the list.'

She growled in her throat. 'Hubris,' she spat.

Era laughed. 'We *are* hubris. We are against the gods.'

'Who are you, lady?' Zos asked again, and the bear growled.

'This is Druku, God of Drunkenness and Orgies,' Era said. 'You witch. We're against *all* gods.'

Dite-Druku gave a small shrug. 'I came to help,' they said. 'And in mortal form, I'm as human and vulnerable as you. Cut me with your star-stone, my darling, and I'll bleed red, not ichor.'

Era tested it, cutting very lightly to the woman's shoulder, and a seam of red mortal blood appeared.

'Ouch,' Dite said.

Zos looked over the wreck of the agora, the two dead gods, and the masts of the ships in the distance.

Pollon narrowed his eyes. 'How do you do that?' he asked. 'Why do the gods and demons … change? What are you?'

'We need to go,' Zos said to Era. 'Although those are some interesting questions.'

'I saved you all,' Dite said. 'I held the power of the sword, *Terror*, at bay so that you could cross the agora. I kept all three of them befuddled while they fought each other.'

She looked from Pollon to Era to Dite, as if they were a jury and she on trial.

'Why are you here?' Zos asked.

'I've defected,' Dite said. 'I won't go back. And honestly, darling, Enkul-Anu will never forgive me after this.'

Zos opened his mouth …

And then the earth shook.

The Temple of All Gods trembled, and Daos emerged and ran down the steps, bounding towards the agora. Behind him, the temple collapsed as if great hands pulled it down into the maw of the earth.

A crack appeared in the marble of the agora and ran from end to end, fully two hundred paces, in a matter of heartbeats. It ran through the corpses of the two dead gods, right between Zos and Era.

The air was full of dust, and flying shards of basalt and marble, and Zos saw Era punched from her feet by a stone striking her in the side.

She lost her grip on Dite and fell, and Zos took a step forward to help . . .

But the crack in the marble pavement had widened into a chasm, and only Pollon's grip on his sword-belt kept him from falling in. Even as he swayed back, the chasm widened and deepened, and the whole of the agora began to rise as if it was held on a soap bubble.

There was smoke emerging from the new chasm at his feet, and it smelt of sulphur.

Daos

The Blue Goddess, Tyka, her beautiful golden horns a brilliant red in the setting sun, walked out from behind a pillar and pointed at Daos where he stood by the steps that led down and down into the darkness.

She smiled, and led him through the great doors of the Temple of All Gods, and onto the portico among the squat pillars. She walked him to a place where two enormous paving stones of black basalt met unevenly.

She pointed, and gave a sharp nod.

Daos raised the trident and slammed it down where she pointed.

Now, run, she said, and vanished.

Era

She got to her feet and felt the whole island move under her. Something hit her, and she fell, and the dust rose like a wild thing around them all.

When she surfaced, Dite had her. The woman was incredibly strong, and her grasp was like love and comfort and happiness all in one.

'What …?' she asked. 'Where …?'

Dite was running on the beach, and then they were in the water.

And then she was being handed up the side of a ship, and her head bumped the side …

She awoke to a crack like the end of the world. It was the edge of night, but something glowed off to her right, and there was fire in the air.

Pollon

The whole of the agora began to rise as if it was being lifted from beneath.

'That can't be good,' Zos said.

'We're cut off from the port,' Pollon observed.

Zos nodded, looking at the hills to the west and the mountain behind them.

'We go west, then,' he said. 'The way escaped slaves go.'

On his side of the fiery crack he had the three nomad warriors, a dozen of the other former slaves, and Persay, as well as Pollon and the boy, Daos. He was bigger; an adolescent.

'There will be a ship,' Daos said. 'It's for you.'

Pollon touched the boy for luck, and then looked at the sky and slung his strung bow on his back.

'I'm out of arrows,' he said.

Zos looked back at him. 'I'm out of everything, including humour,' he said. 'But I know what a volcano is, and I suspect that one of the gods meant this to happen all along. We're tools, Pollon. We did our jobs here. But we've been used.'

Daos shook his head. 'There will be a ship.'

'By the deepest pits of Kur, I hope so,' Zos said, and then ruffled the boy's hair. 'All right. It's a long climb, and we can't linger here. Let's go.'

They ran up the back of the first hill behind the now swallowed Temple of All Gods, and where it had stood there was only a pit, from which heat and a dull glow poured like an open oven into the twilight air.

'Keep going,' Zos spat.

Pollon was afflicted with a scholar's curiosity. He ran closer to have a look and was almost knocked flat by a wave of intense heat.

Ruefully, and lacking eyebrows, he crawled back to safety and ran to catch up.

Zos was already climbing. The others climbed well; the three nomads climbed like spiders, and the Dardanian with the bull tattoo climbed like a mountain goat. The other former slaves struggled.

Pollon felt tireless – as if he'd been given a second youth. He went up the sharp rocks as if he was moving on flat ground, passing the former slaves and catching the nomads.

He reached the top of the first hill and watched Zos disappear into the sharp valley behind it. He eyed the way down in the dying light of the day, picked his spots, and began to descend in jumps.

The magic feeling of youth and vitality lasted until the far side of the deep valley, and about a third of the way up the next ridge, when his leg muscles began to feel as if they were made of molten lead. About half the slaves were well behind them. Zos was carrying the boy, and still a little ahead, and the lanky Dardanian, Persay, was in the lead.

And then he began to lag. Breathing was harder, and his lungs were going like a forge bellows, and they still weren't at the top of the ridge. It didn't help that it was getting darker, nor that there was a growing feeling of heat on his back. Twice he glanced back; the first time, the first ridge they had crossed covered the mouth of the vent, so that all he saw was a reflected orange glow from the ruined marble towards the distant beach, and the last two ships leaving the harbour. He felt a pang for the *Untroubled Swan* and her crew, but climbing, and the present crisis, drove away all other thoughts.

The second time he looked back he was much higher up. The vent was like a burning eye – the red eye of one of the gods – far below him, and waves of heat made it spin and dance. And off to the south, in the last light, he could see the Jeker fleet bearing down on them, the world's wind in their sails.

He slowed.

Zos looked back. They were labouring over boulder-strewn ground, steep enough for some crawling, but sometimes allowing a walk or even a trot, but as the darkness deepened around them the footing became treacherous and small, sharp stones a danger, and sandals were useless. Pollon stripped his off and winced as his writer's soft feet met the volcanic rubble of the island's central ridge.

Soon enough, the pain in his feet equalled or exceeded the pain in his thighs or the fire in his lungs.

And still they climbed.

The mountain shook.

He looked back again, and this time, the staring red eye was obscured by a plume of darkness, and panic made him climb faster. They were going up the narrow pass between the two main peaks; he could still see the top against the sky.

And then the last hundred paces or so had to be climbed – actually climbed. A sheer rock face stood above them, with a soft zigzag of cracks and open fissures where layers of lava had once cooled. He looked up.

Zos was already up, despite the boy on his back, and the three nomads were halfway up. Persay was out of sight.

The smoke plume from the red eye below was now a dense cloud, and he could smell the sulphur and taste the ash on his tongue.

Below him, still stumbling over the loose rocks, were the former slave-soldiers.

Pollon looked back up the cliff.

Somewhere beyond the top of the pass, there might still be light in the western sky, but standing as he was at the base of a cliff, it was dark.

He cursed, and then started up the most obvious cleft.

About fifteen feet up, there was a skeleton. The man had died here, more than a year ago; a little hair stuck to the body, and Pollon felt the power of the man's shade immediately. Doubtless the other climbers had stirred the undead thing, like the passage of a wagon stirring a nest of hornets.

Pollon stopped with his nose no more than a few inches from the skull.

Focus.

He breathed out, onto the skull, even as he raised his ward and pictured his glyphs.

Hatehatehatehatehate.

Pollon felt the emotion, raw and terrible, present, immediate. A strong one.

A slave, trapped and abused …

Oh, yes.

Aloud, Pollon said, 'I wonder how many of the *gidimu* come from slaves?'

It bounced off his wards. He could continue to climb; most *gidimu*, all but the most powerful, were bound to either their own bones or the locale of their deaths.

But there were a dozen men climbing behind him, and he wanted them to live, if there was indeed any chance of anyone living.

He held the unmaking glyph in his mind, rotated it until it was a sword in his hand, and cut. He was not a trained warrior, but the militia had covered the basic cuts, and this *gidimu*, at least, had no real defence. Bone exploded.

Pollon held his position, just breathing, for a moment, and let his wards drop.

Go in peace, brother.

His feet were on one side of the chimney and his shoulders pushed against the other, the bow in his shoulder just outside the rock. He had to wriggle past the rest of the corpse, jammed into the chimney.

But he did it. And it was unable to possess anyone, now.

He got to a shelf above the chimney, and stopped. He was breathing badly, and any feeling of invincible energy was long since gone. He should have thrown the heavy bow over the side of the cliff, but he didn't.

He had the vaguest feeling that his banishment of the *gidimu* had been stronger than usual; he also felt as if he'd earned the right to lie on the shelf and wait for death from this new volcano, which was going to rip the top right off the whole island. He could feel the immanence hanging in the air – the end of things.

I wonder if I'll leave a gidimu of my own.

'Archer,' a voice said, and Persay appeared out of the gloom. 'No nap time, man. Let's climb.' The mad Dardanian beckoned.

'I'm—'

'It's not that far, archer.'

'I'm coming,' Pollon said, like a man being nagged by his wife.

'Here – now. Put your foot here. See the crack? It's easy. No, no. Here. Like this.'

The damned Dardanian's arms were longer than his and the man was obviously stronger than an ox. But his route made sense, and even in the darkness, the rock was pale and the crevice they were climbing was dark.

'You came back for me?' Pollon asked, when he had got over the divide, and could see down to the rocky beach far below.

Persay grinned his mad grin. 'And now I'm going back for the rest of 'em,' he said. 'Don't linger, archer! See the path?'

'If two rocks and a sandy shelf can be held up as a path,' Pollon muttered.

But he was talking to himself. Persay was gone, back down the cliff.

The air was clearer here, with the vent across the high ridge, but there was still a tang of ash and sulphur. He went down as best he could, the tip of the bow tapping against rocks, his lacerated bare feet leaving bloody marks on the smooth stone on this side.

He looked up at the brush of something on his face, and the stars were gone; the emerald Gift had vanished, and the Red Moon was ringed in shining white.

Snow was falling.

No, not snow.

Ash.

Now he knew why it seemed so dark, and why everything smelt like burning and sulphur.

He was reduced to feeling his way down the mountain, for a while, and then a wind came up and blew the ash out over the sea, and he could breathe again.

Below him, almost at his feet, a ship waited, her oarsmen pulling to keep station, just a hundred paces offshore, or even closer in. He could see her length, see her bow rise and fall on the gentle waves.

The sight gave him heart, and he hurried, stumbling over the last rocks.

'Swim!' called a man with a Dardanian accent. 'Jump in and swim!'

The rocks were huge and the water just off them deep and black. Pollon blessed his mother's foresight in making him learn to swim, and jumped, bow and all. He swam weakly, arm over arm, and made it to the slick black sides of the warship.

It was Trayos, the Dardanian pirate, of course. He stood amidships on a little raised deck, while his oarsmen rowed short. Zos stood by him, and Daos, wrapped in a blanket. Strong arms pulled him aboard from the wine-dark sea.

A boy no older than Daos handed Pollon a linen towel and an older man took his bow and began to wipe it down.

'My lord, you have my thanks,' Pollon said. His limbs felt like worn leather, but he managed a deep bow.

Trayos nodded, as if he had other things on his mind.

'How many more, my prince? I want out of here.'

Pollon nodded, fielding the question for Zos, who continued to stare into the ash fall like a man awaiting a visit from a lover.

'This ash is a precursor to a volcanic eruption,' Pollon said with the certainty of a scribe. 'There's quite a long description in the epic *Tale of the Thousand Charioteers*.' He waved, breathing hard. 'And there's a fleet of Jekers just over there.'

Trayos looked at him with narrowed eyes. 'I know it's a fucking volcano, you patronising fuck. I was sailing these seas when you were still shitting green and puking yellow.' He looked at Pollon. 'How close are the Jekers?'

Zos put a hand on the Dardanian captain's tattooed arm above his gold rings.

'I believe my friend Pollon meant only to help.'

The Dardanian's oily civility returned. 'My apologies, writer – I'm afraid for my ship.'

'No apology required, my lord. I'm no sailor – I have no idea how close the Jekers are. They seemed ... almost up to the southern headland.'

'Gods,' Trayos said.

'Good fortune,' Zos said. 'Not gods. We do not need any more gods.'

He went and leant over the amidships bench where Daos sat. The boy smiled. He was clearly exhausted, but still indomitable.

'I told you there would be a ship,' he said.

'And now I have to worry about your mother.'

'Oh, Mama's on a ship, too. I saw it.'

'You said you didn't see this? You told us you couldn't see us rescuing the slaves.'

Daos shrugged. 'Now I can,'

'And did we confound the Huntress?' Zos asked from the command deck.

Daos nodded. 'They're all confused,' he said. 'But I think you simplified something.'

Zos sighed. 'Simplified?' he asked.

Daos shrugged.

There was a commotion on the rocks – two men who

430

couldn't swim. Then splashes and heaving; four men came aboard and went forward, where the three nomad women sat on oar benches, wrapped in cloaks.

'See that man?' Zos said to Trayos. 'He's a hero.'

'He was a slave this morning,' Trayos said. 'And he's mad as a hare in season.'

Zos shook his head. 'Madness and heroism are close cousins.'

Pollon looked out over the side, and saw that Persay was swimming with a man on his back.

'Lady be with us,' muttered the Dardanian captain.

Zos looked at Pollon. 'Why are the Jekers coming here?' he asked suddenly.

Pollon was too tired to think, but he bludgeoned his wits for an answer because it was an excellent question.

Zos pointed south. 'The Jekers come from Umeria, south of Atussa. They raid Akash and sometimes as far as the Hundred Cities.'

Sailors were hauling the non-swimmer aboard – a big man, a westerner with pale skin and blue tattoos. The madman was going back for the last former slave.

Above them, the mountain was beginning to glow.

'My prince, we really need to be gone.'

Zos looked at the Dardanian captain. 'If I am really your prince,' he said, 'then I'm not planning to begin my rule by abandoning one of my soldiers to a messy death here.'

'We may all die,' Trayos said.

'Something that can be said by anyone at any time,' Zos said.

As he spoke, the last man was coming up the side. He had a lung full of water and two sailors got to work on him, but he wasn't going to die.

Persay rolled aboard. 'Lord,' he said, bowing deeply.

Zos threw his arms around the man in a deep embrace.

'You may be the bravest man I've ever known,' he said.

'Try me, lord,' Persay said. 'There's nothing I wouldn't do for you.'

Zos motioned to Trayos, but the Dardanian needed no urging and already the port side rowers were backing oars and the starboard going to full strokes, and the thirty-oared ship turned in its own length.

Zos was looking back along the coast. The ash cloud was beginning to envelop everything, blotting out the sky, but Pollon thought that he saw the flash of oars behind them. Above the ash cloud, there were mast-tops, and even over the roaring wind and the crash of breakers on the rocks, there were the sounds of screams and chants.

The Jeker fleet was coming into the beaches.

The three nomad women took up oars with their usual confidence. Pollon went with Persay and sat on an empty bench close to the bow. He found an oar, dropped it between the pins, and began to row.

After a few pulls, Zos sat down next to him, took the oar from his hands, and brought it inboard.

'I'll teach you to row,' he said. 'But until you learn, you're only pissing off the two men behind you. I need your head, now. What was the plan here?'

Pollon shook his head. 'I can't see it,' he admitted. 'I lack sufficient ... information.'

'The herald-god called them *his* Jekers,' Zos said.

'And said they'd eat us alive,' Pollon said. 'I was there.'

'But *why*?' Zos asked. 'They can't have been chasing us. We're not that important! Why were they coming here *anyway*?'

'Wind's dropping!' Trayos sang out. 'Pull, my lads, because the other options are to drown or be eaten.'

Zos had the oar in his hands now, and he leant back to pull, and Pollon could see the pain on his face. He had burns on his back, and other wounds, visible and invisible; the resin he'd

432

taken hadn't fixed everything. But he pulled the oar so hard that the shaft bent in the sea.

'The Jekers are coming to take Dekhu,' Zos said, at the top of his pull. 'They're not here for us. From here, they're either going to invade Dardania, or Narmer.'

He pulled a few more times. The ash was all around them now, cutting off their view, so that it was as if they were rowing through a silent sulphur fog.

Heaven

Sypa, the Goddess of Lust, lay curled with her intimate friend, Lady Laila, on her magnificent green marble couch in the Hall of the Gods.

It was a stirring sight, made doubly so by the fact that the goddess herself stood, with her hands on her hips and a smile on her face, in Nisroch's Message Room, watching herself disport on one of his supposedly secret god's eyes.

'We really are very beautiful,' she said to Lady Laila, who stood by her, eyes downcast demurely in her tight jacket cut to reveal her whole upper body and her flounced skirts of pure white linen.

'So we are,' Laila agreed.

'It's so ... beautiful,' Sypa said, 'that we can be our own distraction.'

She was looking at the god's eyes. She appeared to know exactly how to manipulate Nisroch's system, which gave Laila a certain pause. In fact, she would have shuddered, if she'd been able to without being seen to do so.

Sypa stopped on the dark god's eyes that had once shown the temples and palaces of Hekka.

She smiled. 'Goodbye, Hekka,' she said fondly.

Laila raised an exquisite eyebrow.

'Enkul-Anu loved Hekka,' Sypa said. 'And he fucked that little golden girl and threatened to make her a god.' She smiled happily. 'I fixed that.'

She lingered on a view of the magnificent and many-horned palace of Cyra on Noa.

'Cyra's turn is coming,' Sypa promised. 'She thinks herself so powerful and important. I'll make her *nothing*.'

Laila blinked.

Sypa was running a finger along the eyes until she reached the last eyes of Dekhu, but they were all dark.

'What are we looking for, goddess?' Laila asked.

Sypa smiled brightly. 'It doesn't really matter,' she said. 'But Resheph and Nerkalush are about to murder Nisroch, and I wanted to watch.'

Laila covered a start. 'Oh,' she said. 'You are indeed very clever,' she added, frightened. She wondered how many of her own little secrets the Great Goddess knew.

Sypa smiled and licked her lips, the tip of her tongue tracing the corner as if delighted to find it there.

'And my idiot god-husband thinks I'm here to spread my legs and do his will,' she said. 'I made sure he banished that creature, that Arrina, to the Outer Darkness, and now I'm making sure her son dies in humiliation and despair.'

Laila nodded, her throat almost closed with fear. *Druku was right. I need to get out of here.* But she regained control, and found an admiring tone. 'Ah. Mistress, you are indeed a great goddess.'

Sypa nodded. 'And the pure delight of the thing is that those two idiots will be the ones Enkul-Anu punishes. Because he always has to have someone to punish.' She winked. 'And my son Telipinu will be there to take their place.'

Laila, who had her own plots, was not having to struggle to look impressed. *I have underestimated you.*

'You ... did ... all ... this?'

Sypa shrugged, and sat back. 'Oh, some of it just fell into place,' she admitted. 'Nisroch's a greedy little shit, but he had a good idea or two – these god's eyes, for example. Now I know everything that Enkul-Anu does.' She nodded. 'And using the Jekers for power.' She rose to her feet. 'Come – any moment now, he'll summon me for a quick fuck.' She laughed. 'That's what he does when he's worried. And he's not even worried about the right things. Like his precious son by that monster.'

Laila nodded. Inside, she was replaying the terrible events of five centuries before, when the new sun goddess had apparently betrayed heaven to mortals and been ... banished to the Outer Darkness.

She looked at Sypa, letting things fall into place in her own well-ordered mind.

Sypa glanced at her. 'I know you're playing with Druku.'

Laila put all of her not inconsiderable skill at dissimulation into her shrug. But terror iced her spine.

'Oh,' she said dismissively. 'Druku.'

'But you do know where he is, don't you?' Sypa asked sweetly.

Laila made a face, portraying a woman scorned. 'Not a word, the bastard. Not a call, not a note. Nothing.'

Sypa's hand for hovered a moment, and Laila was afraid.

'I would be displeased, were you to prefer him to me,' Sypa said carefully. 'Most displeased.'

Laila managed a grin. 'Great goddess, he is but a drunken lout.'

Sypa smiled. 'Good. I was afraid he was coming between us. And I need to trust someone.' She smiled her winning smile at Laila. 'Time to go back to work.'

She turned away and walked to the gateway.

Laila steeled herself. The risks were getting ... terrible.

But ...

As the goddess turned for the gateway, Lady Laila put her hand on the eyes that looked into the palace of the god-king of Mykoax and the lands around, and they went black.

'See something you fancy?' called the goddess over her shoulder.

'Mortals,' Laila said with disgust.

436

Chapter Twelve

Aanat

Even with warning, Aanat could do little but raise his spells and wait for death.

They had cut two good stone anchors loose and left Zos, Pollon and the others behind. Now, with his sail brailed up tight on a perfectly lovely evening, he waited for the end of the world, and it came.

It was too dark to see anything at first. And then, far astern — perhaps fifteen miles away if his spells had served — the top blew off the island of Dekhu with a sound to split the heavens, and fire poured into the sky.

The sound came perhaps a hundred beats of his heart later, and he thought that the great bowl of the world had cracked and the ocean would now run out.

And then the burning stone began to fall from the sky. Pieces hit the water and hissed or shattered as they fell, and more hit their ship. The deck was packed with freed slaves and refugees, crew and friends, and every falling fragment hit someone. Behind them, the glow deepened until the water itself looked bloodstained, and the sky was ruddy and the stars were dimmed.

A huge piece of stone struck just aft of the bow and slammed right through the hull, leaving a gash twice the size of a man's head. Instantly the *Untroubled Swan* began to take water and her bow went down.

Jawala took one of the lines that brailed the sail and swung on it. The main yard was roped down at both ends, but still her weight shifted it slightly, and she swung clear from the aft deck over the holds to land with her feet on the rail of the forepeak. Bravah was already there, and Miti clambered up from the forward hold where she'd been with the donkey and Era's bear.

She had canvas – a big sheet of very expensive heavy wool canvas from Noa. Jawala already had a length of light rope in her hand.

'Thank the Light of the World that the sea is calm,' she said.

Miti stripped her tunic over her head as Bravah brought her four smooth stones. Holding them, she lashed the rope to the corners of the canvas while Jawala stood by, watching her, eyes full of trust.

The very moment she had the last corner lashed, Miti rolled backwards over the side, into the ruddy, blood-coloured waters of the Ocean, the canvas clutched to her chest. She hit the water and vanished *under* the bow. The ship was already moving slowly, sluggishly, and she was a foot lower in the water than she ought to be.

When Miti surfaced on the far side, Bravah was ready for her, taking the two lines as if they did this every day and passing them to Jawala. The woman made them fast to the deck and she and Bravah began to torsion them with oar shafts as Miti pulled herself back aboard.

More falling rock hit the water all around them.

'Pumps! Bale!' roared Jawala as they stretched the scrap of canvas over the hole as best they could.

Every human being on board began to use whatever came to hand to bale. Mokshi showed Dite how to work a pump, and a pair of former slaves took the other one. The pumps were just hollow tree stumps with pull handles, but they were faster than the desperate former slaves with their hats, bowls, dishes, and in one case, a round shield.

The donkey brayed and brayed. And then, unnoticed, it slipped over the side.

More stone fell, injuring a man, flaying the skin from another, killing a third, a big bald man from Weshwesh who would never terrorise a dockside bar again. Miti took a blow to the head that tore hair from her scalp and left her blind for a minute. Pavi, at one of the steering oars, was hit repeatedly, as was Aanat. It was like sailing through a storm of stone.

Behind them, the fire on the horizon grew brighter.

Aanat brought up a very precisely directed capful of wind and placed it straight on his brailed-up scrap of sail. He put the stern to the island, and did his best to blank his mind and ignore the screams of his terrified passengers – themselves men and women of violence who might, under other circumstances, have tried to take his ship.

He pushed his lovely *Untroubled Swan* as hard as his powers would allow, and missed Pollon and Gamash, either of whom might have loaned him a little more *Aura*.

The *Untroubled Swan* moved like a slug. She was full of water, heavy with passengers, too low in the water, and was moving by his will alone, as he kept her stern facing the island.

The orange-red sky behind him seemed to flicker, and he knew what was coming. He went up on his toes, as if they could outrun it.

He knew they couldn't, but he held the ship's stern steady, and then he saw the tidal wave rising behind him. It was moving incredibly fast; he'd caught the first glimmer in the moonlight and the unearthly glow of the volcano, and it was faster than the fastest ship.

It came at him like a glistening black wall. It was so tall that it blocked out the sky, and it went so high that his heart died within him, and he *still* held his little ship on her course and kept her beautifully curved stern to the monster wave.

Mother Goddess, stand by me in my hours of peril...

And then they were flying.

They went up the front of the wave so fast that Aanat didn't have time to experience any *more* terror. The front of the swell was steep; coming at him it had looked like a wall, and yet they seemed to fly up it like a great bird. He heard the hawser stretched down the midline of the *Untroubled Swan* hum as she came to the crest of the wave, and the whole weight of the ship and her cargo was suddenly dangerously balanced in the middle of her back.

He looked back, over the stern, and what he saw remained etched on his mind for the rest of his life.

The island of Dekhu had split in half, like an egg, and from it rose a volcano.

But the volcano was only the beginning. There was a *dragon* rising, a flaming serpent escaping the volcano's maw, vast and red and burning like a torch in a high wind. And from high above, a mighty figure hurled bolts of pure lightning at the dragon, and the dragon belched forth fire...

The hawser stretched...

He thought he saw a tentacled form beneath the waves, massive, hideous, it's glistening arms *supporting his ship*. But his mind shut down, as if he'd seen too much of the supernatural, and he concentrated all his will on keeping his course.

And then they were slipping down the reverse face, and the great wave was racing away into the night, headed north. The next one was rushing down on him like a moving wall, and he had to stay focused enough to keep the ship moving, keep the stern to the next wave...

Jawala slipped under his arms and took the oar. She pushed Aanat free, so that all he had to do was to keep the mage-wind in the scrap of sail. Except that now there was real wind – a hurricane of wind from the same direction as the waves – and still the stone fell. The falling stone was lighter, smaller pieces that stung instead of lethal chunks.

Pavi and Jawala exchanged a glance, and fought the next wave as it attempted to tear the steering oars from their hands, and Aanat used his will and *Aura* to keep them on course. At the top of each huge wave they were in the teeth of the unnatural storm. They could see a crown of lightning playing on the back of the rising dragon, and the dragon belching fire into the sky, and there was no time for terror as they slid down the next wave.

In the depths of the trough between the rushing walls of water, they were utterly becalmed, and in danger of slewing broadside-on, which would take them to the bottom in moments.

Aanat lost count of the waves. But when the sky began to lighten, more like a day glimmer in the midst of an ocean storm than a normal day, and he could see the massive cloud lifting above the now distant island, the *Untroubled Swan* was still afloat. And they were still alive.

Heaven

Enkul-Anu paced heaven, swived Sypa, and then returned to pacing.

In the Hall of Hearing, the sycophants whispered. The eternal fire on the great hearth burned a dark red, and the frescoes on the walls and the mosaic of the floor seemed to shift and move.

'Where is Nisroch?' the Storm God asked, and none could answer.

'Where are Nerkalush and Resheph?' he demanded.

Time passed, and the halls of the gods were silent except for whispers, until Illikumi manifested and stepped forth. They were not a bold god, but neither did they quail in fear like others. The snake god stepped to the middle of the floor.

'Great god,' they said. 'The World Serpent is loose.'

Enkul-Anu looked at the young snake god for as long as a man might mutter a prayer.

'You wouldn't lie about this,' he said. And then, 'Fuck that. I can feel the worm.'

Illikumi bowed.

Enkul-Anu sat back on his throne and put his chin on his hands for a moment, and no more. Then the great Storm God spoke.

'Fetch Ara,' he said.

Lady Laila went, her back straight, her lovely limbs flashing in the evening sunlight as it came through the west-facing portico, lighting her a terrible red.

Enkul-Anu paced until she returned. Sypa lay alone on her stomach, smiling to herself.

'He's drunk. Or drugged.' Laila was on her knees, bent forwards so that her face was hidden. 'I could not rouse him.'

Enkul-Anu straightened. 'Very well.' He looked back at his court. 'Fucking idiots,' he said, almost fondly.

And he went through the golden door behind his high throne and vanished.

He didn't go to lie on his great bed, where he had lately disported with Sypa, his consort. He didn't go to stare out of the great east-facing portico that only he could access.

He opened another door – one hidden from immortals and mortals alike – and walked down a long flight of steps into the side of the mountain. Down and down, first through hallways magnificently decorated, and then into a plain stairwell cut in the rock, down and down, until he came to his treasury above the great beehive-shaped cave at the very centre of the mountain.

And below it, the gate.

He froze. He, the Storm God, master of heaven, lord of all, froze. The ichor in his veins ran like ice for a moment.

Someone had tried the gate. He could smell it.

Moving more quickly, he checked the great double doors to the treasury.

They had been opened.

They were shut and locked now, but someone – not he – had opened them. His rage rose to choke him, and so did his anger at his own foolishness.

Think. Think.

He looked over the treasury in the merciless glare of his white-hot mage-light.

He didn't store gold or silver or pearls from the depths, or precious rubies from the desert, or even stone jars of resin here. None of that was worth so much. The treasury held things that could hurt him, and the other gods. Items forged in generations

443

past, amid the endless conflicts of the old gods: weapons, poisons, armour... and more.

There were the chariots that could fly through the heavens. There was Rani's great bow, and the trident of Nammu Earthshaker, the old god of the sea, and there, safe on the wall, was *Godkiller*, the sword of the Sun God.

Enkul-Anu took the sword and tossed the bright sword-belt over his shoulder. He needed no armour.

'Fucking idiots,' he muttered again. 'If you want something done well, do it yourself,' he added, and started back up the stairs, locking the doors behind him.

This time he placed a trap and a comprehensive curse on the doors, and he cast a long look at the gate.

No one but he should have been capable of trying the gate.

But it's broken, idiots. I smashed it.

At the top of the Endless Stair, he summoned Azag, Captain of the Demons, and the demon appeared without fuss or sarcasm.

'Lord god,' he said.

'Someone's been at the gate,' Enkul-Anu said.

'Not me, boss,' said the lord of demons.

'And right now, someone has released the World Serpent.' The great god looked at his captain. 'Was it my son?'

'Gods,' spat the demon. 'I thought he was just messing with the Jekers.'

'Messing with the Jekers?' Enkul-Anu looked at his captain, who cringed.

'Pardon, great lord god,' the demon said. 'Boys will be boys. He has been teaching the Jekers to worship him.'

'Fucking idiot,' Enkul-Anu said. 'By me and my holy name, Azag, are you all fucking idiots? We have a good thing here. We're on top. And somehow, we seem bent on fucking it away!'

Azag bent his head, which under the Storm God's penetrating stare was crustacean-insectile, not demonic.

'Bring your people, Azag. We need to re-imprison the World Serpent. And rescue my foolish son from whatever plot he's ...' Enkul-Anu blinked.

Suddenly, the Captain of the Demons found himself on a featureless plain. The sky was grey, and so was the featureless ground.

'What?' he asked, terrified.

Enkul-Anu appeared. 'It occurs to me that I can't trust you, Azag. So send your people with me, and if all goes well, I'll come back and release you. If something goes amiss ... why, welcome to your new eternity.'

'No!' Azag wailed. 'I am loyal!'

'Of course you are,' Enkul-Anu said.

And he vanished.

Even the great Storm God had to travel through the air, and even at the speed of a great god, his arrival over the remnants of the island of Dekhu took time.

As a great god, with the intellect to rule the world, he took in the dozens of ships on the wine-dark sea, scattering like mice from an overturned sack of grain. He took in the miles-high plume of ash belching from what had once been the courtyard of the Temple of All Gods.

He took in immediately the smell of the burning demon corpses in the agora, even with the reek of the volcano. And he saw the bodies of Resheph and Nerkalush.

And he saw the head of the dragon emerge from the earth, as the island cracked open around it.

Enkul-Anu had a hundred demons with him. And in his right hand was a thunderbolt. He hurled it at the head of the dragon, and the dragon, slithering from the great magma-crusted rent in the earth, breathed fire.

Demons perished in that unearthly fire that had not been seen in a thousand years.

Enkul-Anu cursed, turned and waved a thunderbolt.

'Distract her!' he roared, and the demons swept in close to do his bidding.

The dragon rose, vast and potent, from the widening crack, which touched the sea at both ends. Steam exploded out as magma cooled, too fast, to rock, and that rock exploded into the air and superheated the waters. The clouds of steam rose into the dark air to mingle with the ash from the vent, and a great darkness fell, blotting out the Red Moon and the Gift and the light of the stars. Demons were caught in the conflagration, parboiled like lobsters or battered with rocks.

But Enkul-Anu rose above the cloud, and he was the lord of the storm, and he smote the dragon with the winds at his command, and with his thunderbolts. Great gouts of auratic majesty – every one the equal of a thousand mortal souls, or ten thousand – and his aim was unerring. Every bolt struck true, and *still* the dragon rose from the liquid rock in which she had been imprisoned.

The demons, immune to most weapons, were, by comparison, just mortal creatures, and the superheated steam and the incredible white heat of the dragon's breath decimated them.

Enkul-Anu drew *Godkiller*. And instantly knew the depth of someone's betrayal.

It's a fake!

His roar of anger could be heard from Narmer to Mykoax.

The dragon beat its vast wings and rose into the black air.

Enkul-Anu rose with it, hurling his thunderbolts. The great adamant shield in his right hand functioned perfectly, turning its fire, so that the two rose, higher and higher, clawing at each other.

The demons had dropped away. As helpless against the terror of the dragon as mortals, they had broken for home and what they perceived as safety.

The dragon turned over the ocean. They were high, now – so high that they were reaching the top of the vast cloud – and yet Enkul-Anu was almost blinded by something as dull and earthly as ash and steam.

The dragon's fire did not abate, and some of its breath went home, and he felt pain. Some of his thunderbolts went home, and the dragon bellowed; there was a great rent in the feathers of one wing, and a burn down its long, serpentine body.

It was many times his size, but Enkul-Anu managed that by increasing his own size and mass. Then he attacked, going close, wrapping his arms around the great snake wings and holding it tight as they both fell.

Its huge talons flayed him, and his thunderbolts were hammers now, pounding at its flesh.

Great pieces of it fell away, burning like meteors...

He took wound after wound from its raking claws.

And far below them, the island exploded.

Enkul-Anu was fighting for his life, and then, suddenly he had lost the serpent, and he was falling, alone, in utter darkness, buffeted by insane winds as if the world itself had broken. He had heard of such things.

He restored his shield, turned his body, slowed his fall towards the sea and then flew. As he flew, he began to realise the extent of the damage he'd taken. He was raining ichor on the sea below him.

He grew new wings – vast predator's wings – and beat them hard, rising clear of the choking cloud, to see the vast ring of the titanic waves released by the island's death rolling out like rings from a stone cast in a pool.

The dragon was gone. It had run away to hide.

Good idea.

Enkul-Anu turned, burning like a comet in the heavens, and flew for home. He wondered if he would make it.

How did this happen?

Book Three

Hubris

Chapter Thirteen

Era

Era awoke to a chilly grey day, and a storm-tossed sea, but she wasn't cold. She lay on a straw mat on the deck of the *Untroubled Swan*, between Miti on one side and Dite on the other, and the latter had her arms around her, curled tight to her back.

Every muscle in her body hurt.

Her right hip, the one currently against the straw mat, hurt like fire, and her lower back felt as if she'd been kicked repeatedly by the donkey.

But she was warm, and very comfortable, until she woke up enough to remember who and what Dite was.

She got up, groaning all the way, and left the other two women asleep. There were dozens of people crammed on the little merchant ship, and there was a patch in the bow, and they'd taken on water. Era went to the bow and looked into the forepeak, but the Dry One wasn't there. That was lucky, as the bilge was a foot deep in dirty seawater. She leant out and relieved herself from the cathead, and then made her way aft, looking down at the bear and the donkey curled together – perhaps the oddest sight she'd ever seen.

Aanat and Jawala were at the steering oars, looking as if they'd aged almost as fast as Gamash ...

Poor dead Gamash.

Era had a hard time mourning him. She'd lost so many people over the years, she was hardened to it; and he had been, despite his heroism, a godborn aristocrat, a magos, and in many ways, the epitome of her enemies.

But he died well.

That was godborn thinking. Did dying well outweigh a life of being an oppressor?

Jawala waved from the steering oar.

'Think you could wake Miti and Bravah?'

'Where's the Dry One?' Era asked.

'In the aft cabin,' Jawala said. 'With the wounded.'

Era nodded, asked no more questions, and went to wake Bravah.

Later, she looked out over the stern while Pavi and Mokshi expanded the sail above them.

'We're going to miss Zos,' Miti said. 'He was as good at the helm as Jawala.'

'Where are we going?' Aanat asked.

He was catnapping on the helm-bench – worried for his ship and his cargo and his passengers, and possibly for his clan and his whole way of life.

Era was looking at the massive plume of ash that rose into the odd, grey daytime air. Everything smelt of sulphur.

'We were headed for Dendrowna,' Era said.

Aanat nodded. 'It's a miracle the bow has lasted this long. Another night like last night...'

'Mother of gods,' Mokshi said. 'May we never have another night like last night.'

'Dendrowna is twenty days' sailing to the north. More.' Aanat gave her a worried smile. 'Or never, if we have a bad wind. One big wave right now and we might just sink.'

'You want to run for port?' Era said.

'Rappa is off somewhere on the port side,' he said. 'I don't really know how far last night took us. I think we were moving very fast indeed – so perhaps we're coming up on the coast between Rappa and Daro. Fifty little towns there, all with good harbours.'

Era shrugged. 'Fine.'

They fothered a second sail over the hole as soon as they'd eaten, and then Aanat took his weary ship in a long, careful turn to port, taking the cross-waves on his damaged bow. But the *Untroubled Swan* rode the sea like her namesake, and they ran north and west all day and all night, with Jawala constantly testing the depth of water in the bow, and volunteers baling and pumping. Some copper ingots were tossed over the side.

On the third day since they'd left Dekhu, they saw the low coast of Rasna. Pavi hailed it, and the Hakrans sang a hymn to their land, and the ox-eyed Earth Goddess who protected it. And many of the men and women they'd rescued joined in, learning the words and tune as they went, because they'd been so terrified of the great rollers on the deeps and the obvious gaping hole in the bow for days, and the sight of land raised everyone's heart.

Until they got close enough to see the coast.

Even from miles offshore, they saw the floating tree trunks, and after they nudged one and almost lost the fothering on the bow, Miti stood like a figurehead, calling out directions.

Era, leaning out over the side, could see worse: floating straw roofs from houses, and once, an overturned boat; a whole length of cedar fence; a broom; five well-stoppered storage pithoi, floating together, bobbing like corks on the surface of the water.

And closer in, the bodies.

453

A few at first – a dead dog, a big bloated ram, and then an old man.

And then a lot of them. Tens, and then hundreds.

'Oh, mother of gods, the wave,' Miti said.

As they closed in on the coast, the damage became more obvious. The heartland of Rasna had been ravaged. The coastal dunes were gone, and the trees on the low hills behind the dunes, and the fishing villages of the coast…

All gone.

The Hakrans wept openly.

Era went to Aanat and took him by the shoulder.

'I agree this is devastating,' she said. 'But we are alive, and we have forty people to save, and we need to land and repair this ship.'

'Land where?' Aanat asked. 'Repair how?'

But he was, despite his pacifism, essentially a fighter, and even as he spoke he wiped his eyes, and rose from squatting by the ship's rail.

'We'll land on the open beach,' he said. 'There'll be driftwood, and we have tools.'

'We'll need guards,' Era said.

Aanat made a sign with both hands. 'Era, these are my people. We will not turn to violence.'

'Starving people will do anything for food,' Era said. 'I've seen it. We have soldiers.'

'Jawala will never allow it.'

Era was canny enough to avoid offending Jawala, even a tear-stained Jawala who looked every day of her forty-plus years. So she sent out scouts, as soon as the ship landed, hard-eyed men and women who had recently been slaves and still saw her as their salvation.

The rest of them dragged the little ship clear of the waves and propped her up on the wet sand. It was all wet – wet as far as she could see – and dunes had been rolled inland to cover what had been cotton fields.

Her first patrol came back with a pair of kittens found floating in a box.

The man who'd led the patrol was a Py like Dite, from the far east beyond Narmer. He seemed to know how to scout; he spoke Trade Dardanian with fluency, and he'd found himself a bow.

'What's your name?' she asked.

'Taha, Lady.'

Era shook her head, because the title 'Lady' didn't apply to her in any way, even though she had placed herself in authority.

'No people, Taha?' she asked.

'Inland, about ten stadia, there's a . . .' He searched Trade Dardanian for the word. 'A tide line. Many dead there. Wood, houses, cows, sheep, men, women.'

Era felt a cold in her gut like a sword thrust to her heart.

Jawala, usually a rock of calm and purpose, was kneeling on the sand. She wept, and raised her fists to heaven, and Era feared that when she began to recover, she was going to blame Era for everything.

Era had her own problems, which included the loss of her adopted son and the hundred immediate problems of survival.

'If you cross the tide line, do you think you could find us food?'

'Long trip back with whatever we find,' he said.

Mokshi seemed less devastated than the others, and it was he who had the most useful suggestion.

'There will be pithoi of grain in the ground in most houses,' he said. 'Find the stone foundations, we'll find grain.'

Dite put a hand on Era's shoulder.

'I'll go,' she said. 'I'm strong, and I can . . . see things.'

Every time Dite spoke to her, Era was touched by a raw lust

that she wouldn't have wanted to examine too closely. Giving orders to Dite – treating her like any other survivor – felt strange.

Let me kiss you . . .

'Excellent. You have a village site in mind?' she asked.

Taha nodded. 'I've got one, Lady.'

'Good luck,' she said, and turned to her next task: starting campfires.

She masked her despair; the loss of comrades, the failure of plans. She walled it all off to concentrate on the *now*; survival. Food. Water. Healing.

She wanted to lie down and weep.

But just before nightfall, a sail was sighted, and before the last light went out of the sky, Hefa-Asus jumped into the waves and strode ashore, followed by Atosa and Nicté and a dozen more makers.

And after she'd embraced each one, she allowed herself to face the distant stars, and think, *We're not beaten yet.*

Pollon

The nomad women insisted that at the height of the storm and the wave, a sea monster with tentacles had seized the ship and held it above the water.

Pollon just nodded. He'd been awake for too long, had too little sleep, and he no longer cared if they were saved by sea monsters or undead porpoises. He was awake enough to see the great scarlet dragon-serpent rise out of the ruins of the island of Dekhu, but he no longer had the energy to be afraid. When the Storm God came on the wings of night, and threw his thunderbolts at the magnificent dragon, Pollon watched, but his blistered hands were on his oar. From his seat, he watched the whole of the drama in the dark sky. The dragon and the god were lit, as if from within, by the effervescence of their powers. Fire and ichor and thunderbolts filled the sky and rained on the waters below.

Pollon kept rowing. Zos was next to him, controlling the oar, watching the sky, and behind them in the stern, a Mykoan kept the beat with hand claps as the light pulsed with every thunderbolt.

The dragon turned, almost above them, and breathed fire while the dying island belched more ash and fire into the air.

The great Storm God appeared like a vision of wrath from the ash and darkness, and locked his arms around the serpent, and they fought, and fell, and ichor sprayed across the ocean, and magnificent sea-flowers and sea-monsters were born. Fire fell from the heavens and killed them. And behind them, a lethal backdrop of fire and ash and rising seas.

The main yard took the strain of the rising wind and drove the bow down into the brutal sea, but the bow was built for it, and the little ship raced on under a scrap of canvas.

The beat of the stern oarsman faltered as the god and the dragon met again in a long struggle, and Zos began to sing. He sang an old song, a song almost everyone knew about the birth of the world from the void in fire and stone at the will of the old god Ranos. Other voices took up his song, singing about the ordering of the world, the dividing of the waters, the raising of the land, as if by the power of their shared song they could drive away the chaos of the war in the heavens above them.

And every moment they survived was a victory.

Eventually Pollon couldn't think – couldn't even really see. He could only add his weight to the oar at the top of the pull, and try to keep the ship moving. It seemed that he was locked in eternity, cursed to row forever in the stygian darkness and sulphur smell of Kur, the deepest pit of the underworld.

*

At last, morning came – a grey morning on a mountainous sea, with enough ash in the air that it looked like snow. There were burn marks on the deck, and finding a dead man amidships explained the odd drag on the ship that all the rowers had felt; killed by falling rock, he'd fallen over his oar and trapped it against the ship.

The wind was steady now, not coming in deadly gusts. Zos was asleep on his oar, the shaft drawn in and tucked under the opposite bench, where one of the nomad women was similarly asleep, head down, arms crossed over the shaft of her oar.

Pollon glanced around to find that all the oars were in and crossed, so that their blades seemed like wings rising above the deck, their shafts locked down under the opposite bench. Most of the crew was fast asleep, a cacophony of snores and snorts speaking volumes for their exhaustion.

The boy, Daos, was right behind him on a seat under the forepeak. He was awake, and his eyes looked fevered.

'You all right, boy?' Pollon asked.

Daos looked as if he might cry. 'She's gone,' he said.

'Who's gone?' Pollon asked, but his heart was sinking.

'The Black Goddess. The Huntress. She's ... gone. She spoke to me ... all the time. Through Bror, and then just in my head. And now ...' Daos looked at him, and his eyes were huge.

Zos awoke and groaned, and Pollon handed him a canteen of watered wine.

'Oh, gods,' Zos moaned.

Daos looked at the warrior with his eyes wide. 'Are you injured?'

Zos looked at him blearily. 'Everywhere.'

He shook his head, as if shaking off a blow. He made to rise from the oar-bench and he winced and fell back.

'Fuck,' he said again.

Pollon nodded. 'Sleeping on a bench ...'

'I think I've pulled or strained every muscle in my gods-forsaken frame,' he said. 'Bull-leaping is for young people, and I'm not...' He looked at Daos. 'What's the matter?' he asked the boy, instantly solicitous.

Daos shook his head. 'I've lost... my connection... to the Huntress.'

Zos sighed and took a long pull on the watered wine.

'Perfect,' he said.

'You didn't trust her anyway,' Pollon said, and wished he hadn't.

Zos drank more watered wine. Then he handed the canteen to Pollon.

'Fuck,' he said again, and began to turn his head back and forth. 'Have you ever lost the Huntress before?' he asked the boy.

'No,' Daos said.

Zos glanced at Pollon. 'You're the one who worked with the gods,' he said. 'I mostly tried to ignore them.'

Pollon shrugged. 'We're as far outside my territory as yours.'

Zos looked back over his shoulder at the surface of the sea.

'I don't think any of the gods planned this,' he said, but he was looking at Daos' trident. 'No, let me try that again.' He glanced at Daos. 'The Huntress gave this to you, yes?'

'Well, no,' Daos said. 'Really, it was the donkey.'

Zos blinked, nodded, and then said, 'And told you when and how to use it?' Zos asked.

'Yes, sir,' Daos said.

Zos looked at Pollon. 'Whoever did that never meant for us to get away,' he said flatly.

'But we did,' Pollon said. 'We... We won. Didn't we?'

Zos smiled grimly. 'We *lost*. People died. A lot of people, I assume. Most of the slaves we rescued are fish-food now, Pollon, and that wave will have killed... fuck, I can't imagine how many

459

people that wave has killed. Era ... Hefa-Asus, maybe. And the Huntress and her friend the donkey thought that was fine.'

Pollon looked away.

'They're all the same, Pollon. All the fucking same. We're just tools to them. Even to her.'

Pollon swallowed heavily. 'Fuck.'

He was crying, thinking of all the dead: his own dead, like his scribes, and Mura — and, for all he knew, Era and all the Hakrans.

He looked up at Zos. 'I'm not thinking clearly.'

'Nor am I,' Zos said. 'And I really have no idea what's going on. But I can tell you this — if we're going on with this rebellion, I'm not getting suckered by the gods — any gods — again.'

Pollon nodded. 'If we arrive in a port, I can read — maybe read — the god's eye network.'

Zos nodded, took the canteen, and looked at the boy thoughtfully. He took a pull of watered wine, handed the canteen to the boy and got up on the amidships catwalk with an ungraceful grunt and several colourful curses.

It almost hurt Pollon physically to see Zos, the male epitome of control and grace, barely able to walk. And watching him hobble and stumble as the little ship climbed the next wave was even worse.

'Perhaps she'll return,' Pollon said to the boy.

Daos nodded, and then, in a very adult gesture, raised an eyebrow.

'And perhaps she won't,' he said. 'I think she's dead.'

Pollon started. 'Gods can't—'

The boy made a hand gesture. 'We killed two,' he said. 'It's fairly obvious that they can die, isn't it?'

Pollon, who prided himself on his rationality, had to smile.

Zos came back with Trayos.

'I'm not used to having command meetings in the bow,' he said, and he smiled.

Pollon thought, *a man with a sense of humour after the last few days is a good man.*

Zos collapsed on his oar bench. 'Any idea where we are?'

'At sea?' Trayos asked.

'I might still have the energy to come for you,' Zos said.

Trayos smiled. 'All right, my lord. I would guess we're a day's sail from the Lion. Perhaps less.'

Zos sat up. 'Really?'

Daos asked, 'Sir? What's the Lion?'

Trayos nodded. 'There's a long peninsula that sticks out of Hergos,' he said. 'The very tip has a mighty rock shaped like ... a lion crouching, ready to pounce.' He shrugged. 'I mean, from a certain angle.'

Zos was looking at the captain. 'A day ...?'

Trayos nodded. 'The waves will have hit them.'

Zos stroked his beard. 'Not as badly as other places. Hergos sticks out like a thumb to the south – the harbours should be protected. Trin, at least.'

Trayos added, 'We can probably get in, buy some supplies, and slip out. I'm well known – you can stay hidden ...'

'No.'

'No?' Trayos asked.

'No,' Zos said. 'We'll weather the Lion and land at Trin.'

'My twenty and your fifteen together, no matter how brave ...' Trayos looked at Pollon, as if for support. 'Today is not the day to retake your father's kingdom.'

'I'm not going to retake my father's kingdom,' Zos said.

'Ah,' Trayos said. 'I worried. I will support you when the moment comes—'

'I am going to kill the king of Mykoax,' Zos said. 'After that, we'll just see what happens.'

Heaven

Three immortal days passed in heaven. Lady Sypa tended to her lord and master's wounds, rousing him from time to time and using her gifts to avert his wrath, which burned hot.

On the fourth day, he flung her from his arms and rose.

'Get you gone, slut,' he growled. 'I have work to do.'

'Slut?' she shouted.

He slammed her into a marble wall, and she subsided.

'Don't annoy me, Sypa.'

He dismissed her with a patronising little wave and donned the purple kilt and gold torque of his rank, and the high crown of the King of Heaven.

'I can help …' Sypa said.

'Begone,' he said. 'Before I test my powers on you.'

'I am your sister!' she spat. 'I am your peer!'

'Really?' he sneered, and waved his hand again, and left her sitting on a featureless plain.

But even condemned to the Outer Darkness for a while, she was smiling.

He walked through the golden door into the Megaron, where he was greeted by a choking silence. He could feel their fear and uncertainty.

Enkul-Anu made himself smile.

'Gods!' he said. 'We are at war.'

Throughout the hall, they came to their feet.

'You!' He walked towards the Huntress, who stood with some of Sypa's handmaidens. '*You traitor!*'

She stood her ground. 'I am the Enemy,' she said. 'It's my job.'

'*You suborned my son!*' Enkul-Anu roared.

The Black Goddess made a face. 'No ...' she said. 'I didn't.'

'*You stole from me!*'

'You alienated your own son,' the Black Goddess said. 'The same way you and your sycophants alienated Narmer.'

'*You released the fucking World Serpent, you stupid witch!*' he roared.

He was face to face with her now, his immortal spittle flicking at her face. He was delighted to finally see her flinch.

She shook her head in confusion.

'No,' she said, perhaps a little too honestly. 'That was no part of my plans ...'

His right hand shot out, and he grabbed her. With his left hand, he opened a rent in the fabric of reality, so that beyond the tear, black shone – pure black, featureless black – and now she fought to escape him.

'Go be fucking immortal in the Outer Darkness, Enemy.'

Enkul-Anu threw her through the rip in reality. She screamed, and then went limp and fell away.

He closed the rent in reality like a woman doing up her skirt, running his hand along the seam.

'So much for the Huntress,' he said. 'Any of the rest of you want to try any form of revolt, that's where you go. Into the Outer Darkness, to tumble forever in the cold and dark. Am I making myself clear?'

They were silent.

'We are loyal!' said one of the godlings of the Goddess of the Utter Deep.

He raked them with his eyes.

'You'd better be fucking loyal, you useless shits!' he spat. 'This isn't a squabble between courtiers. Two gods are *dead*. My son Nisroch is missing.' Enkul-Anu took a breath. 'I have to assume that he was in league with that witch. No more plots. No more crap. Anyone who's involved in this, now is the time to own up.'

'Where's Druku?' asked another of Timurti's brood.

'Where's the other Enemy?' Laila asked. She was brave. She also had Enkul-Anu's ear for other reasons. 'The Blue Goddess?'

'She's powerless,' Enkul-Anu said with a dismissive flick of his fingers. 'It was *that* one we needed to fear. Now fetch me Ara. We're going to destroy Narmer.'

Laila glanced at Sypa, and then at Enkul-Anu.

'Narmer?' she asked. 'Isn't it the greatest of the human kingdoms?'

Enkul-Anu nodded. 'Time for us to knock them back. Perhaps when they are left with nothing, they'll be more pliant. If not, we eradicate them and replace them with something else.' He smiled mirthlessly. 'Anyway – it's not about them. They're insects. It's about us and our little quarrels. I think getting rid of the Black Goddess should do the trick. I should have done it an aeon ago. But once more – be warned. No more plotting. No more fighting. And find Druku!'

He looked them over, and was appalled. Two hundred and fifty godlings; perhaps another hundred either afraid to appear or out on errands, and some of them had no powers at all – they simply had the ability to remain alive. They were functionally immortal, unless something killed them.

But most of the gods of his own generation were lost to the decay of their minds. Timurti had never been a match for the real depths of the sea; Sypa took her role as Goddess of Lust too seriously to plot, or even help him fight. Grulu, green-eyed Goddess of Spite and Envy, was still lost in some internal narrative, and her servants feared coming near her; she lay on a pallet deep in the mountain, and no one touched her.

Gul, now. The Storm God looked at the God of Death. Gul and his mate Urkigul were powerful, and still in possession of their minds … Only that Nerkalush was their son, and their rage was not yet calmed.

Ara, God of War; a drooling idiot.

Uthu, the replacement for Arrina; he couldn't drive the chariot of the sun, and he couldn't generate a powerful light spell, much less a ray of gods' fire. Worthless.

Anzu, the god of rage. He'd stopped returning to human immortal form, and now stayed as a giant winged lion, killing whatever came under his claws. Rumour had him living in the mountains towards Sherem, ruining the tin trade. All of his sons and daughters looked like lions, with thick manes of tawny bronze hair and oversized incisors. And a tendency to kill. They were so dangerous that he'd banned them from court. It might be time to invite them back.

Because most of the young were not fit to hold the swords of their parents. Most of them excelled at fucking slaves and eating ambrosia and drinking nectar. And that was it...

And yet someone had stolen his sword. Someone had tried to open the *gate*. Someone was playing with fire. *Immortal fire.*

The Storm God looked at his subjects, and they cowered in abject fear before his righteous wrath.

But inside the circle of his brow, Enkul-Anu feared that his son was not the victim. He had begun to fear that his son was the perpetrator.

'Fucking idiots,' Enkul-Anu said. 'We had it so good.'

Read on for a preview of

Storming Heaven

Book 2 of the Age of Bronze cycle

The Outer Darkness

Temis, the Dark Huntress, spun through the endless, featureless darkness of the void. She couldn't breathe, but then, as a goddess, she really didn't need to breathe. The cold was a limitless, terrifying thing, but where a mortal body might have frozen, or exploded, she merely endured. The cold, even the absolute cold of the Outer Darkness, was not going to kill her.

She withdrew into herself, thinking her own dark thoughts, most of which were about how her sister Tyka, the Blue Goddess, had set her up for the fall and walked away unscathed. And she spent an unfathomable aeon trying to imagine how Enkul-Anu thought that she was in league with the Jekers when Temis herself had warned him of the whole plot.

That had provided her with some entertainment.

And then she began to imagine the revenge she'd wreak when she returned, but that led, with a kind of awesome finality, to the thought she was trying to avoid...

Return meant rescue. There was no return from the Outer Darkness, not unless you were released. Enkul-Anu, the ruler of heaven, had loved Arrina, and he'd sent her to the Outer Darkness, and the poor goddess of the Sun had never returned.

And Enkul-Anu had been obsessed with Arrina, whereas he flat-out hated the Dark Huntress.

She cursed, trying to see where it had all gone wrong.

It had seemed like any other petty crisis among the gods. Enkul-Anu had ordered the death of an over-mighty mortal, Gamash of Weshwesh. The Huntress had made use of Gamash herself; he was just the sort of ambitious fool that the gods loved.

But one of the insane godlings had got his orders mixed up, and killed Gamash's daughter Irene instead. Why had *that* mattered so much? Temis spun in the dark, thinking.

Tyka, the Blue Goddess, had promised the man revenge, so the two sisters had found star-stone out in the edge of reality near the Outer Darkness, and thrown it to earth. It was an old ploy – something they did to annoy the gods. Mortals would make weapons that could threaten the gods, and the gods would react with war, terror and repression. Enkul-Anu didn't know any other way. And the repression fostered further revolt, the ripples spreading...

Temis might have shrugged – the story was so familiar – if she hadn't been so utterly cold.

And then there'd been another mistake: the same godling, sent to support one mortal kingdom against another, had instead managed to destroy the kingdom he'd been sent to support – *and* had been wounded by a mortal.

Oh, how I savoured that.

In response, her blue sister had rescued the mortal and some others – her own strange choices: a craftsman, a bureaucrat, a dancer. Not the heroes they usually chose. And she'd put them aboard a ship full of pacifist Hakrans. Another very strange choice. As she examined the steps that had led to her expulsion into the Outer Darkness, the Dark Huntress realised how much of the action had been driven by Tyka. How many of the choices her silent 'sister' had made.

She winced.

I thought I was in charge.

Then Nisroch had plotted against his father, Enkul-Anu.

And the insane godlings, Nergakul and Resheph, had plotted against Nisroch.

And the puny human ship had washed up on the beaches of the dead island, Dekhu, seat of the old gods, whom she thought of as *dead*, and everything had gone straight to hell. Someone had killed the godlings; someone had released the ancient World Serpent that pre-dated the realms of the gods.

All of the gods.

The island had exploded; the resulting cataclysm had probably hurried the environmental collapse, and it had certainly thinned the human population. The tidal wave alone would have killed so many ...

The Dark Huntress' tears froze in her eyes.

I didn't release the fucking World Serpent! Who the fuck did that?

She spun in endless, perfect darkness, alone, considering it all, as time passed.

She revisited all her own parts, and those of others.

She repented her errors, but not her rebellion.

She imagined revenge.

She longed to return.

And more time passed.

Revisit.

Repent.

Revenge.

Return.

'How long until I go mad?' she wondered after six or nineteen cycles of repeating her own thoughts.

Not that long.

And then, with malign satisfaction: *Without me, the wheels will fall off. Even now, the whole environment is collapsing, and the Jekers are an accelerant, and the Dry Ones are creeping in from the desert edge. A couple of centuries more, and ...*

That's all I can hope for. A complete revolution, with the winner inviting me back. Nisroch? Not really up to it, and maybe dead, anyway. My sister Tyka? A plotter without power. Clever, though.

Sypa?

For the first time in forty cycles of self-recrimination and desire for revenge and return, the Dark Huntress had a new thought. About Enkul-Anu's affair with Arrina and the former sun goddess' spectacular fall from grace, when it proved that she was secretly leading an insurrection among mortals and trying to give the mortals the secret of the resin that fed the gods.

What, five hundred years ago?

I always believed that story, the Dark Huntress thought, spinning silently in the dark. *But with nothing to do but think, and consider it, Arrina was banished to the Outer Darkness... but who was she a threat to?*

To Sypa.

Whose son Telipinu took over the resin works.

Fuck, how did I fail to see this?

Regret

Revisit.

Repent.

Revenge.

Return.

How long until I go insane?

Zos

The damage from the explosion of the island of Dekhu and the resulting titanic wave was visible everywhere on the headlands of southern Hergos. The islands off the coast had been washed clean of trees and shrubs, and the floating olive trees were a hazard to even the simplest navigation; their heavy wood lay

472

deep in the water, invisible to any but the sharpest-eyed lookout. Above them, the heavy clouds of ash and the storm of heaven hid the stars and the sun, until the world seemed to lie under an iron-grey light.

'Tree!' roared Makeda. She was one of three nomad women from south of the Hundred Cities, a proven warrior with long scars on her forehead and torso and a fluttering black veil hiding her nose and mouth; her eyes were sharp enough to penetrate the gloom and the reflections on light on the waves.

At the stern, Lord Trayos made a precise gesture, and his two helmsmen turned the damaged ship slightly to starboard. They all felt it as the waterlogged timbers scraped through the sunken tree's branches. Leaves boiled to the surface, as if the tree was a living monster spitting yellow-green bile.

Everyone on board had seen so much worse in the past days that no one reacted, beyond an exhausted sailor spitting over the side.

Trayos turned to the man standing by him on the command deck: a tall, whip-thin man in a stained linen kilt and a sword-belt wrought in gold and ivory, bearing a sword so magnificent as to contrast sharply with the man's rumpled, filthy kilt and his salt-stained brown cloak. Trayos was more richly dressed, with two gold rings, a fabulous amulet that glowed like a peacock's tail, and a salt-stained kilt of his family's red and gold tartan, but the man wearing the magnificent sword had the perfect carriage of a dancer and the muscles of a veteran warrior, and his face was set.

Zos looked forwards over the bow at the sharp brown hills of his native land. As a young man, he'd left them vowing never to return, his disgraced and humiliated mother a weeping bundle at his feet as he piloted a small boat into the Great Green, the endless sea, towards distant Narmer.

Zos could almost see that bitter young man now. Indeed, he

had the strangest vision: the past overlaid on the present; the fishing smack sailing on the opposite tack. He blinked it away.

When they reached past the long point where the mountain met the sea in the shape of a great stone lion... When they passed it, then he'd see the enormous bay of his father's kingdom. His dead father's fallen kingdom.

And Trin, once a mighty fortress topped with a palace, would be a ruin. He knew it would be a ruin; it had been one throughout his adolescence, when he'd been kept as a sort of hostage by the great wanaxgod-king of all-conquering Mykoax.

And yet, deep in his heart, he had expected to see it as it had been in the days of his youth: the temples shining and white atop tall walls built of stones so huge that men said that the gods must have wrought them.

'Tree!' Makeda roared again.

The helmsmen turned the ship a little to port, and she glided over the next wave, the reaching branches of a dead oak whispering against her sides like all of Zos' ghosts asking to be remembered.

'You are determined to do this?' Trayos said.

He'd asked the same question four or five times since dawn had revealed the Dardanian coast, and it was clear that they would survive the storm.

Zos didn't turn his head, or answer.

'It's a waste, my prince,' the Dardanian pirate captain said.

He received no answer.

Pleion was the port of ruined Trin and now, of Mykoax. The huge wave that had been born from the death of the island of Dekhu had broken on the long headland of the Lion, but the harbour had not escaped. Everywhere on the waterfront, the rising water had destroyed the tavernas and warehouses. Fifty war galleys were thrown high above the beach, and most were broken. The water was full of corpses and sea-wrack: wrecked ships; floating straw roofs; waterlogged bales of the famous Mykoax wool, and everything else – pomegranates and harvested grapes, half-submerged bales of grain, whole forests of cut timber rising and falling on small waves.

Above the beach, perhaps half a hundred men moved like *gidimu*, animated corpses that necromancers used as eternal slaves. Above them, just visible from the deck, a man in a chariot shouted orders.

He was motioning at the line of destruction at the high water mark of the tidal wave, or its aftermath, but even three hundred paces away, Zos could see that his head was turned to watch the ship come in.

Zos allowed himself a small smile. He understood the man's amazement, because no ship should have survived that storm.

The rowers rowed, and the black ship crept in, her pitch-covered hull taking water in half a dozen places, her oar-banks on both sides thin from losses – dead men, thrown over the side at the height of the waves and storm.

He must wonder if we are a ship of the dead. He must think we are gidimu.

'I'm coming with you,' said the boy, Daos.

Zos lifted an eyebrow. He'd been training the child, a little, but not enough for the boy to survive in a fight.

He shook his head slightly, but his eyes widened.

'You've …' He felt like a fool. 'You've grown.'

It was true. The boy, a whip-thin pre-adolescent of perhaps ten years, now looked like a muscled mid-adolescent. Narrowing waist, enhanced upper body …

When did that happen?

Zos had spent months contending with the supernatural – gods, demigods, the World Serpent – and yet, somehow, a boy achieving five years' growth in forty days at sea seemed the most remarkable feat of all.

Daos looked down. 'It's confusing,' he admitted.

Zos remembered his own adolescence, which had also seemed to happen at a ridiculous time dilation, and his slight smile became rueful and broad.

'It's always confusing,' he said.

Daos shrugged. 'Anyway, I'm coming,' he said. 'I'm your *papista*.'

'Boy,' Zos said without anger, 'every *papista* I've ever had has died. In combat.'

Daos shrugged. 'I won't die,' he promised. 'And if you take me, you won't die either.'

It was moments like this that made life with the boy so very difficult.

'The Dark Huntress told you this?' Zos asked.

The boy shook his curly head. 'Oh, no. Her voice is silent now. I just know it.'

Zos looked at the boy – really, at the young man. Behind him was Persay, the heavily muscled former slave with the bull's head tattooed on his chest. His mad eyes were too open, too glittery, to be normal. But the man put a hand on the boy's shoulder as if they were old mates.

'I'll be coming, too,' he said.

'As will I,' Makeda said. 'And my sisters.'

Zos closed his eyes and took a breath. Opened them and exhaled slowly, trying to blow the unreasoning rage out through his nostrils.

Behind Persay, the man in the chariot was motioning to the men around him, and to the ship.

Zos looked at Persay, and then at Makeda.

'It's over,' he said. 'Whatever adventure we thought we might have, it's over. The revolt against the gods? It fucking died in the volcano. The plan? Fuck it, you don't even know the plan.

It doesn't matter. You're free people. Take your freedom and go and live your lives.'

'Great,' Persay said. 'I'm free to choose. I'm choosing to come with you.'

Zos felt a great sadness replace the rage.

'Friends…' he began.

Makeda shrugged. She didn't speak in Dardanian, and she didn't show any sign of understanding it. Instead, she spoke in Betwana, the trade tongue of the far east.

Pollon stepped up behind her and translated.

'You are our war leader now. We choose you. We make war when you make war.' She crossed her hands on her scarred chest.

Pollon looked at her, and then at Zos.

'Nomads aren't good at taking no for an answer,' he said, spreading his hands.

'I'm going to die,' Zos said. 'Tell her that.'

Daos shook his head. 'Not if I come, you aren't!' he said. 'You don't die. And anyway, Era is still alive, and so are Aanat and Jawala…'

Zos froze. 'What?' he spat.

'Nanuk sent a sea monster to save Aanat and the ship,' Daos said.

Trayos made a sign – a forbidden sign. 'Nammuk, Lord of the Sea, is dead, killed by Timurti,' he said. 'It is forbidden even to mention his name.'

Daos shrugged. 'Nammuck was never exactly a god,' he said in his crackly adolescent voice, a voice that should have carried no conviction or authority at all. Daos was cursed with sounding like every assertive young male who'd ever lived, which most older people were long used to ignoring. 'Nor did Timurti kill him.'

But his words …

'They're alive?' Zos grabbed his *papista*'s shoulders.

Daos grinned. 'And quarrelling among themselves.'

Pollon muttered, 'That sounds believable.'

Zos puffed up his cheeks and exhaled explosively.

'So,' Daos said, 'we all come with you, you do this thing, and then you make a plan and we ...' He looked across the sea. 'And we go to Narmer.'

Trayos brightened. 'I have friends in Narmer,' he said. 'What does this boy – this *ephebe* – know?'

Zos, caught between rage, revenge, hope and some other emotions, felt he had to defend the boy.

'He is a seer,' he said simply. 'An oracle.'

Trayos looked at the boy, touched his peacock amulet, and made a face.

'Of course you have an oracle,' he said. 'Boy, do I die?'

The boy looked at him. Finally, he said, 'Do you really want to know?'

Trayos flinched. 'No!' he admitted.

Daos smiled. It was a wintry smile, and it never touched his eyes.

'No,' he said. 'Really, you don't.'

Trayos looked out to sea. 'Do I go ... with glory?' he asked.

Daos smiled again, this time with his usual youthful pleasure. 'At the moment of victory, on the deck of a ship,' he said.

Trayos snorted. 'Can't ask better than that, lad. And I thought I was going to die as a merchant.'

'No,' Daos said.

In the end, they all came: Lord Trayos; all his surviving oarsmen; the six former slave-bullies; Parsay, Daos, Pollon, the three Nomad women and Zos. They beached the damaged triakonter in the ruins of ten other ships and hauled her ashore over the driftwood.

478

While they tethered her to a piling set well above the normal waterline, a scared-looking man approached cautiously.

'The priest-lord tells me to say this.' The man spoke in careful Dardanian. 'What land are you from? Are you living men or a ship of the dead? Are you friend or foe of our god-king Agon of Mykoax?'

Zos was up to his knees in filthy water, looking at the chipped black pitch and the deep wound below it in the boards of the ship.

Trayos was no slouch about work; he was also knee-deep in the water, despite its being full of dead things, but his hand was on the stem where it met the keel.

'She'll have to be rebuilt,' he said bitterly. 'Or burnt.'

One of the blows the ship had taken had torn the stem away from the planking on the port side. It didn't look as bad as the other damage, but it was in fact a deadly wound for a ship.

Zos ignored the herald, or speaker, or whoever he was – perhaps just a scared slave – and sloshed over to Trayos.

He waved over the harbour.

'We could build ten good ships out of these.' He pointed at a pentekonter, a fifty-oared galley floating upside down and looking like a giant turtle, or a basking shark of monstrous size.

'I'll wager we could right her and row her away today.'

Trayos' jaw worked. He clearly loved his own ship.

Zos glanced back at the herald.

'We're busy,' he said. 'When we're done, I'll be happy to answer your questions. But we're living men, just like you.'

Daos, very cheerfully, said, 'You should run away and hide until sunset.'

The man looked at Daos, and the boy shrugged. 'It would be the best thing for you.'

Zos looked at Daos. 'Are you just going to oraculate all the time now?'

Daos shrugged. 'No idea. It comes and goes, you know?'

Zos smiled. 'No, thanks to all the gods, I don't know.'

The herald was still looking at Daos. But then he turned and went back up the wreck-infested beach, and a moment later they could hear his respectful tone.

Zos looked at Trayos. 'This will keep,' he said. 'If we live, we repair. If we're dead, who cares?'

Trayos sighed. 'I loved my ship.'

But he and his oarsmen picked up their spears and shields and followed Zos, as did everyone else.

Zos had a pair of javelins, an old bull's-hide shield that Trayos had loaned him, and no armour at all. But he led the way, and Daos carried the shield, They negotiated the rubble, the storm rack, the shipwrecks and the corpses, bloated and venting gas into the fetid air.

Zos glanced at Pollon. 'You really don't have to come, old man.'

Pollon had his bow, and a handful of arrows. He shrugged.

Zos shrugged back. He looked back at all of them. He wanted to make a speech – to say something grand, about time, and revenge – but mostly he felt sick to his stomach and light-headed. He hated the sheer waste of all the death and destruction, and he wondered, with a sort of hollow guilt, if it was all his fault.

Persay clapped him on the shoulder.

'You are in a black place, my lord.'

'I am,' Zos said.

'Lay waste your enemies.' Persay smiled. 'You'll feel better.'

Zos shook his head. But the madman's words raised his spirits for reasons he could not fathom. And he stepped over the obscenely swollen body of an old woman, and managed not to step on a dead dog. Then he was in a clearer area with the man in the chariot and a few dozen of his workers, or slaves, or whatever they were. They looked as if they hadn't slept or eaten; more than half were naked.

He walked towards the chariot.

The man in the chariot raised a hand. 'Stop there,' he said.

Zos kept walking.

The man's charioteer was young, but he had the marks of the godborn on him.

'When my lord orders you to stop, you stop!'

Zos kept walking. He was perhaps ten paces away.

The man in the chariot raised his bow.

'Last warning, stranger—'

Zos threw his javelin into the unarmoured man's chest. It wasn't a perfect throw; instead of a killing shot it went in low, just over the groin, and the man rolled over it and screamed.

The charioteer tried to gather his reins, but it was too late for that. He reached for his short sword, and Persay killed him from his blind side, a single cut up into the thigh. The boy bled out in seconds, a look of puzzlement on his face.

Zos stepped up into the car. He hadn't been in a chariot in years, but one didn't forget; his toes engaged with the laced sinew in the bottom of the car, and the car rocked under his weight, but his knees flexed like a sailor in a storm.

'Daos?' he asked. 'Can you drive?'

Daos smiled. 'Of course, Lord Zos.'

He put the bull's-hide shield on his back and stepped past Zos in the small car. The two chariot horses were unremarkable, but very steady, unmoved by blood and death – warhorses.

Zos hardened his heart and used his right foot to dump the young charioteer's body onto the bloody gravel.

The workers and slaves were open-mouthed.

Zos nodded. 'I'm Zos of Trin.' He hadn't identified himself as Zos of Trin since he was nine years old. 'I'm a mortal man like you – we survived the storm. In answer to the priest-lord's questions, I'm from here – my father was king of Trin. And I'm neither friend nor ally of the god-king of Mykoax – I'm his enemy, and I intend to kill him.'

Some of the locals were flinching away now; none of them were smiling.

Zos leant on the chariot rail, and smiled.

'Best thing you can do is run home and hide until I leave,' he said. 'I'll be done in two or three days.' He crossed his arms and glanced at Trayos. 'In which case, we're recruiting and we'd be happy to pick up seventy or eighty good men of Trin.'

Terrified silence greeted him.

Zos nodded. Then he stepped down from the chariot and pulled his javelin from the priest-lord's corpse. It took more effort than he'd expected,

'Let's go up to Mykoax, then,' he said.

The road from Pleion harbour to the old citadel of Trin was straight and well-paved with huge blocks of stone. A thousand years of noble chariots and peasant wagons had worn ruts in the stone, but the ruts only made the travel easier, and the horses' hooves were hard from a dry summer and rang like iron on the old stone.

Trin was still a ruin. The walls were intact, of course; their titanic stones would be virtually impossible to move. Off to the west, Gosa towered over the olive-tree plain, the mightiest fortress of them all. The old king of Mykoax had taken Gosa by stealth and treason, massacred its inhabitants and burnt its palaces, but none of that was visible from here.

The old god-king Atrios had burnt the palace, as his son had burnt Trin. No palace was allowed to stand except mighty Mykoax, rich in gold, and for his success, Atrios' son Agon had been rewarded with the ambrosia of heaven, the title God-King and the promise of immortality.

Zos looked back, amused at his own insanity. He was planning to storm Mykoax with thirty men and three women.

Not so much planning as coming on the wings of the storm and making it all up as I go, he thought. And then darker thoughts leapt in. *Just here, they took my mother. Just there, I was made to ...*

He had had sixty stadia of chariot riding to remind him of his home, his country, and his anger. Four hours, rolling along at a walking pace with his friends walking behind him, until the ground above Trin became too steep for the chariot to roll easily while fully loaded. Zos had stepped down and walked with Pollon while the boy, Daos, drove.

'Where did he learn to drive a chariot?' Zos asked quietly, trying to fight his own demons.

'When did the skin on the back of our hands return to being smooth?' Pollon asked.

Zos looked down and felt a stomach-turning moment of shock.

Pollon, in his pedantic way, went on, 'The Dry One didn't just heal us, my friend. He gave us the ambrosia of the gods. Or rather ...' His voice held a variety of strong emotions: discovery, curiosity, anger. 'Or rather, it now seems to me that the entire rule of the gods rests on a single product – the Dry Ones' blood. Indeed, I might theorize about the so-called Godborn ...'

Zos, whose head had been lost in the memories of his and his mother's endless humiliations, snapped back to the present.

'Huntress!' he spat, and then managed a smile. 'What will we do for swear words if we have no gods?' he asked.

Pollon raised an eyebrow. 'An excellent question. Perhaps words that refer to copulation and defecation – they were quite popular with my contemporaries.'

Zos blinked slowly. 'I wasn't *really* asking,' he said, with almost a grin.

Pollon smiled. 'I know. But it's a useful talking point. And I made you smile.'

The ghosts of Zos' past edged away. 'Bless you, brother.'

'All kidding aside, I have a point.' Pollon said.

'And...?'

'We should strike the resin supply. Somewhere, somehow, the gods must take and store resin.' He looked at Zos. 'I fully admit this is only a theory. But if my theory is correct, the gods are simply mortals like us, with endless access to the blood of the Dry Ones.'

'Fuck, no wonder they hate us.' Zos shook his head. 'Pollon, you're brilliant.'

'It's only a theory,' Pollon said. 'But look – I've made you smile again.'

'Storming heaven sounds even more foolish than storming Mykoax,' Zos said. 'Untenable. But striking against the source of their immortality...'

'Unless I'm wrong,' Pollon said.

Zos fingered his beard, thinking of the demons and the shapes they'd taken in combat.

'You know what, brother? A year ago, I thought I knew a great deal about how the world worked. It was cynical and dark, but I understood it.' He looked up at the enormous fortification of Mykoax high on the mountain above them. 'And now I wonder if I understand anything at all.'

Pollon frowned. 'I feel exactly the same. Are all godborn warriors as thoughtful as you?'

Zos shrugged. 'Are all palace bureaucrats as brave as you?'

Pollon met his eye. 'I'm not brave. I just cannot bear to desert my friends.'

Zos took a breath of air, looking back at his little army of men and women, and at the road that fell away down the hills to the iron-grey sea under the iron-grey sky. Suddenly, his mood was lightened. Suddenly, he didn't want to die. Revenge seemed petty.

'That's all courage is,' Zos said. 'Making up excuses not to run away.' He looked back up. 'But you know what? I think Daos is right. I don't think we die today.'

The road ran past the magnificent gate to the underworld that was the Tomb of Atrios, the enormous doorway capped by a monolith as large as a house.

'Incredible,' Pollon said.

'You've never been to Narmer,' Zos said.

They walked up the dusty road to the citadel of Mykoax, standing on the windswept mountain. There were people on the road – beggars, and pilgrims going to the tomb with carts of produce. All made way for the chariot, because only the godborn had chariots, and they were lethal.

Zos had remounted the chariot as they passed the Tomb of Atrios. He didn't make an offering, or salute it, which made him feel odd, as he had always done so with all the other godborn and the bull-leapers.

Persay gave a mad laugh as he passed the enormous gate and its bronze doors.

'Dead is dead!' he called out. 'No matter what you put the corpse in.'

Pilgrims in the road made the sign of aversion, and a woman made the evil eye sign.

They walked on. The chariot rumbled over the smaller paving stones – the god-kings of Mykoax had never invested in roads as heavily as the god-kings of Trin, and Zos could feel it in his bones – but then they took the last turn in the road, and there was the Great Gate. Above it, lions stood to either side of a massive stone pillar, their onyx eyes gazing out at the travellers.

It was clear that even here, the storm had done damage – perhaps not the lethal damage of the great wave, but there were roofs off houses, and just inside the gate, a tiled, whitewashed stone house had been reduced to rubble by a titanic stone flung off the wall. The high winds and scouring pumice had driven most people inside, and a continuous wailing from the temple atop the highest citadel suggested that many people were invoking the gods.

Zos was a veteran of this particular palace—fortress and he knew that most of these people were palace professionals: scribes like Pollon, craftspeople like Atosa, entertainers like Era, warriors like Zos himself. He glanced up at the megaron that faced the temple at the highest point in the town. His goal lay within its red pillars.

There were guards at the gate, of course – four men in bronze, none of them a day over twenty, all with the marks of a night spent on watch and a day spent in fear. Too young to know him.

Men in armour. Odd …

In his day they'd have been bull-leapers – warrior-athletes in training, naked but for a kilt and a sword.

Zos raised his hand in greeting. He didn't have a plan past this point. He was still a little puzzled by the ease with which they'd come up the mountain. The mighty storm must have done more damage even than he'd reckoned.

'My lord,' said the *phylarch*. 'I must ask you to dismount and hand over your weapons. This is a very … difficult … time.' He didn't smile; he was clearly a young man who took himself and his role very seriously.

Zos looked at him and realised that this young man was about to die; it was almost like being Daos. There was no peaceful way that he was passing the gate; there was no possibility of mercy. And he didn't like that.

But it didn't matter, because when the chariot rolled to a stop,

486

it all unfolded as if the future really was a predestined thing. Perhaps, if he hadn't taken the chariot…

No. He wanted his revenge. He wanted this. Even though this serious young man had never done him any harm.

Zos shrugged. 'Kill them,' he said.

And it was done.

Because it hadn't really occurred to any of the four men at the gate that they'd be attacked, they didn't land a blow. Persay killed one and tripped another, and the three nomad women finished them, and it was done. There was a surprising amount of blood on the cobbles, and the horses remained unperturbed.

Zos found that if he went with the inevitability, it was less unpleasant.

'Drive on,' he said to Daos.

The boy was smiling.

'Jawala makes some good points,' Zos said.

Daos glanced at him, a very adult smile on his young face.

'She certainly does,' the boy said. 'And yet, sometimes, someone has to put down a rabid dog.'

There were enough bystanders to the killings at the gate that there were screams in the town.

The chariot rolled in past the sacred enclosure, where the old god-kings were buried; in the ancient days, they'd buried their kings inside the walls, and a circular tunnel led to the underworld.

Again, Zos had to fight the urge to propitiate their shades and make his reverence. He was done with all that. So the chariot rolled by, and none of them made any sign of respect to the dead.

'I can feel their anger,' Pollon said.

'They're about to be much angrier still,' Zos said.

Somewhere above them in the town, a woman screamed, and a man called, and someone beat a bronze bell.

Zos' chariot rolled on. The horses were flagging, but it was an offence against the wanax to ride a chariot in the upper town, and Zos had always imagined entering the citadel in a chariot.

Halfway up the Sacred Way that led from the circle of ancient graves to the upper town's temples, a line of armoured men barred the road. The road was narrow; it ran from the magnificent stone wall on the right to the cliff's edge on the left, with a seven-hundred-foot drop.

'Ready?' Zos asked his charioteer.

Daos grinned. 'Born ready,' he said.

The chariot was going up a steep slope behind a pair of tired horses who'd walked all the way from the sea and probably had walked half as far again that morning, and yet, as Daos tightened the reins, their heads came up. He said something to them in a language that Zos didn't know, and their tails swished, making an eerie sound.

Zos didn't need to look back to know that his little war band was gathered behind him.

'Go,' he said.

The two chariot horses leapt to full stride without further word or whip – fatigue apparently falling away. The cart lurched forwards so hard that Zos, trained from youth to fight this way, was almost flung from the car.

Daos, leaning forwards, toes curled over the axle, looked like the living embodiment of a charioteer, reins in his left hand, and his long trident held aloft in his right.

The bronze-clad warriors waiting in two ranks across the cliffside road had perhaps a few seconds to decide how to deal with the oncoming horses. Chariots did not usually attack men in formation; they were too lightly built to survive the collision, and horses didn't like planting their delicate legs among squirming men.

No one had told these horses, or this driver.

Perhaps ten paces from impact, about half of the warriors, including all those closest to the cliff edge, elected to shuffle back, or away from the edge.

Zos said, 'I haven't done this in a long time,' and dropped his cloak.

Perhaps three paces from the dreaded impact, he leapt up to plant one foot on the chariot rail, flung a javelin *down* into one of the bronze-clad warriors from above, over the man's tower shield, like one of Enkul-Anu's thunderbolts...

And went forwards *over the rail* to land on the chariot pole between the horses. His landing wasn't perfect, and he used his free hand on the offside horse's back to stay on the pole as they burst through the disintegrating formation. His second javelin took a brave man in the mouth as he tried to rally his men, and they were past, racing up the long curve of the Sacred Way as the rest of the men who had tried to hold the road were finished in a cloud of dust.

Daos hauled on the reins, slowing the horses, but they trotted all the way to the top. Only the three nomad women and Persay could keep up; the rest of his people and Troyas' sailors were left behind.

At the top of the Sacred Way, the road forked; to the left and right it ran to the palace quarters, but straight on, through the High Gate, lay the palace megaron and the temple.

To the east, out over the sea, lightning flashed in black clouds, and thunder clapped.

The chariot rolled to a stop just short of the gate, and Zos put his back against the chariot rail and rolled back into the car.

'Are you hurt?' Daos asked.

'A bit,' he admitted. 'But only because I am not as practised as I used to be.'

In fact, his lower back was on fire and his groin...

'Let's do this,' he said.

He leant forwards, and the chariot passed through the open gate of the sacred enclosure, and people began to scream.

To his right rose the Temple of All Gods, the Pantheon. Like every other pantheon in the world, its great frieze depicted all the great gods in their aspects: Enkul-Anu sat in judgement; Sypa, his consort, lay on a couch, divine and beautiful; Druku lay opposite her, raising a bunch of grapes; Ara, God of War, stood by in armour; Timurti somehow stood on her fish tail, arm around a trident. At the other end of the portico, the Dark Huntress and the Blue Goddess were alone, angry.

Because he was in the chariot car, Zos was almost at eye level with the priest raising his arms to the enormous golden statue of Enkul-Anu that stood at the east end of the temple, where it could be seen on a clear day from far out on the Ocean. Behind the statue, the cliff fell sheer for six hundred feet to the rocks below. In front of the statue, a dead boy lay across the altar, his throat cut, his viscera spread across the altar for augury. The empty carcasses of two more child victims lay where they'd been thrown from the altar like rubbish.

Zos smiled, not because he approved or relished the scene, but because any scruples he might have felt about what was about to happen fell away when he saw the rubbish heap of children.

A tall man in the prime of life, handsome, bearded, and wearing a long robe of magnificent Tyrean red, embroidered with poppies and ravens, came to the steps, his face red with rage.

'You defile the sacred places, stranger, and for that your life is forfeit.'

Zos was not a splendid figure, as he'd often imagined himself in this moment; he didn't have a scarlet cloak billowing, nor a mighty bronze helmet on his head, nor golden armour. Instead, he was splattered with blood, naked but for his filthy linen kilt.

And his back hurt.

But the smile stayed on his lips.

'I'm not a stranger, Agon,' he said. 'I'm your humble slave, Zos, son of Urystes, whom you killed.'

Zos stepped down from the chariot as Daos stopped the team, and walked up the temple steps. The nomads were still in the gateway; Persay had followed him more closely, but stood, relaxed, by Daos and the chariot.

Agon narrowed his eyes. 'You fucking idiot,' he said.

'Kill him,' he said to his guards.

There were a dozen or so around him, and more across the great marble square, on the steps of the megaron, the palace hall. And more were coming up the side steps from the barracks.

Zos waited, savouring the moment. For the first time, perhaps, he *believed*. He believed that they might overthrow the gods. Because he was in arm's reach of Agon, and no one had stopped him.

Two huge men pulled Agon to safety behind them, and then the guards drew their swords.

And then Zos drew his.

There were mortals who were relatively unaffected by the sword *Terror*, the sword usually carried by Ara, God of War. Men and women who'd faced their direst fears, or even those who'd succumbed to them and then re-emerged, battered but unbroken: they could face the sword *eventually*.

But when Zos drew it, it was like a punch in the gut, or lower. The more noble and thus more unsullied a person was, the less resistance most of them had. The godborn guards fell away like chaff before a wind. The nobles and palace functionaries thronging the temple screamed almost as one, as if the scream were some continuation of their hymn, reaching for their distant and terrible gods.

Zos began to kill them. He was sparing and cautious, like

the trained warrior he was. He didn't waste energy on leaps; he used simple thrusts instead of heavy cuts.

And *Terror* killed, and every death fed the dread sword, so that the waves of terror rolled every stronger, reaping any strong heart and leaving it destroyed. Some of the older people simply died in fear; many leapt from the temple wall to end themselves on the rocks far below.

Zos didn't worry about the worshippers. He killed the guards. And out in the courtyard, Persay slaughtered the other guards, apparently unmoved by the lethal waves of fear. Even the nomad women paused in the gateway, gathering themselves, but Persay *danced*. And blood flowed on the white marble.

Zos found it all curiously anticlimactic.

And finally, as he'd always imagined, he had Agon before him, thrashing on the stained marble. The man was screaming in fear; he'd fouled his clothing, and writhed, unseeing.

Zos nodded. 'I only hope that your worst fear was me, returning.'

And then, with the remarkable strength that the Dry One's healing had given him, he lifted his former captor, carried him to Enkul-Anu's altar, and threw him onto it. He ran the god-king of Mykoax through the throat bole, neatly, and permanently, so that the great king's blood mixed with that of the children his priests had just sacrificed.

Zos looked up at the statue. He raised his arms like a worshipper.

'Hear me, Enkul-Anu,' he said, and the statue flickered.

Zos still held the sword, *Terror*, naked in his hand.

Agon's blood continued to run down the carved channels in the altar, feeding the link to the gods.

'Hear me, Enkul-Anu!' Zos called.

The statue's features began to grow in animation.

'*Hear me, Enkul-Anu!*' Zos roared like the power of the sea, the magical third time.

And the great god was made manifest.

'You dare?' the god bellowed. Only his head was animated, of course; the rest of the statue was stone.

Zos spat into the great god's face.

'You're next.'

Heaven

Enkul-Anu cut the link to Mykoax and fell back onto his couch, shaken.

He was almost alone, except for the three sisters who waited on him night and day – unimportant human slaves. But none of the other gods had witnessed this humiliation. One of the slaves bent to wipe the spittle from his immortal face, and he killed her with an angry swipe of his hand, hurtling her broken body across his private hall.

A *mortal worm* had dared…

And he had the sword, Terror.

And here I lie, wounded by the World Serpent.

This isn't funny any more.

Credits

Miles Cameron and Gollancz would like to thank everyone at Orion who worked on the publication of *Against All Gods*.

Editorial
Gillian Redfearn
Claire Ormsby-Potter

Copy-editor
Steve O'Gorman

Proofreader
Patrick McConnell

Editorial Management
Jane Hughes
Charlie Panayiotou
Tamara Morriss
Claire Boyle

Audio
Paul Stark
Jake Alderson
Georgina Cutler

Contracts
Anne Goddard
Ellie Bowker
Humayra Ahmed

Design
Nick Shah
Tomás Almeida
Joanna Ridley
Helen Ewing

Finance
Nick Gibson
Jasdip Nandra
Elizabeth Beaumont
Ibukun Ademefun
Afeera Ahmed
Sue Baker
Tom Costello